BOTH MY SONS

A NOVEL BY

KEN YODER REED

Also by Ken Yoder Reed:

MENNONITE SOLDIER
HE FLEW TOO HIGH

BOTH MY SONS

A NOVEL BY

KEN YODER REED

© Copyright 2016
All rights reserved

BOTH MY SONS

A Novel by

KEN YODER REED

Library of Congress Number: 2016908689
International Standard Book Number: 978-1-60126-499-2

Masthof Press
219 Mill Road | Morgantown, PA 19543-9516

TABLE OF CONTENTS

PART 1 | THE FIRSTBORN

CHAPTER 1: The Paxton Boys, Lancaster, July 12, 1755 3

CHAPTER 2: Franklin Deals with the Mennonists, Lancaster, April 29, 1755 12

CHAPTER 3: Bod Cameron, Commander, Lancaster, April 29, 1755..21

PART 2 | THE OLD COUNTRY

CHAPTER 4: The Unfortunate Forester, Waldhilsbach, 1706.................................35

CHAPTER 5: In His Father's Grave 47

CHAPTER 6: The Mennonist.............................60

CHAPTER 7: The Desperate Need for Revenge, Sinsheim, December 10, 1709................................67

CHAPTER 8: The Voice Speaks.............................77

CHAPTER 9: What? Forgive? Sinsheim, March 5, 1710......91

CHAPTER 10: Meeting the Murderer............................100

CHAPTER 11: Mutti and the 600 Reichsthalers, Heidelberg 113

PART 3 | THE INDENTURED GIRL

CHAPTER 12: Sold! The Philadelphia Harbor, 1718 131

CHAPTER 13: The Pequea Settlement, 1718–20 147

CHAPTER 14: The Fateful Snowstorm,
December 1719 160

CHAPTER 15: The Judgment of the Preachers,
March 1720 174

PART 4 | THE WIFE'S STORY

CHAPTER 16: On the Pequea, July 1755 191

CHAPTER 17: What Is a Wiedertäufer? Switzerland,
1696–1715 195

CHAPTER 18: Never Trust Your Life to a Man, The
Kraichgau, 1715–17 209

CHAPTER 19: The Resurrected Wife,
Pequea Settlement, 1722 224

CHAPTER 20: Making the Best of It, 1722 236

CHAPTER 21: The Miracle Babe, 1738 245

CHAPTER 22: Butchering Day, 1742 259

PART 5| JANEY'S FLIGHT

CHAPTER 23: From the Pequea, December 1742 279

CHAPTER 24: To the Scots-Irish, December 1742 292

PART 6 | THE SCOTS-IRISH

CHAPTER 25: Taking Care of Bod, July 12, 1755 313

CHAPTER 26: "He's the father!" Harris' Landing,
July 12, 1755 327

CHAPTER 27: A Funeral, Interrupted, July 13, 1755 342

CHAPTER 28: Vision of Locusts and the Savior 355

PART 7 | THE SECOND SON

CHAPTER 29: Janey Again, the Pequea, Sunday,

January 4, 1756 369

PART 8 | GREENYWALT'S JUSTICE

CHAPTER 30: Benjamin and the Will, Sunday,

January 11, 1756 385

GLOSSARY | 399

ACKNOWLEDGMENTS | 408

—◆◆◆◆◆◆—

MAP OF THE OLD WORLD | viii

MAP OF THE NEW WORLD | 410

The Old World

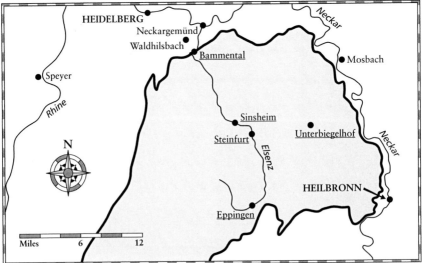

The Upper Kraichgau

Underlined names—Some key towns where
Swiss refugee Wiedertäufer settled between 1648 and 1700

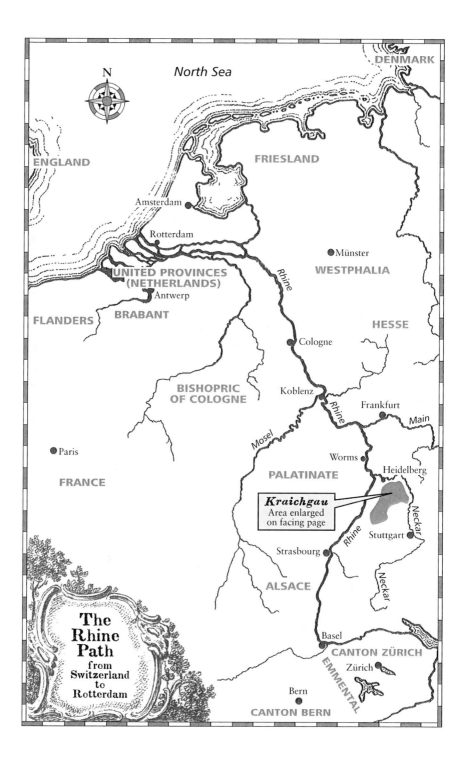

North Sea

ENGLAND

FRIESLAND

DENMARK

Amsterdam

Rotterdam

Münster

WESTPHALIA

UNITED PROVINCES
(NETHERLANDS)

Rhine

Antwerp

BRABANT

FLANDERS

HESSE

Cologne

BISHOPRIC
OF COLOGNE

Koblenz

Frankfurt

Rhine

Main

Mosel

Paris

Worms

FRANCE

Heidelberg

PALATINATE

Kraichgau
Area enlarged
on facing page

Neckar

Rhine

Stuttgart

Strasbourg

ALSACE

Neckar

**The
Rhine
Path**
from
Switzerland
to
Rotterdam

Basel

CANTON ZÜRICH

Zürich

EMMENTAL

Bern

CANTON BERN

PERMISSIONS
AND CREDITS

- The Old World map by Jan Gleysteen, courtesy of Lancaster Mennonite Historical Society, Lancaster, PA.

- A Map of the Province of Pensilvania by Thomas Kitchin, 1756.

- Maps are the work of Kerry Jean Handel, Millersville, PA.

- Original Text of the Ausbund song, 'Wer Christo jetzt will folgen nach' by Jorg Wagner, 1527, in the Ausbund. Translated by David Augsburger, 1962 in the Mennonite Hymnal.

- Lyrics of 'Das Zurich-Lied' by Hans Rycher were quoted in Christian Neff's "A Hymn of the Swiss Brethren", Mennonite Quarterly Review, July 1930.

- Lyrics of the Schabab Song by Benedict Brechbühl were written in 1709 and appear in translation by John Landis Ruth in The Earth is the Lord's, courtesy of Lancaster Mennonite Historical Society, Lancaster, PA.

- Back Cover artwork of the John Harris Homestead on the Susquehanna. This watercolor by William S. Reeder, done in 1839, shows the John Harris, Sr. cabin at Harris' Landing about 1719. Used by permission of the Dauphin County Historical Society.

- All Scripture quoted in the novel is King James Version, 1611.

Author's Disclaimer

BUT IS YOUR STORY TRUE?
COUSIN SANFORD ASKED. . . .

This book is a novel and the central character, Greenywalt, is an invention of the author, a composite of several Pennsylvania pioneers. The scenes and conversations of his life are imaginary.

However, the main events and people in Greenywalt's world are real. Benjamin Franklin did threaten the Mennonite farmers. William Penn's secretary James Logan sold Pennsylvania land, including 6000 acres known today as the Pequea Settlement, to Mennonite settlers and ordered the burning of Scots-Irish squatter cabins. "Fighting Parson" John Elder organized the Paxtang Boys militia to defend the Susquehanna River settlers and John Harris sheltered the traumatized settlers in his stockaded house in 1755. Benedict Brechbühl, Hans and Christian Herr, the Wiedertäufer and the dungeons of Trachselwald Castle are historical figures and places. The Great Freeze of 1709 and religious harassment triggered the mass migration of perhaps 40-50,000 Swiss-German refugees to the New World between 1710 and 1750, while the Church of England's persecution drove tens of thousands of Scots-Irish Covenanters/Presbyterians to the New World in the 1720–45 time period.

PART 1

THE FIRSTBORN

CHAPTER 1

THE PAXTON BOYS, LANCASTER, JULY 12, 1755

O N THAT JULY MORNING, the stars of heaven tumbled onto Klaus Grünewald's head.

How does a father prepare for the death of his child? When it's the favorite son, the one most beloved, once the heir apparent of his life achievements, the heart detonates that much more brutally.

Did the fact that the boy ran away fourteen years back change anything? No. His heart still displayed the bleeding holes left by the boy's roots ripping out. Did the truth behind "the Bastard" label make any difference? No. Nothing made a difference. He loved the young man.

Bad news didn't trot in jiggity-jog like a pony cart ride on a Sunday afternoon. Bad news came at a gallop, with a summer thunderstorm violently driving it.

Greenywalt (his name as Penn's secretary Logan misspoke his family name Grünewald, and it stuck) was feeding his team in the corral behind the Mennonist conestogas, eight of them backed up to the market tables between him and Penn Square. The horses thrust and parried with their noses in the long box, going after last year's ground corn and oats as it tumbled from the scoop. The Boy Benjamin had already toweled off the heavy dew and turned to move out the five-and ten-pound sacks of white flour, imprinted with the Greenywalt's Mill label. The farmers in the other eight or ten waggons were also up, rising with the sun, and setting up their own tables.

The mare's upturned ears and nicker alerted him. He heard the far-off tattoo of horse-hooves well before his eyes could figure out anything.

"What is it?" he called the Boy Benjamin from the corral.

"Raiders!" Young Herr, in the neighboring booth, spilled the basket of apples he was carrying from his waggon to the table. He wheeled and hallooed the other farmers. "Boys!" He scrambled onto his table to see.

Greenywalt's rifle lay right there, an arm's reach away on the waggon bed. Rifles were fine to go after the wolf or rabid groundhog but not to aim at men.

"I see them!" The Boy Benjamin pointed, his eyes sharper than the rest. The farmers abandoned their tables and collected behind his, as if a wooden table could offer any protection. "Five of them."

A dust cloud the size of a man's hand materialized at the far end of West King Street, the direction of the River and Wright's Ferry. The dark set of clustered heads rose and fell in boiling thunderheads of dust that their seemingly legless mounts drove out of the rutted streets. Five of them. Or were there more?

"I see six," the Boy reported, "only no rider on the sixth."

"Not savages," Herr shouted down. "They're wearing hats."

"Redcoats?" a farmer insisted.

The sound became a steadily rising drumbeat, and the heads of the horsemen moved apart, spreading, at a full gallop, to take up the width of the street between the brick two-stories, the legs of their mounts still not discernible in the dust.

Only minutes from the first sound of their hooves, the riders and their mounts became visible, hats to hooves, in the traveling dust cloud.

Not savages, but the riding style of savages, he thought. Their spurs and hand whips slashed their horses.

"Who would treat a horse that way," Herr asked, "but the Scotch-Irish?"

They didn't slow when they hit the cobble-stoned Square but crossed it, charging the market waggons. Hardly two lengths away, the lead rider sawed on the reins. The begrimed horse, perspiration glazing her flanks and running like suds from under the halter, rose on her hind legs, forefeet clawing above the tabletop, her eyes popped and rolling. The other riders followed his lead. A dense cloud of clay swam by the lead horse's breast and enveloped the farmers, distributing a patina of red particles on their tables, fruits, and faces.

Young Herr choked, spitting bits of clay.

"Dummies!"

The lead rider paid no attention. Perhaps because he didn't understand their dialect. In fact, he seemed to not even notice the farmers. He dismounted, took three steps to Greenywalt's table, and doubled down with the reins to loop them around the heavy wooden leg.

Greenywalt saw the rider's face, now that the cloud had passed and the man crouched only a tobacco-spit away. Trail dust coated the whiskered face, from which his eyes peered out of whitish sockets like the eyes of a coon. Whatever color his clothes had been, he was now painted ochre from the eyes to the moccasins. His hands and face looked Shawnee.

The man snapped his fingers as he rose from his crouch. At the sign, the other four threw their legs across their saddles, and eight shoes thudded simultaneously on the cobblestones. The riders' eyes were focused, every one of them, on the sixth horse.

Now Greenywalt noticed the sixth horse among them, its reins trailing from the saddle horn of the second horse. In place of a rider, a long baggage lay roped sideways across the saddle, a flannel blanket concealing whatever its contents, secured at both ends by a rope snugged tight under the mare's belly.

Wordlessly the second militiaman loosened the reins of the riderless horse from his saddle and tossed them to the third, who tied a half hitch around the leg of Herr's table. The other three riders encircled the horse. They were filthy, their shirts and breeches and sweat-darkened hats, their faces and arms caked with ochre dust. While they moved in unison to untie the baggage, the lead rider ripped a folded Union Jack from a saddlebag.

Greenywalt knew that Jack. Memories of the sea trip some forty years gone. The Jack, the Colours of the English Queen, lashed to the bowsprit of the *Mary Hope*. Now dry in a fair wind and flapping. Eight weeks, like Abraham, going out he knew not where.

The four horsemen seized corners of the flag and stretched it taut, revealing burn holes and stains, while the leader ran beyond the riderless horse to lever up the long package. The mare stood still, nose tilted out of curiosity. He shoved it upward to the tipping point, then skipped around to the other side, between the open flag and the horse, where he heaved again. Shoes appeared at the top of the envelope as he rested its bottom end on the taut flag, between the two riders. It somersaulted slowly, the blanket dropping away to reveal a scarecrow figure, the shoes skyward and lashed together, long-sleeved arms flapping side to side, and then it thudded heavily on the flag and sagged it, hammock-like, between the straining arms of the militiamen.

The men staggered, the flag slung between them, toward Herr's table.

"Move the bags!" the lead rider snarled at the Boy, who stood goggle-eyed at the end of Greenywalt's table, with the farmers ranged out to his side, staring at the spectacle.

The Boy had organized the flour sacks in neat rows, the five-pounders, the ten-pounders, with a propped handwritten sign declaring the prices. At the rider's command, he began consolidating the sacks toward the far end.

The rider stepped up, combative. "No! Completely off!" He swept an arm a foot above the table to demonstrate what he wanted.

The Boy stood flustered and gawked around in his confusion.

"Toss them to me." Greenywalt moved into the gap between the market table and the waggon, his back to it. "He wants it empty."

The Boy tossed a bag, and the farmers joined, several of them throwing while Greenywalt and two men dropped the sacks into the waggon bed.

The riders staggered, the Colours slung between them, toward his table. The burden came up over the edge of the now-empty table and trucked steadily the full length, then dropped onto the table-top. The table joints sighed. It was a man, a white man, stretched the length of the table, with mud-caked shoes at the far end, hands flung helplessly off both sides, and the head lolling, face downward, toward him and the Boy.

The lead rider pulled back the flag to expose the man within. He was dressed like the rest and similarly begrimed. One leg of his breeches was cut away to expose a grievous wound on the back of his left thigh. The leg was swathed in linen bandage, and the blood flow had attracted more dust onto the wet bandage, then caked dry. It was impossible to gauge the severity of the wound.

The man had been scalped. His head slumped over the near end of the table and showed a blackened, lumpish, and teacup-sized hole in a rough circle where the hair had been torn away on top, while his remaining hair, ochre like the rest of him, frizzed away on all sides. The hair pulled back from his temples into a tail, which trailed across his neck, looped with a skewed black ribbon.

The militiamen wrapped the man in the flag, meticulously tucking flaps under the legs, then under the arms. The lead rider grunted once, and the five strained as one man and rolled the body onto its back.

Within the swaddling flag, the man's chest rolled upward, darkly striped. Streaks covered the now visible chalky face, from the scalp scar downward to the chin. The stripes ran blood-black, but in the early light, some gleamed fresh and iron-red.

"Is he . . . ?" Young Herr broke off, the question still hanging.

"I don't think . . . "

The lead horseman slapped his hands. Two of his men leaped forward to retrieve muskets from behind their saddles and jogged back to position themselves on either side of the slain man's head, their muskets at present-arms position, upright against their noses, triggers forward, glaring through the onlooking farmers.

The Boy Benjamin stood next to Greenywalt, between their waggon tongue and their market table. The man's head at their end of the table hung upside down an arm's length away. The boy nudged his father with his knee.

"It's him." He said it closemouthed and intense, driving the words through his teeth.

Greenywalt stared. The boxed jaw and Roman nose. The powerful chest. The frizzed hair that showed rust-colored at the roots and tied in a black bow at the nape of his neck. The missing dogtooth in the mouth that sagged open.

"Bod?" He said the name with no intonation, no strength. The other farmers studied the slain man's face and turned to watch Greenywalt. Their faces creased and furrowed and distorted with pity.

He leaned in and his trembling fingers sought the man's face. If it was Bod . . . .

The rider on the right used his musket butt to swipe away the hand. "Don't touch him."

"Dutch dog!" the lead rider accused him from across the table. He'd superintended the movement of the figure in the flag and the setup of guards, directing the action with his outstretched musket. Now he took off running and, with one enormous leap, landed in a half-crouch on Herr's table. His traveling legs kneed over two more baskets of Herr's apples, which scattered like breaking billiards and dropped onto the cobblestone. The riderless horse immediately seized them with its teeth.

"See this, Chicken Hearts! Quaker Scum!" The rider denounced them into the morning sky. "Look what you done. Come see, everyone!" He jabbed his musket at the Courthouse tower on the north side of the Square. "Ring 'em! Ring 'em!" The remaining riders leaped away to carry out his order. The rider lofted his musket and fired. "Wake the dead, I say!"

Young Herr turned to Greenywalt for translation. "What did he say?"

Greenywalt felt the blood drain cold from his hands and feet and down the surface of his face. His knees lost their mettle, and he could feel them crumble. The cobblestones floated up as, right then, Young Herr's hands gripped his armpits.

"Let me go!" Herr's hands fell away. The cobblestones collided with Greenywalt's rear end. Herr's long uncut black beard appeared directly above him, almost brushing his nose. "That's my son!" Greeny-walt shouted and slapped the beard away.

The church steeples on the periphery of his sight swam in and out.

Why me? Why my boy?

It's daytime, but the stars fall around me. Meteoric showers. What next? The Heavens roll up like a scroll, that's what the Book says happens next. He studied the blue vault. He waited: Where would it tear loose? When would it begin the rolling up?

His head sagged back against the waggon tongue. A lone cloud traveled along, pushed by an invisible lumbering breeze. It would thunder and lightning and pour down by 3:00 p.m., certainly. It did every day when it started like this, with the air so sopping and still and sweltering that you tasted it. Only the locusts loved this weather, mating weather, and they were shrieking right now.

He had dreaded that it would end like this. Bod was too brave, too impetuous to live to old age. He'd taught Bod to use the rifle and how to wait for the prey at six and gifted him the Mylin rifle at eight, and when he did, he knew. The man would carry that rifle on his last day.

He could only imagine that last day because he had no facts yet.

Bod the waggoneer, a master of forest trails. Bod the scout, always out front, studying the night sounds and the messages left in the trampled leaves, the broken twigs, the prints in the mud on the creek bank. Bod the marksman, shooting the king's face off the deck of cards at two hundred fifty yards.

The shot that knocked him from the saddle could have been fired from behind any oak or maple of Penn's Forest, and once on the ground . . . once on the ground, on your back . . . your precious rifle taking wings away in the shock of the hit . . . once on your back . . .

He could see the dark face poised over his son's. He smelled the bear grease and crossed with the enemy's pitiless eyes as the enemy pulled the long red ponytail back with his left hand, planted a foot on the supine shoulder, jabbed the scalp with the iron blade in his right, swung the biting tip in a circle, and cried the terrible whoop as he pulled up on the trophy and left enough that the man would survive a few days.

The Boy Benjamin's face hovered over him, his moving lips posing questions that he didn't comprehend. Not the boy he loved but the younger one. He should have sent this one instead.

"Your brother," he said. "Your brother . . ."

"Hnnnnh?"

At that moment, the bells! The air itself seemed to split apart to make passage for the peals that assaulted the farmers. In the Courthouse tower, the massive leaden bells lurched forth and back. The cacophony of notes ran on and on, deafening.

The Mennonist farmers stood transfixed, wide-eyed, a herd of whitetail caught in the open field by braying hounds. They clapped their hands over their ears. In the corral behind the waggons, their horses reared and plunged and broke boards with their hind hooves.

CHAPTER 2

FRANKLIN DEALS WITH THE MENNONISTS, LANCASTER, APRIL 29, 1755

BETWEEN HIM AND THE MARKET TABLES, the farmers bunched in a fervent, quarreling huddle. They were men of the soil, not scholars or lawyers, and the long white handbills they waved and jabbed looked out of place, scrunched between their massive, callused, and worn fingers. Young Herr summed it up for them.

"Tell him again." His foot-long and unshorn beard a few inches from Greenywalt's face, his left hand ticked off the points on the fingers of his right. "No guns. No soldiers in uniform."

"Oats and corn only."

"Oats and corn only." Herr repeated the farmer's interruption. "Provisions. That sort of thing. Tell him that!"

Greenywalt turned. The gaps in his spine compressed and pinched every time he moved. He sucked air. He needed to sit down. There was no chair.

On the lone chair—a throne-like cathedra with curled arms, feet carved as lion's paws, and an ivory-inlaid back—the man Franklin sat before him, his legs crossed, sporting white-stockings below the knee breeches. The two redcoats stood erect on either side of Franklin, their muskets at present-arms.

Greenywalt veered away from Franklin, drew down on his sinuses several times, and spat into the old bandanna. "Sorry." It was the mill dust, thirty years of it.

Franklin dismissed the impropriety with a flick of the hand. "Go on."

"Sir." It was one of the first English words he'd learned, a useful word. "Sir. They're saying they won't ferry guns. Or soldiers in uniform. Only—"

Franklin's chopping hand cut him off. "Why do I keep repeating myself? I told them yesterday." The hand with the large-stoned ring banged twice on the chair arm.

"They weren't here yesterday, Sir. That was a different group—"

"You people don't talk to each other?"

"Of course, but—"

Franklin unfolded slowly upward, a magnificent profile in the mustard waistcoat with twin rows of pewter buttons that rose to the snow-white lace cravat, gold-embroidered buttonholes opposite on his open waistcoat and French cuffs, nut-colored curls tumbling to his shoulders. His lips pressed and he waited.

Greenywalt turned again. The farmers babbled all at once, their faces and hands slanted toward him.

"What's he say?"

"We won't do it."

"Until he promises, no waggons." Young Herr took his customary spokesman role. He used the scrunched handbill to gesture toward the queue of draught horses and conestogas that began at the market table where Franklin's son and the Paymaster stood and ran westward for a hundred yards, one team after another.

"He said he answered this question yesterday. And I was here. He did. And the handbill says it." Greenywalt snatched the handbill from Herr and read the relevant passage first in English and then roughed it out in Deitsch. "No drivers who take care of horses are obligated to perform military service in addition to looking after the loads and horses—"

"Aha! Aha!" Herr's hand swiped the handbill again, and he bumped it twice against Greenywalt's lips. "The Devil hides himself on the back side. We won't be fooled again. Like they fooled us with the Oath of Naturalization."

"Right! Right!"

"I wasn't the one who explained the Oath to you. It was your father."

"Maybe it was. Maybe it wasn't. You can't dupe us twice—we're standing on principles. Tell him we'll cough up the waggons and horses for his general—and drivers too. But we don't support this war. We're a defenseless people. Five generations, all the way back to Switzerland. He needs to promise us—"

Greenywalt shifted back, and molten tears of lead coursed from his hip toward the knee. "Sciatica," the Lancaster doctor said. He chomped his lip and tasted blood.

"Mr. Franklin, you need to say it again. They want to hear you say it."

"All right." Franklin's pudgy frame fell into the chair. "I'm doing them a favor, do they know that?" His face veered away as he addressed the Paymaster. "Not that they have a choice. I have the General's word: they do it voluntarily or . . . he'll send Hussars to take the waggons. And their sons."

Greenywalt waited, in pain. Franklin's face came back, and there was no anger, just a bemused smile.

"So therefore, the answer is No. No guns on the waggons. No soldiers in uniforms in the waggons."

When he translated, the farmers nodded among themselves, satisfied. The deal was struck.

The first waggon was Young Herr's, and he signed and extended an open palm for the pay, fifteen shillings a day, with seven days' advance and the rest to come from the General when the campaign ended. The waggon wheels turned, lurched forward, one after the other, their beardless and lean drivers barefoot, shuffling alongside the blinkered horses, the reins light in their hands.

Three of the driver boys bunched by Oberholtzer's team and barked at each other over the backs of the horses, glad for action after an hour of nothing.

"Franklin's a genius! They pinned a gold medal on him in London. All the steeples in Europe are putting up his lightning rods." The lanky, awkward boy, who wore a pair of Franklin's spectacles, spoke.

"Says who?"

"*The Gazette.* I read it."

"My pop says they're an offense to God."

"Science!" the awkward boy said. "Electricity! That's what he discovered. If it's in the clouds, if it's the vapor that sparks and jumps when you rub your slippers on the rug. It's the same thing, he said. He ran up a kite in a thunder shower and collected the lightning in a jar—do you believe that!"

Greenywalt knew. He'd pointed out the lightning rods on the Statehouse in Philadelphia to the Boy. He hung on every word the Boy was saying now. It added another hundredweight of grief to the burden he was already carrying, the dread he'd carried about this day. I can't lose him. He's all I got left.

The queue had emptied, and it was Greenywalt's turn. What could he say? He walked to the table where Franklin's own son bent over his checklist, reviewing the horses and condition of each waggon as it was presented, before tossing up his assessment to the Paymaster, who then dipped his quill and wrote a receipt for the transaction, collected the farmer's X or signature, and cracked his wooden box to count off a small stack of coins with King George's face. Yesterday there'd been trouble at this stage—disagreements over the assessment of the waggons and horses. Today it was going too smoothly.

Lord. He could say it in the dark wet cellar of the mill, with the millwheels at eye level, their rumble nearly deafening him. He could say it in his waggon, under the white canvas top with the rain drumming while he drove home from Philadelphia. He could say it in Penn Square with Benjamin Franklin and twenty Mennonist farmers trafficking around him, guessing he catnapped, as he stood still, one hand propped against the table, his eyes pinched shut. He could mouth it under any circumstances. Sometimes the blue dome overhead cracked with thunder and the skies pulled back to reveal a path that led right to the Throne. Not that he *saw* anything. But he knew. He was going to *hear* the Voice.

Lord. I can't lose him. I lost Ichabod fourteen years back. Benjamin is all I've got.

Lightning had struck the family, a bolt flung from Heaven that breached the family like the oak in Strasburg. The oak survived too, deeply fissured, blackened, massive twisted keloids on the faces of the two forks that now leaned away from each other like quarreling sisters.

For the sake of your name, O Lord,
Forgive my iniquity, for it is great.

For a long time now, he'd heard nothing. No Voice. No cracking of the Dome. The clouds continued to scud across its closed, voiceless, concealed entrance. No Voice.

The waggons rolled forward, one team at a time. Young Franklin was doing better with the farmers today: there were no arguments. The farmers were happy, in fact. They collected their advances, and their hired men or their sons drove the contracted teams to the far side of the Square. Young Herr stood just beyond the Paymaster's table, debating farm values in the dialect with the other farmers.

All the men who came forty-five years ago, they're all gone now. All the men on the *Mary Hope*, and most of their wives too. Who's left of the Original Ten? Old Hans, and he's home in bed, paralyzed on the left side, they say, and mumbling his words out of half a mouth. And then there's me.

Franklin ordered the soldiers to lift his chair and turn it around, facing west, him still in it, with his back to the now high and generous April sun. He sat warming himself like a box turtle. He'd ripped off the nut-colored wig, thrown it onto the counting table, and donned a large tricorn hat to keep the sun from baking his brains. He was occupied with dictating letters to a shriveled, earnest secretary, who renewed his quill furiously in the well he'd brought, toiling to keep up with a torrent of words. Ever since the waggon rentals had begun, Franklin's entire entourage sat arranged around the market table.

Franklin glanced sideways from his slouch in the chair, his legs outstretched to encourage circulation. "So, what do we have today, William?"

"Sixteen."

"Plus yesterday's thirteen, that's twenty-nine teams. Are we all in?" He pulled himself together and rose to look around the Square.

"How about that one?" His walking stick fingered Greenywalt's waggon and team, tethered alone at the far end of the Square.

Greenywalt's reverie ended abruptly. "You can take the waggon, Sir, but . . . mmm . . . I've got no driver."

Young Herr turned from the farmers. "He wants your waggon? Don't upset him. We have to do this, right? Or he just *takes* the waggon and your son. And you need the money."

"I can't anymore. Four hundred miles." He spoke Deitsch now. "I'm just not capable."

Young Herr's chin lifted, his gaze directed across the Square at the drivers on the far side, squatted down among the waggons, bragging and laughing among themselves. "The boy. He's tall and smart. Hey, Benjamin . . ."

Benjamin spanned the Square at a full sprint.

"Can you drive that waggon?"

"You're joking! You mean . . . *with them?*" The Boy's thumb backward indicated the already waiting and queued waggons on the far side, where his two comrades stood cracking their knuckles, watching.

Franklin studied the little drama, puzzling out what was going on behind the alien language.

"Dat?" The Boy's eyes rose to his father's.

Right then he heard the Voice. For the first time in months. *Let him go.*

No! No! If I knew you'd say that, I would never have come today.

"Mem says we need the money," Benjamin said.

Send the Boy.

Impudence and disrespect! Blabbing our finances to the whole world. And No, I can't, he told himself. But his mouth said:

"Go."

The Boy danced the five hundred feet to their parked team. Yet Greenywalt knew. It was a mistake. He should not have said it. The bully-ruffians of the highways and weeks of nights with the British lobsters, hardly any safer than the highwaymen. Him just seventeen, and wearing spectacles. Six weeks through the troubled forests. Then the battlefront. He'd be murdered. They'd truck his body back to him in the bottom of his waggon.

But his mouth couldn't compose any words.

Franklin's men processed his team, inspecting the Belgians and the waggon, then produced the receipt, and Benjamin brought the receipt and quill for him to sign and wormed the bag of coins into his hand.

Words assaulted his throat, massing on his tongue now, but his tongue mutinied, refused to pronounce them. The Voice had said, *"Send the Boy."*

The waggon wheels turned, squeaking on the cobble. Now the Boy's frame was passing and now his back was turned and he could see that the Boy was skinny and elongated, not compact like he himself at fifteen: a narrow waist, a V back, and at the shoulders the bunched muscles playing beneath his shirt on that day, faraway and long ago in the Kraichgau, driving off with the Mennonist miller's cart while the kneeling Barbara Grünewald sobbed for her son, shamelessly, outside the house's front door. The Boy's brother was built like me, but this one? Him survive in the forest? Wearing spectacles, of all things.

The Boy was going and he knew it. He would never see him again. How could he permit this? His mother—she'd had no idea, when she urged him last night to go this morning: "We need the money." When she learned what had happened here . . . He was going to shout now. He was ready to bellow it: Stop!

Franklin was back on his feet. "I think we're all done here. Tomorrow in York." With his walking stick he banged the guard's shoe, to his right. "All right, I guess. We're ready."

The guard jerked erect, heels clicking, the musket lifted off his shoulder and out in front, as if he'd sighted one of the Canada geese that regularly routed north on the Susquehanna Flyway about this time of year, and he pulled the trigger. A tongue of fire leaped from the flintlock, and a white cloud the size of a man's hand floated away.

CHAPTER 3

BOD CAMERON, COMMANDER, LANCASTER, APRIL 29, 1755

FRANKLIN SWUNG the walking stick toward the Courthouse Building and the street beyond it. Like Moses' rod flung out in the Pharaoh's court, the stick seemed to conjure forth a company of mounted riders.

Their horses cantered from the shadow cast by the impressive two-story Courthouse in center square.

It was a sight unlike any he'd seen in forty years on the Pequea: a company of mounted, armed, well-shaven men on horse, in some semblance of discipline. The men wore similar hunting frocks of off-white linsey-woolsey and dark felt hats, a turkey feather or a piece of brown-and-white bucktail stuck in the band. Rawhide strips crossed their shoulders and suspended canteens, powder horns, and shot bags at waist level. They rode smartly, one-handed, their fowling guns stock-down against their thighs and pointed at the cloudless sky. Riding among them, a half-horse length in front, the commander differentiated himself by the redcoat officer's jacket with a double row of pewter buttons that rose in precision to an ascot looping his chin and a black tricorn hat that he poised a handsbreadth off his forehead in a salute to Franklin as they passed him. His horse was even more striking, a powerfully built stallion whose proud gait mimicked the commander's pose. The commander's hair matched his mount's, deep russet and pulled back into a tail tied with a black ribbon.

Young Herr and the Mennonist farmers had nearly finished packing to leave, now that their waggons and drivers were dispatched in the care of the youthful drivers, mostly hired hands. They stopped to gape at the intruders.

The horsemen caught Benjamin halfway between the Courthouse and the train of waggons on the far side of the Square. Benjamin, on foot beside his team and waggon, jerked the team to a halt to stare at the commander and then the riders, who surrounded him. One leaned in to slap his shoulder, laughing.

"We don't bite. Keep moving."

Greenywalt worked to keep up with the Boy and the conestoga, but the pains kept shooting down his leg, which he dragged with a lurch each time. The Boy had slipped out of reach, and when the riders came around him, the Boy was a hundred feet off. Greenywalt poised again to shout "Stop," and the word travailed on his tongue.

Benjamin and his escort reached the waggon train. The conestogas stood queued for their trip, with waggons and teams in a semicircle that began in front of the tavern at the corner of Queen and extended to the head waggon and team, several hundred feet down King Street in the direction of Wright's Ferry, the river, and the eventual meet-up with General Braddock's army of three thousand British regulars.

"We're here to keep you company!" the commander shouted at the drivers. "Make sure none of you gets lost between here and Fort Cumberland!" He laughed. The drivers laughed when he did, although a number of them didn't speak English and didn't comprehend a word he said. "We're Paxton Boys, all of us!"

One of the riders had already dismounted beyond the waggon train, by the well and watering trough in front of the tavern, Swan's, on that corner. The rider wrenched a bullwhip from his saddle and scampered back between the waggons to a point just in front of the commander, where he uncoiled the whip and flicked it overhead, the pop of the whip better catching the attention of the drivers than the commander's words.

"When Captain Cameron speaks, perk up!"

He snapped the whip again and gave the cheer.

"Captain Cameron!"

The other rangers had deployed themselves along the lined conestogas, one every twenty-five feet or so. On this shout, they raised their muskets.

"Hip Hip!"

"Captain Cameron!"

"Hip Hip!"

"Thank you, Aengus." The commander perched on the stallion's back, looking down on the drivers, who waited and shifted from leg to leg to ease the heat from the cobblestones on their bare feet. None of them had any experience with military manners or expectations, but they anticipated it now: they were about to hear the expectations and protocol of the trail.

The Ranger Aengus instructed drivers in mid-train to unhitch their horses and lead them to the watering trough, where he had already cranked the windlass arm to haul up a brimming bucket, which he tipped into the iron trough for the horses.

"Gentlemen and Fellow Soldiers!" the commander said. The drivers who did understand English stared into each other's open mouths, astonished at their ranking in this new world order.

"I need first to put you to mind the cause for which we have gathered. Is it not to maintain the honor and just right of our glorious Sovereign, George the Second, and the protection of our country? You have all cheerfully embraced this opportunity to serve your King and Country and in so doing, secure the welfare of our families, our wives and children."

The drivers raised their eyebrows. Most of them were unmarried.

"The enemy is *out there*." He stabbed his riding crop in the direction of the River, the Blue Mountains beyond, the Alleghenies further beyond, and all the wooded hills and vales in between. "In our neighboring provinces, bloody barbarians have butchered some in their grainfields, some in their beds, some at their meals, in some unguarded hour. Shall we tamely look on and suffer them to exercise hellish barbarities on our children and wives?

"You were born to liberty, with all the glorious rights and privileges of a British subject!" He paused and let their status in the world cloak their shoulders before delivering the punch. "Our Quaker government, however, has infected our province with the disease of Quaker non-resistance."

"Hear! Hear!" The rangers stabbed their muskets.

"Forever shame! Today I adjure you: Lift the drooping head of Pennsilvania and restore her to health and vigor!"

Greenywalt arrived at the well in time to assist Benjamin as he led their team to the trough. But he stopped, riveting on the commander on his horse, beyond the line of waggons.

The shock of recognition coursed down his spine like the lightning charge down Franklin's kite string. Down the great trunk nerves, out into every neuron, and across every synapse.

It was *him*. It was *Bod*. First it was the voice, the man's nasal twang, which he heard before he saw the face, while he still threaded his way around the end of the last waggon in the train. Then it was the conviction and forcefulness of the man's words, then the hair like the sumac leaves in October, the only one with hair like that in an assembly of twenty-five riders and drivers. But now, as he came to the well and moved into direct line of sight with the man, it was *his face*: the boxed jaw, clean-shaven.

The recognition flooded his senses. It was fourteen years back, the last he'd seen him, on hog-butchering day one frosty Saturday in late November, in his own orchard on the Pequea, the day this son plunged the butcher knife into a hog's head and led the children in the chanting, "Don't mess with the Dutch!" His own wife had cried out: "We don't want you here. Go join your people at the River. The ones who have the war spirit."

Where had they gone that same night, when they ran away, Bod and his mother? He'd changed his name, too. Captain Cameron. That's why he couldn't find him because he kept looking for Grünewald, the name he'd bestowed on the boy at birth. "Has anyone see Bod Grünewald?" "No, and did you mean Bob Grünewald? Robert?" Old Harris at Harris Ferry said. "No, Bod. Ichabod." "Ichabod? Really? Ichabod?" "Ichabod, I said. Have you seen him? About as tall as you and redheaded. Nineteen, about, and costumed like a waggoneer?" "No," he said. "I ain't." If not at Paxtang on the River, then where might they have landed? Where did the Scotch-Irish settle, because that was certainly who his mother would seek out, herself a Scotch-Irish. New York? The Shenandoah Valley? So it went at the next place and the next and the next. He got the same story everywhere. "Haven't seen anyone like that in these parts." Then he turned up. Today. In Lancaster's Penn Square, fourteen years later, in the outfit of a militia commander.

"Now, Gentlemen, as I've laid our cause clearly before you . . . On my honor, you will receive pay for every day you do service. And on behalf of the people of Pennsilvania, and on behalf of His Majesty Himself, I salute you!" The commander tipped his hat to the barefoot drivers who stood before him.

Aengus stopped the windlass crank and lifted his musket.

"Hip! Hip!"

The other rangers raised their muskets.

"Huzzah!"

They fired in unison.

"Nancy, you're up!" The commander turned on his horse and seemed to address an empty square, since no one else remained there. But they all heard it, a tinkling of sleigh bells and banging of tin pans and a sorry nag materialized in the Courthouse shadows. The nag pulled a waggon in jerks. The waggon resembled a miniature conestoga, with white canvas stretched over its hooped back and barrels on both sides riding on shelves in front of the rear wheels, each dangling a noisy tin dipper. The woman on the high driver's seat was a dumpling, dressed in a red-and-black checkered skirt and a mob-cap with frills all around. She was a woman who spent her days under the sun, and the deeply tanned face carried smallpox pits. Black hair streaked with gray frizzed from under the mob-cap in front and behind.

Nancy pushed her knees wide to maintain her balance and flogged the carriage whip to send the nag up alongside and behind the commander's horse, where it suddenly braked with its front legs stiff. The waggon stopped. Nancy gathered her skirts, leaped over the side like a waggoneer, and went around the back. She plucked a long pole anchored along the bed and poked it skyward to strip back the canvas that covered the rear half of the waggon, all the while with her eyes on the watching driver boys.

"Anybody for apple pie? With a splash of milk on it?" She dropped the pole and now lifted up, balanced on her outstretched palms, two large pies. "Come on." She wheeled the pies around to the built-in shelf at the rear of the waggon and reached overhead into the massed tin cups and bowls hanging on racks that hinged and rattled as she opened the racks outward.

"We take care of our boys on the road." The commander swung down from his horse. "Line up, Boys, it's a long ride yet till supper." He tossed the reins over the saddle and walked toward the well and the watering trough. The horse followed voluntarily, its nose tucked into his armpit.

"We're going to give back," the commander addressed the drivers, who eyeballed him, sparrow-mouthed. He lifted away the tricorn hat, and his fingertip drew a savage line around the top of his head, burrowing into the hair. He seized the hair and yanked upward, as if doing so would pull it off as a trophy.

"We'll take the scalps of the Frogs and their Indian toad-eaters. You have questions?"

The commander stepped through the line of waggons, and his own horse sniffed the water. It nosed urgently past him and thrust downward into the trough. The commander lifted his head.

Their eyes met. Greenywalt saw the shiver of recognition cross the man.

"Dat!"

"Bod!" His hands floated up by themselves.

"Dat!"

They rocked back and forth, arms around each other. He heard the first catch in his son's throat, the first muffled sob. Or was it his own voice? His shoulders shook in spasms. The commander stood a foot taller, but he bent forward, and his hands fumbled the old man's head against his chest.

He noted his son's smell. Fourteen years and he still smelled the same. It was a good smell, like trees. Like the Pequea forest trees. He felt the dimensions of the man's shoulders, well-muscled. He cupped his son's stubbled and perspired face between his hands and pulled it downward and kissed his lips, brushing the smartly cut mustache. His son's eyes were chips of the clear sky itself.

"When did you come here?" he asked his son.

Bod's eyes flicked sideways, as if self-conscious.

"Speak Deitsch, Dat." He said it in the dialect.

"Sure."

"I thought you'd gone to New York. I looked everywhere."

Bod's hand thumped on his back, reassuring.

"We live here. My Mem too. We have a farm in Paxtang."

"Why didn't you communicate? Visit us?"

His son had developed crow's feet around the eyes, and the boyish roundness of his face had firmed into angles.

"Your wife didn't want us on the Pequea. Did you forget? She hates my mother. But let's not talk about that." Bod pulled back from the embrace, and they stood by the trough, each man waiting for the other to somehow salvage the conversation. The ranger Aengus stopped the windlass crank and emptied another bucket into the trough. The stallion nosed another waggoneer's horse out and consumed the entire bucket in noisy draughts.

"I still have the gun." Bod said it through a huge smile that softened his face and revealed the gap in his teeth that the sailor had opened with a brick fifteen years ago. He reached behind the horse's saddle.

"He's beautiful." Greenywalt gestured at the horse. Who rode stallions, anyway, but generals? "Is he yours?"

Bod tipped his chin up in affirmation. "Eoch. His name's Eoch." He added that in English. "My brother Aengus named him." His hand wave indicated the man at the windlass. Aengus's face cracked into a smile.

"A stallion. Is he hard to—"

"Manage? Of course! But not for me. Here." He rolled the gun sideways so his father could see the stock, the fine etched-out swirls in the wood, and the signature scribed into the metal of the bar that held the cockpiece. "*Martin Mylin*. And I know what to do with it." He lifted the muzzle, sighting away at the Courthouse across the square. "Watch me." The rifle belched fire, and across the Square, an impossible distance for any ordinary musket or musketeer, the bell in the Courthouse tower suddenly emitted a leaden ommm.

"Nobody has a gun like it. Rifled. Not so good in battle, maybe. It takes more time to reload. But I'll get him on the first shot."

"You'll get him?" Greenywalt said. "I hope you mean a deer. Or a groundhog. Like I taught you."

"They're coming to burn and scalp our women and children, Dat. I don't believe like you do anymore." He hauled the rifle back and replaced it behind the saddle.

"Who are these men?" Greenywalt waved his hand over the other riders, who paraded slowly along the line of waggons in twos, on horseback.

"Hey, Men!" Bod veered away and addressed the men on horseback. "He wants to know: who are you?"

"Brothers in Christ!" the rider directly across the line of waggons shouted.

"The sword of the Lord and of Gideon!" the rider Aengus shouted, behind them at the well.

"I'm a captain now," Bod said, returning to Deitsch. "I command these men."

"Come home with us for a night before you go on this trip."

"I'll invite you up when I get back. You can meet my family."

"Your family?"

"You'll see."

He felt the reserve in his son's voice and saw it in his stance opposite. That was new. The boy Ichabod had never shown a modicum of reserve, but something had happened over fourteen years.

They stood still, a few feet apart, and gazed into each other's faces. A lilac bush in bloom stood directly behind the well, where Aengus cranked on the windlass again. He hadn't noticed it, but now the smell of the Pequea in April, an exuberant honey aroma, drizzled over him. Masses of purple blossoms, the size and outline of grape clusters, hung profusely among the green-black heart-shaped leaves.

He would remember this moment, again and again and again, every time he encountered blooming lilacs in the springs to come. The aroma would cause his heart to bleed.

"Well . . ." He glanced sideways and remembered. "Your brother Benjamin." Benjamin had hitched his horses to the waggon again and stood by the lead mare's head, caressing its muzzle.

"Benjamin!" Bod plucked off his hat and crossed the short five yards to the Greenywalt team and waggon. "Benjamin, you were a little shaver. You rode behind me on Casper."

The rangers in earshot around the well lifted their eyebrows in surprise. They were hearing Bod speak Deitsch for the first time. Perhaps it seemed odd to them, out of the mouth of a smooth-shaven redcoat officer. Bizarre, perhaps like a freak of nature, an apple growing on a walnut tree.

Benjamin glanced up. "I did?"

"Remember me?"

Greenywalt observed the jarring differences. Could they both be his sons? A muscular, imposing ranger in a redcoat jacket who barked orders and a gaunt, bookish lad who didn't smile and glared out through his spectacles like a fish hawk.

"I remember by your hair," Benjamin said. "Carroty pate!"

"Good!" Bod extended his arm, and Benjamin seized the commander's hand and pumped it.

Greenywalt sensed the opening. Since the Boy was going, this was a godsend, wasn't it? He would accompany a man who knew the forest, who thought like a scout, who knew how to deal with the bully-ruffians, the perverse men of the highway.

"Can you look out for him, Bod? Franklin conscripted him and the waggon. He's all I got left."

Bod reviewed him and the request.

"No, even better. Go home." He directed this to Benjamin. "Go home. I'll drive the waggon."

Benjamin suddenly stirred, energized. "No! I want to go. Dat! I've committed. What about your fine speech? 'Lift the drooping head of Pennsilvania.'" He directed that in English at Bod. "I'm ready."

"You have no idea." Bod whistled, and the stallion tossed up his head at the trough and immediately broke into a fast walk toward him. Bod looped the reins to the back of Greenywalt's waggon. He stepped to the driver's spot alongside the conestoga and took up the long lines that rested there. "They'll be killing out there. You don't want to see it. Aengus, lead out while there's lots of daylight. I'll be right here."

Greenywalt stretched his hand to his son, his older son, and Bod took the hand with his left and squeezed it.

"I'll invite you when I get back," he repeated.

The ranger Aengus mounted, crossed the line of the teams, and rode out into the Square past Nancy's escort waggon. "All done here? Okay, Gents. Will's Creek and Fort Cumberland. By Sunday evening. We have some driving to do."

The foremost waggon and team pitched forward, and each waggon followed in its turn. Bod gestured with a small hand wave.

Greenywalt stood by the well with Benjamin. He put his arm around the boy's shoulder, and the boy didn't resist. They watched the waggons move out. It was then he felt the heavy downward drag of the pouch of coins in his pocket. It was a horrific trade. He didn't want the coins. He wanted his son. The other one. He'd had him for a brief hour, and now the man slipped away again, like the magical stag that only appeared once every decade.

What would he have done differently if he had known then that it was the last he would see Bod alive?

PART 2

THE OLD COUNTRY

CHAPTER 4

THE UNFORTUNATE FORESTER, WALDHILSBACH, 1706

H E WAS NOT GOING TO BAWL: he'd vowed that up front. No sobs of weakness that his future employer, the Elector Palatine, might see. No red eyes for the little ones to stare up at: they needed him strong. Like Father. Or as he once was.

This afternoon, his father's long, rangy body filled up the box, pillows wedging him up so the mourners could view his face from the side. Mutti had scissored off the caked-blood uniform and dressed him in a new one, forest green, woolen. His once capable hands that had instructed the boy's, step by step, how to pour the black powder down the throat of the flintlock, then the ball and square cloth, how to tamp it all with the ramrod, then prime the flashpan so they were prepared for any creature when they headed into the forest—those hands were now curled stiff like claws, and Mutti's hands caressed back and forth over them, skipping occasionally to the gouge on his forehead, which she'd hidden with lots of her cosmetics, now running in chalky creeks down his cheeks.

Raindrops—the size of his tears if he could have saved them from yesterday—paused all over his father's face like smallpox eruptions. Some trickled into the horrible gash. The streaks of chalk, the Imperial coins weighing down his sightless eyes, his mouth fixed open in a leer—Klaus didn't think he knew this man anymore.

Thank God, the blow that killed, the huge axe gouge, was on the back, out of sight.

"Kaspar! Kaspar! Kaspar!"

He'd never in his life seen his mother cry, and it ripped him. Like vomit propelling up the throat, it burned. Correction. It ripped him the first ten times, but today, after twenty-four hours of hearing it, when he heard her cry, he felt nothing. He was numb. But she carried on, pleading with his father's remains.

"Kaspar, what now? I thought I . . . No! If you . . . Kaspar, if you'd warned me last week he'd threatened you, I could have . . . What could I have . . . ?"

He considered his mother elegant. Not glamorous, like the women of the Elector's Court, but more refined than any other woman in the village.

But this afternoon, she was disheveled. She and Grossmuttchi wore all black today. Her bodice, the mantua trimmed with black ribbons at the elbows, the skirts that trailed in the grass, the rain cape she and Grossmuttchi had both thrown over their heads when they looked out this morning—all black. The cape had slipped off her shoulders, and Heidi picked it up and carried it. His mother's repeated slapping of her forehead with both hands and ramming her hands through her hair as if she might smear the events of the last week out of her brain had ripped loose several tresses the length of his arm. They trailed across the face of the dead man. His brother Helmut (wearing the new black waistcoat Mutti had commissioned a week ago when it became clear her husband was sinking and would never recover from his wounds) stood like a toy bodyguard by her side, and after each emotional outburst, he patted her back.

"Kaspar, four little ones! What am I going to do?"

"Five, dear God!" His grandmother's eyes rolled upward. She stood at the head of the coffin, holding the hands of Trina and little Rudi. He had learned enough about the world in the last two years to know what she meant. The bulge in the front of Mutti's long black gown meant they'd been doing it. Sex. He'd done his part and left. *And us?*

"Why, Kaspar? He was jealous, that's why! They said it was the fruit trees. The Elector's little apple trees, which you defended with your precious life. But it wasn't, Kaspar, was it? It was jealousy! When Daadi died and you took the Mayor's seat, he couldn't stand it. It enraged him. And he hunted you down like a stag—"

"Barbara," his grandmother said, looking around, as if the trees might be embarrassed by the woman's outburst.

"And I curse him!" Mutti said.

"Barbara."

"I curse him. Andreas Ziegler, I curse you!" The dark sky shadowed her terribly white, puffy face. A mad wind circled the inside of the walled cemetery, tumbling the already fallen red and yellow oak leaves ahead of it. The sky threatened to let loose any minute and drench them.

"And where is he now?" she said. "And the whole village?"

He knew exactly where they were. Ziegler was Mayor now, and if he said no one dare honor the family by attending the dead forester's funeral, no one would come. They'd held a lonely wake last night, with just the family and Heidi, whom they paid to show up.

"Where is Pastor?" His mother moved heavily and leveraged herself up off her knees with one hand on the coffin, causing it to tilt on the sawhorses. She reached vertical and flung the question around, aimed at no one in particular the first time, but then at the elegant carriage beyond the cemetery wall, the twin white horses, and the long figure next to the carriage.

He'd regarded it as the honor due a man of his father's stature in the Elector's far-flung forests and towns, when the carriage wheeled in. The courtier stepped out with ceremony. His black hat trailed yards of black crepe back into the carriage, and when he arrived at the bottom of the stairs, he reached sideways and doffed the hat, one high-heeled shoe pointed toward them, his right hand resting on the hilt of his rapier. The boy didn't know him. Neither did his mother—just one of a dozen pretty faces in the Elector's Court—but the fact that he'd been sent by the Elector he took as a wonderful omen.

It had not yet occurred to him that there could be other reasons for the man's coming.

"Where is Pastor?" his mother repeated, this time to the Elector's man. "You! Why didn't you bring him?"

The courtier replaced his hat and tilted his face slightly, gazing down the road toward Gaiberg, the direction the Pastor would certainly come from.

"So he can ring the bell." Mutti whirled back to the mute face below her. "To summon the village, Kaspar. The village you served so bravely. To the end."

"Pastor went to get permission, Ma'am," Heidi said. "Now that we share the church with the Catholics—"

"The village won't come," Grossmuttchi said. His brother and sister clutched her legs, frightened by the spectacle of their mother falling apart.

"The village won't come," Mutti repeated to the stiff figure. "Why do they hate us, Kaspar? Why? When you worked so hard for them. Fifteen years!" She flung it, like the Turks flung Christian heads from their catapaults—so he'd been taught—at the Elector's man: *"Fifteen years!"*

The Elector's man's face furnished no more emotion than the dead man's. The coachman passed a long clay pipe to him.

"Fifteen years!" His mother's voice was not plaintive or defeated; it rang imperious and angry. "What will his pension be?"

The Electoral prince exhaled, opening and closing his mouth precisely to form two perfect smoke O's.

"Ask him for me, Klausi."

He stood fifteen feet from the drama unfolding around the coffin. If someone had pried the face off the village clock tower and dropped it down on the graveyard, with the drama at the center, where the hands attached, with the long dark empty hole in the ground and the mound of dirt beyond it in the direction of six o'clock, the ruined Kapelle beyond the stone enclosure wall at nine, and the Elector's man at twelve, where the lane looped off the road that stretched between Gaiberg and the town, then he had chosen to stand over the wall at four, where he could watch them all because he had a foreboding.

"Klausi, ask him. Did he bring the pension he owes your father?"

His entire boyhood, his father had drilled into him the importance of the Elector and his business. Villagers might grumble about compulsory work, compulsory hunts to bring game to him, but for his family, it was different. Someday he'd be the Elector's forester, like his father and his father before and the great-grandfather he'd never known. They were all foresters, although they'd worked for other Electors in other states. He'd guard his forest, his deer, his timber, and his orchards of fruit.

This man wouldn't answer the distressed simple question that his mother had asked. Surely not because we're Reformed. Was the courtier Catholic, like his boss, the Elector Palatine? Of course. Still, no reason for disrespect toward the wife of a faithful employee.

"Sir! You heard my mother. Our pension."

The Elector's man removed the pipe. He was only a youth. The massed blonde curls of his wig framed his round pink cheeks and made him cherubic.

"His Highness has already informed you, Frau Grünewald." The Elector's man reached for his hat again and lifted it to a point three inches above the blond waves, tilting his chin slightly in Mutti's direction.

"Ask him to tell us, Klausi."

"You've gotten everything you're getting," the Elector's man said. He wheeled, extending his pipe at arm's length, to indicate the Gaiberg Road. Now Klaus heard it too, the rumble of wheels, punctuated by hoofbeats.

"The Pastor!" His mother turned to face Gaiberg Road, one hand falling back to the coffin. "He's here!" But it wasn't their Pastor seated by the driver and riding on the uncovered waggon that crunched to a stop at the gap in the cemetery wall. The man who leaped over the side of the waggon wore long black robes, which he hiked up with one hand, while the other trailed a porcelain crucifix with the Savior cemented to it. A boy in white robes scrambled after him. The four laborers on the waggon wore dirty smocks with arms either too short or too long. They perched like obedient hounds, watching for a signal. The two cart horses snorted and stamped their feet.

"Not you, Papist!" Mutti's voice turned angry again. He strode directly toward her, and the long cords that wound around his waist dangled and banged his striding legs.

Klaus knew him, of course, from his visits. "The Jesuit," Grossmuttchi said, spitting when she said it, although the priest insisted that people call him "Father Kneitz."

His parents' marriage was mixed: his Catholic father had married into a Reformed family. Grandfather hadn't only been Mayor; he was also an elder among the Calvinists. His headstone, upright behind Grossmuttchi right now, was white marble, taller than the boy himself, and more handsome, he thought, than any other stone in this dilapidated chapel cemetery where, for two hundred years, Müller family members had been laid to rest until Resurrection Morning. The headstone proclaimed his importance, didn't it? The stonemasons had constructed it in three sections, with a stone urn in front at ground level for flowers and a tall white panel above, engraved with his life facts and his name, ERNEST MÜLLER, prominent at the top, beneath a small engraved cross. A large blackish marble slab grafted onto the top of the white, with a bas-relief carving of two angels with their heads bowed, under a carved awning that supported four-inch-high filigreed leaves of marble. The red earth still showed, raw and untrampled, between the clumps of sparse grass over his spot, a reminder to all how quickly their family fortunes had changed.

The Jesuit had come through their doorway last summer, uninvited, the day after they'd buried Grandfather, with the evening sun backlighting him. He pointed at the children. Mutti turned at the clavichord in shock at his unannounced entry.

"Why haven't they been baptized?" he asked. "Three, four . . . Any more?"

"They have," she said.

"Not in the Holy Catholic Faith! Not by a proper priest."

His father stood stricken, as the boy had never seen him stiffen before any other man except the Elector Himself, his eyes sticking to the floorboards at his feet. "Of course, of course. Well, of course," his father said. (But he had no power to follow through with it because he'd been attending with Mutti and the Calvinists since he moved here, and she was in charge of the family's spiritual welfare.)

And now, Father Kneitz was back in their lives, triumphant.

"Who were you expecting?" He didn't slow but kept walking, around the foot of the coffin.

"Our Pastor. He promised me—"

"Your husband was a baptized Catholic, wasn't he? I passed your Pastor on the road here. Horses travel faster, you know." A reminder of the fact that their Pastor couldn't afford one. "And I informed him so. This one is mine."

"And did he agree to it?" she shouted.

Kneitz paused directly opposite Mutti, his feet only a yard away from the open grave behind him.

"That doesn't really matter, does it?" he said. "The law says he belongs to the church where he's been baptized. The law also says his faith rules his children too. Doesn't it now, Frau Grünewald?"

The pimple-faced boy in white sidled along, just off his elbow, and lifted a metal canister.

The priest gazed into Father's face and began his speech.

"Kaspar Grünewald. Kaspar Grünewald. 'Grant this mercy, O Lord, we beseech Thee, to Thy servant departed, Kaspar, that he may not receive in punishment the requital of his deeds who in desire did keep Thy will, and as the true faith here united him to the company of the faithful, so may Thy mercy unite him above to the choirs of angels. . . .'"

His mother stood erect across the coffin from the priest, unmoving, arms crossed over his future brother or sister, and Grossmuttchi stood the same, at the head of the box. Neither of them spoke, but he knew exactly what Mutti was doing: she was biting down on her tongue.

"'. . . delivered from the pains of Hell and inherit eternal life through Christ our Lord. Amen.'"

The priest turned, lifted the canister from the hands of the boy, and held it preciously, like a gift he was receiving, while the boy un-lidded it. Water sprinkled across the body from the open hand of his bare, long-boned arm.

"Have they said their good-byes?" He turned back, his eyes probing.

Mutti didn't flinch or cry out. She hadn't shed a tear since her exchange with the Elector's man. She stood poised, staring. "Yes."

He motioned. The men on the waggon tumbled off, carrying two coils of rope, which they brought to the coffin. Two of them lifted the lid, settled it loosely onto the box, and then received the rope ends offered them beneath the coffin from the other two. They straightened up again, waiting for a signal.

The priest moved to the foot of the coffin so he wouldn't block their work, sprinkling water over the coffin with his right hand as he walked, the white porcelain cross in his left grazing the unprotesting body within. "*Rore coelesti perfundat . . .*'" None of them heard the rest because a loud thunderclap overhead drowned out his words, but did it matter? None of them knew Latin anyway.

The boy understood what his mother wanted. He saw the priest wasn't going to grant it. He took off, high-jumping sideways over the enclosure wall and coming down in time to see the priest's hand flap and the coffin come up off the sawhorses, lifting his father, the box balanced on the two ropes and swaying heavily. He saw his mother's clenched hands, for she hadn't released his father's hands but gripped his cold claws beneath the partly closed lid, yanking them toward herself. She sobbed loudly now:

"No! I want Pastor! I want Pastor to bless him first!"

As the men lifted and stepped sideways to straddle the open hole, her downpull and draped weight against the side tilted the coffin, and at that instant the unthinkable happened. The coffin balance shifted sharply downward and right. The lid rose as if it were Resurrection Morning, and his father appeared, his bare feet coming first and kicking the lid aside, and then, as if he were sliding out of bed, the rest of him came over the completely tilted box edge. Responding to the weight shift, the two northside gravediggers made wild one-armed grabs for the tilting edge of the box, but he was already over the side, the three pillows tumbling around him as his body picked up speed, feet downward toward the open hole, clearing the edges of the earth as neatly as a diver, his coarse dark hair straining upward. Except for the fact that his hands were still folded, frozen on his chest, it looked like he was enjoying the ride. He went out of sight, and a loud splash followed, then a second and smaller splash, then silence.

But only for a few seconds because the sparse, remaining leaves overhead began to rattle furiously, as if on cue.

He reached his mother as her knees buckled, and she fell backward into his arms.

"Go!" The priest pointed his men toward the waggon. The empty box, the ropes dangling downward into the hole, landed on the dirt mound behind them. The rain fell in torrents, and the men ran helter-skelter, tumbling back up onto the waggon, which was already moving out as the last man hauled himself over the edge.

Grossmuttchi glared at the priest, while Rudi and Trina wrapped themselves in her skirts against the rain.

"Ingrate!" Kneitz delivered his verdict on the widow. "Ingrate!"

"This is outrageous! You knew what she wanted," Grossmuttchi shouted. A line of clear water streamed off her nose.

"You don't worry. They'll be back to finish," Kneitz said, tramping steadily through the tumbled and worn headstones toward the gap in the wall. "Although you deserve nothing further."

The Elector's carriage wheeled around smartly, and the princeling leaped out and held the door open. He lifted his hand and hat and swept the hat almost to the ground in a grand gesture toward Kneitz, who walked, deliberate and unhurried, through the headstones, up onto the carriage steps and disappeared inside, without a backward glance. His white-robed assistant scrambled behind, and then the Elector's man went in, the door clicked shut, and the carriage rolled off.

They'd been dishonored. Treated like Jews. The carriage leaving with three men inside in the dry, abandoning two ladies in a driving rain, was only the latest insult from the ambitious priest and the Court lackey, and it all looked deliberate to him. Letting a man lie dead and exposed at the bottom of a water hole like a trapped and bludgeoned varmint. Sending a Jesuit to perform the funeral of a man whose family were faithful Calvinists. Rewarding his father's fifteen years of service, at such great risk that it ended in his murder, with a paltry five Reichstaler, thirty days' worth of his former salary. Someone had planned this.

He longed to pursue and pelt the men in the carriage with rocks, but it was pouring rain on his family, Mutti lay half-conscious against his chest, and Grossmuttchi was beside herself with fury. No one was in charge of their little party, and right then he recollected what Grandfather would have done.

"Helmut." Helmut was two years younger and dependable. He knew that fact about him.

"Take Mutti home. I'll be along later."

"Yes, that's good, Klaus." Grossmuttchi revived and seized the hands of his brother and sister. Chocolate rivulets were gurgling down the waggon path already. Helmut led Mutti by the hand, and Heidi, the servant, walked on the other side with her arm around his mother's neck, stretching Mutti's cape up to cover her head. Grossmuttchi followed with Trina and Rudi.

"Klausi?" Grossmuttchi turned at the gap in the wall and called from beneath the rain cape. "What about you?"

"I'm staying."

"Come with us!"

"Someone needs to watch him. Till it's closed up."

"Klausi," his mother called. Her voice was weak. "Klausi . . ." She didn't have the strength to turn her head. "The pension. What did the man say about the pension?"

CHAPTER 5

IN HIS FATHER'S GRAVE

HE DIDN'T WAIT for them to get out of sight. He wasn't su-
perstitious. He towed the coffin off the mound of dirt, down
into the grass between the rows of headstones, and crawled beneath it
to wait for the Jesuit to keep his promise and bring the gravediggers
back to finish the job when the rain stopped. Rain drummed on the
boards; the carpenter deserved credit, making the bottom watertight,
and not a drop seeped through the joints.

Unfortunately, the box was up top and his father was down below, lying in several inches of water, and Klaus tried to imagine a way
to get him back into the box. He worked his way through several
scenarios.

He could tie a rope around the man's legs, fasten a block and
tackle to a tree limb, and use the pulleys to drag him up and back into
the box. If he tied several spaced loops into one rope, fastened it to a
tree, and lowered himself by using the loops as steps, then he could
use the second rope to tie to his father and climb out before pulling
up the corpse—but then what? How could he safely lower his father
in the box? Four gravediggers couldn't keep him from falling out and
into the hole. And who would loan him pulleys or a horse to pull

the weight out of the grave? But then, how could he try any of these things if he couldn't get out of the pit himself?

Night was coming, and the hole needed to be covered. Otherwise . . . otherwise, what? Dogs, wolves . . .

He'd seen them in these woods.

The Elector's private forest extended all around. This was his father's territory, as Oberförster.

What benefit had the man's loyalty brought him and his family? His murder. The injustice of it physically scorched his chest, as if he wore a shirt full of live coals. The injustice of it! The man who did it, caught in the act of stealing the Elector's fruit—hadn't he swung his woodman's axe into Father's skull? That man was telling everyone he'd found no witnesses to the crime he'd discovered in the Elector's orchards. That it was certainly a gypsy who did it. Or a highwayman. "But who stood to benefit from his death? Who stood to become mayor in his place?" Mutti had asked. "Who assaulted him last winter before the town councilmen gathered in his tavern, and helped his sons to throw him into the street? *Andreas Ziegler.*"

As the evening came on, the rain ceased against the coffin. He had just crawled from beneath the box when he heard what he had dreaded. The animal wail came from the left, from behind the Kapelle ruins. Then an answering whoop from dead ahead, the massive oak tree beyond the wall on the packed dirt lane, where the Elector's man had parked his carriage.

A pack of them. How many in a pack? Five? Ten? Twenty? Fire— they're afraid of fire, . . . but there is no firebrand or live coal to light one, and all the fallen branches are surely soaked. A good hefty stick, then.

He couldn't take the chance of leaving the walled cemetery to find one in the woods beyond because they were already close. Too close already.

"Awwwwhooooo!"

He leaped around, certain he'd catch the yellow eyes, the gray ears, the tongue pink and drooling out between the long white eyeteeth, but No. Unless . . . a shape moved behind the oak that grew just inside the wall, and instinctively he lifted his foot and thrust it twice, sharp and hard, against the interior of the coffin. Pine was a poor weapon but perhaps just the sight of the board in his hands, in the dusk . . .

The human wolf stepped completely free from behind that oak. The human wolf, Ziegler himself. Not the tavern keeper, no. It was his son, the one actually named Wolf! He moved a step toward Klaus, half-crouching as he motioned with an uplifted hand. The pack materialized from various angles, six of them, barefoot, ragged, none older than Klaus himself.

"Hey, Cully! Kneitz said we'd find you here."

"Bing avast!"

They were ragamuffins, all of them. Unschooled, except for Ziegler, who went to the school Kneitz had opened here in the restored Kapelle so Catholics needn't go any more to the village school in Gaiberg, the one run by their Pastor. Laborers' sons, all of them except Ziegler, and destined to be laborers like their fathers because their families owned no land and couldn't pay to apprentice them out in a trade. In that way, he and Ziegler had everything in common: each had a future, each had a skill.

"What you want? Bing avast!"

"We want you!" Ziegler laughed easily. His shoulders shook and they laughed with him. The other six were spread apart, like the numerals of the clockface, all coming through the headstones toward him as he stood by the broken coffin; the hole with his father at the bottom was two long strides behind him, and beyond, with the dirt mound between, was the wolf behind his back.

"Why?" He chose to focus on Ziegler. They would not do anything without a signal from him.

"Why not? Who thinks he's superior to us? The Chief Forester's son? Who wears the gold rum-kicks, the holiday clothes? The silk drawers, the coat and lace . . . the cravat . . . ?" Ziegler chopped at his neck. "And the shoon with silver buckles?"

"Yeah." The wolves at twelve o'clock and nine o'clock echoed him.

"Who's navel-tied with the Elector and gets to eat one of his prized deer, maybe at Christmas? Maybe at Easter? While we get what?"

"Turnips!" shouted the wolf at nine. He was the one behind Klaus now. They were closing, about ten feet away.

"Who plucks juicy apples from the Elector's orchards? And plums?"

"Not us! Not us!"

"Whose old man conscripts our fathers to cut timber for the high and mighty . . . *Elector?*"

He swung his coffin board carefully, letting it slap loudly against his free hand.

"Watch him, boys." Ziegler was six feet off, moving just beyond a headstone. The wolf on his left had climbed the earth mound and seemed to consider a running jump across the open grave, which would land him on Klaus's heels.

"Whose old man makes us work for *him*? Treats our village like his personal puppy dogs?"

"His old man!"

That was a lie. Only two of the boys were from Waldhilsbach; the others he'd never seen before.

"But my old man hushed him for good."

"Sooooo. . . . You admit it!" The blood kettle boiled over in his brain. "Your father says he didn't, but you just said it: he killed him. My father protected the Elector's forest. And your father murdered him."

Ziegler stopped, eyeballing Klaus, just beyond the reach of his board. He was also scoping the position of his troops. "Picking his apples in Hell now, I suspect." He smirked.

"I'll kill you, Ziegler." His voice held even and steady. If he made the first move, he stood a better chance. What should that first move be?

"Ohhohohoho!" Ziegler threw back his head, laughing. "He'll kill——"

And he squashed the laugh, with one enormous leap onto Ziegler, crunching his nose with his fist, dropping him backward and then sweeping his free hand around with the board to catch any risk-takers. The board caught the leg of the wolf who had just leaped across the grave and landed awkwardly, one leg down the hole. He teetered on the edge, grasping bunches of grass with both hands to get out. The grass in his left pulled loose.

"Help me! Help me!"

Ziegler sat up, blood streaming from both nostrils and dripping from his chin onto his shirtfront. He unfolded upward slowly, wiped his nose with a sleeve, and Klaus made the mistake of looking around toward his left flank. Ziegler made his move, closing the four feet between them, his head horizontal and head-butting Klaus in the gut. He went heels up over the back of the toady, who'd pulled himself out of the hole and cleverly dropped onto all fours directly behind while Klaus was distracted.

They swarmed him when his back hit the ground, tearing away the board, sitting on his arms.

"Unrig the cull!" Ziegler shouted. The other two pulled everything down that would come down, leaving him naked on the soaked mud. "Look! He's hairy!" They guffawed but seemed unsure what to do next, how much damage to inflict. Incidents like this would reach the Elector's ears, and he would avenge his employee on their parents, as he'd done before. Klaus pulled loose, scrambled to his feet, one hand yanking the breeches upward, the other wrenching the board back and forth with one of Ziegler's wolves.

He was yanking and wrenching and back-stepping as Ziegler came in small steps toward him, a grin spreading slowly. Too late, he learned why, as his reaching foot came down over the open hole, and he sank backward, the same journey his father had taken feetfirst two hours earlier. The smack of landing, six feet down on his back, drove the oxygen out of him. He clawed for air like a man drowning.

Their open, laughing mouths wove in and out over the grass fringe of the grave cut., Their hands raised and the balls of clay they threw clobbered his half-naked body and he rolled to protect himself. The mud kept coming.

"Bury them both!"

The mound of dirt by the hole had turned to soggy mud. They had no shovels, only the coffin board and their bare hands to scoop up a few cups worth at a time.

His situation became clear. He lay face down on a sort of dais, his hands in chilly, ankle- deep water, filled with leaves. His nose was buried in a patch of green wool that reeked like a soaked sheep. It was his father's forester jacket, and the rocks that protruded into his stomach were the man's clenched bones. The clouds overhead had ripped apart and the full moon lit up the hole.

He bolted upright, and the face stared back. The body hadn't landed completely flat but with its upper back and right shoulder propped against the grave wall. The Imperial coins had fallen away, and the fall had jarred one eye open in a demonic stare.

"Ahhhhhhhhhhhhhhhhhhhhh . . ."

In the walled-in hole, the scream was deafening. He scrambled to escape it, clambered against the far wall and ended with his legs thrust straight out, the ochre water surging all about and between them, while right about the knees and the top of his black silk stockings, ten white toes of the corpse's bare feet protruded from the ochre water.

"Ahhhhhhhhhhhhhhhhhhhhhh . . ."

It punished his ears. He begged it to stop. All at once he knew— it was his own voice. The instant the screaming ceased, the raucous laughter began. They'd been watching. Ziegler's voice overpowered their laughter.

"Bury him, I said."

Mud trickled into his ears. It oozed out of his hair and across his line of sight. He felt it chunking on his legs. It was chunking on the dead man's legs as well.

The horror of it began to appear, burning through like the sun burned off the mists over the Neckar. *How far.* He gazed at the face at the far end. *How far you have fallen. We all . . . Tumble tumble tumble.* Over the coffin edge feet first because of Mutti's hands. And me backfalling because tricked there. And more. Much more.

Murdered. Point of an axe into the soft yielding back of the head. A gouge so deep . . . That pink and yellow pudding, dripping onto the floor. Was that your mind? As we dragged you in by the shoulders. Shouting crazy words. While the killer. . . gone where? Tossing away the brain-stained axe. Where? In the river? Under the logs? While he ran away, through the apple trees. Smashing the fallen apples under his fleeing feet. Like foresters' heads.

And more. Much more. The Elector Palatine. Mighty on his ivory chair in Heidelberg Castle. Arch-Treasurer and Elector of the Holy Roman Empire. Duke of Bavaria, Juiliere, Iberres and Berg. Count of Veldentz, Spanheim, Marck, Ravensburg, and Molours. Lord of Ravenstein. Et cetera. Et cetera. Wasn't I rulered in fifth grade for leaving out just one of those? His white wigged head nodding. His pudgy fingers outstretched to mine, across from him in the royal carriage: "Our next Chief Forester! Delighted!" Applause all around. Huzzah! Huzzah! . . . *Can't reach down here to shake my hand now. Won't touch won't even look.*

And more. Much more. The whole family, Müllers and Grünewalds. Little and big. Tumbled together from the height of happiness. Never happy again. We will be no more. This huge sadness. I will be no more.

His demon eye upon me matters not.

Never happy again. And what are these, cutting paths through the encrusted mud, turning chocolate like the mud? Falling wet on my hands. Tears, yes, tears. Cry! Cry your eyes out! We will be no more.

He cried, finally. Huge sobs. He fought to hide them, couldn't let the wolves see them.

He heard distant shouts over his sobs. Maybe they weren't distant. Everything sounds distant six feet down. He listened and realized, the mud had stopped. The hole was silent. They were gone. He was alone. No—not alone. Together with a corpse.

He huddled in the earthen corner, wondering, had they run off? How soon until they came back? The hole smelled like a cistern, and it had gotten dark.

They returned. Dirt crumbs splashed in the water between his legs. They weren't talking, and he didn't look up to give them the satisfaction of seeing his tears. More crumbs. They moved around the hole, assessing, perhaps. He threw his arms overhead to protect himself.

"Well, I never . . ." He didn't know the voice, deep and masculine. It was not his tormentors. "What is it? What are you?"

He only understood later that the man had judged him, in the darkness, to be an animal of some sort, trapped and unable to get out. "Do you speak?"

Was it Ziegler himself, the old man, come to eyeball his mortal enemy's son? Triumphantly. Did he have his axe with him?

Then silence. He had gone. That was worse. The man didn't care if he lived or drowned. He didn't care who he was or why he was trapped.

A rhythmic patter started. Rain fell again. And something more. It hit the wall by his hand and splashed alongside his leg—a small sound, not a rock, not a clod of dirt.

"Grab ahold."

He saw nothing in the dark at the bottom of the hole. Above the opening circle in the forest, where the church and its cemetery were niched, formless storm clouds had moved in and blocked the light.

"Grab ahold!" the voice commanded.

He trailed his hands around and brushed it, sunken in the water, a rope end as broad as his big toe. When he pulled on it, he felt an answering tug.

"Do you have ahold?"

He wrapped the rope around both forearms, the end between his clenched hands, and tugged again.

The rope tightened abruptly, and his body lifted, clods of mud dropping noisily off his legs and down into the water. His shoes—the good buckled ones Mutti had bought for the wake last night—clawed the wall for a foothold, catching a root here and there and pawing loose more dirt. Abruptly his body exited over the lip of the grave, and an enormous palm and fingers grabbed his seat, pinched it sharply, and propelled him forward with such force that his face skidded through the wet grass.

"A boy, huh?"

The final effort had dropped his rescuer arse-down in the grass by the grave, facing Klaus. He saw the man's silhouette, staring, but words failed him. Grass and flower petals were crammed into his mouth, his nose, his ears, and he deeply inbreathed their greenness.

The man went away. He knew he'd returned when a sack landed on his arms, still outstretched and helpless on the grass.

"Dry yourself."

Loose flour embedded in the sack flew up. The boy sneezed three times, one after another. The man laughed. It was the first indication that he might be friendly. He pushed up on his forearms and daubed his face, his arms. He sensed the man's dark shape but didn't look.

"Why'd you jump in?"

Ridiculous conclusion! He jerked up to stare into the man's eyes. The man's dark clothes melted into the night so that he didn't have an outline. His hat was dark too, a curious type of flat, broad-brimmed hat that he'd seen now and again as he roamed the woods with Father. A long frock coat covered him to midleg. He puzzled out the shape of a large, untrimmed beard. Overall, the man looked squarish, and his muscles bulged his coarse stockings and thighs.

"I'm not here to hurt you. . . . You can talk to me." The man seemed to understand the emotional drain that a couple hours in a grave—he didn't seem aware of the other body down there—might put on someone. He paused politely before the next question. "You fell?" And then a second flash of insight. "Ahhh, the boys! They pushed you! And the mud"—he described Klaus's entire body with his hand—"all over you."

Klaus noticed the man's dialect. It was a thick mountain accent, from up the Rhine.

He nodded. It wasn't exactly true. He'd fallen under his own weight. But for this man's purposes, yes, they'd pushed him.

"Come along." He stretched up, and Klaus's original guess was correct. He wasn't tall and angled like his father. He was more of a rectangle. Rather short, rather wide. He lifted a leg over a headstone, moving toward the exit gap in the cemetery wall. A whinny broke in the gloom beyond the wall, and the high-pitched tinkle of small bells. Bells! Like Christmas. Or sleigh rides.

Klaus tossed the bag aside and unfolded upward. The rain had ceased, and now overhead clouds abruptly tore apart again, and a bolt of moonlight shot down. He turned back toward the open grave. Moonlight lit his father's body at the bottom of the hole, although his face, propped at that angle, was shadowed.

The man looked around. "Are you coming?"

He only stared at his father. He knew the answer was No. He couldn't leave him. He couldn't go anywhere and abandon his body. Kneitz's gravediggers weren't coming back tonight, that much was certain.

"I can't leave him."

"Him?" The man took a step toward him, then picked up speed and stood over the hole, the moonlight falling over his shoulder and onto the bony hands and the ten protruding toes of the body below, half-sunken in the water.

"Did you know him? Who is he?"

His tongue ripped loose from the roof of his mouth, where it had been stapled in shock. "My father. He fell"—his voice shook tremendously—"out . . ." He looked at his rescuer. Klaus felt incapable of running away.

The man waited as well, silent. The moonlight that illuminated his father's corpse also illuminated the man. The hat, flat, unadorned, old-fashioned. Bearded, unlike any men he knew and the beard untrimmed. The Swisser accent. *A Mennonist.*

"I want to put him back"—he darted toward the coffin box, still upside down in the grass, and hoisted the end; the side panel he had kicked out lay some yards away—"in the box."

The Mennonist folded his arms and pushed fat, stubby fingers through his beard. Now that he had turned, the boy saw eyes. The moon lit his face. The eyes watched him steadily. He was considering the impossible request. Abruptly his hands dropped.

"We'll do that," he said. He came alongside, lofted the broken coffin with one hand, and revolved it to parallel the hole, then dropped it and bent and retrieved the rope that lay sprawled in the grass. His chunky hands moved adroitly to make a bowline knot. "We'll do that!" he repeated and clapped Klaus's shoulder with his large free hand. "Can you make a knot like that?" He tugged the knot apart and retied it, step by step, giving each step a number. Klaus followed his lead, took it apart himself, and retied it, repeating each step's number.

"A quick learner! I'll lower you down." He pointed to the bottom. "See. I get a good grip, and you take this end and put it under his"—he stared full into the boy's eyes—"under your father's armpits. Understand? Tie it on top over his chest. In a knot like that. And you don't pull this end of the rope until I say, or you'll put me down on top of you." Klaus nodded. He turned his back to the hole, the loose rope end between his hands, and rappelled down.

It took some time to do the job. The body, heavy with water and mud, seemed cemented in the clay bottom and tears swarmed his eyes, making it impossible to see, even with the moonlight. He sobbed as he pried the body up from the clay, threaded the rope under his armpits, and looped it over his chest. Then he looked into his father's face, and it seemed the eye was moving, alive. But friendly now. The eye talked to him.

CHAPTER 6

THE MENNONIST

THEY HAD JUST COME riding out of the forest, into the clearing over a narrow valley. His father turned, high in his saddle, and fixed his eye on him.

"I need a drink," Klaus had said.

They'd been riding since breakfast, inspecting the Elector's forest. Two rabbits hung by their hind legs on a string off the boy's saddle. The man was teaching his son "everything you need to know," he said, "on the day when he appoints you his forester."

"Over there!" Klaus pointed the muzzle of his flintlock, the one his father had gifted him on his twelfth birthday, across the perfect lines of vines, hanging thick with purple fruit already. A neat little *Hof* nested in the valley beyond the rows of vines. "I see a well."

"Let's go!" His father dug his heels into his mare, and her hooves kicked up clods of dirt as she leaped forward on the path that led upward past the vines, away from the direction the boy had indicated.

He sat still in the saddle, confused.

His father turned his head back at full gallop, one hand on the reins, calling back over his shoulder. "Come on!"

But he stalled on the pony. "I need a drink!" He headed the pony down the farmer's path between the rows of vines. He clucked her into a gentle trot. It wasn't disobedience if it was purely a matter of opinion, like whether to go which of two equally good paths that led to the same place. But he had misread his father. The mare came charging past, and his father's hand caught the pony's bridle as he passed and abruptly ground both animals to a halt. Only the boy's full downward hug of the pony's neck kept him from pitching over her head.

"I said, Come!" His father's usually easy voice sounded harsh, uncompromising.

"Father! There's a well."

"There's a well. There are lots of wells. There's another one up ahead fifteen minutes."

"What was wrong with that one?" They were mounting the hill again, and his father led, a few feet ahead on their way to the ridgetop trail, away from the Hof.

"Mennonists," he stage-whispered. "You don't mess with them." He kicked the mare and slashed ahead.

The boy let the topic drop. His father had his reasons, no doubt. But he couldn't really drop it. He asked Mutti, in the evening, after his father was in bed.

"Sure, Klausi. They're people. But they're different people. Your grandfather—well, you knew your grandfather. An elder with the Reformed. The Mennonists won't come to church. Baptism—no, they won't baptize their kids because—I don't know why. Your grandfather got the constable to break up their midnight meetings in Gaiberg. But Karl Ludwig—and he was a broad-minded Elector Palatine, not like the Papist we have now—Karl Ludwig invited them from Switzerland. Thirty years ago, when I was young. They were refugees when they came to town, in rags, with all they owned on their backs, homeless, parts of families—a wife by herself here, two children and a father there. But marvelous farmers. Did you look at the farm when you passed?"

"I did."

"Wasn't it wonderful? Big gardens with beans and melons? Healthy cows? But you have to guess something is wrong with them or why would . . . why would the Swiss expel them? *They won't defend the country, that's why.*"

"They won't fight?"

"In the army. Or otherwise. Where would we be if our boys hadn't defended the wives and babes against Louis Fourteen's dragoons?"

"The French slaughtered us anyway."

"They'd have slaughtered more if we hadn't defended, . . . and they'll come again. Your Grandfather always said the French have a bloodlust. Because they're Papists."

—⁓⁓⁓—

The Mennonist waited, his rectangular body looming over the hole, as the boy finished the bowline knot.

"I want you up here when we do this. So you don't get hurt. Get ahold of this rope."

When he reached the top, he found the Mennonist had prepared everything. The rope he'd taken down was no longer tied around the coffin but threaded over the long extended arm of the oak tree that flung out above the grave. From there, the rope led down to his horse and hung tethered to her traces, as she faced away from them.

"Stand clear."

The man clucked, and the horse stepped away. The rope groaned, then creaked overhead and went taut. A loud sucking sounded at the grave bottom, and his father's body rose headfirst out of the clay, streaming mud and water, rising steadily until his bare feet cleared the grave lip and his body hung over the hole, swinging slowly to and fro. He'd seen gypsies and Jews hung in Heidelberg, for crimes. To see his father swing like that . . . Mud rained down on the gravestones.

"Bring the box."

He towed the box between the headstones and spotted it beneath the body, which hovered just off the grass a few feet from the hole. The Mennonist, his hand on the horse's halter, clucked the horse backward, a step at a time, while Klaus steered the descending body and planted his father's bare feet into the foot of the box; slowly the rest of him angled down, plank-like, until the body lay completely inside, at rest. Water continued to run through the broken side of the coffin, and he fetched the loose board and fitted it, pushing his father's leg against it to brace it in place.

The Mennonist had a complete plan. He directed the boy to retrieve the lid while he untied the rope that had lifted the body.

"A forester," he said, examining the dead man's outfit. "Your father was a forester." He gently swabbed the face of the body with the flour sack Klaus had used twenty minutes earlier. Klaus could hardly bear to watch, and yet he couldn't tear his eyes away. The rag paused. The Mennonist stared at the gouge at the back of the man's head.

"Murdered!" Klaus snarled it. He hurled the word as if it were an axe, sinking it crushing it, burying it in the back of Ziegler's evil and treacherous skull.

"It's a cruel, godless world," the Mennonist said.

They fitted the lid on the box, and then the man rigged it up again, a rope around each end of the box, with slipknots on each rope. He sent Klaus shimmying up the tree this time to position both ropes over the branch in the shape of an A. Back on the ground again, the boy extended his hands in imitation of the man's, steering the box, as the horse high-stepped slowly backward and the box swam out of sight, so easily and gradually that it made no splash when it reached bottom.

"Untie it," he said. Klaus went back into the hole for the third time.

When he surfaced, the Mennonist extended the handle of a shovel. "You want to finish, I think."

It took thirty minutes to shovel the dirt pile into the hole. He mounded it, toward the end. His schoolboy's hands were not accustomed to such work. Blisters formed and broke open, and then the broken skin rubbed off at the base of all eight fingers. Blisters swelled and broke between his thumb and index fingers as well. His salty sweat streamed down his arms and burned in the open wounds.

The Mennonist stood wordlessly at the end of the grave, one hand on the horse's bridle. Wasn't this respect? Wasn't this man showing greater respect to his father, his mother, and his grandmother than the Elector's own prince? The only sound was the steady chunking of dirt as it fell into the hole. The silence didn't bother him. He had nothing to say. When the hole was nearly full, the Mennonist spoke.

"Where do you live, Son?"

Son?

"Waldhilsbach."

"What you aiming to do now, now that . . . you were apprenticed? You had your heart set on forester, didn't you?"

The boy's loss was too great for words. He had thought of that, of course. It wasn't only the loss of his father. And his income. It was also the end of his career as a forester. Too many boys his age stood in line for too-few forester careers. Not that Mutti had money to pay for an apprenticeship for him, in any case.

"Loyalty's a good thing. I like that about you," the man said.

They walked side by side out of the cemetery, him leading the horse with the ropes coiled on the saddle horn, the boy carrying the shovel and the grimy flour sack. His feet squeaked, sloshing water in his shoes. He was unbelievably hungry. He was also curious about this man. He didn't want to say good-bye when they got to the man's waggon. But what else was there to talk about?

The Mennonist hitched the horse to his waggon, there in the lane where the Elector's prince had parked his carriage only a few hours before.

"Get under the tarpaulin." A light rain began to fall again.

Klaus stepped up on the waggon tongue, into the waggon, and around the seat. He lifted the tarp and found five or six fifty-pound sacks of flour in a double row.

He didn't duck completely under but sat on the board floor and pulled the tarp over his head like an awning, so he could watch the man.

The Mennonist steadied himself up onto the seat, and rain shot backward off his hat when his head tipped upward. He lifted the reins, but before signaling the horse, he turned to gaze right at the boy, seated below him on the floor. The tarp stretched across the boy's forehead like the horizon.

"I need a boy at the mill," the man said.

"Mutti has no money for that. Father's pension—" Klaus shrugged his shoulders.

"Who said anything about money?" The man threw a huge laugh at the dark sky. He laughed some more and clucked.

"Turn a sack on its side and spread an empty bag on it. Here." He pulled one from beneath his seat and handed it back. "It'll soften the bumps."

The rain came harder and rattled on the tarp. The horse lowered his head in the direction of Waldhilsbach. The boy studied the man's great square shape as it shifted on the waggon seat. What would Mutti say about this? A Mennonist.

Without warning, the man began to sing. The voice was melodious and deep, and the notes curled and spiraled out into the wet forest like a stream of butterflies.

> O blinded World, how mad you are,
> How to our God offensive!
> Though you are full of mirth and lust—

The song went on and on as the horse and cart descended the trail through the woods toward Waldhilsbach. It seemed to have an endless number of verses, which the man knew every word of. Some of the words seemed foreign, although Klaus found himself liking the tune.

> What think you, in the Final Day,
> An answer to be givin'?
> When you your neighbor treated thus,
> And let him die of hunger!

And that was how Klaus began his worldly trade as a miller and entered the life of the outcast and heretic Mennonists.

CHAPTER 7

THE DESPERATE NEED FOR REVENGE,
SINSHEIM, DECEMBER 10, 1709

IT WAS HANS HERR'S FAULT that he ended up in America. Maybe "fault" isn't the best word because it was a happy day when he decided for the New World!

The Kraichgau was the Old Country, and the Old Country lay under a curse that year of 1708, a curse every bit as abominable as one of the Ten Plagues Moses delivered with a thrust of his rod at the Pharaoh and the trembling land of Egypt.

On Christmas Eve '08 the curse fell when the mercury plummeted and stuck below freezing for three months straight. By January 3, the Seine and the Rhone had frozen solid, and the Thames in London—he'd heard the stories—froze so thick that families put up tents and booths on the ice and held Frost Parties there. Snow fell every day in January. Birds dropped dead out of the sky, their fragile bodies chilled to the point that they couldn't stay airborne. Hunters found healthy deer, frozen stiff in the woods. Three-quarters of the beautiful vineyards up and down the Rhine died, the sap in their roots turned to ice and bursting the rugged root skins.

All of this after the latest incursion by Louis Fourteenth's armies from May to September of '07, pillaging and burning the Rhineland as they'd been doing for forty years now, pushing the boundaries of Catholic Europe into former Lutheran and Calvinist territories. Did any of that lessen the taxes that the Catholic Elector levied that year or the next? Did the Lutheran landlords of Sinsheim and Heilbronn reduce the annual work service requirements for their peasants? No.

Tenant farmers went broke and had no money for seed grain in the spring. Who had any grain to take to the mills for grinding? Speculators roamed the countryside, on the lookout for stored grain to wheedle from desperate farmers and turn into big profits at the city bakeries for the breadlines. Groff, the Mennonist miller, closed his mill four days every week and only operated on Fridays and Saturdays. What he was able to grind was so precious that Young Klaus took to carrying his fowler with him on deliveries, without his employer's knowledge, to ward off the desperately hungry men who concealed themselves along the forest trails.

That Saturday afternoon the temperature fell below zero again, with ice skins forming along the banks of the Neckar when he arrived from delivering four sacks of valuable wheat flour to the knights of Neckargemünd. Was another winter like '08 coming on? He tethered the pony and cart to the ferry railing and dumped several handfuls of oats into the trough fixed to the floor below the railing. Even oats were scarce, and the flesh had sunk away from the pony's ribs. She looked up at him with large luminous eyes like those of the gypsy beggar children in Heidelberg.

Only moments before launch, he saw the sleek mare step up to the rail, alongside his pony. The rider stood on the far side, tethering, his head dipped out of sight. He noticed the bulging saddlebags.

The rider's shoulder and battered tricorn rose, and their eyes met over the back of the mare. Above the man's luxuriant black beard without a thread of silver and chapped cheeks that announced a man of the outdoors, the curious black eyes peered fiercely. The man laughed.

"Terrible year for business, huh?" He worried a sack of grain from beneath the saddlebags and emptied a pile of mashed oats and dried molasses mixture into the trough for his mount. "Do thirteen thousand Palatines know something we don't?"

"What thirteen thousand Palatines?" Klaus asked. He sensed the man wanted to talk. But first, there must be a little game, a little foreplay to test if there was safe ground between them.

"In London." The man returned from the feedbox. "I read the English papers. Thirteen thousand of your neighbors camped out on Blackheath because the English Parliament passed the Naturalization Act March 24 saying Protestant aliens who come to London, take the Lord's Supper with an Anglican priest, and swear allegiance to the Queen will get transport to America and expenses paid. Free. After last winter and the rumor of Louis's armies coming again, who wouldn't be ready to pack up and put his life in the hands of God and good Queen Anne? But where are the thirteen thousand today? Hounded out by the mobs in London and shipped home to the Rhineland again."

The man's voice seemed cynical, maybe even cocky.

"We can't blame them for trying," Klaus said. "Most are landless. Tenant farmers."

"Well. Me and the wife went too. Now what do you think?"

"You!"

"I saw the Queen herself, her royal personage. I shook her hand." The trader, which is what he appeared to be, raised one gloved hand and waved it side to side, as if the royal perfume still hung on it. "And now I'm a believer. Next time we're going the whole way."

"Next time? Whole way to where?"

The trader rummaged in his saddlebag. He lifted out an oblong paper package looped both directions with a fat green satin ribbon and untied it. Between gloved fingertips he held the paper corners over a swatch of filigreed lace hearts and flowers.

"Venetian lace for the Lady?"

And then a goblet, with the silhouetted head and shoulder-length blonde curls of a nobleman in a medallion held by naked cherubs, all glazed over with transparent green enamel.

"A goblet for Milord's nightcap? You see what I deal in! I ride a thousand miles to deal with shifty, greedy middlemen in Venice, and all for the dining board and parlor of our Elector. The crates follow by pack train." He gestured the east to indicate the direction the pack train would come from.

"Or for the missus of your shopkeeper." This time he yanked a canvas sack from beneath the saddlebags and opened the sack enough to reveal ornamented handles of a set of pewter knives and forks. "No one has Reichstaler to buy anymore, so they're headed to Frau Herr's table for Christmas. It's only two weeks off, you know."

"But here's what—" This time he brought up a leather volume, tattered as if it had been handled and pored over many nights, with underlines and asterisks at the key passages and perhaps passed between many who couldn't believe the story it told unless they saw the inked words planted on paper. "Kochertal's *Palatine to Charolina,* the book he wrote of his trip last year."

"Charolina?"

"The New World. His voyage there in '08. A Lutheran minister of the gospel, so he's obliged to tell the truth, am I right? He knows God is watching!"

"Can I see?" He reached, but the trader snatched it back from his fingertips.

"Ahhh! Got you interested now? Heh, heh, heh!" The trader laughed a belly laugh.

The Ferry bumped the far shore, across from the city, and tumbled them both forward against their mounts.

When he recovered, he wheeled and thrust his arm across the mare's back to the trader, who was occupied, tying up his package again. "I'm Grünewald. Klaus."

"I know." The trader's face flashed into a smile. He seized his own glove between his teeth and shucked it before extending his arm back and shaking the offered hand. "Herr. Hans."

"I'd like to hear more about this fellow Kochertal. Well, I'm interested in America." Klaus untied the pony and tugged her head around to his chest, pointing her toward the gangplank and the shore.

"There's the inn, left up the street in Böckingen," Herr said.

"All right." His passion to examine the Kochertal book, which he'd heard mentioned a dozen times over the last year, was battling right now with an inner voice of caution. One couldn't be too careful. The Elector's men were everywhere, keeping tabs on the Mennonists and Jews, noting who was doing what. Might the man take him for a Mennonist? Groff's brother, who wasn't one, had been hit with the Mennonist Recognition Tax of six guilders for three years running now because the Elector's spies reported the fact he'd spent nights at the mill with his brother Isaac, who was a Mennonist.

He tied the pony to a hitching post at The Neckar and went inside, out of the chill, and ordered a pint, which he carried to a table by the window that overlooked the river and the hitching rail outside. Aside from protecting his fowler, which he'd toted inside with him, he had nothing else to protect, now that the cart was empty. In a few minutes the man Herr came looking for him, dragging his saddlebags along the puncheon floor.

"Can't be too careful."

"You *know* me, you said." He had waited until the man was seated.

"Ahh. Yes!" Herr's voice descended to a whisper. "You work for the Mennonist miller. What? Four years already?"

Klaus leaped to his feet. "What is this? Who are you?"

"Hush. Hush. I'm a Mennonist myself." Herr still whispered, chuckling. "You didn't recognize, huh?" He pulled off the tricorn. "This fooled you, did it?" He replaced the hat, glancing around. "So you want to know about Kochertal." He positioned the book on the table between them.

"First, how you know—"

"I've heard good things about you from Groff. Through my brother. Christian Herr? The Preacher?"

Klaus gave the question an empty stare.

"You don't know any of them, huh? That's good. The miller's being careful." He thumped the leather book with his open palm downturned, showing the cracked, red, and swollen fingers of a man who had spent days and nights on horseback in the snow-filled passes between the southern German states and the seaports of northern Italy. "You ready for Kochertal?"

Cracking the book open now between his chapped hands, Herr reviewed the list of contents and launched into his digest version of Kochertal's trip to America in 1708.

The land was completely empty and uninhabited in Charolina, Kochertal had written. Except for the Indians, "who live with our people in perfect peace. And they are decreasing in numbers." Herr read the quote and went back to summarizing. There was culture of the vine, but you needed to bring your own live slips. The land was fruited with wild peach and grape, but settlers were also bringing slips of quince and pear. Cattle, horses, sheep, and pigs multiplied easily, living in the well-watered meadows and oak forests under whose mighty branches the ground lay an inch thick with acorns, on which the pigs fattened. The meadows ran green most of the year, for Charolina winters were like April or October in the Kraichgau, Kochertal said.

As for native animals—"I see you carry a proper rifle," Herr interrupted his story. A man could hunt waterfowl: swan, geese, and ducks. Or bison and deer in the forests, which covered all of the American provinces. "You live off game until you have cleared your garden, sown and harvested the first crops on the same." Kochertal also described the "Welsh chicken," a bird weighing thirty-some pounds, thereby similar to the German bustard, but with a full fan of tail feathers on the male and making a gobbling sound.

"No taxes. No service to the knights and lords. No serfdom."

"What about the trip across? Does he say anything—"

"Once you get to London, he says to book with a ship captain. For five to six pounds sterling, he will transport you and your chest of seven to ten stone and all the food you buy for the trip. If you don't bring your own food, the trip price may double. But here's the rub. If you bring your own and you exhaust it, what with contrary weather and a long trip, the captain may not have any more to sell you, so you will starve.

"But against that risk, there's this," Herr said. "After a few years in America, no head of family is poor. Each one owns a hundred or even several hundred cows and pigs."

Herr slapped the book shut. "We have a better plan than Kochertal's. Penn's Woods. The Rhineland has gone daft over the Penns, Klaus Grünewald. Have you heard of Penn's Woods?"

"Not much. Go on." He was completely immersed in Herr's story now, hanging on every new detail.

From the beginning Mutti had argued that there was no future in Groff's mill. "In his will, Groff will pass the mill to his sons, and then what?" she said.

Klaus had a little stash for his own mill now, and he was certain that Groff would help him with the plans, maybe even make a pledge of surety when he went to buy the millstones and build the mill. But where to make such a start? In America?

Herr propped both elbows on the table and leaned in closer. "The English king deeded forty-five thousand square miles to Penn. And for settlers, Penn likes the Palatines. How do I know that, Klaus? Because I read the English papers. 'Treat the Palatines with tenderness and love,' it's said he wrote his secretary in Philadelphia. He knows our Mennonist people, and he calls us 'a sober people who will neither swear nor fight.' Now who does that sound like? Penn's own Quakers! There you have it!"

"I'm not a Mennonist."

"I know that too. You should be one. We need a miller in Penn's province."

"*We?* You're going?"

Herr made an avuncular smile, and this time Klaus thought: How young the man is. All the foreign cities he's seen: Venice, London, and now the New World. He can't be past thirty. Close, perhaps. We might go together. We might be neighbors in Penn's Woods.

"Ahh, you're hooked. Let me unhook you," Herr said. "Why go? If it's to get wealthy, consider the Scriptures." He quoted the passage from memory:

> But those who desire to be rich fall into temptation
> and a snare and into many foolish and harmful lusts. . . .
> For the love of money is a root of all kinds of evil, for
> which some have strayed from the faith.

What faith? Klaus mulled that. Maybe the Mennonists have it. Me? Nah. Wealth sounds good to me.

"But if daily life is dangerous here in the Kraichgau, what with fear of French dragoons or persecutions by the Papist Elector. . . . Or if it's the will of God you go, then take hope. But first consider the hardships. The storms at sea," Herr said. "Consider the expenses. Waiting in Holland or England for fair winds to sail, you may see all the savings you planned to use for equipment on the far side get eaten up on this side.

"How about the hardships in the new land? No house to come home to. No warm bed. Maybe just a lean-to in the woods and a bed of pine needles for months. No cart and pony. No household tools at the start—pots and pans, bake ovens, ploughs. The land you are assigned, that you've paid for, still wild and overrun with great trees, each of which takes days to whack or saw, and a team of horses, which you don't have yet, to jerk out the stump. Overrun with vines as thick as your ankle so you can't even see the ground to put down your little grapevines. You still want to go? Have I unhooked you?" Herr slapped his shoulder with a familiar swipe.

"I'm practically nineteen. What is life for if not for deeds of daring and conquest? But if I leave here—?" His eyes met Herr's as he paused.

"What?"

Should he vocalize it? Vengeance, that was it. Could he leave without fulfilling his promise to Mutti that Old Man Ziegler would never go down to his grave in peace but would go with a musket bullet between his eyes or an axe blow or choking over a glass of poison? Desire for vengeance burned continuously in his belly like a live bed of coals out of sight in a winter stove.

The other issue was a wife. Four years with Groff in Sinsheim had generated no candidates. The burghers' daughters, the shopkeepers' daughters whom he passed every Sunday on the way out of the great Church—none would stop when he hailed them. They knew, even if he looked like any other eighteen-year-old: *Grünewald lives with and works for a Mennonist.* If Herr and his band all went as families, and he supposed that's what they'd do, where could he find an unattached German girl, once he left? What chance that he'd find a wife in the forests of Penn's Woods? An Indian woman, how about that? There was always the Quakers; surely they had daughters. Quakers were shopkeepers and merchants, he'd heard. Would a Quaker father give his blessing on a non-Quaker son-in-law?

When he lay awake in the still night, thinking this way, he grew more and more confused, and he hated confusion.

Herr seemed to probe his soul, across the pint of beer.

"Made you think, didn't I!"

"Mmm."

Herr's hands came across the table and seized Klaus's hands between his.

"We're going, Klaus. Twenty-eight of us are going when the Rhine turns passable *in the spring*, and we have room for one more like you. It will cost. Maybe fifteen pounds. Do you have that much saved up for the mill you plan to build someday? We're going to Penn's Woods in April, Klaus. You want to come with us?"

He sat speechless.

"Come to Groff's mill Saturday night at six and ask for me. I'll be there." Herr stood, picked up his saddlebags, and turned toward the door. As if he'd thought of one more thing, he turned back, crossed the room, and threw one arm around Klaus's shoulders.

"I like you. We could be neighbors in America. Think about it."

CHAPTER 8

THE VOICE SPEAKS

NOW IT MADE SENSE, why he'd been sent home to his mother in Waldhilsbach every Saturday at noon since his first week here four years ago, with Isaac even providing his precious pony to make the trip. The Mennonists held secret meetings in the mill loft, and Groff was guarding the secret that couldn't be shared, at great personal cost. Clever idea of Groff's: the pony. She always sounded the alarm five hundred feet out from the mill, breaking into a trot and a whinny. He'd returned once without forewarning at Saturday midnight and was stopped at the door to the mill by Groff, fully dressed and directing him to sleep elsewhere "because of a problem with the children."

The pony nickered as the gray outline of the three-story mill materialized ahead in the fog. It lifted from the snowy meadows and hulked against the hillside, the hill that birthed the spring and brook and cuddled the now ice-bound pond. She nickered again as her hooves hit the wooden bridge, just below the spot where the brook fed into the larger creek. There it was, Groff's alarm system.

He pulled her into the shelter of the shed behind the mill and marveled. If there was a meeting, where were the horses and carts?

Had they all come on foot, in this chill? Impossible. From town it was a thirty-minute walk, in below-freezing darkness. No footprints showed in the new snow by the path leading to the mill's shop door. Had they come single file to avoid a telltale collection of footprints?

Perhaps he'd misunderstood. Perhaps Herr meant another Saturday night? He arrived at the door and reached for the latch. Only right then, he noticed the crack, and it stopped him. The door stood ajar an inch, and simultaneous with that realization, the crack sprang wide and a single hand gripped his advancing arm and pulled him through. The door pulled noiselessly shut against his heels.

"Hans?"

They stood momentarily bunched in the dark on the inside of the door, and the man was shapeless opposite him but not silent.

"Shhh!" The man propelled him through the shop, his hand in the middle of Klaus' back, applying steady forward pressure.

Not that he needed any guidance, even without light, as they exited the mill office and entered the darkened Meal Floor. He had memorized the layout during his first week because Groff forbade candles in the working part of the mill.

"Explosions," Groff had said. "The powder off the floor. That's how Binkelei lost his mill. Blew his whole operation and himself inside to a pile of rocks and rubble."

To his right, they passed the unseen spouts for sacking the flour, the task of Groff's sons. Beyond that the great stones, bed stone and runner, lay silent, tethered by a vertical axle to the lantern pinion that caught each tooth on the gear wheel, bolted to the great ever-cycling (except in the worst of winter and except after work hours) waterwheel. He'd marveled once upon a time at the genius of it, how rushing water could translate to raw grinding power that made the flour in every muffin, biscuit, and slab of bread in Sinsheim and its villages. And then for many, many years he cursed the work that it generated: the stones needed sharpening, the main shaft needed grease every morning, the water buckets wore out year after year.

His hands found the stairs upward, rising at a forty-five degree angle, without handrails to guide one's steps. He'd mastered these too, and he could descend them in the dark with a full bushel of wheat over each shoulder.

The man followed, one hand against Klaus's belt line. Klaus's uplifted hands touched the loft door, lying flat and shut. He bunched his head and shoulders together to butt it upward, his usual method.

The door lifted away and revealed the amazing scene above, half lit by two lanthorns resting on waist-high hogsheads, their wicks burning steadily behind glass walls. Had Groff winked at this breach of safety? To the north the grain bin squatted, neck high, and that was his workstation, where he tore open the full sacks of wheat and let their contents stream away.

Only this much was ordinary. Everything else in the room looked rearranged.

Pairs of eyes, floating disembodied in the darkness, pivoted toward him, each with a miniature lanthorn flame dancing in it. There were dozens, as if he'd stumbled into a nighttime migration of lemmings. Each pair seemed not to belong to a body but instead to a chimera whose amorphous body slinked along the length of the loft. He only realized later that it was their bundling, layer upon layer of coats and blankets, that melded them into a mythological many-eyed monster. Winter nighttimes, when he slept here, his freshly washed chemises froze into rigid pipes on the clothes line stretched across the room, but tonight, the forty or fifty bodies had raised the temperature. The odor of soap was discernible and sweet.

His guide pushed him along the row of shapes beyond the loft door. He trailed his hand across the broad shoulders, seated and turned away from him in the direction of the grain bin. Three, four, five . . . and then a blank spot.

"Sit here!" the guide stage-whispered, and now he was certain it was Herr.

He dropped, and the full wheat sack rose up to collide with his buttocks and simultaneously a powerful thumb and forefinger pincered the muscle in his upper leg. He stared at the dark form. In the gloaming, they all looked the same, with their long Swisser beards and dark coats.

"Klaus!" the man said.

Groff's voice sounded a note of comfort. It *was* Groff's mill and it *was* the Mennonist gathering. The miller shifted his muscular shoulder familiarly against Klaus's.

He stared about the loft, at its strange transformation into a meeting room for the heretics. Double rows of bodies sat on wheat sacks laid out in a large L to face the twin glowing lanthorns. Low whispers drifted in from one direction, now another. At the far end of the loft, a boy bunched himself by the input door, the same door Klaus regularly swung out for waggons unloading their sacks of wheat via the block and tackle fixed in the gable end. Why was the boy there? A small whimper across the room, on the other leg of the L, drew his eyes. He saw the woman's white breast, round and full, gleam in the half-light and then disappear beneath a small burrowing head.

So, the women and children sat separately. He noticed other differences from his mother's church. Could this even be labeled a church?

His grandfather had taken him numerous times to the Heilige Geist Kirche in Heidelberg. "Our church," Grandfather said. The

Müllers owned a pew, and they sat together as a family on the polished wooden benches with their upholstered pads. As a boy, he rested his neck on the bench back to gaze in awe at the splendid pink marble columns that rose like a forest of oaks to the far-off ribs of the vaulted ceiling. Diffused light filtered through the columns of the nave. Beyond the triumphal arch, the choir loft hung in the streaming sunlight, with a massed choir in robes hymning great anthems on Easter and Christmas Sundays. All that before the organ lit the air aflame and sucked the oxygen out of the room and out of his lungs; he sat spellbound by the tumbling melody and bass that chased each other like schoolboys. Grandfather called him "the Genius of Germany," the choirmaster named Bach who wrote such music of Heaven.

In the cathedral, his family alongside, he felt holy. Surely God dwelled in cathedrals like the Heilige Geist Kirche.

What kind of God would dwell in a mill loft?

The loft door flapped upward again, and the face Nicholas rising over the floor line dangled an entirely white beard to the man's mid-chest. Saint? Perhaps they'd invited the saintly bishop to bring gifts to the children, like they did at the Heilige Geist Kirche? Except it was already a week past his saint day, and where was his sack of gifts? The old man struggled to maneuver his overweight and crippled body through the loft opening, reaching up for helping hands and getting a push from below.

What was that behind him? Boy Ruprecht?

"Follow the brother, Dat," Boy Ruprecht said and passed the elderly man on to waiting hands. Boy Ruprecht pulled himself up through the loft door, dusted his breeches, and walked to the "front," between the lanthorns. He moved deliberately, doffing the flat Alsatian hat, splaying his great Bible on the table, the noise of his fingers turning pages the only sound in the room. He stood at an angle, as if an invisible ceiling right above his bald head pressed down on it and caused him to stand bent. Now stretching out his arms to prop himself on the table, he spoke at half volume:

"The peace of Christ be with you."

Their chorused response was not the terrified squeal of the harassed and huddled rabbits that they looked like. The voices rang confidently, unified, restrained: "And also with you!"

Hans said he'd know him by the hooked nose. "That will be my brother Christian." Christian was younger by three years, he said, "and more spiritual than me." The man had a hang-gallows look: the protruding face bones made him look hunted. Or was it a look of grief? Hans said he'd had a twin who broke through the millpond ice and drowned when they were running from a sheriff years ago. "He hasn't been the same since."

"Dearly Beloved!" Herr gazed over them.

This was their Pastor? His breeches looked old and his chest bulked out. He seemed to wear two or three layers of waistcoats against the cold, like everyone else, including Klaus himself.

The Reverend Doctor Faust wore floor-length black robes when he climbed the spiral stairs into the carved cherrywood box at the Heilige Geist Kirche. "Finest orator in Europe," Grandfather had said. As a boy, Klaus loved the funny stories he sprinkled over his sermons, which were otherwise a compendium of wise thoughts about a topic of the day, an exposition of certain Greek words that appeared in the Bible verses he used, reference to parallels in Greek and Roman mythology, and all delivered in his fine-timbred voice, which matched the pipe organ in its capacity to command the nave.

This man's voice was pitched too high.

"We have news. A letter." The Preacher unfolded an oil paper onto the tabletop and reared back to get the text in focus. "From our

Brother Benedict." An audible sigh of recognition rose in the dark. "You know him, don't you? From the little 'excursion' with Hans Burki here last year." A slow, sardonic smile spread across Herr's face. "You know what I mean by 'excursion.' An excursion sponsored by the Town Council of Bern, who dragged them in irons to the border and expelled them. But courageously, they returned to their families. Courageous, I say, because there was a sentence of death if caught again." His fingertip traced the words on the letter below as he read. "Listen."

"Twelfth of January this year the government of Bern—this is Brother Benedict writing—sent seven provosts with an officer of the court to my house right about dawn. We saw them coming and my wife and I, we ran to hide. I hid in the haystack. They searched every cranny of the house. Finally they got to the hay and thrust their swords into it, so that they poked me and detected me. As I emerged, they seized me by the throat and demanded my name, which I told, and whether I was a preacher of the Mennonists, which I admitted.

"They then pushed me into my kitchen, where the court officer slapped my face, roped my wrists behind my back, and led me out the front door. My children cried and wailed so piteously. A heart of marble would have felt something. The provosts, however, were full of joy they'd captured me."

Herr glanced up. "I won't read every word. They sold his farm to pay bounties to the betrayers. Chained him in the Hole, hands, feet, around the neck, for eighteen weeks. Then another thirty-five weeks toiling every day from 4:00 a.m. to 8:00 p.m. carding wool, together with Brother Burki. Of course, we've heard worse. The Schlachter boys, who were sent to row the galleys on warships in Venice for the rest of their very short lives. Durs Aebi, who returned homesick from forced exile, and they burned the big bear of Bern onto his back with a cattle iron. Then they drove him back across the border, but he survived! And now, they will exile Brother Brechbühl, he writes, for the rest of his earthly life. Alone, without his family, to the Spice Islands, no doubt."

Jail? The galleys? Branding with a cattle iron? Exile? It was one thing to work for a Mennonist miller. Attending their meeting was a very different thing. A crime, in fact, in the Elector's Palatinate. I could be jailed. Sent to the galleys. What am I doing here anyway? All because of Hans Herr's invitation. Are they really going to America? These people? How stupid was I to think of going with them?

However, hadn't he already thought this point down to its logical conclusion? He would never go to America. He had a vow to fulfill to his dead father: the death of Andreas Ziegler. How was that coming along? Miserably. The tavern keeper of Waldhilsbach still walked the face of the earth.

That thought brought to mind his other griefs. His career as a miller. The apprenticeship was up, and no opportunities had presented. "We need a miller in Penn's Woods," Hans Herr said, but that option only brought him full circle to his dilemma. His unfulfilled vow to his father.

Then there was the problem of a wife.

Preacher Herr opened the large Bible on the tabletop. "Our text is First Corinthians 4, Ten to Thirteen." The light was weak, even directly under the barrelhead lanthorne. Herr labored to read the printed text.

> We are fools for Christ's sake, but ye are wise in Christ;
> we are weak, but ye are strong; ye are honorable, but we are
> despised. Even unto this present hour we both hunger, and
> thirst, and are naked, and are buffeted, and have no certain

dwelling place. . . . Being persecuted, we suffer it; we are made as the filth of the world, and are the offscouring of all things unto this day.

Christian's dark-ringed eyes, like the hungry eyes of a badger, fixed them. His words came slowly, deliberately. "I will be very bold, Brothers and Sisters. I'm going to say these words of the Apostle are for here, today, the church in Isaac Groff's mill, in Elector Johann Wilhelm's Kraichgau.

"Now why should we be the refuse of the world?" His eyes criss-crossed the people. "Why shouldn't we be princes and princesses, dancing minuets in the Elector's palace in Heidelberg?

"Because we follow the Prince of Peace, Jesus. He said—you'll remember this, I trust—'Blessed are you when men revile you and utter all kinds of evil against you falsely on my account.'

"What were you expecting when you joined us?

"Does God see? Does he care? Does he notice when heathen men—tell me, dare we call them heathen if they were once baptized and say they believe in Christ? Jesus said: 'The hour comes when who-ever kills you will think he is offering services to God.' He who would follow Christ must bear a cross, like the Master did." The preacher stopped and lowered his head toward the book. His extended arms still propped him up at the table. The people waited. His face came up. When he smiled, the bearded preacher seemed to Klaus like a ge-nial Saint Nicholas, his eyes wrinkling and beaming.

"Brother Brechbühl has other talents, and he's had lots of time to practice them in that Hole, in leg irons. He sent us a song. Brother Isaac."

Groff's hand pushed down on Klaus's shoulder as he levered himself up from the sack.

"He calls it 'Schabab,'" the preacher said, "after the little garden flower they have in Switzerland. Maybe Dat, you knew this flower as a boy? And to a tune we all know well, 'In the Beautiful May.' Brother Isaac."

"Schabab? Yes, a flower, but didn't it mean the shavings, the sawdust, the wood scraps, too?"

Groff came alongside the preacher. He lined out the first stanza in the mellifluous bass Klaus had heard many times on the mill floor:

> Schabab: this is a flow'ret small
> That from the earth is growing—

The congregation joined, vigorous, sotto voce, like the disciplined choir of the Heilige Geist Kirche.

> In color red as blood itself—

Right on "blood itself," a whoop broke from beyond the mill wall. The song died across the loft.

His body took flight well before he picked up the whispered word "Sheriff." How he got to the second-floor access hole, he couldn't say afterward, but he was scrabbling on knees and hands over the cover, wrestling off the wheat sack that barred escape to the mill floor below, when muscular arms wrapped his torso, a second body crashed heavily across him, and all lights in the loft went black.

"Let me go. Or I'll . . ." Callused fingers snuffed the words and smelled like horse across his lips, and now he lay, his cheek jammed sideways against the trapdoor while his fate unrolled like magic lanthorn pictures.

Ankles chained to a heaving deck. Stripped to the waist and my blistered hands burning, straining against a pair of oars. Shoulders and back bloody from a foreman's bullwhip. No, branded! Glowing, searing iron pulled from the forge and thrust between my shoulders. Odor of my flesh, smoking. Scream after scream until my voice box breaks and oblivion swallows me. Maybe irons. Irons pulling wrists and ankles into open lesions as they drag my body, naked side up, over frozen cobblestones. The leering mouths of jailbirds thrust between bars to spit on me: "Damn Mennonist! Goddamn Mennonist!"

And then stillness. There was no sound. Except the drip of water from the tethered waterwheel. And the mouse, still somewhere on the floor. As if there were no one in the loft but him.

But now a crashing! Bushes trampled somewhere below. Shouts. Thwacking, again and again. A hoarse cry. A cow's cry somewhere directly below. More crashing. Then the double whoop.

He knew. Before the boy at the little wall door cracked the door to hear the message shouted from the ground, he knew everything.

"Loose cow. Looking for her calf."

Low laughter tided across the room. The fingers and arms and body pulled off and away from him, and Groff's lips pressed against his ear, whispering wetly, "Sorry. But we couldn't chance anything. Farmer Kropf, you know. He could be out there."

He felt his way back to the seat on the sack, touching backs and shoulders and the hands that extended, helping him along. When the lanthorn light returned, he was already seated.

Don't look at me. No! Don't look at me! But the eyes hadn't turned his direction. Not even the children's. Their faces tilted sideways toward the flower table. Had no one seen his great act of cowardice? Were they used to such scenes?

"Who would join us?" Preacher Herr lifted his hands. "Who chooses to follow the outcast Christ in this world? But stands a prince in the house of God?" His question lay unanswered on the tabletop and consumed the air slowly, like the wicks of the relit lanthorns.

Brother Groff took up his song again, lining it, then leading them in the response:

"Schabab am I, too, in the world . . . ," Isaac sang.

Now he grasped the meaning of it. They were the wood scraps, the shavings. These people! "Schabab am I!" Their unseen mouths echoed it more softly, in the event Farmer Kropf had discovered his cow was missing.

By everyone rejected;
In God is set my confidence,
He never will forsake me.

It was during the song that he heard it: *"Follow me, Klaus."*

No one's mouth moved his direction, not that he could see or notice. Yet there was no mistaking. Someone had spoken, and he had heard it. He knows my name. A Presence stood beside him. Or hovered above? Or around him? No face was visible. Yet it had a face without features that was turned toward him. The Voice seemed nearer than the man's shoulder on the sack in front of him: *"Ten thousand years from now, you'll be glad you did, Klaus."*

Ten thousand years from now? This was an unbelievable piece of information. How old would he be?

He sensed personality behind the Voice, and the personality loved him. He didn't wish it to leave. Its presence filled him with a surge of confidence; it emboldened him. Was it real? Mutti's eyes! It was dark in the room that night too, but he felt her eyes, burning through the sheet across his cheeks and mouth. She bent over him in the dark. They had dragged his father in that night, mortally injured, and he lay in the dark, completely bereft. She voiced his name—Klaus—just as the Voice had now spoken his name. It was the way she said it. She knew all there was to know about him and what had just happened—and he felt what he felt now.

"Who would follow this Christ?" Preacher Herr asked it again.

A burbling spring opened somewhere in his core, in the arid landscape littered with bones down there. The smoldering rust-colored stones opened a crack, a mouth, and pure water poured upward from the crystalline underground aquifer, a river he had not known existed. IwillIwillIwillIwillIwill. It plashed in the open air, the drops catching sunlight and displaying the whole spectrum of colors. IwillIwillIwillIwillIwill.

He didn't stand, he leaped to his feet.

"I will."

Preacher Herr closed the oversized Bible. He hadn't noticed Klaus. The women and children on the other side of the L, they had noticed him. Their eyes with the flickering lanthorn lights in them had turned toward him. Groff noticed too, and for the second time this evening he signaled disapproval by pulling sharply on his waistcoat. Now the preacher noticed him approaching and tilted his head.

"Did you want something, Friend? We're about finished, if you can wait a few minutes."

He was not part of them. Not Brother or Sister but Friend. He brushed off the unintended slight, the phrase that made him only a guest, as if it were a mosquito, because he needed to tell the preacher. "You said, 'Who would join us?'"

"Yeees?" Preacher Herr studied his face.

"And I'm here."

Years later, when he lived in America, he took the decision apart. He was not conscious of making a decision that night. The Voice seemed irresistible. He could have said: I won't. Yet perhaps he had no choice. Love in the Voice was a flame, and he the moth that circled the flame. That didn't fit, however, because moths destroy themselves in flames. As he looked at the Decision like a gemstone, from many angles, he came to believe that when he said "I will" to the Voice, he crossed a line. The love in the Voice seemed more real than anything else in his flesh-and-blood world. It spoke from another land. That land was more real than the world of blood and flesh, grinding millstones and vows to a dying father. That land was more real than the one he lived in, where Electors imposed crushing taxes and compulsory labor to build lavish palaces, where men stalked men and bludgeoned them to death.

When he said I will, he entered the reality of the land where the Voice lived. A land ruled by a God-King who came downward and walked among the people in the blood-and-flesh world. That King had addressed him: "Klaus. Follow me."

Everything good in his life happened after he said "I will."

CHAPTER 9

WHAT? FORGIVE?
SINSHEIM, MARCH 5, 1710

H E WOULD KILL ANDREAS ZIEGLER and avenge his father. It was a pillar of his credo, as solid and necessary as the marble columns of the Heilige Geist Kirche in Heidelberg. He'd made the vow with his hand on his father's crushed forehead at fourteen, with Mutti watching him through her unbound and disheveled hair, her tears cascading. That vow was as firmly planted as the other pillar of his life: I'm a miller, and I will someday own and run a mill of my own that grinds men's bread.

But here was this man Hans Herr saying No. No what? No avenging his father's murder? No keeping of the vow he'd made on the man's deathbed?

—◦◦◦◦◦◦◦—

The pond that supplied Groff's mill froze solid enough to walk across before Christmas, and the mighty wheel that turned the shaft that spun the grindstones sat disconnected and mute, awaiting weather warm enough to let the race run. Groff, his wife, and two sons were camped before a roaring fire in the living room, a ground floor room of the mill, eating chestnuts.

He paused the pony on the hilltop, its nostrils blowing huge plumes of vapor. He'd come three miles from the village of Weiler and the Tower overlooking the town. For two of those miles, his pony's footprints were the first tracks since last night's new snow. In all directions from the hilltop, the miserable frozen stubble of last summer's failed wheat and corn crops stretched off to wooded patches. Below, at the far side of the basin formed in the valley between the two cultivated hills, he saw the Unterbiegelhof for the first time.

The Hof's existence seemed incredible, even after years of tramping the Kraichgau forests with his father and another four driving his cart with flour bags to the cities. Here, only a forty-five minute walk from town and civilization, a set of handsome buildings surrounded a central courtyard, with a steaming manure pile in its center. The key buildings were two-story, with multiple windows and doors, each connected to the next via a roofed-over passageway or smaller building. It seemed enough living space for three or four families. Did a whole clan live here?

He'd heard of the Hofs. There was that memory of one he'd seen with his father. "Keep to themselves," Father had said. "Big gardens with corn and melons. Healthy cows," his mother had said. "They came as refugees and created those farms out of the war rubble."

Now he slanted the pony down the hill and across the enclosure with the manure pile, reaching the door of the big house. The maw of the door cracked, as if on cue.

"Aha!" Hans Herr himself filled up the doorframe, his face round and jovial and hedged completely by his beard and black felt hat, flat in the Alsatian way like the one he himself now wore. "You decided to pay us a visit. And look at you." Herr swiped his own untrimmed beard. "Something grows there, anyway. Heh heh!"

At least a small, irregular red bush had finally appeared on his chin. The day after his baptism, he'd taken off the elegant tricorn hat and military waistcoat and put on the dark breeches and black waistcoat. It raised the question to the discerning onlooker—was he Mennonist?—and he knew it and studied people's faces for the signs.

Tiny hands appeared on Herr's pantlegs and attached to them, a blonde, pig-tailed girl, a chicken drumstick in the free hand, and simultaneously a boy of seven or eight appeared on his left.

"Have you met my children? John." The boy nodded, unsmiling. "Franny." The small, pretty face shrieked and disappeared behind Herr, the chicken leg still clutched against his leg like a strange fleshy tumor. Herr said something unintelligible, and the children disappeared.

He motioned Klaus in, stepping back in the doorway, then abruptly changed direction and charged out through the door. "Let's go to the barn. I want you to see. And I don't understand." His hand gripped Klaus's arm above the elbow. "I thought you were interested in America."

"Who said I'm not?"

"You haven't come to our planning meetings. You haven't said anything since I told you. I guess you'll stick with Isaac Groff and the mill, hmm?"

"I can't go now."

"Why not?"

"I just can't."

They crossed the courtyard, skirting the manure pile, and Herr led him in a large circle along a well-trodden path through the snow, around a barn and outbuilding to a shed, in front of which a number of unhitched carts and waggons sat, empty. Low voices filtered through the latched door.

Herr stopped at the door and clapped his shoulder again. "You can't shut me down like this. I thought we were friends."

Klaus pointed at the door. "I'll tell you why later. Who's here? " "Don't forget to!"

Herr lifted the latch and shouldered through. A sweet smell of burning tobacco and heated air floated past them.

The huge warehouse was a warren of strategically placed piles of goods, with a few long-bearded men here and there among the piles, bagging things, sorting things.

"Look what I found!" Herr said.

The nearest longbeard swiveled and extended a hand. Not tanned and muscled like Hans's hand, but finer fingers, uncallused. The pale face moved right up into his, the blue eyes and nose growing until the man's mouth touched his in a sudden kiss. "God bless you. Meili. Martin Meili," the man said with the kiss.

It made him uncomfortable. They all greeted that way, he had noted from the day of his baptism. The men, that is. The women had their own practice. It caught him off-guard the first time, the night at the mill, when Christian set down the baptismal sprinkling vessel and leaned in to kiss him on the lips. He'd pushed back with both hands, indignant, forgetting why he was there, unsure if it was a trick or a test until the next man, the old patriarch Hans Herr, Senior, reeled him in with one arm, and he tasted the horror of shaved upper lip and cold sweat against his mouth.

"I'll fix you up with a real rifle," Meili said, his face still only a foot off and backing away. "I hear you're a deadeye. A forester's son, right?"

"He makes them," Herr said. "Modified Jägers."

"Is he coming with us?" Meili asked. "Are you?"

"I'm working on him," Herr said.

With Herr leading, they threaded their way through piles of saddles, harnesses, bridles (all well-used), collections of plows, iron pots broad enough to cook down a small pig, copper and cast-iron kettles for various purposes. Every item carried an identifying tag, a family name, tied with hemp twine to the item. Someone had neatly divided the floor into sections, and now Herr led him past gunnysacks with small leafless fruit trees protruding; gunnysacks misshapen with seed corn, seed wheat, seed barley; and wooden boxes with cast-iron plates of disassembled stoves.

"Takes a lot of supplies to set up nine households in America," Herr said.

From his crouch, the man bagging fruit trees stretched up an open hand. "Jacob Miller. From Zurich."

"You get your passports yet?" Herr asked.

"Next week," the man said.

"See! See what I volunteered myself for when we made the decision to go?" Herr said. "The trip guide gets to remember everything."

"The organization!" Klaus said. His opinion of Herr was jumping up.

They arrived at a five-plate stove against a chimney beyond the partition wall. The glowing interior indicated warmth. Herr rounded up two chairs and moved them side by side, facing the stove. Gesturing to the other chair, he kicked off his shoes and stretched his stockinged feet toward the stove. He pulled a long-stemmed reading pipe from his waistcoat pocket, emptied a little stream of loose tobacco into the bowl from the other pocket, grabbed the idle tongs that swung on the side of the stove, and fetched a live coal to ignite the tobacco. Transparent blue smoke curled out of his hand.

"All right," Klaus said. He'd determined to tell the story to this man, who seemed to be extending friendship.

"You don't have the habit?" Herr lofted his pipe.

"Some evenings, but I didn't bring—to answer your question, I promised my mother. That's why I can't go."

"What kind of promise?"

"Actually to my father. I promised him justice."

"Justice?" Herr said. "In such a world as this? He asked you to do this?"

How much of his story did the man know? He'd always supposed the miller Groff had told everyone how he'd found the boy, orphaned and deprived of a future, trapped in the grave pit in the Waldhilsbach cemetery. Was that assumption true? Especially for a man like Herr, absent on trading trips much of the year. Perhaps he'd never heard.

"No. He wasn't conscious. He was near dead. But Mutti heard me make the promise."

"What's it mean—justice? You're speaking of the courts? The courts in your hometown?"

"Justice means I kill the man who killed my father." He laid it down like a cold utensil, without a shred of emotion. There it lay now, on the table, so to speak, the ugly burden he'd been stuck with since he was fourteen.

Herr looked back, his mouth paused on the pipe stem. His eyes burned. Some silence followed. Herr drew down on the pipe at last, and twin purls of smoke exited his nostrils.

"You have a plan, I suppose?"

"I do." He needed to add the wretched truth. "I did. Helmut and I—that's my little brother Helmut who's joined the Elector's bodyguard. I doubt he thinks of this anymore. It's been four years, and he has a woman now. But I will never forget. It was my deathbed promise. To Father."

"Firstborn, huh?" Herr chuckled.

"Loyal to my Mutti," he said.

"Why didn't you do it? Is it so hard to make a man disappear? A marksman like yourself?"

He nodded at the compliment. But the wretched truth interfered again.

"It's not 100 percent sure it was him. I can't prove he did it."

"Hmm."

He didn't have to tell anything, he knew that. Over the years, how many people had he told this story? Fewer than the fingers on one hand. To tell the story diminished the fire. Brooding alone on the story fed the demons, the guardians of these memories, and they danced more furiously each time he fed them. Nevertheless, gazing on Herr's open, unjudging face, he plunged on.

"He drug father back to our house, see. Said he found him in the Elector's orchard. It was late in apple season, and Father was patrolling the orchards when—they drug him in. Ziegler and two of his men, and Father had a hole in the back of his head and his brains—"

He paused. Whether he just relived the picture in his mind or told it out loud, the emotions of that night flooded him. It started at his feet, like a step into the scalding mineral waters of Bad Wimpfen, and rose, driving his body temperature up until his head filled with fierce thoughts that careened across his consciousness like red-hot bits of fireworks.

"Why him? If he was the killer, wouldn't he hide the evidence?"

"Maybe. Maybe. But he pinned it on gypsies. He wanted us to believe he cared for our family. Cared so much that he brought him home."

"I'm sorry for you and your mother."

He could answer questions with a straight face, but even a single word of sympathy for his mother pushed the emotion bucket to the tipping point.

"Yes, Mutti. No one knows how she's suffered." His mother's face filled his vision. Worry lines carved her forehead and made a vertical groove between her eyes. Wrinkles puckered her mouth into the shape of a prune, her cheeks furrowed, blotched and rosy from weeping, her eyes hunkered hollow with sorrow. "Mutti has—" He buried his forehead between his hands and his shoulders shuddered.

"She's the one that believes he did it. Ziegler." He blurted it ferociously into the hands that covered his face. "He stood to gain. He got the mayor job if he got rid of him. Father was acting mayor after Grandfather. Ziegler sued. Father sued back over his land dealings, and finally they met in Ziegler's Tavern: this murderer, his wife, and sons ripped my father's clothes half off and threw him into the street in the middle of a thunderstorm."

"They were rivals?" Herr said.

"Rivals for the mayor job."

"What would it take to prove he killed him?"

"Helmut and I, we had a plan." He came out of his hands for air. Herr's eyes were quiet, still unjudging. "We were going to put a gun in his mouth or plant the muzzle on his wife's temple with him looking on and demand he tell the truth."

"But you never did it."

"No. And now with Helmut off—"

Herr's pipe had died, and the sounds from the big room beyond the partition had ceased. It was suppertime, and apparently everyone had gone home. Herr did not seem to be in a hurry. Their chairs sat bumped against each other, facing the five-plate stove. Through the joints of the plates, he watched the flames flicker.

"Klaus, listen. I don't know what to advise you. What have other men done? Someone like you, with a grievance. Does vengeance really work? Have you heard of Dirk Willems?"

"Willems?"

"A Dutchman. The story's in the *Martyrs' Mirror*."

He'd heard a half-dozen martyr stories since his baptism, enough to know that such stories were branded into the souls of these people. But not this one, no.

"Can't say I have."

"Willems was Doopsgezind—what they call the Mennonists in Holland—and the mayor of his town was in bed, you might say, with the Romish priests and sent his thief-catcher after Willems, who escaped across the frozen canal. But the thief-catcher, being heavy, broke through. Willems had a choice. Let him drown? God's revenge, you're thinking. Or the Jesus way? He chose the Jesus way, went back across the ice, and pulled the man out. Saved his life. Yet the mayor, on the bank of the canal observing all this, ordered the thief-catcher to bring Willems in. Which he did. They burned Willems at the stake. Think it over, Klaus. Revenge? Or a forgiving heart like Willems. It may be the only way out."

"You mean me? Forgive who?"

"I'm not telling you what to do. What did someone else do when face-to-face with an impossible predicament. The Savior himself. What did he do? They were hammering nails through his hands, and what did he say? Was ever a greater offense given than that?"

He labored to understand the intent of Herr's stories. *Is he saying Me forgive?* The man I want to see wallowing in his spilled brains while his wife wails hysterical screams until she faints. That's what I long to see. He says Forgive? What about the vow to my father? What about that?

CHAPTER 10

MEETING THE MURDERER

Wer Christo jetzt will folgen nach
Muss achten nicht der Welte Schmach. . . .

He who would follow Christ in life
Must scorn the world's insult and strife
And bear his cross each day . . .

HE SHOUTED THE SONG at the Elsenz, which gurgled and surged alongside the cart path. It ran milk tea brown, the waters reaching even with the bank tops to his right, which still lay frosted with snow beneath the overhanging trees. Snowmelt. Spring was coming, even if the pony's breath blew white and visible this afternoon and the air felt leaden. Might it snow again before he reached Neckargemünd?

Wer Christo jetzt . . .

He pictured the Mennonists, huddled together in the dark on the top floor of Groff's mill, singing it out. No fear crouched behind their eyes, even as the watch boy at the closed window sat poised to investigate any strange sounds on the ground outside below.

He had said good-byes to Mutti two weekends earlier, her last in the *Forsthaus* where she'd birthed and raised her little brood, himself first of the litter, over a ten-year period. He had spent the weekend helping her box her belongings, which were few now, with all the children gone. Her beloved clavichord had gone a year ago to pay the taxes. The four oil paintings she'd inherited from Grandfather Müller went the previous year. Even the cherry table with lion's claw feet was up for sale at the auction last weekend, which he'd missed. She'd have plenty of help from Helmut and his fiancée, and Tina, she said.

"I don't need you for the sale. But how can you leave me?" She'd begged him, there in the empty house, with everything boxed or labeled with a price tag. "Don't go! I'll never see you again! America. It's like the moon, Klausi!"

What could he say? He promised he would come back, after he'd settled. That was reasonable. He knew people who'd gone and come back. Even Kochertal, who wrote the book on Charolina. . . .

What he didn't mention was Andreas Ziegler—that he had given up the grudge and vow of vengeance.

That was between him and God. Well, also between him and Hans Herr. Without Herr, would he have abandoned his vow and promise to avenge his father? No. If not for Herr, would he be here now, with his sea chest and all he possessed stored in it, driving Groff's pony and cart to the wharf in Heidelberg, to meet the Mennonist band and the Rhine boat that would take them the first leg to America?

Muss achten nicht der Welte Schmach.

The words tumbled out in his tuneless growl, and each clacking turn of the cartwheels on the graveled path matched a word of the song and lent a rhythm to his song:

Muss. Achten. Nicht. Der. Welte. Schmach.

Der Welte Schmach. The world's humiliation of them. His family, in particular. Yes. He would forgive him. That's what he'd told Herr. The impulse to do so bubbled up spontaneously from his gut to his mouth, and he told him: "I will forgive this man." And he would go to America and never see the man again.

Go tell him that.

The message came out of nowhere, it seemed. He didn't need to ask who *him* was. He'd just been thinking of the man, Andreas Ziegler.

Tell him you forgive him.

It was a thought that he dismissed promptly as perfectly ridiculous. He would not go and tell him that because it was unnecessary. He'd forgiven the man and said so to Hans Herr.

In another hour the Elsenz would dump into the Neckar at Neckargemünd, and from there he'd swing the pony west along the Neckar to Heidelberg, where the boat waited, and he'd be done forever with this blasted, damned, and cursed land.

The Kraichgau was history: the past, the olden days, the heretofore, and from the moment his feet stepped onto the Rhine boat, from that moment he lived in the New Day.

What did he leave behind? Plenty.

Ice-destroyed vineyards and fruit trees, including these dead ones in the overgrown-with- weeds-and-brambles orchards along the Elsenz Road. The Catholic Elector and his Jesuit lackey Kneitz. The taxes and prohibitions on the harassed Mennonists. Andreas Ziegler, the tavern keeper and mayor and the only one who knew the secret of his father's death. (Unless he counted the man's unreliable son Wolf and his taunts that day at the Kapelle.) Even his beloved Mutti in her new lodgings with the family servant, Hans Abraham, in Gaiberg— all of this is the cursed past, and I will sail away, sail away to a new unmapped forest. Like the Hebrew slaves, now free, now crossing the Jordan into the Promised Land.

> So I have come down to rescue them from the hand of the Egyptian, and to bring them up out of that land into a good and spacious land, a land flowing with milk and honey.

If this is what the *Schmach* of the world looks like, bring it on! *Go tell him. You're going right by his house. . . .*

The message rabbit-punched him this time. Its discordant, disruptive voice fell on him, and he moved to throw it off his back.

That's not true at all. This road does not go by his house.

He knew the weakness in his argument. Waldhilsbach and Ziegler's Tavern lay right on the other side of the wooded hill, and the cutoff to the village was coming up, perhaps ten minutes further along the cart path.

He argued with the message now.

It would be ridiculous to go and meet Ziegler. What if he kills me? The man had shown how he handled his enemies. What would stop him from doing so again? On the other hand, . . . Kaspar Grünewald, the renowned forester, had gifted Klaus with a rifle, which he'd mastered, and now he reached beneath the seat to retrieve it. He pointed the muzzle at the foaming current and at the slick-haired, shining back of the beaver riding its waves 150 feet away. Klaus braced his elbow on his knee. The cart jolted and he waited, waited, and at the precise moment, tugged the trigger. The beaver's head jerked away, and the animal suddenly rolled over beneath the current. A white cloud the size of the pony's head rose from the fire hole, but the pony didn't flinch. He'd trained her well.

He reloaded, pouring the powder down the throat of the gun, then the ball and the ramrod to tamp it in place.

What if there were men with him? Of course there would be men. Ziegler's tavern was the social hub of the village. His own father had taken him to meetings in the large open dining room and court sessions with out-of-town justices. If none were scheduled today, there were always the farmers, especially on a winter Saturday afternoon like this, with tilling still a month or more off and the farmers just passing time, exchanging the news. There was plenty of news to talk about, with the emigrations that had begun last year already in full throat this year. Who would move next? Perhaps they just stood around, nursing mugs of beer from Ziegler's barrels.

And with him too apparently a Mennonist. Eighteen years old, just mature enough to produce scraggly red growth on the chin while the farmers all shaved theirs, wearing the Mennonist breeches and leggings and waistcoat stretched tight and outlined over the muscles of his chest, his thighs, and his calves, the muscles built by years of carrying hundredweight sacks of flour down the mill steps, and tossing them onto the cart, off-loading them at one of the Elector's castles, lugging them to a second-floor pantry.

Yes, everyone in the tavern would wonder what he was and turn and stare when he came in. A Mennonist? The ones who don't fight. Not even to protect their women and kids. What's he doing with the gun?

So, he couldn't take the gun inside.

Who was he arguing with, anyway? He wasn't even going to Waldhilsbach. He would drive straight ahead when he passed the cutoff because he had a date in Heidelberg and a trip to take to America.

Then he thought of Jonah. Jonah the Hebrew prophet. The one who got a message from the Lord and ran away. The one who boarded a ship! And the great storm on the Mediterranean that threatened to break up the ship and the lot-casting and the lot falling on Jonah and the only way to calm the sea: he knew—how did he know?—it was himself. "Throw me into the drink and it will calm. This storm is my fault"; and they seized him, they tossed him overboard, and the roaring of the sea ceased.

It will happen to us on the North Atlantic. I am running away from a message, and the Lord will send an unquenchable storm.

If not that, then failure in the New World. The Old World followed, and his New World would be blasted, damned, cursed, because he . . .

He pulled the cart to a halt. *What ails me, anyway?* He was too young in his new beliefs to know that voices come to every man after decisions of conscience, to test the decision, and much too young to discern the difference between the kinds of voices. Those that could be trusted, those from the infernal regions.

If it's you, Lord . . .

He decided on a simple test. The road to Waldhilsbach was a minute away, around the wooded corner where the road bent to follow the river's curve. He replaced the rifle onto the cart floor, dropped the reins over the hook screwed onto the cart's front rail, and lifted his hands free of control. The pony would decide. God spoke to a donkey once. Couldn't he speak to a pony?

'Gittup!"

The pony tossed her mane and strained, and the cart moved obediently forward. The woods curved, and now the cutoff came visible on the left, a break in the trees and a less-travelled cart path, while the main road to Neckargemünd continued straight ahead along the Elsenz.

The pony approached the cutoff and then, without any slowing of pace, leaned left and brought the cart smartly around and onto the smaller road, leading up through the woods toward Waldhilsbach.

The hairs on his arm stood up, and an ice ball came together in his stomach. He watched in astonishment as the road unrolled ahead between the pony's ears, the familiar path and roadside boulders as he crossed the ridge to Waldhilsbach. He was going to meet Ziegler.

The pony trotted up the streets of Waldhilsbach. On the corner of the road leading off to Gaiberg, the Forsthaus sat, neat, three-storied, its half-timbered structure like the Tavern's, a block away, except that the timbers of Forsthaus were painted black and those of the Tavern an oxblood red. The house sat lonely, empty, and SOLD, the sign nailed across the front door said.

The Tavern's chimneys, in contrast to the silent, cold chimneys of the Forsthaus, puffed wood smoke.

It wasn't too late. He could cluck once, and they'd be off. No. He couldn't cluck once. *Go tell him*, the Voice had commanded.

There were other waggons parked, but their horses had all been led off to the barn, meaning the owners were here for the afternoon. He eased over the side of the cart and tied the pony to the hitching rail. He wouldn't be staying long. In and out. "I forgive you."

He threw a blanket over her back and brought a scoop of grain from the saddlebag. The hand on the scoop trembled, and a shower of kernels missed the trough and yellowed the snowbank at his feet. He opened the chest, thrust the rifle inside, and padlocked the lid.

Jesus, I need strength.

Inside, the scant light of the weak, northern, late afternoon sun only half-lit the room, and coming from the brightness of the open air, his eyes needed to adjust.

Yes, there were diners at several tables and a pair of farmers playing cards at a table by the slow-burning open hearth. The air smelled sweetly of their pipe tobacco and roasting beef. He'd forgotten the other widely known reputation of the Mennonists. Unlike himself in his previous gay clothes, they didn't patronize taverns. The farmers glanced, noted, and commented on him among themselves.

He advanced toward the bar and was intercepted by the barmaid, who passed with two steins that astonishingly didn't spill their over-the-top suds.

"Sir! Welcome! Can you wait until I . . . ?"

He gazed at the mounted stagheads over the fireplace and remembered the one on the right, a sixteen-point red stag that the Elector himself had shot, with his Father leading the hunt in the Streitwald ten years back, and donated the magnificent trophy head to the village for Ziegler's wall.

"Hello."

Her eyes, hazel like the woods themselves, engaged his first, and then she faced him, her twin braids dark and neat, foaming steins balanced at the end of each outstretched arm so he could look directly from her eyes, down to the steel cross that lay against the broad expanse of vibrant and pink flesh between her embroidered dirndl top and the white puffed sleeves of the X-laced bodice, which hardly restrained her matching breasts from escaping *into my cupped hands as I lean against her from behind.*

He scuttled the thought.

"Afternoon! Will you be sitting?"

She was thinking he looked good, that he looked no younger than herself, that without the Mennonist hat, he might be a man.

"No. I'm here to see the Mayor."

She nodded and disappeared. I knew a girl like her in a Sinsheim tavern. Before I joined the Mennonists. And I did all that and more with her.

She returned from delivering the glasses and came up and reached for the hat and lifted it away.

"Better!" she said and laughed, the hat out and away and teasing his outstretched hand. "He's meeting some litigants. Let me get you a drink while you wait. Beer? A glass of Burgundy?"

He noticed a clarity of gaze in her eyes that he liked. Had he simply been bewitched? He hummed the song:

Wer Christo jetzt will folgen nach . . .

"What's that?" she asked. "I like it."

He felt the blood retreat, felt his resolution and purpose return. He looked at the floor when he answered.

"I'll just wait for him. Oh, and my hat."

She led back the passageway and handed back the hat.

Ahead of them, the door opened, and a man and wife he guessed to be his mother's generation emerged and passed; then he and the girl, with her leading, entered the private meeting room of Andreas Ziegler, the proprietor. He sat before a large round table, with documents piled on it and on the floor beside him.

"Mr. Mayor! You have a guest." Turning back toward him, the barmaid said, "I didn't get your name, so please introduce yourself." She pulled the door behind her as she went, and it latched.

I'm alone with him. With Andreas Ziegler.

The Mayor looked up. He remembered the man's face, but it appeared that the reverse was not true. He hadn't seen Ziegler for six or seven years, not since before his Father's death, when they often met in his father's rounds, but he was fourteen then, and dressed like his father, in a forester's suit and hat.

The man was in his fifties, balding, with long iron-grey locks falling to his shoulders behind, a large paunch that distended the red waistcoat, and a reading pipe in hand, which he was in the process of lighting.

"I'm Klaus Grünewald, the Forester Kaspar's son."

"Look at you!" Ziegler leaped to his feet. "I would never have guessed." He stretched out a hand in greeting. "Your mother." He sucked deeply on the pipe and then gestured with it toward the chair across the table from him, one of which the couple had just vacated. Klaus remained standing. He wanted to deliver his message while he was erect and in a position to do whatever needed to be done next.

"Your mother sold the Forsthaus last Saturday, and I think she did well. That was the couple there; we were finalizing the deed. But so sad. She didn't want to sell, I think. Sit! I said. Sit!"

He needed to deliver his message, without mincing it. O God!

"I'm here to tell you something important." He felt Ziegler's eyes linger on his. "I once hated you. I had a plan to kill you, like my father was killed. But I'm here to say 'I forgive everything. I forgive you.'"

Ziegler's demeanor didn't change He still lounged in the chair across the table from him, as easily as if he'd just heard the news that supper tonight would be served ten minutes late.

"So. You've joined the Mennonists?" Ziegler said. "How does Mother feel about that? And your sister's joined the Mother Church. Ahh, children!"

"I've joined the Mennonists, and I'm on my way to the New World. Charolina or Penn's Woods."

"Sit down!"

He sat this time and placed his hands loosely on the tabletop because he thought it supported his statement that he forgave, that his hand was not in his waistband, fumbling for a revolver.

"Amazing! Really!" Ziegler said. "Do you think more will go this spring? How many of you are there?"

"Twenty-nine. Mostly from Sinsheim."

He hadn't expected a conversation. He had expected a violent reaction to his statement about killing and revenge. Perhaps the man would go for his throat. Or reach for his weapon, the musket that hung behind him on the wall.

"Your father," Ziegler said. Again, he hadn't shifted nor changed his easy posture. "We had our disagreements, as you may remember. Ahhh, yes. You're Wolf's age. You knew each other, I think."

He wondered if the old man had heard the story of the Kapelle graveyard and his fistfight with his son. He imagined he had.

"He was a bit fanatical about his work for the Elector, I always felt. Your father. It wasn't good for the village. We went back and forth. He threatened me with his gun: did you know that?"

Ziegler stood up and began to pace in front of the window that overlooked the street. "Listen, the Zieglers had every right. For twenty-five years before your Grandfather Müller, my father was magistrate. When your Grandfather passed on, I held as much right to the mayor job as your father. But he got appointed mayor pro tempore first.

"Then he took me to court. He brought in the administrator from Gaiberg, Kauffman, and sued me for defamation and slander because I said his work was shabby. Which it was. He lost the case and showed up at the tavern to pick a fight, and the boys and I threw him out.

"Like I say, the Zieglers had every perquisite, as a magisterial family. That means firewood from the Elector's forest when we need it. Or fruit from his orchards."

Klaus bit his tongue. The hypocrite! For a year now, his mother had told him, Ziegler had charged her for firewood that Hans Abraham had collected for her, although his family had magisterial rights as long as his mother lived, the Elector had promised her.

Ziegler stopped his pacing. The dying afternoon light silhouetted him so that his facial expression was difficult to read.

"So there we were, in the Elector's orchards, which I had every right to, and your father, . . . he was a zealot, a legalist when it came to the Elector. I was picking apples for my family, and he comes out of the trees unannounced, jumps off his horse, and abuses me to my face. He'd take away my tavern, he said. Et cetera, et cetera. Then he pushed me, I pushed back, and he went for his gun in his saddle. I had no intention to hurt anyone, but when he went for the gun—"

"You did it?" Klaus said.

He stared at Ziegler. The man stared back. They both realized the import of the conversation, that it contradicted the story that had been handed down to the village.

"I heard you say—" Klaus began.

"You heard nothing," the older man said. He came back to the table, sat down and took his pipe, which lay among the document piles, and found a bag of loose tobacco.

"Look, you're part of a heresy. You come here and accuse me." He began to load the pipe bowl. Klaus noticed dry leaves falling out of the bowl and landing on the tabletop. The man's hand was shaking. "Why did you come, anyway? No one believes you. You're a Mennonist."

"I said at the beginning, I forgive you. Christ forgave the men who nailed him to the Cross." He stretched his hand to the proprietor.

Ziegler folded his arms. He drew sharply on the pipe and blew a huge cloud at him. "Just go. Just get out."

He left, walking by the barmaid, who stopped and watched him walk past.

The pony was waiting patiently, and they would need to move swiftly now. The light was fading. It was going to turn dark somewhere between Neckargemünd and Heidelberg, and didn't the city close its gate at nightfall? It was too raw to sleep in the cart with just a blanket.

But his heart sang loudly.

Wer Christo jetzt will folgen nach . . .

He had listened to the Voice, and now he felt certain he'd done right. The details of his father's death were more clear now. Did it matter? Yes. More important, he'd said good-bye to the memory. He'd killed the demon that had taken up residence in his room at the mill the day he moved in, and that demon wasn't coming with him to America.

CHAPTER 11

MUTTI AND THE 600 REICHSTHALERS, HEIDELBERG

HEIDELBERG!
The rust-colored tiles of a thousand roofs gleamed in the dawn drizzle as he marched up the Hauptstrasse toward the west gate, where it pierced the fortified walls and opened the way to the Rhine Valley.

He thought now of his first visit to Heidelberg.

The Elector's Annual Deer Hunt came every September. As his Chief Forester, Kaspar Grünewald organized the hunt; repaired the fences that ran from the hilltop to the river in successively narrowing walls, hired the beaters to drive the animals out of the forest and into the runs, and set pens across the Neckar to force the trapped wildlife to swim in circles before the Elector and his invited guests and their guns.

The carnage dazed his six-year-old eyes: magnificent roebuck and tusked boars splashed wild-eyed in the bloodred water at his feet while the Elector and his guests loaded, fired, reloaded and fired, and the trophies piled up on the moored barge behind them.

The Elector drove him back in his own carriage, leading the procession of guest carriages and the long train that carried the trophy animals. The Elector himself sat opposite in full hunting outfit and pointed him out to his guest, similarly bewigged and outfitted.

"You'll be my forester next, my Boy!"

He remembered the rush of pride. "Yes, Sir!"

His father, beside him on this triumphant early evening, beamed continuously at the Elector and massaged Klaus's shoulders.

The carriage entered the half-moon west portal of the fortified wall of the City that evening, the reverse of the route he was walking today; a dark tube lined with armed men on both walls of the huge gateway, and they emerged a minute later on the other side into the autumn sunlight as it beat on these same city rooftops.

"Heidelberg, the home of princes!" the Elector said. He laughed, and Kaspar Grünewald and the guest minister both laughed precisely the same amount. He'd noted that.

All his other memories included Grandfather Müller, who hated the Elector only slightly less than he hated the French armies and their king, Louis XIV, the Sun King of France.

In those memories, Grossdaadi's man drove their carriage up the steep walled stone path that led to Schloss Heidelberg. The green bells tolled the hour as they drove up, even as they tolled the hour now. The isinglass windows blurred the outline of the rust-colored roof and spire of the Heilige Geist Kirche, where the bells swung, out of sight.

"He's a Papist," Grossdaadi said. "He built that wall to divide the church into his half, our half, because his councilmen wouldn't permit him to seize the whole church for the Pope. Your father works for him, and all I can say is 'God bless him.'

"I will say in his favor, 'He's a German!' When Louis's armies took revenge on Heidelberg, . . . when they herded our people into the church and torched it, and only thanks to Pastor Schmidtman prying open a secret door were we spared a great massacre—to that this Elector protested.

"Yet to no avail!" Grandfather's brandy-face, his voice angry and relentless, cowered Klaus into silence.

"The Sun King said, 'Burn it to the ground!' They set gunpowder boxes and blew our castle and the entire city—look at me, Klaus!"

He gazed into the man's blue eyes. He was eight and sitting on the man's knee. Grossdaadi's eyes burned cold and steady. "These eyes, Klaus." His fingers tapped his closed lids. "These eyes saw it burning. These eyes saw them fix bayonets. Saw them run down the women and children who got through the exit door of the church." He stabbed empty air as if his arm were the bayonet. "What do you think of the French now?"

He hated them, of course. With pure and perfect hatred, without a single strand of mercy or pity in it. He hated them as he hated the Devil himself. He took turns those days with Helmut in the neighbor's pumpkin patch, shattering French heads with their clubs.

His hatred was an artifact of the past that he now dropped at the foot of the Cross, where the Savior hung. He gazed upward into the Savior's eyes, the one who spoke to him.

"Not just Andreas Ziegler. The Sun King too," the Savior said.

He looked back toward the turrets of the fortress on the hill. The nearest tower, like a roebuck from the Elector's Hunt, hung split from top to bottom. The left half still hung while the stones lay in a pile like its guts, below.

Could he say it aloud to him, as he had said it to Ziegler? He addressed the shattered tower, over the roofs of the city. He addressed the spirit of the megalomaniac himself, wherever he strutted this afternoon.

"I forgive you!"

The mother with her two boys in tow who approached him on the street paused.

"I forgive you, Louis!"

She stopped her sons from mocking by covering their mouths with her hands, as he passed.

He walked on, out through the city gate and into the scattered fields of farmland beyond. The devastation of last winter showed everywhere. Of course, it was March and nothing green had sprouted yet, although the sensible heat today was over the frost point, and the drizzle that slowly intensified was liquid, not flakes. The vineyards to his right and to his left lay dead and unkempt, with dried weeds as high as his shoulders between the carefully staked vines that hung, lifeless, their roots exploded by the winter of 1708. The house on the edge of the right vineyard sat empty too, abandoned, its front door unlatched and banging back and forth in the light gusts of drizzle.

An hour back he'd said good-bye to the Mennonists at the Neckar wharf in central Heidelberg. Hans Herr was everywhere on the dock, giving orders, working to load the riverboat that wallowed slowly in the fetid and foul water in the inlet off Hafenstrasse. The strange colors of Holland flew on its forward mast. All of his hurrying with the cart and pony from Sinsheim last evening had been unnecessary. The ship would camp for a week, Captain said, to wait for a second party of Palatines from Heilbronn.

Seven days to do what? Fraternize with men with whom he would spend four months on the North Atlantic? Why not visit Horsch, his old school chum who lived downriver in Bacharach and ask the other emigrants to pick him up when their ship came down the Rhine in a week? Herr agreed to the plan. He turned over the cart and pony to Groff and said farewell.

After his good-bye to Mutti last weekend, it could only get easier, he'd thought. He never thought he'd cry over anyone but family, but there he stood with the miller, the man's hands gripping his shoulders.

"I will never see you again," Groff said. Tears trickled steadily into his beard.

"I'll come back."

"You think. . . ." The miller's hands squeezed repeatedly. "God be with you."

He might never see Heidelberg again, this city that seemed to be the personification of his soul and the life and times of his family. Was it true that the land had been cursed? He wheeled and continued walking backward, drinking in the Kirche and its spire, the exploded towers of the fortress on the hillside, and the familiar streets. When he was a boy, riding home from Sunday services with his family, he would contest Helmut as they passed through the city gate. Who could hold the air of Heidelberg in his lungs the longest? He always won. He inhaled deeply now, the blessed air of the city filling his lungs.

He was still holding that breath, his eyes on the spire of the Kirche, when two flapping objects entered the periphery of his vision. They grew and grew and resembled arms, and he thought he heard his name: "Klausi! Klausi!"

Yes, someone was calling.

"Klausi, come back!"

He'd been gone four years now, but the round whisker-dark and eager face of Hans Abraham hadn't changed a bit. The man came at a gallop, his arms pumping. Hans Abraham! Hans hoisting his body to release his head and bruised throat from the forked tree where he'd been caught, when he was—what? He didn't know. Before he went to school. Hans rolling him in the grass to extinguish the flames consuming his breeches when he was eight. Hans extending his hands toward Klaus, hands cradling the miniature horse and rider he'd carved.

"Hans Abraham!"

His arms wrapped the man's shoulders, but Hans pushed back and away. He stood bent, inhaling great gulps.

"Your mother—"

He shook the man's shoulders. "Quick! What's wrong?"

"No . . . No . . . There!" Hans lifted and spun around, pointing back toward the city gate.

"Here? She's here?"

The man's white head nodded, and then he folded completely double, his shaking hands propped on his knees for support.

"Take your time!"

"Come!" The old man, gradually recovering, seized his hand and pulled him back in the direction from which he'd just come.

"How did you find me?"

"Saw you! From the gate." Hans stopped, heaving again, one hand against his chest.

It took fifteen minutes to reach the city gate, and by then Hans had narrated how Mutti, distraught over the house sale yesterday, the day he had left Sinsheim for Heidelberg but three days after his last visit to her, now insisted she must see her son once more before he left for America, and they'd driven at a furious pace from Waldhilsbach this very morning, only to reach the ship after he'd gone and "that Mennonist" told them Klaus's plans to walk to Bacharach. They'd rushed off in that direction, driving the old berlin that once belonged to his grandfather, decrepit and rickety because there was no money for repairs; just short of the city gate, a carriage wheel broke loose and rolled off downward into the rain gutter. He started the repairs, and she'd walked through the gate and spotted Klaus, a mile off but recognizable in his forester's cap as he turned to stare at the city. And she'd compelled him, Hans Abraham, to race pell-mell through the puddles on foot. Him, sixty-three years old, short of breath, and not run since he was fifty-one, when he'd chased down a thief.

Klaus wanted to smile at the chase, but he thought better and repressed it.

They came through the dark semicircle in the wall, and there she was. Her carriage, anyway. The horse, still healthy but uncurried and unkempt, had been loosed and stood head down, eating dead grass at the gate. The carriage, a forest-green berlin that matched the horse in looking unloved, stood crossways on the street, leaning toward the gutter. The once-fashionable coach, which normally suspended neatly from its two chassis rails between the smaller front and larger rear wheels, now looked sick, listing deeply on the front left. Captured in the front glass, Mutti gazed in their direction and waved one gloved hand frantically as she saw Klaus and rose from her seat.

She appeared briefly in the glass of the door, but as she moved, the carriage tipped more sharply downward on its three good wheels , and her face slid sideways out of sight.

Hans Abraham opened the door and reached. An arm, black-gloved to the elbow, appeared, and then the red hair frizzing out from the black rain cape that tied beneath her chin. Hans braced his back against the carriage to keep it from rocking, while offering his hand.

Klaus presented at the door.

"Mutti!"

She fell into his outstretched arms. He lifted her feet free from the carriage, and for a moment her full weight staggered him as he caught the aroma, the expensive French perfume she always wore on trips to the city.

She couldn't speak, and he didn't want to. Her face nestled into his shoulder, and he stroked it. How odd they must appear, him in the dark Mennonist clothes, instead of the military waistcoat, elegant tricorn and buckled shoes he'd worn as recently as four months ago. He did sport the forester's hat today, because the wind didn't lift it as it did the flat felt hat. Then too, the beard . . .

"Don't go. Don't go, Klausi."

Her face pulled back. He saw the red, puffed lids and worried eyes.

"Mutti!" He caught a frizzed wisp of hair between forefinger and thumb and smoothed it under the cape. "Mutti!"

"I'll never see you again," she said.

"Mutti, you make it hard." Was the perfume in her hair or on her neck? He remembered searching for its source, as a child. "If I come home with you, my heart will still be in the New World, and I won't be able to stay."

She exhaled hugely and twisted the white lace handkerchief between her gloved hands.

The drizzle suddenly ceased falling on their heads. Hans had opened her umbrella over them.

"I'll take it." She lifted the umbrella from Hans. "Go ahead, Hans Abraham. Can you fix it?" Without waiting for his reply, she added, "Come with me, Klaus." Her gloved hand led him away. She pulled him into the dry space under the city gate.

"The sale was so hard, Klaus. I didn't know that—when the auctioneer said 'Sold' and gaveled down, and he sold our kitchen table, the table where you and Helmut and Tina and Rudi—and your father and I, of course. Sometimes Grossmuttchi, after Grossdaadi died—and this sniveling courtier in a purple cloak—and why not? You know how beautiful and rare it is, solid cherry. A deep vermilion too, not the black kind. With lion's paw feet, four of them, and expandable with four leaves so you could seat sixteen people. I just . . .

"Your father and I, Klausi. We moved there in 1701."

"I know the story, Mutti. I was there." He rubbed her cheek.

"The Forester's House," she said. "A proper place for a forester, for a nobleman, of course, to raise a family. And then he got himself—you know. . . ."

Tears leaked from her pinched, downcast lids and stained the purple, lace-trimmed bodice.

"I just don't know how we'll survive."

"Yet you do. You're strong, Mutti. I don't know any woman as strong as—"

"We do have a place, of course." She glanced up. "Hans Abraham—" Her gloved fingers motioned toward Hans, on his back on the wet ground beneath the carriage. "Hans Abraham invited us to live with him. Me and Rudy and Tina. Of course—" She smiled weakly, and her voice dropped. "He owes me. So he'd better. When things were good, I loaned him so much—"

He noticed her anemic cheeks. That the cuffs and collar beneath her cape were frayed. Clean and starched but worn heavily, with a clump of loose white threads on the lace mantua pulled loose and conspicuous against the purple bodice.

"My eyes too." She saw he was reviewing her face and appearance. "They blur sometimes." She shucked a glove and used two fingertips to press and move the eyeball beneath the darkened lids. "It's the needlework, I guess." Her fingertips were thickened and dark red. They'd been pricked often.

"How soon, Hans Abraham?"

Hans was back on his feet, the carriage wheel upright in its place at the front of the carriage as he tightened the nut. Hans paused the wrench and turned to address her.

"You can get back in." He swiped his hands on the white kerchief hanging from his pocket, opened the carriage door and steadied her with one hand as she stepped up onto the stirrup.

Klaus followed his mother into the carriage, facing front in the old Berlin. The leather upholstered seats showed heavy usage. The leather around the buttons was cracked open to reveal the white batting. She noticed him finger the cracks.

"Well, it's not fancy, but it's served our family well. Lots of noble families I know don't have a carriage anymore."

Hans hitched the horse while they sat in silence. Her hand nestled in his, and he rubbed the back of it with his free hand. The door opened, and Hans's solicitous face appeared. "I'm sorry. We'll go very slowly. I'll lead the horse. Need to keep an eye on the wheel, My Lady. It's a temporary fix. And where to?"

She glanced at Klaus.

"The wharf, I guess," he said. "It's too near dark to go on. They'll be shutting the city gate."

"The wharf, then." When the door latched, she added, "He's a good man, Hans Abraham. Five children to support and one a mere babe. He got a late start in life, but he's got a young woman. Sally Ann. She's good in the kitchen, too, but I said, 'I don't expect that. Tina will cook for us.'"

The carriage rolled away from the gate and began to rumble as they passed onto the cobblestones of Hauptstrasse, going eastward, toward the wharf.

"Things are so much worse than when you lived with us, Klaus. I hate to complain, but—"

"Mutti, you're not a complainer."

"We used to get together all the time, you remember. Even after Pappi's death. Easter. Christmas. Birthdays. Parties and so much happiness. Now it's all falling apart—that's what I mean by not survive, Klaus. Not the money so much, although God knows, that's—but the family. Where is the family? Helmut especially, since he joined the Elector's Horseguard. I paid his apprenticeship as a tailor. But did he follow through? *No.* Six months, and the Elector's recruiter comes by and promises handsome duds and adventure in the Horseguard, and he walks off the job. What if there's another war with France? You never know. Then there's that Papist girl Hilda. Her father, the rich lawyer, insists that any man his daughter—not that she's so righteous—" Her hands spoke her meaning, tracing a pregnant belly in front of her. "The father, he says his daughter will only marry a Catholic, so what does Helmut do? He renounces our Reformed faith, and will our neighbors let me forget it? No.

"And Tina, now she's fifteen. Going to that monster Kneitz—yes, the one who ruined your father's funeral. Kneitz! How could she? Doesn't she remember? But of course, she was only eleven, yet still, we've all talked over the years and such a terrible insult—but Kneitz, he's got her convinced she'll meet Catholic boys. There you have it. Boys. It's true, I don't have much for a dowry, but Klaus, I've fixed her up—"

Mutti stopped. A faint smile flickered around her mouth.

Am I missing something?

"They taunt me all the time, Klausi." She came back to her topic with a vengeance, her finger shaking in his face. "'Papists. Your kids are Papists. And Klausi now a Mennonist. Why didn't you raise them right?'"

She sank down, threw her head against the seat back, and stared at the ceiling.

"Mutti." He rubbed her bare arm with his fingers. The glove still lay scrunched in her left hand. "Mutti, they're wonderful people. The Mennonists. They love God!"

"I didn't say they didn't."

"Groff rescued me from my own father's grave and apprenticed me without a penny from you and look! I'm a journeyman. We'll need a mill in Penn's Woods, they say. Not right away. It takes plans and a lot of money to build one, which I don't have. He's been, well, a father to me."

"A father?" Her eyes hooked and latched his. "You have a father. Your father was a nobleman, an official in the Elector's Court. Not a peasant. A nobleman, Klaus! This man got you a career, but he's not your father. He is not equal to your father." She lifted her hand and repeatedly banged the large amethyst on her ring finger against the carriage window frame as she said it. "This man's a heretic!" The carriage stopped, and Hans' face appeared in the doorway, his collar, his sleeves, and his hair dark from the drizzle.

"Madam?"

"Tell him to go on," she said.

"It's nothing," he told the coachman. "Proceed."

The horse started and they rode in silence for some minutes, and then she began again, her whole body curled downward, as if she were addressing her own heart.

"You know what that man Ziegler did? How much he hated your Father. How much he hates me. He fined Hans ten guilders. For what? Because Hans cut firewood for me, which I asked him to do. It's the only benefit left me from Kaspar's stipend, which all ended with the first and only payment. Except for free firewood, as much and as long as I need. And now Ziegler says—he's Schultheiss, after all, in charge of Waldhilsbach, although we voted twice to censure him for moving his pasture fence into our village meadow. He has the gall! . . . *He has the gall!* To say free firewood no longer applies to me, since we've got a new Elector.

"Klaus!" She came bolt upright, her popped eyes drilling him. "When will you take this man down for me? This man murdered your father, and you vowed that day . . . you promised, do you remember? I don't care how you take him down. You're good with the rifle, Klaus."

He stared at her. Was she actually this thirsty for blood? The answer, of course, was 'Yes.' There was no way to handle this but to walk directly forward with it.

"I forgave him, Mutti."

It was her turn to stare. Her mouth sagged into a look of utter disbelief.

"Forgave him?"

"I forgave him. The Lord said, 'Forgive,' so I went to Waldhilsbach, to his tavern, and I told him so."

"Klaus! You didn't. You can't. He must die."

She pummeled the window frame of the berlin with both fists, and Hans Abraham's eyes appeared, twisting down, in the gap between the carriage and the driver's seat. Klaus shook his head.

"How could you say that? You have no right to say that." Her eyes bulged with anger.

"Christ himself—"

"Don't talk about Christ. He's God."

"I'm his follower. He set the model. I follow."

"Klaus, you've gone mad. See what the Mennonists have done to you? You betray your own mother. Then you abandon me." Her voice clogged with tears and distress. "You go off to America and leave me—"

"Mutti!" he roared into her face. He was an animal, his paw suddenly pincered in a terrible iron trap.

She recoiled.

The carriage rolled slowly on. Neither of them spoke. They'd crashed into each other, and now they both fell back, conscious of the crevasse between. It was not possible to repair this crack in the earth that had been opening between them for a long time. She might throw herself into the crevasse. She might stand back and wish him well. But he'd made his life choices.

The harbor and its putrid smell of decomposing fish reached them. The wheels ceased their rattle on the cobblestones as the carriage turned onto the planks of the wharf. The planks whimpered under the weight.

"Stop the carriage." She spoke in a tiny voice, her face turned toward the window and the outside evening.

He banged on the front window frame. "Stop here."

He fell back onto the seat. It was dark, the early evening of northern Europe in the late winter. His hand fell onto her bare arm. "I'm sorry I disappoint you."

She pushed her hand under his and intertwined their fingers. The other hand, clutching her white lace handkerchief, blotted her eyes.

"You're the only one I can count on, Klaus. The others . . . I don't know."

"I'll come back to visit. Once I build the mill, I'll come back and bring you to America."

She shook her head. "I'm too old."

"What? Forty-six? Groff's forty-seven. It's not old."

"I don't know anyone there."

"You know me."

"Friends, I mean. And family. They speak English. I don't know English. I don't want to know it."

He opened the door and threw his legs over the side of the berlin, propping himself with one hand against the carriage as he leaned back in. "I want you to meet them. Come. I'm going with them to America. They're my friends." Their flat hats bobbed on the wharf. They were still out there, in the cold drizzle, although otherwise the dock was empty. They'd gotten all the baggage on the ship. He extended his hand into the carriage.

"Why would I want to meet them? We're nobility, they're—"

"In America, we don't have nobility."

Like the evening darkness, the awkwardness between them gathered strength.

"Come back in." She thumped the seat beside her. "I have something for you, Klaus."

"What?" He stepped up on the stirrup and slid back into the seat, pulling the door shut behind him.

"No, open the door. Hans, bring the box."

Hans knew what she meant. He dropped the horse's reins and walked the length of the berlin to the elevated seat directly over the rear carriage wheels, his perch when it was in driving condition. Through the window behind, Klaus saw the man's arms thrusting, pulling, adjusting something, something heavy that resisted mightily. It slid into view, blocking the rear window, a long box, and then it lifted up and away, and they heard it land heavily on the planks outside the side door.

"What is it?" He saw a black box on the ground below, the length of his forearm, with side handles, heavy iron hinges riveting the lid irrevocably to the box. It was plain and undecorated.

Mutti fished a brass key from her purse and passed it to Klaus for Hans. "Open it, Hans." Hans turned the key in the padlock that bound the lid to the box. He lifted the lid. Six rows of golden Imperial Reichstalers lay arranged in neat rows. Hans held up a coin for him to see.

"From your grandfather's sale," she said. "I was going to divide it equally among the children, but after Helmut . . . I saved some for Tina's dowry, as I said. And some for Rudy, if he turns out right. I'm hopeful. But Helmut? Nothing!"

He stared. "How much?"

"Six hundred."

"Mutti. You could have saved Forsthaus. You could have paid everything you owed."

"I didn't want to. It's for my children. You'll need it in America." Her bare hand hardly covered half of his muscular, callused one. "You listened to me. I asked you to stay. And you said you can't. That's all I needed to know."

His tongue fumbled for words, and no words were there.

"Hans! Help him carry it down to the ship."

That was how he would remember her, in that gracious, perhaps discriminating act of generosity, sacrificing her own well-being to live with the servant family and passing on the entire (as far as he knew) inheritance money to her children. And of that, most of it to him.

He would think over that a lot, as he purchased his first land in Pennsilvania with Imperial Reichsthalers. He would think a lot about it when he built his mill.

Part 3

THE INDENTURED GIRL

CHAPTER 12

SOLD!
THE PHILADELPHIA HARBOR, 1718

SINCE MY PAPA went to be with Jesus the 23rd of August—without so much as a Christian prayer his poor, withered, and lifeless body splashed into the Atlantic and disappeared—I suffer these spells.

I was indeed suffering such an attack in Philadelphia Harbor, flinging my bereft, orphaned self onto the rough pine shelf so familiar after sixteen weeks at sea. The distressing millstone of my fate pressed so heavily on my chest that I could hardly breathe. Instead, I made huge, sucking gasps, and all the while tears were coursing. In addition, this morning being the eighteenth anniversary of my nativity, I had reason to recall the last October 3rd, when Mama was still in this vale of tears and Papa played the good nurse, keeping up a cheery aspect:

"Suze, any hour now you'll be up and about and begging for a wee bite of smoked salmon."

All that day I steered my eyes out the window toward the lough that borders Lurgan Towne. Couldn't let his eye catch mine. Couldn't show I was already certain Mama wouldn't be entering Canaan Land with us. On the other hand, weren't we happy? We were together still.

I wouldn't be getting my own private tutor for Latin and Greek, as he'd promised me when I'd completed my studies under him.

America, after all, is not Ireland, where the poor Irish Lazarus supports Dives the Bishop in his Dublin mansion, where he spends the Irishman's rent money on balls and theaters and coaches with footmen. No, Papa told us, his little flock in Lurgan. We have been called out of Ireland, our Egypt, to the Promised Land, the land of honey and milk. We believed him, every one of us. The other families got to go first because of Mama's sickness, and they wrote back—real letters delivered to us by the Irish sea captains they'd entrusted them to—letters saying the stories were all true. They were staking out large estates on the River and waiting for their beloved preacher, my Father.

My grief for them—that they would in this life not see their preacher again, and I had memorized a speech to convey when they came aboard the *Polly Walker* to welcome us and pay our passage— that grief was now devoured by the new and bigger grief. They had not even come. Had our letter never reached them?

Ten days now rocking with the river in Philadelphia Harbor, and this truth a horrible cesspool into which I had tumbled and could only keep thrusting my nose and mouth desperately above the rising sludge. How long till it overwhelmed me? Another day perhaps, the Captain said yesterday. And then?

"Nobody wants you. Irish paddywhacks—"

"I'm not. We're Scots—"

"Ooooh. A temper."

His big fingers grasped my bottom cheek familiarly through my skirts, and I wheeled and slapped away the offensive hand. I wanted to go for his eyes with my nails.

"She's a vixen, Boys!"

I rushed off to a group of German youths waiting on the aft-castle deck while a shopper for indentureds decided whether it was four or five he needed for his mill. Only a dozen of us were left on the ship anymore.

So as I said, I suffered, stretched on my back in the dark bunk shelf, the unbearable weight sitting on my chest like an animal. I was sucking air audibly in the dark when a shaft of light suddenly shot downward at the far end of steerage, and through the opening hatch, descending the four steps that separated the deck overhead from our deck, I saw uniformed legs, which I recognized as Captain's and simultaneously that it was No Time for Spells. I might be in serious jeopardy. I leaped, looking which way to flee. I figured I had the advantage of size. Only a child could walk below deck without walking jackknifed, and the Captain was a large man.

"Jane! Jane Cameron!" he sang out like a foghorn, and there was no one else to hear him, but temporary blindness from exiting the sunlit world prevented him from seeing me.

That's when I saw he wasn't alone.

"Come up, Jane. Someone for you."

I knew right off it wasn't one of our Ulster congregation come to welcome me. This man stood on the bottom stair behind the Captain and even his shoulders didn't come even with the Captain's shoulders. His breeches and knee socks were stuffed with his muscles. He paused on the step, like I'd always imagined a tiger cat would, his body one contiguous sinew, poised. As I approached, guessing it safe since the Captain wasn't alone, I got my first peek at the face, under the flat black hat, which I thought meant he was a Quaker: the carroty pointed beard, oversized ears that cupped forward, and sharp nose holding apart the two riveting eyes as blue as the eyes of a painted dolly face. I laughed out loud—it was one of our Irish leprechauns!

The leprechaun extended a hand, well-muscled like the rest of him, and voiced his name, which was not English. It resembled "Greenyvald," which I shortly found was close to the correct sound, although his name in German was somewhat more down the throat. He pumped my hand, up-down up-down, like men shake with each other, which I thought quaint until I discovered that all his people did so when they met. No kissing of the lady's hand or seizing just the fingertips. They had a sweet, bucolic way about them. Sometime later I even saw men kiss men, instead of the handshake.

And I realized he was here to buy me.

We climbed the stairs to the Captain's cabin. I'd never been invited in before, so I must have gawked at the large oil of the King because the Captain hailed me.

"We're waiting, Jane."

They had both already settled into the enormous wicker chairs at the equally enormous oak table, and the Captain tepeed his hands over a large parchment document. He pointed his chin at a chair below the oil painting. Before I even sat, he began:

"*This Indenture witnesseth that Jane Cameron, of her own will and accord . . .*" He eyed me significantly. "*. . . in payment for her passage, and in consideration of the sum of sixteen pounds sterling—*"

"Sixteen pounds!" I wailed the obscene figure. "It's seven pounds ten. You're taking advantage because I'm—"

His forefinger made a zipping motion across his lips. "And seven pounds ten for your father's passage. Past the halfway point when he perished, and that's the agreement, Missy. Plus ten shillings for the extra food these two weeks in port. Plus ten shillings interest for payment made *after* the trip."

I gaped, my mouth wide, I'm certain, desperately wishing Papa were here to use his infinite wisdom and persuasion on this man.

But of course, he *was* there in the Lion's Arms in Dublin when we signed the contract last Christmas Day. And he protested that first night with the Captain.

"Our people will come to Philadelphia for us and pay. There's no need for a contract."

The Captain looked captainly in the Royal Navy uniform and bars and acted completely like a Captain Grand. "If you don't pay up front, you sign a contract. Insurance for our Owner, if you will. He wants full payment, and you either pay sterling when we get to Philadelphia or sell your services. Like everyone else. A gentleman of the cloth, huh?"

We took the quill and filled in our names. Papa first, then me.

In exchange, he agreed to transport our bodies, our souls, and the big chest from Dublin to Cowes, where he took on provisions for the trip: bread, butter, cheese, flour, peas, rice, salt bacon, dried fruit. And barrels of fresh water. Then from Cowes to Philadelphia, across the North Atlantic.

Those first days at sea, Papa and I sat topside, on the aft castle, every evening an hour before dark. It was Ascension Day when we left Cowes, and balmy. Most evenings he asked me to read psalms to him, but now and again he'd return to his favorite passage, Joshua 1. I read it with deliberation, so he could savor every phrase:

> Now therefore arise, go over this Jordan, you and all this people, into the land that I am giving to them, to the people of Israel. Every place that the sole of your foot will tread upon, I have given you, . . . all the land of the Hittites. . . .

After two weeks I didn't need to read anymore because it was branded onto my memory, and I recited it with my eyes wide open as dozens, then hundreds, then thousands, then tens of thousands of lights pricked the black dome and swelled as the night deepened, until the dome seemed hung with festival lamps, large and close.

We didn't know anyone on the ship. The ten German families talked and ate among themselves, in their tongue, naturally. There was also a knot of young women and men who were English. Some of them were attached. The girls who weren't played games with the sea crabs in the dusk, as they called themselves, sat on their laps, and shortly the sailor would lead the girl below deck, their arms around each other's waists, laughing in a carefree way.

"'The ungodly are not so, but are like the chaff the wind drives away,'" Papa said. He needn't explain. I understood his mind. He thought those girls unworthy of the Promised Land and therefore, somehow, they would be driven off like chaff before we reached shore.

He was right. What we didn't know then was this: he wouldn't get there either. We sat on the aft-castle deck, talking of our new home, and his voice rose more and more intense, until he graduated to his preaching voice.

"It's our exodus, Janey. We've left Pharaoh's Egypt. We're in the Wilderness. Some will worship calves here. Some will murmur. Some will turn to whoremongering. But wait. It won't stay smooth the whole journey. When the Wilderness threatens to eat us, will we lose our hearts? Will our eyes no longer fix on Canaan Land? The last verse again, Janey."

So I said it again" "'Have I not commanded you? Be strong and of good courage; be not frightened, neither be dismayed, for the Lord your God is with you wherever you go.'"

Nine days out, the troubles started. First it was seasickness. The decks turned slimy because the sailors couldn't wash them off fast enough. The sick fell and wallowed in their own vomit. The air in steerage grew putrid. The sun came up out of the waves a fireball and grilled people on the top deck and baked them in steerage. Whole families got sick, and it wasn't seasickness any more.

"It's the meat," people said. The meat had soaked in salt so long that it became impossible to swallow, and the salt in all the food drove us wild with thirst. But the water stank, after the first week, because the barrels mildewed. If you sucked a dried apricot with the water, it partly masked the smell. So we did that.

Four weeks out, a wave of bloody flux swept steerage, and the continuous diarrhea made the air unbreathable and left many unable to walk, moaning on their fouled bunks. The malady spread. Through the water, some said. Through the food, some of us believed. The oversized kettles out of which they dipped our food were open, and the healthy and the sick jostled together around them, coughing and sneezing. No, it's touching the sick, still others said. Maybe it was all of these.

Papa and I both came down.

The children were first to die. Stiff little bodies were carried topside every morning. In all of that, a woman in steerage gave birth. The abdominal contractions of the flux forced the baby prematurely, and we heard screams most of that night, now softer and softer until they ceased about dawn. No one would touch the body. No one had strength to carry an adult body four steps up for proper burial at sea. Two men draped a blanket around her to avoid touch, broke open a porthole, and pushed the body of the mother out. Followed by the little bundle, like a bag of rubbish.

It wasn't enough. The Almighty was going to test us. He sent a Jonah Storm. It blew out of Newfoundland, the sailors said, with winds that shrilled through the rigging like the *bean sith*, so we clapped our ears, down in steerage. The ship rode the sea like a stallion, lifting his forefeet and pawing the air, then suddenly dropping forward with his hind hooves almost vertical. Down in steerage a poorly tied chest broke loose and became a missile, racing breakneck forward and back. In the darkness, one could only hear it coming as it smashed the whole length of steerage before a man threw his body across and roped it at the bottom of a plunge.

I stood over Papa. My own legs wanted to buckle, but I hooked arms around the vertical bedposts with the thought that he's worse than I. I worked to hydrate him, feeding him the apricots with the terrible water. He drank and immediately hurled it all out across the floor. His voice turned raspy, then muffled and weak. I knelt in the foul sputum. I planted my ear next to his lips. What did it matter? I already had the disease. I heard a hoarse whisper:

"*Arise; go over this Jordan, you and all this people, into the land. . . .*"

"Hold fast, Papa. They're waiting for us. All of them. We'll go in together." It was too dark to make out his eyes and too dark for him to make out mine. I was glad about that.

The storm exalted over us for six days. By the fifth he could no longer move his legs, even with help. No one would help me carry him to the heads. He soiled the blankets with the tiny amount of water and blood and feces still inside. I cleaned him up. When I finished, he sighed, "Be of good courage, Janey."

Two large luminous eyes fixed me in the darkness. Those were his last coherent words. He hung on, his spirit unwilling to orphan me, but his mind flung itself, like the runaway chest, back and forth. He called out to my lost mother.

"Tell them to fire up the stove for service."

"Suze, any minute now, you'll be askin' for a wee bit of salmon."

The morning of the sixth day the storm ceased. The sun rose out of the sea, cheerful and undimmed by any clouds, as if nothing had ever happened. It was too late for many, including our dear papa. They didn't push him through a porthole, thank you, Savior God. The sailors stretched him full-length on the deck, and I wrapped a sheet around him toe to head for a shroud, turning the clean side out. Two unattached girls lay stretched out on either side of him. It wouldn't have made him glad. The sailors started at the far end of the corpses, one at the feet, one at the heads. Lifting, tossing. Lifting, tossing. His body sank slowly in one big circle, like a maple leaf in October. I tracked him by the sheet. The white bundle grew smaller in the translucent aquamarine until it looked no bigger than one of the baby bundles, and then it was no more.

—◦◦◦◦◦◦—

"Hath bound and put herself Servant to the said Klaus Grünewald to serve him in the Province of Pennsilvania for the full term of five years . . ."

"I need a girl." The blue eyes in the leprechaun face across the table corner latched onto mine. "English is better. You read, of course?"

When I nodded, he said, "For contracts, patents, English is better."

"Are we fine with this?" the Captain catechized me. The feather end of his quill tapped on my fingers. "Otherwise, you go back with us to London. My men might like that."

I plumbed the blue eyes of my Potiphar. What was in there? What if he had a wife like Potiphar's? (Little did I know.) Five years? I would be twenty-three when I went free again.

I took the quill and signed my name. Mother always said my penmanship was the best of any she knew.

—⁓⁓⁓—

I came back up from steerage in the only other outfit I owned, the Lowlands dress I'd been saving for the celebration with our parish, a tartan skirt, blue and green plaid, white blouse with starched poufy sleeves, the blue bonnet tam.

"Whoa ho!" The Captain smacked his hands.

Usually I wore it proudly. Today I ignored his display and headed for the gangplank. From topside, I could see across the city four-stories, all the way to a long line of purple hills. My new master was three paces before me, up the quay, up the embankment, and then onto Fishbourne Street.

I found Philadelphia homes to be large, four floors of red brick, and all spanking new, a very big contrast to the ancient houses in Dublin. Men dressed like back home. Well, maybe not Lurgan Towne men but certainly Dublin men. They wore powdered wigs. The women wore petticoats with red or blue ribbons, and all with white aprons covering their skirts. I saw a woman with three strings of precious stones around her throat, and I touched the beads around mine. They appreciated fine things. Mama would have been happy here.

Most surprising were the Hittites. They came single file down Broad Street, without a sound, on bare feet, on the packed dirt. I stared, never having seen a people whose skins were blackish-orange. In all other aspects, their bodies seemed constructed like ours. Each carried a horse blanket over one shoulder that hung loosely front and back and revealed the single shocking fact that the Hittites were *naked* beneath their blankets. They had smooth hairless bodies, and because the blankets masked their anatomies, how could I tell which were men, which were women? Perhaps they were all men? Several carried woven baskets that rested on the napes of their necks and attached by bands around their foreheads. I saw animal skins in the baskets. Were these the women?

How my new master knew I wasn't following, I don't know, because he appeared to be walking without minding me. Maybe he stopped hearing my footsteps. Anyway, he stopped at the street corner and turned to observe me staring at the Hittites. He raised one arm and motioned.

Shortly we arrived at a large three-sided shed. Waggons were queued along the front, and twenty-some horses were tethered, under the overhang, to a long rail inside. Which was his? Here came another huge surprise: the size of his waggon. We have lots of waggons, hansoms and carriages in Dublin, but none to compare with the *conestoga*. This strange vehicle resembles a four-wheeled barge with a canvas cover stretched across a series of hoops to protect the contents from rainstorms, which I came to find out were frequent and often without warning. This was further indication that my master was a man of means. His waggon was already loaded with casks of nails, lead, several sizes of new copper kettles, bolts of colored cloth, and he was hitching two pairs of massive horses to it.

I queried whether he owned the waggon as I stepped up into it, and he affirmed that he did. To my surprise, he didn't onboard himself but stepped alongside with the horses, somewhat guiding them with a twenty-foot leather strap fixed to the cheek of the lead left horse but depending more on a series of "Gees" and "Haws" that he uttered in a conversational manner to the animals.

I was disappointed to sit cooped inside this waggon and unable to see the Mister, as I chose to call him, and therefore, unable to ask my questions. While I debated what to do about it, we came to a river several hundred yards across. It looked deep. I couldn't imagine horses swimming it, all the while towing a loaded waggon of the type we had. But Fear Not! Mister gave a halloo that seemed directed at no one, and yet in five minutes a large flatboat came poling through the rushes and cattails along the bank to the edge of the beaten path where our lead horse, like Joshua's priests, awaited the Lord's command before dipping its feet. We rolled onto the flatboat, which conveniently had a wooden rail on three sides, for tying lead horses. Although it tilted side to side, I never felt in danger of upset.

To this point I had not seen a reason for fearing Mister, other than the major reason that he would now be my owner for five years and might take my questions to be foolish women's chatter, as ignorant men do by instinct. Papa, however, had reared me from childhood to speak my mind in concise sentences, with nouns and verbs and without the laborer's "ums and ahs," making no distinction between male or female, low or high, slave or free. As the Apostle put it in his Letter to the Galatians.

He had eased up by the lead horse, a pipe of some sort pressed between his lips and burping bubbles of smoke while staring at the river's uncertain bottom. I approached mostly fearlessly and asked if I might pose a question or two. I was frankly uncertain of the man's comprehension of the English language because of some oddities in his speech.

"Why, sure."

He turned his red-bearded chin my way and removed his pipe. I noticed that he wasn't more than a youth, maybe ten years older than myself.

"Where are we going?"

"Home. The Pequea." At this moment our pilot poled the flatboat into the current, and we were off.

When I asked exactly what the Peck-Way was, he described a settlement in the forest some sixty miles to the west, where he and twenty-nine others from the Rhineland had settled some nine years earlier. He'd built a gristmill on the Pequea, he said, and ground flour for the neighborhood farmers. He also owned this waggon and delivered the produce of the same farm to a Philadelphia merchant on a regular basis and returned with store goods. However, some years earlier the settlers had dispatched him back to the Old Country, and he had led some 360 of his people to Pennsilvania and was now engaged in land transactions for them. For this reason, he needed someone with excellent English, a person who spoke the language natively, such as myself, to keep his books and represent him before the Governor's land agents.

My estimation of this rather humorous-looking man rose. I'd discovered a merchant of the first order, and I congratulated myself on locating such a good person to start my enterprise in America, since it had become painfully clear since arriving in Canaan that I would not locate the Ulster emigrants for some months, and I began to put out of my mind the fantasy I'd had of their help in my redemption.

At that point we collided with the far bank. The Pilot unlatched the rail at the river's edge, swung it wide on its hinge, and Mister drove his procession off the flatboat into what appeared to be the very Dark Wood of Error itself.

Enormous oaks rose beside the narrow double ruts as our waggon came up the sloping bank. Their branches swiped the far side of the waggon. Their tops drooled over us, their matting leaves so densely interleaved overhead as to make it instantly twilight, although it was hardly later than one or two in the afternoon. I remembered Dante:

What wood that was! I never saw so drear,
So rank, so arduous a wilderness!
It's very memory gives a shape to fear.

Were there other travelers on this path? Did one ever meet a waggon? If so, were there rules on who backed up or turned out? Otherwise it was impossible to pass.

Except for the creak of the turning wheels, the scraping of branches, the occasional snickers of the horses and Mister's clucks, the woods were still and dark as a Lurgan cemetery.

I must have fallen asleep in the back of the waggon because I jerked perpendicular when the waggon lurched. I could hear nothing, see nothing, and in the moment, I couldn't remember where I was.

"We're here." The voice poked through the black oval opening of the waggon front.

"Home?"

"Milltown. We'll overnight here. Here . . . my hand. Now your foot here." His hand led my shoe onto the waggon tongue. "Jump. Now go in. Over there! I'll be in shortly."

With a Gee and a Haw, he and the waggon headed away, crunching around the side of the large edifice that blocked my way, its presence shapeless and dark, except for a tiny light somewhere deep inside, which illumined the outline of a doorway ahead. Voices called here and there. With my open palm I tested the door, not sure if I was welcome or not.

"Hello? Hello?"

The aroma of beef and onions hung in the dark room and reminded me that I was famished. A light came now, bobbing, and a swishing of skirts, coming toward me down what seemed to be a hallway. I waited motionless, three steps inside the doorway.

She was middle-aged and bosomy and walked right up and brushed against me as she lifted the smoking lanthorn to fully illuminate my face.

"Law for me! A girl! What brings you here this time a night? I never see a woman on the road so dreadful late. Who are you? Where you going?"

Startled, I stepped backward, but fortunately the door swung behind me in the dark, and my master strode past into the flickering light.

"Lawful heart, Greenywalt. How de do? Where in the world you going with this woman? Who is she?"

Greenywalt didn't answer but found a chair, dropped into it, and fumbled his pipe out of his breast pocket. "Give me a light, Debb?"

She vanished away and returned, thrusting a flaming splinter to the Mister, and he curled over it until the little flame jumped on his tobacco. I heard his long suck and exhale, and the sweet tobacco smoke filled up the entryway, obliterating the beef and onions.

The woman Debb turned back on me. "Who are you? She don't look like your kind, Greenywalt."

I told her she was being rude, not offering me a seat. She scoured me up and down, then trotted off and returned with a chair. After that, she fetched plates of the same beef and onions, still warm, one for each of us. We ate with the plates in our laps.

Greenywalt dismissed himself. "I sleep rough," he said, and I wasn't sure what it meant but guessed I wouldn't see him again until next morning.

Debb motioned me to follow through the hallway to its end and waved me into a little room filled side to side with the bedstead. I climbed a little stepstool to get myself into the blessed bed. Blessed, I say, for after sixteen weeks at sea, this was the first bed with pillows and sheets and quilts since I'd left Dublin in May. Nor did I inspect to see if they were clean or filthy nor grumble about the other traveler Debb's lamp revealed, a woman my age on the wall side of the bed, with her back to me, one arm around a pillow, and soughing slow and regular.

I didn't mind. I arranged my weary bones, and before I could notice the passage, I had journeyed from my first day in the Promised Land into the River Lethe of forgetfulness and slumber.

CHAPTER 13

THE PEQUEA SETTLEMENT,
1718–20

I MADE UP MY MIND to be as useful as I could to the new Master and set aside my grief, recalling Jeremiah, instructing the Hebrew children to seek the welfare of the city of their exile. He also said: "Take husbands and have sons and daughters; . . . multiply there." I didn't imagine this part of the verse applying to me.

Accordingly, on my second day there, I asked Mister to fully acquaint me with his plantation. I'd already been shown my quarters, of course, on the third floor of his mill, and found the drip-drip of water off the tethered waterwheel to be a sort of lullaby through the night. Of course, if the wheel was running and the millstones grinding, the whole building vibrated, and it was quite a different matter, but that was never the case during the night hours.

He responded kindly and walked me to the top of the hill that sloped up and away from the creek until we got to a good overlook and I saw just how the stream—Beaver Creek, so-named--bubbled out of the hillside, ran into his millpond, and from there down a race and dumped its cargo onto the overshot wheel, a good twelve feet in height. He explained how the wheel caught the stream in little bucket boards, and the water's weight drove it round continuously when the race was open, which in those days he did every morning at eight. The wheel rotated a shaft the width of my leg that in turn drove a millstone by way of a second shaft, and also a windlass to hoist the sacks of grain to the dormer window on my floor, which became a workroom during the day. Around this mechanical system, he'd built the whole mill with limestone rock.

Even as he waved and pointed there on the hilltop, I espied one of his neighbors, a black hat and a beard like the Mister himself, pull up with a waggon and hook his sacks to the pulley. They hoisted them up to the loft window, where a young man, Christ, an indentured like myself (I later found out), put his arms around the incoming and disappeared with it back inside. The grain, the Mister said, fell downward through a feeder onto the millstone on the meal floor, was ground fine, and poured out the meal spout into burlaps that Gerhard, another indentured, held beneath it.

The mill snuggled into the hillside, two stories tall from the side we were viewing, with a cellar on the far side, away from us. He himself lived on the walk-in cellar floor, allowed by the slope.

"But when the Missus comes—"

He would always refer to her as the Missus, although her name was Maudlin, an oddity because in English—but I doubted that his English went that far.

"When the Missus comes, she'll live *there*."

The cabin was constructed with peeled logs and its stone foundation banked into the hillside like the mill itself. It didn't look finished; only half the logs were chinked with moss and mud. I guessed it rather draughty right now, although he said he'd lived there eight years until he finished the mill last year, but never got to properly finish the cabin.

"So when you have time, do you sew?" he asked. "It needs curtains. And coverlets."

I said it wasn't my strong suit. "And begging your pardon, where is the Missus?"

"In the Kraichgau."

Up to this moment I had never heard of "Mennonists." Right then he introduced me to them, saying he was one, that the whole Pequea Settlement was made up of Mennonists, refugees from the dungeons and prisons. I wondered, but didn't ask: Might they be a criminal element, thus justifying such treatment? I didn't imagine so, seeing his plantation and considering my impressions of the man so far. He said they'd been imprisoned for breaking the law, refusing baptism for their babes in the Church of the land. They so wanted to worship the Lord in the right way that they gathered in grottoes and at midnights in the forests. I felt a pang of kinship in my bosom. "It is our story as Covenanters in the Lowlands of Scotland," I said.

He seized my elbow and brought his leprechaun face right at mine. "Your people then too?"

The hand ripped away. He pulled his face back too. I guessed it was that neighbor on his waggon down there. What was the Mister doing with a strange and pretty woman on the hilltop, his hand on her arm?

He recovered real quick. He'd married the Missus two years back, he said, when he was in the Rhineland, but the Kraichgau law also forbade Mennonists from multiplying. So they couldn't stay there, married. Yet she also couldn't leave, he said, as her father lay in the Swiss prison. When he was released, they'd both come.

"I'll show you the letter," he said. "My mother's coming also. I'll show you that letter too. Can you read German? Well, I'll show you."

That day I learned that my chief responsibilities would be keeping his records on the mill operations, in English, and fixing up the little bower of bliss for the Missus when she got here, which he believed would certainly happen during the upcoming sailing season, as they'd already released some prisoners, including the man whose cabin we could see looking north from the hilltop, "Brother Brechbühl," as he called him.

Why records in English? I asked, as he himself spoke German natively.

"For Logan."

I was assembling the jigsaw puzzle of this man in my head. Logan, I found out when I rode with the Mister to Philadelphia some weeks later, carried the mortgage on the mill. He was a Philadelphia swell, a topping man of the Quaker party; he'd even been the Governor of the Commonwealth for some years. Logan was also what we back in Ulster familiarly called The Bacon, a man who seems to be everywhere and creates a sizzle wherever he goes, to stick with that metaphor.

Most of what I learned about Logan the Mister shared in dribs and drabs over the next several weeks, as I set up the books. Up till then, he'd kept his records speared on a scrap board with a nail and on pieces of paper that every night he threw into the great ship trunk that he kept locked with an equally great key.

Mister was contracted to this Logan, he said, to fetch white flour and garden vegetables and fruits from the German farmers for the tables of Quaker English families of Philadelphia, and for export on Quaker ships bound for London and Jamaica. That was the flour, in particular, and the grain in liquid form—an inferior whiskey, any Lowlander would have judged. And this called for a Book of Shipments, with dates, weights, invoices, and payments.

He had also contracted to buy land from Logan, who served as land agent for the Very Honorable William Penn and his family. The land-agent responsibility was horrible, Mister said. Logan administered the land Penn had once purchased from the Hittites—he called them Indians—who once owned it, and then sold it to Germans, Irish, Welsh, the Scots-Irish, . . . and the business was looking like the Tower of Babel. Germans, he said, were honest and paid for their land—which I took with the time-honored grain of salt, as he himself was German, and I did discover shortly that he winked at some who weren't on time or had missed their payments altogether. The Scotch-Irish—and that was how they referred to us Scots here—squatted without paying at all. Logan was sending troops to remove them—and did I know Logan was Scotch-Irish himself?

To settle the problem, the Penns refused to deal with any more newcomers, and instead sold the land via Logan in big parcels to Mister and other brokers like him. Keeping track of that called for a Book of Real Estate, with entries on land purchased by Mister, parcels sold, payments received, payments outstanding, annual quitrents for the Proprietor Penn collected, annual quitrents outstanding, et cetera.

Within a week I was asking myself: How had he managed without me?

About the third week, he asked me to attend the evening meetings he held in his new cabin. The Mister and a Mister Hans Herr, who was a partner in this enterprise, presided. The mill closed at five sharp, and by five-thirty every evening two or three teams and families were queued in the lane, waiting to hash out the status of the land they wished to buy for farms. They all spoke that terrible language that growled. Even the women growled. The men all sported unshorn beards, often to the mid-chest, no wigs, and large nail-studded shoes. The women carried babies inside or out and wore simple aprons over their long skirts and cute white German caps. I kept a record of the requests made and the decisions agreed upon.

A most unexpected blessing fell into my lap by way of the meetings. I met Mr. Herr's wife, Frony, a cute nickname from her christened name Veronica, which they'd also named her daughter. Frony was a very sweet dumpling and I mean no insult by that: she was shaped like one. But then, many of their women were dumplings. Their food, I found, wasn't lean and from the sea like our Ulster cuisine, but great feasts of potatoes, stuffed sausages, ham and bacon from their pigs, cheeses and butter and yoghurt, pickles of every type: pickled melons, pickled beets, pickled cucumbers and meats. They filled pies with every berry or fruit imaginable and baked a bread they called "sourdough" with slabs of honeycomb on it. The women made beers and served it all up with the produce of their magnificent gardens: eggplants, white and yellow corn and squash, plants I couldn't have imagined existed—foods the "Indians" had introduced to the Quakers.

But to Frony! We spoke with our hands and pictures at first, since my German was only bumbling phrases, to which she time and again responded: "*Vass? Vass?*" On her side, she knew no English, but I didn't expect any. My entire time in the Settlement, I met only a few who spoke more than a couple phrases, except for Brother Herr, as we called him, whose English was passable, and Mister, of course, who was mostly fluent.

She'd been to London the year before they came to Pequea, she said through her husband. But—and she giggled—she let him do all the talking in London. She seemed quite pleased with herself about that arrangement even now whenever they were in the room together. When asked a question in his presence, she would tilt his direction and smile cherub-like, and her mister would nod and proceed to an-

swer as if the question had been directed to him. He and Frony had birthed and reared five well-scrubbed, well-fed children, the oldest two in their teens, the two middle ones girls (Veronica and Anna), and the youngest, Christian, was six. She volunteered to show me the Settlement on my day off, which was every Sunday. We agreed on 2:00 p.m., after their services, which Mister had not asked me to attend, as I knew no German yet, those first months.

From the Mister's great surveyors' maps, I knew that the Settlement was five miles long. I supposed that we could walk it out and back in an afternoon, but Frony had other plans. About two that beginning-of-November day, she arrived at the mill. I was reading my Testament. I had almost no time for it during the week, as we were working days and evenings and I also cooked breakfast and supper now for Mister in the large room on the ground floor of the mill, which doubled as his bedroom. It required building a wood fire every meal and usually splitting the wood chunks for it as well. My contract hadn't specified my responsibilities other than *"behave obedient and faithful in all things as a good and dutiful Servant ought to do,"* so there was nothing he couldn't ask for, I supposed. In all fairness, he also had obligations: To provide me with "Meat, Drink, Cloathing, Lodging, and Washing," as well as the sum of ten pounds sterling on the last day of my contract, six years hence. To date, he'd met all the necessary except Cloathing, which I hadn't needed yet, although the daily washing of my one work outfit, out of sight in my room, was shortly going to wear it out.

She hallooed me from the lane, and I ran out and saw her seated in a small pony cart with her two youngest blondes on the back bench. The Mister had lent us Gerhard for the afternoon. He sat astride one of the big draft horses, barefoot even in what looked like a rainstorm later, and followed a respectful distance back the whole afternoon. We could talk in private but know he was near enough to ward off any savages.

She thumped the seat by her side with her free hand to indicate that I should jump aboard. As soon as I did, she made a kissing noise that set the pony in motion, then turned to exclaim over my outfit. I was wearing the Lowlands dress, the tartan skirt and blue tam, and I suppose my red hair, loose to my mid-back in those early days, gave the whole outfit a snap.

"*Ah, wie schön, wie schön!*"

I did understand that and thanked her. She produced a little hand-drawn map with a few English words and spread it on my knee, beside hers. I recognized Mr. Herr's writing and appreciated the effort, although "House" and "Street" are quite similar in the two languages.

Anna and Christian weren't like English children, under orders to speak only when spoken to. They chattered away, pointing out things. Frony began a narrative too, of which I caught occasional words, but she believed in "total language baptism." She was definitely immersing me.

She wore the ubiquitous dark skirt and white apron. What was unusual was her flat straw hat, which topped one fat braid that fell past her waist behind, the hat tied under her chin with a deep blue ribbon. It was the only time I'd seen her hair outside the cap. The other unusual piece was the purple woolen shawl with white tulips and pink birds with red beaks knitted onto it. In a bucolic sort of way, it was lovely.

Frony was in gay spirits, even more than her usual cheerfulness. She relished the job of showcasing the Settlement. Those days the forest was still everywhere: we drove through deep shadows between massive oaks for periods, and abruptly a cabin would appear around a bend, constructed like all the others with notched logs, a little springhouse in one direction or the other, and a stream trailing away, sometimes the stream only discernible by the rich streak of vegetation. Each cabin had a main floor with grease-paper window, a loft under the sloping roof, and often a lower floor that one didn't see if the house fronted away from the road. Each cabin was roofed with closely packed straw-thatch bundles, now gray from the rains, and the logs were chinked immaculately with clay. On both sides and behind the cabin, a large garden (all of them appearing dead by now) and some fields stretched away until they bumped the line of trees, where the eternal forest began.

And then we entered the woods again.

I unfolded the map further. The Settlement was a series of parallelograms sketched the width of the paper, eleven of them, lined up east to west for five miles, with names and acreages written in each box. The trail labeled Conestoga Road ran in a mostly straight line from the eastern edge, where we got on it, all the way to the farthest plot, which like the first plot was labeled with Greenywalt's name. Acreage was also designated, not in morgens, which I never understood, but in English acres, beginning with Mister's plot of 1,080 acres, now divided in two, with the Swiss Pastor Brechbühl on the north side of the road.

From Mister I had learned that the total acreage of the 1710 purchase was 10,000, which they purchased for 500 £; they'd sold 3,600 acres off to the Huguenots, and the remaining 6,400 acres were purchased at the wonderful figure of five pounds per acre, 100 £ immediately payable and the remainder to be paid over a six year period, with interest. But a year later they paid off the full amount, plus 40%, still, at seven pounds an acre, an astonishing bargain, Mister said, "And only because William Penn fancied us Mennonists and said so when we met him in London."

The tracts followed one another, connected to each other. Hans Funck's tract, Hans Miller's (where we crossed Pequea Creek on a rough puncheon bridge), Wendell Bowman's, and abruptly, Frony and Hans's 530 acres. The Herr Plantation included "the German barn" with a whitewashed wall-enclosed yard.

Herr's was the first such barn, but soon I could easily identify the German barn—a massive building as large as our Irish lords' manor houses—because every farmer along the Conestoga Road had one. You accessed the first floor via Dutch half-doors, its walls of Pequea limestones twenty-four inches across, which Herr's children coated every spring with a skin of white lime. The second floor, the haylofts, hung out over the first and could be accessed from within the barn by a stairway of notches cut in a single large log or from outside by a sloped embankment, up which Herr drove his teams pulling wag-gonloads of hay or wheat shocks. It was a marvel to me that family men like Herr built more beautiful homes for their cows than for his wife and children.

In addition to the barn, like all the other Settlement plantations, the Herrs had an outside oven and a small squat building that I'd come to identify as the springhouse, the spring being most strategic in the locating of the cabin. An orchard surrounded all the buildings, although stripped bare today of all but a handful of apples that were out of reach and already blasted brown by the hard frosts.

"*Unser Haus!*" Frony beamed. She clucked and the pony moved on.

We came up out of the trees, over a rise, and met the pièce de résistance, as the French say, of our community: --a three-story house of brown limestones and wood shingles as pretty as any I'd seen in Philadelphia, but *here*, in the heart of the heathen jungle.

In later months, I got to see the inside when I attended services with the Mister, as services were held in his house. "His" being Christian Herr, the Pastor of the Settlement Mennonists. Sunday after Sunday, fifty of us stuffed into that front room of his, the men to the right, the women together on the left, on backless benches, while Christian stood behind a small table, his back to the large brick and cement-plaster tumor in the corner that poured forth heat.

That particular Lord's Day in December of my first year, the woods were deep with snow, and men and women had all come bundled in dumpy black coats and hats. Inside Christian Herr's living room, our cheeks glowed red from the heated air. That and the sickly sweet smell of women's bodies made my head swim, and all at once, things went dark. As I began to feel myself again, I found my body stretched on a rope bed in the rear of the home, covered with someone's overcoat, and I gulped up the frosty air in the room. Frony's face was bent over me. Her hands were resting under mine, and she burst into chatter when she saw my eyelids flicker. She pressed the rim of a mug to my overheated lips, and I tasted cider, still slushy with ice.

It may have been that story that started the saying going around that Irish women weren't strong, which I resented as I was not nor ever was nor ever would be *Irish*. The fact of one's living on the same island as the Irish no more made me one than living on the Rhine in Germany, as these people had, made them Dutchmen who also lived on the Rhine and built windmills on dykes and wore wooden shoes. We are *Scots-Irish*, from the Lowlands across the North Channel.

—✗✗✗✗✗—

All this right before my first Christmas resulted in my falling into a prolonged spell of homesickness, resurgent grief over Papa, and weeping every day. Christmas in Ulster was gay and festive, bedecking the house with holly berries and holly leaves, lighting a candle for Mary and Joseph, singing carols. The Mennonists did none of these and instead went to church, wore black clothes, and held their traditional feasts.

My Ulster clothes had long ago worn out by then, and Mister gave me replacements, sewn by a woman in the Settlement, so that I now resembled all the other Settlement women: navy blue skirts to my galoshes, with a white apron over top.

When Mister shouted up the loft ladder with why was I still abed at noon that Lord's Day before Christmas? I said I wasn't coming down, that I didn't fit in. When he asked why, I said because they didn't like my red hair. I needn't mention my beads and jewelry and perfume. I'd stopped them a year ago. They were *frowned upon.*

Brother Herr used that phrase when I asked why the women stared at my jewelry. What could be wrong with beads and little golden earrings to set off what the Lord had made with such exquisite design? Brother Herr was happy to show me in the pages of Scripture.

> Whose adorning let it not be
> That outward adornment of plaiting the hair
> And of the wearing of gold, or of putting on of apparel.

How could I have missed First Peter 3 in all my years of catechism?

Mister appeared at the top of the loft steps, peering at me with his own brilliantly red beard.

"What is it, Girl?"

I turned on the pillow because I didn't want to look at him, didn't want to explain. Surely being a servant didn't mean I had to leave all my feelings at the dock in Philadelphia when I signed the Indenture.

"Janey?"

"What!"

"People are concerned. You've been in such a sour mood—"

"Why can't I be in a sour mood? Is that in my contract?" Immediately regretting the fact I'd raised my voice to the Master, I fell back on the bed and said: "They don't like me; they're judging me. They think I'm worldly."

I spoke English, although my German was good enough by the second Christmas that I could have said it that way. But he always spoke English to me, so I always spoke English back, and since he was the only one capable of that in the Settlement, I found it a relief to speak my native tongue.

"Well, I'm sorry about that. And I don't think it's all true. But I'm an outsider too. I was a Calvinist the first eighteen years, but maybe that was different. It meant nothing to me."

His head lowered back down the loft hole, but for the next several days he treated me uncommonly kindly and gave me a Christmas gift, he called it, of a golden guinea to spend as I wanted and two days of holiday.

Maybe it was good what happened, as it softened up his heart to suffering right at the point when he was about to suffer.

It was June 1719, and the first Atlantic ships of the season had already docked in Philadelphia, and he came back from the Philadelphia market trip empty-handed.

"I don't understand." He spooned the bowl of stew I'd made for his return. "No letters. No letters now some twelve months. Since you came here. Captains say there's a war on—did they raid the Rhine again? Or pirates? Trained killers left with no one to fight since the War of Succession. They're grabbing ships up and down the Atlantic.

"Could be *they* seized our letters. The ones coming to us. Maybe the ones going to them too. Could be!" he said.

CHAPTER 14

THE FATEFUL SNOWSTORM,
DECEMBER 1719

T HIS IS HOW I CAME into possession of the letter that would alter forever my course in this vale of tears.

I sat in the library of His Honor James Logan, Governor of our Commonwealth, closing up the Quitrent Books, and I'd gone over every entry with Mr. Logan, to validate the owed sum, which I'd piled in British pound notes on the table beside the books.

A blue cloud enveloped Logan's head, capped by the flat black Quaker hat he wore in house and out, --and I reflected how sweet the smell of burning tobacco when his back swiveled in the chair, and I saw the visage many call "morose" or even "melancholy."

"You've done your Master well, Janey." The long pipe dropped to his lips while he dragged. "Do you know how much I love this man, Greenywalt?" He released another small cloud.

"I taught him the King's English, you know. It was I who led him to the Pequea, introduced him to that royal piece of land. You know, I read men like books." His fingers traveled back and forth overhead to draw my attention to the books behind, a multitude of leather-bound volumes, shelf above shelf. I'd heard some call it the best library in the

Colonies. "And I saw a man who feared the Lord and"—he jabbed a bony forefinger across the desk that separated us—"could read men like books. *Like me.*" He bestowed his only smile of the afternoon on me.

"I thought to myself—this was the winter of 1710 or so—he can handle those fur trading devils for me, the Bezaillons, Martin Chartier, the LeTorts. The Proprietor said, 'Fur trade is the smart way to wealth in Pennsilvania.' But I came to see after a bit—it isn't furs, it's land. Land is the indispensable basis of wealth. Your Greenywalt is worth more to me as a broker of land than he ever was as a trucker of furs.

"That's how we come to where we are." He leaned across and tapped the bowl of his pipe on the Quitrent Books and spilled ash. "Sorry." He retrieved the pipe while I brushed the still-warm ashes into my hand. He was bent head-down, rummaging the drawers of the desk.

"Here." His hand appeared with the letter. "And I'll take those." I pinched the letter and saw the name "Klaus Grünewald" on its face as I dropped the ash crumbs into his extended palm.

"A man Horsch gave it to the captain in Rotterdam." He unfolded upward arthritically and reached to shake my hand, as if I were a man, a freedman.

—✎✎✎✎—

The Mister needed to see this, immediately. He wasn't in the bay of Logan's warehouse on Fishbourne and Second, where I'd left him a couple hours earlier. My eyes adjusted slowly to the dark warehouse. Huge pallets parked everywhere in the gloom, piled to the ceiling. The air was unbelievably toxic and thick, much ranker than the odor of a pig butchering, but my curiosity kept me going.

Deerskins. Bearskins. But feel these! In the gloom the ermines shone pale and lustrous, skins for the robes of a queen. Or a king. Didn't Louis the Sun King wear floor-length ermine capes in the paintings?

"Here! Look at you! . . ."

I was not prepared for the slap on my thigh. I recoiled, and yes, it was the lecherous captain of the *Polly Walker*, our fateful ship some two years past.

"So you married the Little Swisser? That's why you traded your fancy Boglander clothes for these . . . these scullery rags?"

"Where is he? Greenywalt?"

He flapped a hand southward, to indicate another building. The captain looked quite ordinary and common when he wasn't in his naval uniform. My chin high, I marched straight by him and out the open doors.

"Might be an important letter." His foghorn voice pursued me. "That's what the dandy said in Rotterdam."

I found the Mister in the bay of the next warehouse, most of him out of sight in the back of his conestoga, pushing burlap sacks of shelled corn into the waiting arms of two longshoremen. The very same *Polly Walker*, rocking slowly, could be spotted through the open door at the far end of the warehouse.

He noticed the longshoremen avert their eyes my direction. The Mennonist clothes did nothing for me, but was my face still pretty? He angled from the back of the waggon and saw the missive in my upraised hand.

"A letter! Is it from . . . ?"

The Mister tumbled off the waggon, with both hands seized the letter, and used his teeth to peel the red wax seal in one continuous motion. He unfolded it, read it, his body dropping back and down onto a hogshead, and now his clenched fingers hopscotched up the page, and his eyes followed the fingers to the top and down again.

"Janey!" He jerked around.

I came near and saw the tears leaping out of those blue wells.

"Janey!"

This was most unusual behavior for the Mister. He only rarely voiced my name, but today he not only repeated it but reached from the hogshead and gripped my arm with his miller's hand like a vise and repeated my name the third time. "Janey! She's been sold to the galleys."

"No!" I hardly knew what else to say. "No!"

His shoulders shuddered rhythmically while he held up the open letter directly before his face as if he could alter the text on it by staring at it, and he began to wail out the message.

"My friend Horsch—my mother told him." He backslapped the letter. "Father Aebi was released from prison! But went straight back to Switzerland and got rearrested. Not just him. His wife. His two boys. Maudlin! All shipped in chains!" He stabbed the inked words with his forefinger. "In chains. To the galleys in Genoa. Janey! No one comes back"—his head fell back, and he bayed the words at the rafters overhead like a foxhound—"alive! From the galleys!"

—⁓⁓⁓—

The six weeks from that day until the fateful snowstorm, time stood still at the Mill. Of course, the usual work went on:

The mill kept grinding wheat into flour for farmers. The two indentured, Christ and Gerhard, saw to that.

The Mister took a loaded conestoga once every ten days to Logan's warehouse in Philadelphia.

Nights when he was home, land buyers queued their teams and crowded around the table in the cabin under the hanging lanthorn, working out details on land purchases with Hans Herr and the Mister.

I built wood fires and cooked suppers for him, delivered cartloads of farm tools, bolts of cotton and muslin and tins of molasses, sugar, and tea to the homesteads. Evenings under the lamplight I recorded neat columns of collected quitrents and new transactions.

I also fought off the attention of Christ, the indentured, who was transparent about his romantic interest in me. My declaration to him was straightforward: "We can talk about anything, but I will not hold your hand or walk in the woods with just you."

Like Joshua at the Battle of Gibeon, the Mister's sun seemed to have stopped that day in Philadelphia. He wouldn't move forward. He ceased smiling. Whenever he found me available, he interrupted to go over his loss once more.

"Janey!" We were in the mill room where he slept and ate, me standing by the pots in the fireplace, whose chimney rose the whole three stories of the mill and warmed my bedroom on the top as well. As the year descended, the frosts returned, and the clouds rolled in wet and leaden from west of the Blue Ridge. He paused over the sausage I had served him.

"Janey!" Reaching up, his hand seized my wrist as he had the day he got the letter. "I built that cabin for her. And for our children. And she's—"

In the lanthorn light, his blue eyes held two little flames that danced and demanded a solution from me. His tears couldn't quench the flames. His hand dropped back to his fork, but he didn't spear anything with it. He went on, his eyes leaping back and forth from a fixed spot on the tabletop to my eyes, and I listened, unmoving, as I had once listened to my own father.

"I built this cabin for her! To see her look when she sees it the first time. The fireplace, to make apple butter. The bake oven for pies—she's a real baker, Janey! The curtains with daisies that Frony is sewing, to pretty it. The garden plot. When she puts in a seed—you should see her garden in the Kraichgau. Eggplants, gladiolas . . ." His voice trailed and choked off. Abruptly he crossed to the coat hooks on the wall, behind the door.

"I need to chop the horses."

'You didn't eat."

"The horses. They're hungry." The door banged against his heel as he went out.

But in the morning when I descended the stairs into his room, the food on the table had disappeared, the dishes had been scrubbed, and they were lined neatly upside down on a dishtowel.

—◆◆◆◆◆◆—

The snowstorm started about ten o'clock on an overcast Saturday morning. The Mister was gone to Philadelphia, by now returning, I supposed, since he'd been gone since Wednesday, and he always aimed to be home Saturday night to ready up for Sunday services. The English Harvest Feast—which the Germans didn't celebrate because they had their own holiday in October—had come and gone, and I grieved the loss of it again this year, as I did every year.

In the beginning the flakes came capricious and very fine, like a cloud of mosquitoes falling and rising in the front yard. Unlike the week before, these didn't melt but began to add up almost imperceptibly. The wind picked up. It whipped them like mashed potatoes into ridges and banks that curved around buildings and flung long shoals across the road. By three in the afternoon, the bank in front of the millhouse main door was above my knees, and millions more flakes were flying in. I imagined them to be the angels around the Throne itself. Thousands upon thousands and tens of thousands. How many did that add up to?

The Mister always asked for his favorites when he came back from a week on the road: Pannhaas and sausage from the fall pig, Frony's sourdough bread and apple butter and mashed potatoes. By five, his mantel clock was tolling it, the meal was done and set to the back of the raised hearth to keep it warm, and still no sound of the horses.

I waited an hour before starting the final Saturday night chore: toting the kettle of ever-boiling water from the crane hook over the fire, I mixed in buckets of cold water from the millrace and filled the wooden tub. Our routine was I drew his bath first, and then he read his Scriptures in the cabin while I took mine, before I doused the lanthorn as the signal. I kept my own lanthorn in the loft. The Mister prohibited any of us from carrying one lit around the mill. "Too many mill explosions happen that way," he said. Through the darkness I would feel my way to the frigid third-floor bedroom.

It looked increasingly like he wouldn't show at all tonight: the road itself was no longer visible through the shifting banks and escarpments of snow, four and five feet high now.

The cedar tub sat perfectly round on the flagstone floor, and I sat in the wonderful liquid, knees pulled up to my breasts, and reached side to side with a tin dipper to stream the water in cleansing rivers over my ears and eyes and hair, while steamy rivers buried the aroma of Frony's lavender into every locket of hair. I thought about the wife of the Proprietor Penn himself, off in her London manor. Could she be any happier than I right now? Could her bath be any more delicious?

Thinking about that, I missed the first dog bark and the second. It was the insistent bells on the collars of the team that jolted me out of my reverie. The Mister was home. and where were the waggons?

"Belle! Trixie!" They rounded the mill, their bells ringing smartly up the slope, minus any sound of waggon wheels, heading to the horse barn. He'd be through the door in ten minutes. I created tidal waves as I stood, reached for the lanthorn to extinguish it and blacken the room, and in no time I was bent over the hearth, my robe belted around me, to stoke the fire under the Pannhaas and sausage, when the door swung in savagely and hit the wall with a thud.

It was him, stumbling ahead of the howling gale. His white head came through first, the stuff still clinging unmelted to his beard and eyebrows, falling in chunks off his hat and shoulders. He made huge sucking sounds, as if he'd escaped from a fight with Grendel herself, with only five minutes left in his lungs. The lanthorn swung and threw large shadows of him. He thrust it down on the flagstone and with the same move pulled off coats and sweaters that landed heavily and waterlogged. He peeled the shirt over his head, dropped seat-first on the flagstones to strip the boots and woolen breeches, then for the first time seemed to notice me.

"Sorry. So wet. Freezing!"

When he reached the chemise layer, he unfolded up like a jack knife and balanced with one hand against the hearth to stop himself from falling into the fireplace. The flames were licking his knees, and steam began to rise from the wet leggings that ended in the bare toes.

"I'll go." I moved toward the stairway at the back. "The food will be hot in—"

"No, no! Stay. I got a robe too." He hippety-hopped to the back wall where it hung, each foot recoiling from the cold flagstones. His hopping, red-bearded (now that the snow was melted off) shape in yellowish wool chemise from neck to knees and then the clinging woolen leggings brought to mind my initial impression of his leprechaun likeness. I laughed.

"Heh heh."

"What?" He'd tossed the gray flannel robe around his shoulders and trussed himself around the middle with a yard of rope.

"Your supper—you're hungry?" I'd come back to the hearth again.

"Janey!" He dropped into the chair by the table he built himself, the little table for two, in contrast with the big table that sat eight in the new cabin. "This storm—I couldn't leave the horses out in it. Couldn't see my way—wind whipping the snow in my eyes. Tea! Do you have anything hot?"

"How about cider?" I poured a tin full, redolent with cinnamon.

He slurped cautiously. "Took me three hours from Paradise to here, two miles, and I kept losing the road, whited out and all, and going dark on me. Belle, she knew the way whether she saw it or not. I dumped the waggon at Brechbühl's and walked the team the rest of the way. Through drifts"—he measured off a chest-high drift—"and all."

"You're exhausted." I spread the pots before him on the table, so he could help himself. The potatoes, the Pannhaas, or fried meat pudding. He devoured them.

"Not physically so much," he said. "It's the heartache. Why am I doing all this?" He pushed back in his chair and bent double toward the fireplace. "I ask myself. Why am I doing all this?"

I felt compassion. It rose up the fronts of my legs and arms and face like the blush of the bath's hot water. He'd lost everything. He was like me now. Alone in a howling wilderness. His dreams, melted

I guessed. Like mine, only mine didn't melt. They got tossed into the North Atlantic by the sailors on the disease-ridden *Polly Walker*, and they sank down, down, down, circling until I could see them no more.

I felt compassion. But what could I say? Or do? I did what I realized later was the worst thing to do: I touched him. I came from behind and lay my two warm hands on his damp shoulders, and his cold hands stretched and seized mine. They reeled me in against him.

"Janey!" His voice crackled, like an adolescent boy's. He spun the whole chair and buried his face between the folds of my robe. I stood, motionless. His lips began to move, kissing the skin on my chest.

The Book says Sarai gave Hagar to Abram as a concubine, and "he went in to her." So it happened, and when it did, it seemed the natural and inevitable outcome, as the gloved hand stretches to receive the ball tossed to it and closes around it. No joy came with it. Our bodies collided, and my feet came off the floor as his powerful arms upended me backward onto his bed. I didn't struggle.

And then we fell apart. I pulled the robe back around me and ran for the stairs, and behind me he sat up in the shadows on the bed. The skin of his naked body reflected the lanthorn rays, like the lustrous ermine furs in the warehouse did.

—◊◊◊◊◊—

The storm went on for three days. The valley in which the Settlement lay turned unbelievably white. The gale winds had stopped, but the snow kept falling the second day. The mill was shut down: no one could come in on the road, and we couldn't go to services either. I came down the second day and prepared his evening meal, the only thing he required of me on the Lord's Day. I climbed back to my room and sat on a bag of wheat, gazing out though the third floor port of the mill—which I'd propped open—at the wide Pequea Valley. Even the creek was gone, frozen and covered with the white stuff like everything else.

When it was about dark, I heard footsteps on the stairway to the loft. I didn't turn around. I knew it was him.

"Janey." The footsteps came closer.

I looked up and full into the leprechaun face, the little beard, and the blue eyes. What was behind those eyes? He placed both hands on my shoulders and knelt before me and said my name.

"Janey."

> Let him kiss me with the kisses of his mouth:
> for thy love is better than wine.

He kissed me on my mouth and I kissed him back.

This time we didn't get up. It grew dark, and still we didn't get up. His legs wrapped around my body and mine around his.

—〰〰〰—

On day 3 the storm stopped. It was Monday, but there was little that could be done other than sleep and eat, and for me, think about what had happened.

I opened my eyes, and it was as if it was all just a dream. I was alone. I could see my breath, and the pitcher of water that I kept by the cot had a skin of ice. Had I dreamt it? Why would such a thing ever happen? Because I wanted it—I couldn't discard that idea. Yes, I wanted it. And what was this? A man's sock, lying beneath my covers, across my leg. Indisputable evidence he'd been here, lying in my bed.

I am his wife. I knew it now. The other woman was gone, God knows where. Perhaps dead in Genoa. Perhaps just never to be seen again. As he had said, "No one ever returns from the galleys alive." And he needs a wife. "And the Lord God said, 'It is not good that the man should be alone. I will make a help meet for him.'"

I heard a river of joy and purpose splashing. I took out my Papa's Bible and went again to the book I had discovered in the Snowstorm, the Song of Songs, which is Solomon's.

> I sleep, but my heart waketh:
> It is the voice of my beloved that knocketh, saying,
> Open to me, my sister, my love, my dove, my undefiled:
> For my head is filled with dew,
> And my locks with the drops of the night.

Did my father feel like this when he looked at my mother? Did he feel this tumbling fountain of joy?

From my trunk, I dug out the one article still left from Ireland, the white Lowlands blouse with poufy sleeves, although no longer starched and quite worn, and not a great match with the blue work skirt I'd received after my immigrant clothes wore out. I hung the ruby earrings Mama had given me, real rubies from India—the holes hadn't closed! We didn't have a proper mirror, only a polished brass plate, but I saw my reflection well enough to know: I'm still Jane Cameron. I brushed the red hair out to my waist. I hadn't worn it that way for two years because the Mennonist women didn't wear theirs loose. I pinned the tam, blue as the blue of our Scottish saltire, on my crown.

I descended the two flights to the door above the cellar mill floor. I heard the mantel clock toll ten through the door. I knocked. I heard an unclear response and pushed the door open and came down. I came slowly, knowing deliberate motion best shows a woman's beauty.

He sat before the fireplace, his stockinged feet propped on the hearth, perhaps drying them. He'd been out already to care for his animals. He certainly heard me, but he didn't look up from the tin of something, steaming, that he cupped between his still-mittened hands.

He must feel what I feel. I had to know. I had to tell him what I felt.

The Mister dropped one hand to the tabletop as I approached him from behind. I put my rather soft and well-shaped fingers on top of the rough mitten wrapping the hand on the table.

"Klaus. I love you."

I'd thought a long time about it. I wouldn't call him "Mister." I wouldn't call him "Greenywalt" like his customers did. I'd call him what Hans Herr, his friend, called him: "Klaus."

Nothing happened for some moments. Me with my fingers on his mitten. Him with his mug, his eyes on the fire. Then he jerked his hand away and said, as if he were speaking to the fire, not to a woman, certainly not to a wife,

"It's a mistake, Janey. I made a mistake."

Twenty years later, and I can still feel it: My heart skipped. It bumped out loud. And then it discontinued. The fountain lost power to leap and dropped back into a silent pool. A great urge to wrap his head in my arms came over me, like the wave of compassion the first night of the storm. But my arms hung paralyzed, with no power in them to move.

Klaus . . .

His eyes remained level with his outstretched feet and the fire. "I've been thinking."

"So have I, Klaus."

"Janey." The blue bottomless eyes turned and screwed directly into mine, and I knew then whatever was behind those eyes wasn't friendly, it was strictly business. "I'm a married man—"

"Don't say that. You're not. She's—"

His mittened hand brushed my words out of the air. "Stop!" He crossed the flagstones to the coatrack. His back to the coatrack, he finished his thoughts, looking first at me, then back at the coats. "I'll move to the cabin. Bring my meals there from now on." He clamped on his hat and went for the door.

"Klaus!" Glaciers collided inside, like the ones we'd seen up close from the deck of the *Polly Walker* in the North Atlantic. They collided thunderously, and ice flew everywhere. I was going to scream. I was going to scream until he crawled over me, pushed me down, and stuffed rags into the great O of my mouth.

But he had gone.

I felt the scream rising. I fell forward onto the bed, the symbol of our relationship. I couldn't stifle it. It welled up, just as the fountain had welled up, and the sound of it was piercing. It pierced the joints in the limestone wall of the mill and flew out. It transmogrified. It became a *bean sith* wailing through the Settlement, above the Pequea Creek. The banshee keened on and on and on as it flew wraith-like over the homesteads, over the white forest, the whole way to the River.

My throat ached, and the scream became weak and husky. The pillow was soaked from my sweltering and the unstoppable tears. My limbs were unfit to move, even as the light dwindled, and the last I heard, the scream still rose out of my prostrate body, without an audible sound anymore.

CHAPTER 15

THE JUDGMENT OF THE PREACHERS, MARCH 1720

ALL SNOWSTORMS DO STOP, the sun always comes out, the residual always melts, the creeks always overflow. This storm was no exception. The only exceptional piece was my life, which was no longer the driven, sparkling snow. I had become the dirty melting runoff.

Awkwardness became the rule at the mill. Through the snowdrifts he'd scooped a path that ran from the mill to the cabin. I toted his dinners in a handbasket to the cabin every evening, and he didn't turn from his task: chinking the logs, mortaring the fireplace stones, talking with a would-be landowner. No words were exchanged.

Physically, life improved for me. I no longer had three flights to climb several times a day because I lived on the mill's ground floor now, from the hour I woke on his bed the fourth day of the storm. I didn't ask permission. Who else would live there? Who else would make meals on the hearth and tend to the cupboards of food?

All storms do stop. On the morning after, Jacob discovered it wasn't Rachel, and Leah stood up naked to receive his scornful, hateful look. Bathsheba opened her eyes in the King's bed and remembered her husband on the battlefront. Hagar? I hadn't thought about the phrase "to know" before in my Scripture book. *Adam knew his wife.* David "came in to" Bathsheba. There was no knowing between Klaus Greenywalt and the indentured Janey Cameron. My great sadness had its source in that fact.

I resolved only to call him "Mister" from that day forward.

—⁓⁓⁓—

The hands tried to cheer me up. Christ and Gerhardt returned from preparing seed corn for Hans Herr, and Christ renewed his charm offensive. He assumed my coldness, my glumness, meant I was angry with him, and he brought me a Christmas gift, a mess of bass from the millpond. He'd broken the ice with a digging iron to get his line and bait through.

With the snow melting, the sun glittering on the rivulets along the road, Frony came driving in the pony cart, her three youngest bundled in bearskins. The children threw snowballs of the melting stuff at each other while I entertained her in my new room.

"He likes you," she said, looking around at the room, an obvious improvement over my previous arrangement. When I didn't respond because her words only dragged a currycomb across my wound, she opened her Christmas gift to me. A wicker tray with one hundred cookies in ranks: snowmen with raisins for eyes and walnut halves for buttons, stars with red sprinkles, twists with congealed liquor of brown sugar, butter, and cinnamon.

I sat speechless on the bed, the tray balanced on my lap, and teared up, which she noticed.

"Has he been unkind to you?"

I shook my whole self "No," but my secret remained untouched, unrevealed, and deep within my body.

The New Year opened with new troubles. The first day of the year, when I thrust my legs over the bedside, I felt my stomach wamble, the coats on the wall beyond began to undulate, followed by a series of blinking lights that went around my head and circled back, and my buttocks barely caught the edge of the bed as I buckled, rolled, and spewed up last night's supper. By noon I was fine. But the next morning, browning pork for the Mister's New Year's pork and sauerkraut, it happened again. When it happened the third and fourth mornings, I knew. The worst fate of any indentured girl, its prohibition clearly spelled out in the Indenture Document, had become my fate.

The Mister and I were on civil terms again: a Question, an Answer. No discussions, no familiarity, not even speaking each other's names. I broached an idea I'd had for some time. He was lounging at his dining table in the cabin, his back to the hearth fire, whittling a door latch with a penknife.

"Can I tell you my idea?"

He eyeballed me, the blue eyes devoid of any feeling, but his mouth set in a way that unsettled me. "What?"

"I've been thinking of a store. Instead of my delivering goods to all the farmers, they come here. They come anyway from time to time. They all have carts. Imagine how much time we'd save."

"Where are you thinking?"

"Maybe here. In the cabin." I pointed out the large amount of space about the cabin, which wasn't going to be used anytime soon. The Mister's bed was in this half of the cabin, with the table and benches. I already visualized the other half with a counter, behind which I'd stand on duty, the goods arranged in barrels or shelves behind me.

"Hmmm. . . ." His eyes fell back to the latch. His thumb idly turned it over in his palm, and he began to whittle the other side.

It was the last week of February. The crocus bulbs I'd pushed down last fall in a marching line across the cabin front to surprise Maudlin, when she came—this was a few days before the Letter—now those very crocuses pushed green tops through the rotten bank of snow. I'd seen the first robin. New life was coming.

Yes, I realized. New life. My hand could trace a noticeable *bump*, and the nipples were tender. New life was on its way.

Frony visited on a Sunday afternoon. The pony and cart were tied in the horse shed, and she sat at the small table where I'd formerly fed the Mister his suppers. I turned from the hearth with a cup of cider from the hearth pot when her eyes splayed.

"Janey!" Her eyes fixed on my belly. They raced to my face. "Janey, are you—?" After two years, I communicated easily in the dialect and understood even much of the sermons. I knew the word teetering there on her tongue.

Then they started. Tears from somewhere welled up and over. I stumbled backward, felt the bed behind me, and sank down. More tears. They wouldn't stop.

> Oh that my head were waters,
> and mine eyes a fountain of tears,
> that I might weep day and night. . . .

"Janey, its true, isn't it? There's a little one?"

My head nodded on its own, relieved to share my dark secret.

Frony, the Saint, took my hand between her own simple, unringed, roughened hands and petted it. Her knees bumped mine, and we sat like that with only the Mister's mantel clock interrupting, marking the steady progression toward my destiny.

"I'm the mother of a bastard," I said.

"Janey, who's the father? You have to marry."

"He doesn't love me anymore."

"Was it one of the lads in Philadelphia, Logan's lads?" When I didn't respond, she said: "It's Christ, isn't it? He must take responsibility!"

I only listened. There was more to the secret than I could reveal today.

She looked deeply into me. "You have to marry. He needs to take responsibility for this, or they'll flog the both of you. In the public square."

I didn't respond, so she went on.

"When your time comes, I'll be with you. A woman needs another woman when your time comes."

I only scoured her compassionate and gentle eyes. I was unable to express the depth of my gratitude.

About a week after that, the Mister made his first spring journey to Philadelphia, although the roads were very soft and the creeks ran high. He asked if I could bring Logan the patents we'd been drawing up over the winter. I said I wasn't feeling well. When he returned with a load of goods, I brought up the store idea again. It was becoming a critical issue for me. I had to come up with alternatives.

The tableware he'd purchased in bulk in Philadelphia was spread across the table as he sorted the pewter knives and forks. He stopped when I posed my question and looked up. "Who will run such a store?"

"I will."

"You? You?" He stared directly at my belly, which bulged the front of my apron. He knew, at last.

—⁓⁓⁓—

By the second week of March, it was no longer a secret. People everywhere in the Settlement looked long at me, turning to talk—at church, in the mill, when I drove my cart by. When I took the evening meal to the Mister, he said,

"They're coming tomorrow night to talk about you."

"Who?"

"The ministers."

"What will they talk about?"

"What to do with you."

"With me!" On what planet of the universe was this, that a girl could single-handedly bring into the world another human life? Other than the Virgin Mary herself, who had the assistance of Almighty God?

I stormed out. As I remember, I was screaming. In fact, I may have thrown the Mister's supper into the fireplace.

—⁓⁓⁓⁓—

I intended not to miss the court hearing on my life, even if I wasn't invited. The Mister said nothing further about it. The next day, which was Saturday, he was dealing with customers at the mill, past five o'clock. I took his dinner over at dusk and lit the lanthorn. To cover my tracks, in the event anyone at the mill had watched my comings and goings, I exited the cabin door again and made a point of banging it. In thirty minutes it was dark. I returned surreptitiously, flattening myself against the cabin back and then sidling toward the door. Through the window, predictably, I saw the pots still resting lidded on the table, his plate still clean, and his chair empty.

I slipped in, crossed to the back half of the cabin, and climbed the rung ladder to the loft. I could have run up that ladder once.

Tonight I took one tortuous step, then the next, all the while my eye on the front door. What would I do or say if he did come through? I imagined I would beg his permission to stay, that I deserved to hear my own fate, and I would not betray my presence to his peers. Let me stay, please.

I hauled my awkward torso and swollen legs over the ledge and into the loft, a dark platform eight feet off the floor, the width of the cabin and extending a good twenty feet deep into blackness.

I lay motionless, stretched out upon the platform to regain my breath, and squinting to figure out the series of dark shapes, goblin-like. If I hadn't come here in the light, carrying up goose-down ticks and bags of dried apple schnitz, I'd have been terrified. As it was, I could guess at the shapes. I pulled a goose-down tick beneath me and rolled heavily onto it, humping like an inchworm to turn myself around, my nose now back at the platform edge and peering down over the table where I myself had sat many evenings, drafting patents for would-be land buyers. Would he see me from his chair, with his back to the hearth—the Mister? The lanthorn guttered, and the large shadow it threw tottered like a drunk on the cabin wall. The sharp turpentine smell was much sharper up here, under the eaves. If he turned up the wick, then what? Would the light reflect off my face?

I must have fallen asleep, which was not surprising now that I was feeding and lugging around two of us. I opened my eyes to voices. The Mister was welcoming two or three of them at the door.

"How nice! How nice! It's the first I've seen it since you're living in it." That was Christian Herr, the Pastor, leader of Pequea Settlement flock. His hand lifted the black dress hat away, and his balding head gleamed. I could mark his progress toward the table by the sharp tap-tap of his cane tip as he stabbed the plank floor and heaved his crippled body across the room. He rounded the table, and as he sidled onto the bench, elevated his eyes directly at me, it seemed. My breathing ceased. I let my face slide downward into the tick. Had the light bounced off my forehead?

"Yes, Maudlin would have been pleased," the Mister said.

I waited for Hans's booming bass next but heard only a subdued voice, rather unlike Hans. What had he and Frony been sharing? He took the seat on the bench across the table from his brother.

And finally the old man, Brechbühl, who also hobbled, although his was rheumatism. His back to me, he doffed his hat and shook his white mane. I couldn't see the face now, but in my memory I saw the cherubic cheeks set over the white beard that flowed untrimmed to his breast pocket. Like a pair of fall apples on a pile of ice shavings. Of the four, I knew Brother Brechbühl least but trusted him the most. Christian Herr would have official things to say. Hans was the Mister's friend and business partner but wouldn't stand up to his brother, as I saw it. As for Greenywalt, I expected nothing out of him.

Brechbühl inhabited a plane above everyone in the Settlement, a kind of living saint, although from the cough, it was unclear how much longer he would be a *living* saint. He had a dry, hacking bark. Everyone knew his story: his negotiation with the Prussian king for the Mennonists and then his decision for North America. He had led the 1717 migration with Greenywalt as a guide. Everyone repeated the tale of his prison time in Bern, his expulsion from Switzerland, and his trip down the Rhine, chained and welded to a raft. What would "Brother" Brechbühl have to say about an indentured Irish girl caught, like the woman they dragged before Jesus, "in the act of adultery"?

The Mister poked the logs in the fireplace, and each poke threw up a huge column of sparks that briefly lit up the whole room, all the way to the loft. He sat down again with his back to the fire.

The scene was set for my trial. The four got down on their knees to pray and Christian Herr spoke it for all of them. He prayed for the purity of the church. He prayed about the tiny bit of leaven that now threatened to leaven the whole body. He prayed the Lord to strengthen their hands as they delivered to Satan the sexually immoral person, for the destruction of her flesh, that her spirit might be saved on the day of the Lord Jesus. In my imagination, I saw Anne Boleyn or Thomas à Becket, like me, eyes fixed on the axe that dangled in the hand of the Executioner.

"What shall we do with your girl?" Christian turned to the Mister as he got up from his kneeling position. "You have legal right to release an indentured who breaks the covenant she signed. Send her away. In Philadelphia, they tie fornicators to the stocks and flog them in the public square at noontime. In my mind, that's cruelty. If it's a woman's salvation we still care about, and we do, don't we? Better to send her away with her wages. And do we know who the father is?" He aimed this question at the Mister.

The Mister sat in the posture he'd taken every night for the last four months, his eyes fixed on a knot on the table about eighteen inches out.

"Has she told you?" Christian added.

Hans motioned to interrupt. "She hasn't said. My Frony asked several times, and I've questioned the indentured boys who work in the mill, Christian and Gerhardt. Frankly, I suspected Christian in the beginning; he's had eyes for her, several have said, but he himself insists—"

"Of course he insists. Why would he tell the truth? Un-Christlike behavior is all around us and our own youth. That's what makes it so important that we not send her away quietly because the youth need examples not just of the good but what happens when one deliberately trespasses across the line. Has she mentioned a name to you?" Preacher Herr turned back to the Mister.

I could barely breathe. The image of a mouse had terrified me before the men came in. Not the image of a mouse itself. I'd trapped several with my broom in the mill and delivered the coup de grâce with the iron poker. But the feel of a mouse leaping suddenly onto me in the dark of the platform, and wondering if I could hold absolutely silently voiceless while it traveled, O God, up my skirts! . . . But the drama below me banished all such thoughts, and I anticipated the Mister's answer. Of course, he would say it was a lad in Philadelphia, one of Logan's longshoremen. That's what some were saying in the Settlement. What else could you expect of a girl who had traveled single across the Atlantic for two months? Using every wile in the female toolkit to accomplish her goal of reaching America, some said.

I could sing out—that option had oh so briefly occupied me: rising up on my elbows in the loft, or weeks before this, turning to one of my accusers in the crowd after church, stretching my arm full length and dramatically extending the forefinger. Like those poor wretched girls in Salem we'd all heard about, I could cry, "It was him! It was him that did it!" And the crowd falling back, believing, because it was "the disease of astonishment" that had seized those girls. But at no time did I let that thought take root. I couldn't put my word up against his. I wouldn't. Because in fact, I still loved Klaus Greenywalt. Yes, I did, and I knew it. So I said nothing then, and I wasn't going to say anything now. If he said it was a longshoreman in Philadelphia, then for his sake, I was going to let it be that man.

"Well? Has she?"

The Mister looked up, dead at Preacher Herr, and he was going to say it now, I knew it.

"I'm the father."

The blood drained out of me. He didn't say, "I did it." He said, "I'm the father." Which he was. He had become a father, every bit as much as I had become a mother.

"You?!" Hans Herr tilted his bench backward, as if to move away from this raw, naked, unbeautiful truth about his friend. Klaus Greenywalt was an adulterer. He'd fathered a child by that girl. That Irish girl. The indentured.

"You?" Preacher Herr repeated it.

The Mister lifted his hands in appeal. Abruptly he covered his face with them. "I was lonely. I was distressed. My wife was dead—" He spoke through his fingers.

"We don't know that." Brechbühl spoke in his deliberate way, his first words since he'd come in. "There's no death certificate. Nobody's heard anything for sure."

"Which is even worse," the Mister said. "The galleys. No one ever returns alive. No one ever finds their bodies. They pitch them overboard."

"I have more to say on this," Brechbühl said. "If I'd known you were thinking like this."

"I was wrong. I made a mistake." The Mister pulled back his hands, vise-gripping his face between them like children do to make weird faces. "Brothers, it was me!" I hadn't heard him weep since that day in the Philadelphia warehouse when he got the letter, but his voice was shaking now. "It. Was. Me."

Preacher Herr said something indecipherable and motioned toward the door, and the Mister got up. He back-stepped toward the door, his palms lifted on both sides of his face, as if he still had things to say, which he didn't say. The door closed on his face, looking back in appeal.

The three men now set out to deliberate not one fate but two fates.

Preacher Herr was adamant. His fist banged on the tabletop. "Excommunication and the ban. No business with him. No fellowship until the consequences of his sin are felt by him and the whole community."

Hans grew increasingly restless during his brother's declaration, and he flinched every time Christian's fist hit the table.

"He confessed. With tears, he confessed it," Hans said.

"He waited until we had him."

"We didn't have him. He could have lied. I know Klaus. Klaus doesn't lie. Maybe he waited too long, but he confessed to it. At great cost to himself, I must say. The ban will put this man out of business. We cannot afford that. We, I mean us, the Pequea Community. We cannot afford that." Hans Herr painted a picture of Greenywalt's value. Greenywalt was responsible for leading more than half the settlers here from the Palatinate. Without Greenywalt's help, the settlers would not have gotten any land from the Penns. In fact, he held the mortgages on many of their plantations today. "Suppose he were to ban us back and take away our homes? What then?"

"Well, he wouldn't," Christian said. "He's not that kind of man."

"How do we know what he'll do if you put him out of business?"

"What would you suggest? Overlook it? Keep the knowledge of the transgression to ourselves? Say 'Don't do it again'? What do we tell the Church?"

"I'm torn." Old Brechbühl spoke low and slowly. His back was to me, and I cupped my hand to my ear to hear. "I'm torn. Here's where we differ from our brother Jacob Ammann, who is for the ban. But when we look at Christ and his apostles, Peter, I mean . . ." I wanted to catch it all, but I could only hear snatches: "Our Lord Himself . . . Betrayed him thrice . . ." And there were phrases about the morning on the beach of Galilee: "He ate with him after that. He forgave him, I have to think."

In the end, Wisdom had spoken, and the three agreed on it. They'd decided on the Mister. What about me?

Preacher Herr led out again. "The girl took advantage of his situation, it seems to me. His loneliness. Klaus is rich. Think of her station in life if her child inherits his mill."

"I know the Swisser system," Brechbühl said. "I mean to explain it to Grünewald," he used the Mister's correct German name, "when he comes back in. Just because they threaten the galleys, even haul them off in chains . . . She may turn up yet. In any case, it's the men they put on the ships, not the women."

"And your decision on the girl?"

"We can't know her motives. What options does an indentured have? This is why I've opposed the system and said so. It's too close to slavery."

"He can't marry her," Preacher Herr said.

"Why not?" Hans said. "It's been two years. Would you sentence our brother to live the life of a celibate? With a child who needs a father? Are we considering the child?"

Once again, I experienced shock. Might they sentence the Mister to marry me? What blessed fate would that be? Just as quickly as the spark ignited, Preacher Herr extinguished it.

"Not without a death certificate."

—*∿∿∿∿*—

They brought the Mister back in, after they'd deliberated for almost an hour. I have no idea where he went for that hour, but might he have gone to the mill to tell me what he'd just told them? And not found me there?

He stood, his hands clasped over his waist, while Preacher Herr told him their decision:

1. You will stand before the congregation. You and the girl. Before the congregation you will confess your sins against God and against each other.
2. You will raise the boy as your son until he is of age.
3. The girl will be freed from the indenture immediately, and should she choose to stay on the Pequea, you will support her and the boy and pay the market wage for her work. You will have no relationship with the girl, other than your business relationship, and to talk of anything that concerns the boy.

— ✦✦✦✦✦ —

That was the first I knew it was a boy. But I knew it certainly then, not because Preacher Herr said so, but because I knew that was what the Lord had provided.

I was not a fellow soul to these men, a fellow sinner. I was a special category: the woman who had taken advantage of one of theirs. I would not be one of them, even if I spoke the dialect perfectly and wore their clothes and made mush like their women did.

My glory, like the glory of the snow, had melted, and it was dirty runoff, like the runoff in the ruts on the Conestoga Road. His name came to me in that instant, there in the loft, the name given to the newborn son when the house of Eli fell: Ichabod. The glory of God has departed.

That's what I would name the coming child. Ichabod.

PART 4

THE WIFE'S STORY

CHAPTER 16

ON THE PEQUEA,
JULY 1755

YES, I LIKE MY PIPE. It calms a body down, helps me breathe easy. I like the tobacco smell, if it's out here on the porch and not stinking up the house. I blow the smoke around my head to shoo the bugs off, these summer nights.

I picked up the habit from you, Vetti. That won't surprise you, I guess, but I never smoked while you were alive since you didn't like a woman to smoke, especially your daughter.

So I light it evenings when I'm on the porch swing, just as you did. You loved the swing that Greenywalt built special for you, and you got to spend two years of your life on it. I'm thinking the best two years of your life, your battles over, your soul-case worn out but your spirit strong. I got to pay back the times you made me happy as a girl. I'm a little proud of that. We're not to be proud, preachers say, but surely that kind of pride is good.

I dillydally on the swing and look over my garden, spread out on the hill below as it slants toward the creek. Evenings in July are my favorite. The tomato slips burst with yellow blossoms. The sweet corn shoots an inch every day when we're getting good rain, which we haven't the last three years. I had Greenywalt build raised beds, like we had in the Old Country, and put up an eight-foot fence around the whole thing to keep the deer out. I whitewashed the boards so it wouldn't be an eyesore. I've got a bed for the corn, one for the tomatoes, one each for cucumbers and melons, and a couple herb beds. I planted a row of gladiolas and hollyhocks around the edge for pretty.

The bugs are out tonight over the garden, but you won't see them in the gloaming until their tails light up. Bang! There's another one over the corn tassels. Bang! Pretty soon it's bang, bang, bang, bang. Glowworms, they say on the Pequea.

If I push off with my bare feet, the swing takes me out over the cellar wall, and I spy the gooseberry bush below, loaded with fruit. The green ones are tart and the best for pies. I also fly over my trellis, just full of little green grapes. Reminds me of the verse: "They shall sit every man under his vine and under his fig tree"—that's the prophet Micah—"And none shall make them afraid." That last part isn't true yet in our case. There's plenty of fear going around.

The not-so-Quaker Quaker Logan provoked the province ten years back to build a militia for taking on the Indians and French. It was him started the rumors that a war was coming and that we'd all be victims of an invasion by the French, with their Indian cohort. Now we have this general from England marching west with his army of a couple thousand redcoats. We thought we'd escaped all that by coming to the New World. We had about twenty years of peace and quiet, and then the warmongers in Philadelphia started talking up invasion and conscripting our boys and waggons and raising taxes to pay for armies and forts.

Preacher Herr used to say, "It's just a sign of the times, before the Faithful and True rides forth on his white stallion to conquer the world's armies and capture the Beast." He's gone five years now, and our new preacher Hirschi is one of those that petitioned the Assembly in Philadelphia to say We Mennonists won't take part in this war against the French. I say Bully for him!

So there's a lot I can bring you up to date on, Vetti. Why would anyone stop an old woman who wants to smoke her pipe while she tells a story? Not that I want to dwell on old times—I've never been that sort. But you always liked to ask your people: "What's the news? What's the news?" That's a virtue in a preacher. It means he cares about his people and their lives, and you did, Vetti.

I've got such things to tell you. A lot has changed these twenty years.

Start with Greenywalt. Not much new there. He built the gristmill, which you got to admire. But I opened the store in it, which you never got to see.

The English woman. I got things worked out and threw her and the boy out thirteen years ago. I'll tell you how that came about.

The big news is your grandson Benjamin. Yes, it's true! Our Miracle Babe! We had some laying on of hands and anointing with oil. He's a fine lad, Vetti. He'll make something of himself. He's off with his father at the Lancaster shambles tonight. They'll sleep rough, so they can get up early to huckster flour and some of my cucumbers and peaches that I sent along. There's such a good crop of the white peaches this year.

But there's things I've always wanted to ask, Vetti, mostly about my Mem, your wife, Emmeline, whom I never got to meet. Not that I remember, leastways. Am I like her? I guess I lost my bloom in my fifties. When I sit here now in my *Häubchen* and Mennonist apron and skirts, do I look like her at all? Although I like to put off the *Häubchen* and do my hair in rainwater and vinegar on a Sunday evening and let it flap dry when I push back and forth on the swing. It goes the whole way down to my hips, and I'm thinking she must have had a head like that.

What else is there on a Sunday evening, with it dark now and still half a pipe to go?

Let me start at the beginning, Vetti.

CHAPTER 17

WHAT IS A WIEDERTÄUFER?
SWITZERLAND, 1696–1715

I FINALLY MADE UP MY MIND about the English Woman: she was no more than another piece of furniture. One of the chairs. Or, considering what she did to my husband, a bed.

I did talk to her. One doesn't talk to a chair. She could take some comfort in that. That particular night I had the hoe and was on my way to the garden. It was always good to take advantage of all the extra light summer nights. I passed through the front door, and there she was outside her room in the mill, her head down over a washboard in a tub of soapy water.

"I don't want you fixing Lukey's pants. I'll do that," I said.

She looked up.

"I said I'll do that." I added a bit of tone to make sure she got my message.

"He's still my son," she said.

"Ask Greenywalt about that."

"Bod—" she started in.

I hoed out that noxious weed before it could bloom. "We don't use that name anymore. It's disgusting."

She dropped her face but I knew this woman. Just when you thought you'd buried an issue six feet under for good. . . . "And don't sass me about it," I said to her out-of-sight eyes. I left her with that to put in her pipe and smoke and unhooked the white picket gate in the fence you and Greenywalt constructed around the garden, Vetti.

Over that fence, I could spy you pumping on the porch swing, you and Lukey. I hoisted my hoe, and you waved back. Lukey just went on swinging and didn't flinch. He wasn't sure yet if I was really his mommie or not.

You were probably thinking about the Old Country again. I never missed it like you did because I had the mill and the store and Greenywalt to deal with, and what did you have anymore? Lots of long-ago faces and memories. You would push back and forth on the swing. and There were times I'd catch you with tears running out of control, and Lukey would get upset and say, "Pawpaw!" as he called you.

"Vetti!" It just made me sad to see, and I couldn't stand it. "Pull yourself together."

Still, I did have questions about the Old Country. You told me about your herd and each cow had a large bell strung around the neck. Cowbells were ringing, you said, the morning I was born, Year of our Lord 1696. The fourth child of you and Emmeline, whom I never got to know.

No, it was not a day I remember because my first memory was my Mutti's face as she bent over to pull the stinger out of my big toe. I always loved barefoot. I didn't know anything about clover flowers and honeybees. She pressed her key down on the red spot "to bring the poison to the surface." Maybe I was three or so, and I already knew the story, how she wasn't really my mother, not the one that carried me around in the womb. But of course you knew how sweet she was, being's my Mutti was your own little sister.

"You were *Wiedertäufer*," Mutti said. I had stopped my *brutzing* over the bee bite, and I was cuddled on her lap.

"*Wiedertäufer*," I said back. I had no idea what that was. But I had every detail in my story committed to memory. She and the Reverend going up to the jail in the Castle at Trachselwald, and how she marched in through the gates and picked up the little girl—which was me, about the size of a dolly—out of the arms of the mother nursing it, with her feet chained to the wall. Were you there too, or did they have you chained in another dungeon? I regret I never thought to ask you while you were still with us. And she carried me out through the iron gates, which clanged behind her, in a picnic basket.

"We rescued you," she always put it.

I had lots of reasons to fear the *Wiedertäufer* after I found out what they were. They didn't live like normal people, together in town like us, I learned. They hid in caves and huts up the mountain slopes, like marmots. Most of the time you wouldn't see them but once in a crow's age we got a look at a whole family stroll through town, with its brood of children. The Reverend said they didn't believe in God like we did. I didn't know different: if he said they didn't, they didn't. They didn't baptize their kids, which meant their kids were going to Hell, he said. What kind of parent would send his children to Hell? They gathered by night in woodsy groves, and who knows what dark, illegal things they did together? he said.

Mutti hated the *Wiedertäufer*. So I did too.

And what did it mean, *Wiedertäufer*? To my little unschooled ears, the word sounded like *Wiederteufel*, and I knew about the *Teufel*. The Teufel prowled about naked after dark. He resembled a man, except with claws for feet and hands. In place of a human nose, his swine snout and twin horns pointed at you like a deformed mountain goat. His tufted hair on end, he glared and hissed at the mother and father as he drug their child off backward with his claw-hands. It was all there in the Reverend's book, with a full-page woodcut of the Teufel himself. That must be it. They worshipped the Teufel in those woodsy groves.

What could be more wonderful than the fact I'd been rescued from the Wiederteufel?

The Fuogs lived in town center, down the street from our church. with white stucco walls and bell tower, where the Reverend preached every Sunday, standing in his pulpit above us, in his splendid robes. But you know all that because you came by and saw him in his robes after services, and you saw the house with eighteen rooms, which was the first landing place for *Wiedertäufer* children whom the hunters brought to the Reverend when their parents were clapped in prison. The Reverend's week job was warden. He redistributed those loose children to orphanages and foster homes.

My Mutti was a collector. She collected children who didn't fit in regular school, plus the motherless *Wiedertäufer* children, and she mothered all of us. The drawing room—yes, you came and stood in their drawing room, with fancy French Louis-the-Fourteenth mirrors and sofas—she converted to a schoolroom during the week, where she taught us reading and arithmetic and geography with the help of Natasha and Aimee, your nieces, of course.

The next memory I've got, I was four and Natasha and Aimee were decking me out in their own second-hands: a little pink ballroom dress with lots of petticoats, white stockings up to my thighs, elbow-length gloves (white as swan feathers, of course) and patent-leather shoes that reflected the gas lights. Natasha had a flair for fashion, although—ain't it funny it often works this way?—she was mickle-mouthed and big-boned. Aimee was the fair one. She did my hair. She trained it with a hot iron to fall around my neck in gold ringlets, like her own golden hair. You would have called it worldly, but they loved worldly. Then they whistled for Gerard.

"Come see Maudie!" which is what they called me.

Gerard was very tall, with a muzzy already, and dreaming of a life of service in the Swiss Guard, which is what he became, and he died in the war with the Catholics. Anyway, Gerard saw me and walked right up to me, stiff-legged, like a Guardsman, and he bowed like we were dance partners. Then he lifted my gloved arm with his right and tucked it into his elbow and off we went, him promenading me around the drawing room while he whistled a dance tune.

I could feel their eyes following me, and Natasha said, "Isn't she the pretty thing? Call Mutti!"

So Mutti came down the curving staircase, together with the Reverend, who was dressed still in his black robes because it was Sunday after church, and I remember the Reverend, on the last step of the staircase, saying, "Look at our Little *Wiedertäufer*, Emmeline!"

Gerard and I took another turn around the drawing room, and everyone clapped and said how pretty I was, and that's how I first got into my head what a pretty face the Lord had bestowed on me. It's the kind of fact that once it gets in you, you never forget. I made up my mind right there: I was born for this life. My destiny, you could say. But how could I be pretty and a *Wiedertäufer*? These two didn't fit together in my little head. And I still was a *Wiedertäufer*, the Reverend said. If you were born a *Wiedertäufer*, did you always stay one?

This explains what happened next. As long as it was light those days, I was happy. But when darkness fell, it cast a spell on me. Happiness funneled out of me like water from the pump, and then the first tear and pretty soon the second, and I couldn't stop this fountain that sprang up inside my head. Tears just gushed. They tried to comfort me. First the girls, but I was inconsolable. Finally Mutti took me to her own bedroom and lay next to me. She lay her head on the pillow beside my hot little one, and with the hand that wore the big green emerald ring, she stroked my cheek and said, "There, there, my Pet."

She repeated it again and again, and I could see she felt compassion for me, the Little *Wiedertäufer*. What else could I ask for? It didn't stop my crying, it didn't drive away the darkness I felt, but it comforted me to know this wonderful woman was fond of me, although I was who I was. And next I knew, I'd opened my eyes to see sunbeams dance in through the bedroom window: I felt as airy and cheerful as a sunbeam, and I jumped up to look for Mutti. Until night, and then the same thing happened all over again.

But now that I knew about the *Wiedertäufer*, or *Wiederteufel*, or whatever they were, a bigger mystery presented itself. Mutti let slip a secret about you, Vetti.

All us children knew you were Mutti's younger brother, and we called you Uncle Ulli. You were my favorite man in all of Switzerland, much more so than the Reverend, who always looked me up and down without a smile and talked formal or maybe some disapproval so that I came to wonder: Did I of course deserve to be treated like a problem because I was a *Wiedertäufer* Child?

You, however, romped through the pages of our very ordinary town life like the fairy animals in the tales Mutti read us at bedtime. Like a Unicorn. Or the Frog Prince, which is what Mutti called you, and she kissed you on the mouth every time you came because "one of these days, you're going to change and turn into a prince." The Reverend didn't like it. He would scowl and leave the room when you came. But she loved you. So I did too!

I loved you because you brought a new dolly every Christmas for me. "I made it myself," you said. You pointed out the chisel marks on the wooden head, behind the neck, under the line of real human hair. Every detail about those dollies was dear: Their faces were creamy and shone with shellac. Their eyes opened and shut. One year it was a brunette with brown eyes, the next year the dolly had painted blue eyes and golden hair. "Like yours," you said, and you would pinch my cheek. They were dressed in dirndl skirts, which you said a dear friend had made, and I'm wondering now if it was your daughter, Kirsten. You never said, and I can't ask you now.

"Maybe someday you'll get to meet her," you said. "You look a lot like her." And you kept your eye fixed on Mutti, who didn't seem to like that idea. I should have guessed something from that.

In the second place, I could tell you were crazy about me. When you showed up, you would tease me for an hour and laugh with a big hee-haw laugh that roared around our drawing room. The Reverend's friends laughed polite laughs, which they covered with their hands. You know what I mean, don't you? You threw back your beard, which came down to your breast buttons, and black those days, and laughed at the chandelier. Each time before you left, you would throw your arms wide. I ran straight at you, and you swept me off my feet and kissed me on the lips and tickled my neck with that beard until I couldn't breathe for laughing. But why did you come so seldom and always just appear without a warning *at our back door* in the garden? I wondered things like that.

On this particular day, when I was seven or so—I was reading a book of fairy tales, and that's how I know I was seven—I had just con-fided in the family, all of them except the Reverend, who was away in his study: "When I grow up, I'll marry a Reverend. Like you, Mutti. Or a Mayor." We knew the Mayor; he came to our church and waited every Sunday on the way out just to shake our hands.

"A mayor!" she said.

"Or a king." I'm sure I had my index finger up, and I under-scored my point with a nice up-stab.

"Why do you think the king will pick you?"

"Because she's pretty," Natasha said.

"And she has ringlets," Aimee said.

"She can dance!" the brother said.

I didn't say anything. I occupied the middle of the room, under the gas chandelier, with them all in chairs in a semicircle around me. I blushed and laid my finger across my mouth.

"So cute!" Gerard said,

I stomped my foot. "Not 'cute.' 'Pretty!'" For some reason, this wonderful thought welled up, and I blurted it out, "I'll marry Uncle Ulli!"

"You can't!" Gerard said. "He's a *Wiedertäufer!*"

He immediately regretted that he'd said it and no doubt wished he could stuff that back down his throat. I looked at Mutti in disbelief. Her mouth had fallen open wide. It was clear she and the Reverend intended I never find that out. But there it was, and I handled the news as you might expect. I stormed off to my room and fell into one of my crying spells, although it was only ten o'clock in the morning.

MuttiMüeti ran after to comfort me, as I recall, but how could I be comforted? There seemed a dark side to everything I loved. I seemed to be deeply infected with whatever these people did in the dark forest.

"I don't want to be a *Wieder Teufel* anymore," I sobbed, hysterical.

"*Wieder Teufel?* Is that what you think?" She closed the door so no one else could hear. "Oh my Pet! Did you think you were a devil? No! No! It's *Wiedertäufer*. The Rebaptizers."

"What are they?"

"Rebaptizers," she repeated. "You'll understand when you get bigger."

"No! Tell me now. Why did Uncle Ulli become one? How did they trick him?" I was positive they'd tricked you. Why else would such a good man, who loved me like no other man I knew, become one?

Mutti stared at me. "It doesn't change a thing. He's still a good man. I love him, Maudlin."

But I knew she was hiding something. Why did she hate the *Wiedertäufer* if they were like Uncle Ulli? I questioned her closely, alert to where the hidden piece might lie. But in this case, she'd bolted and padlocked her mind, and she wasn't about to unbar it and let me look inside. What awful thing did lie inside?

I refused to let this revelation change my relationship with you. But I also didn't have the nerve to ask you about this horrible fact. I concluded I hardly knew anything about you. Did you live like a marmot in a cave in the mountain when you weren't with us? Did you have a brood of children? Did you meet secretly in graveyards at midnight and do illegal stuff? Were your children on their way to Hell? I suspect you knew that I knew your secret, but you also didn't bring it up. When you gave me the next good-bye kiss, all I could think was: you and Mutti were hiding something from me.

Then the adults announced that you had moved to Germany. I should say *been moved* to Germany. How you and a group of *Wiedertäufer* were dragged in chains onto a riverboat by the City Council of Bern, and shipped down the Aare into the Rhine, the whole way to Holland, and forbidden to ever return to Switzerland. But I didn't much care by this time, and I feel horrible now, thinking how little I cared. But those suspicions I had about you took your specialness away. You'd also neglected to bring a Christmas doll the winter before. Most of all, I'd turned thirteen, and gymnasium studies and birthday parties and family and just growing up, I guess, overturned all my childhood idols. I wasn't a *Wiedertäufer*—no one ever said so any-more. I was a proper member of the Fuog family.

Or so I'd convinced myself. One of those Matterhorn avalanches was about to break over the Fuog house, and the consequences would one day lead me to the Pequea Settlement. They would lead you here too! Look at me now, a Mennonist, a *Wiedertäufer* by just another name. Isn't life funny like that?

It was Mutti herself broke the news to me. It was a wintry night, just before Christmas and right about the time of year when you used to visit. The house was decorated as much for Christmas as appropri-ate for the home of a Reformed Pastor, which was very modest, as you know. Mutti could hardly even manage that. For some months she'd been withdrawing into herself like a caterpillar into the cocoon. Being a thirteen-year-old, I didn't think much of it (my "sisters" also would go through moody periods) when I found her lying down in the mid-dle of the day, or still asleep when I went off to school with Aimee. But pretty soon the doctor was doing consultations with the Reverend almost every morning, with the door closed, and then I saw the doc-tor leave and get into his carriage with a scowl on his face. Since she always shared everything important with the family, I assumed for the time being there was nothing to worry about. If there was, she'd tell us. Especially she would confide it in me because I was her Pet.

But this winter evening, with the whole family just finishing sup-per— always made by Natasha these days—she announced she and the Reverend had news to share with us. She'd caught cancer in the breast, she said, and the doctors said there was no cure. We all sat thunderstruck. Finally she turned to me, as I always sat beside her at the dinner table, and rubbed her hand on mine.

"I'm afraid I have to leave you, Pet."

"No! I won't let you go!"

That made tears jump out of her eyes, and I hated seeing anyone cry. From the time my night spells had ended, I hated tears, my own or anyone else's. I demanded right there that she stop, and the rest of the family just sat, dumb. Why didn't they say anything?

"Stop it, Mutti!"

"You can't stop me, Pet. But I will always be watching you, even if I'm gone. Up there. . . ." She pointed toward the Heavens over Switzerland.

"I don't want to hear it." I leaped up and plugged my ears with my fingers. "I won't listen to it." I screamed, as I remember it, a really horrible scream, as big as any one of your big laughs.

She followed me. I had tossed myself onto my bed facedown, the pillow clutched over my head. I heard her enter and felt her sit on the bed, next to me. She put her hand under the pillow and on my shoulder. "I know."

"No. You don't know! I'll be alone!"

She pulled me against her, and I could actually feel the tumor against my ribs, hard, like a tulip bulb, and I hated it. I hated the tumor! It was going to kill her. It terrorized me.

The next morning after the doctor had left, she came to Natasha's room, where I was busy working out math problems, with Natasha supervising.

"I want to tell you a secret, Pet."

I pretended disinterest. I didn't lift my head. What secret could possibly be left in the world after yesterday's news?

When she pulled me aside and told me, the news was very big. You were my real father, she said. I was so stunned that for once, not a single word came off my tongue. Not that I was angry. No. Just beyond belief.

She poured out the details. You were a Wiedertaüfer Pastor, she said. You'd been one for many years, and you and Emmeline, whom she called "your other mother," had sheltered *Täufer* runaways. The Bern government, with Reformed Pastors like the Reverend Fuog leading, had determined years ago to crush the *Täufer* and arrest its leaders and they clapped you and my mother up when I was an infant. Your children were scattered, she said, but you had specifically asked my Mutti to care for me. She agreed. But as the prison term passed the eighteen-month mark, my real mother developed consumption in the damp and miserable Insel Prison cell, and you knew she couldn't care for a small child when you finally got released. So you came back to Mutti and the Reverend with a second request: she should mother me even after you were released and the family reunited. Mutti agreed, but only under the condition you would not tell me your true identity until I was grown.

Now I was thirteen, and she was leaving me, she said, and she clutched and unclutched my hands continuously as she said it. She wanted so to see you once more, Vetti, but where were you? She was leaving me, and I needed a father, and we both understood the Reverend had never been a father for me. She didn't know why, she said. He just wasn't drawn to waifs and orphans like she was. So she was going to offer me a choice.

I could stay with her daughters until they married—and Natasha was already engaged to a young Guardsman—or I could reunite with the only man in all the world that I loved. If I chose "Uncle Ulli," she would provide me with the address of Kirsten, whom I of course didn't know yet, who could connect me with you, as you were now in Germany with my mother, she said.

—✎✎✎✎—

That's how I came to the Kraichgau Region, in South Germany, to reunite with you, my blood parents, after fourteen years. As it turned out, it would only be you, because you had already buried my mother. That was no surprise to anyone but me. You'd arranged for her to travel from Switzerland ahead of you, in the company of your friend, in hopes of saving her from consumption, with the help of the smart German doctors in Heidelberg. It was too late. You purchased our farm in Sinsheim, with the house within the town limits and the common pastures radiating out, South German style. My first day in Sinsheim, we went out together, you and I, to see the still- fresh red dirt, under a linden in the field. I hardly felt sad because I didn't know her. But your heart was broken, I saw that. That impacted me so hard. I promised you in our kitchen, "I will never leave you again, Vetti. You will never be alone again."

You asked me to call you *Vetti* now. I was happy to do so.

But the secret you'd kept from me for fourteen years was a very high fence between us, and we both felt it. You spent most evenings away from home, talking with the other refugees about the congregation you left behind in the Emmental. I came to think you loved them more than you loved me. Being a saucy sixteen-year-old by now, I accused you of that. You denied it. You cried when you denied it. I didn't believe you, and I couldn't stand to see a grown man cry.

You were used to the plain farmer's life. I however—I'd lived the town life, with an important Reformed Pastor and his energetic wife, in a big beautiful house. Sinsheim was just a cow town. We lived in an ugly house, and the physical work was endless—milk the cows, shear the sheep, plant and weed, harvest the garden, make meals. Then do it all over the next morning.

I actually learned to like the physical work! Work always makes me feel useful. I plunged into the daily chores and took over managing our simple little house. Every day I learned something new and different: how to raise vegetables, how to butcher a hog and make sausage (I got to be an expert at that), churning butter and cheese, making meals for you and Rolf, who I got to know for the first time because he came to join us in Sinsheim. I could not have had better preparation for the life I live today on the Pequea.

The *Wiedertäufer* problem was different in the Kraichgau: they called us Mennonists here. The authorities harassed us with stupid laws, but we didn't need to hide. Mennonists ran prosperous hofs. I've never been a stickler for religious doctrine. If it was a Reformed chicken or a Mennonist chicken, who cared? As long as it laid eggs that we could eat. The Mennonists were friendly people. Why, I'm still friends with many I first met in Sinsheim.

Which is how I also discovered firsthand that not all Mennonist chickens do lay eggs—if I can still put it that way.

CHAPTER 18

NEVER TRUST YOUR LIFE TO A MAN, THE KRAICHGAU, 1715–17

GREENYWALT CAME to our town the summer I was nineteen. I was in love with Martin Groff, the miller's boy, but of course it's Greenywalt that's the father of our Benjamin. Plus a couple little ones that never opened their tiny eyes and rest now and forever under the apple in our orchard, next to the plot where your mortal coil rests. But their little souls, like yours, "rest on the bosom of Jesus"—the Bible says it that way. I like to think of that: you finally get to hold your grandchildren, you didn't stay long enough to meet Benjamin. Lukey or Bod, or whatever he wants to be known as, doesn't count, of course.

I say "Greenywalt," like everyone does here on the Pequea, but I may have said "Klaus" in the beginning. Or Bruder Grünewald," more likely. "Our Bruder Grünewald, who's come all the way back from the New World." Oh, he was a hotshot when he arrived, wasn't he?

Young people on the Pequea have no idea the life we lived in the Kraichgau. We own our farms here. Soldiers don't come around to torch your house or drag your daughter into the haymow. Our church is over in Herr's House, and they're starting another one in

Neu-Strasburg. We meet in broad daylight, and no one says "Boo" about it. Young folks marry and set up house every spring, and no one says: "Get out! There's too many of you already!'" Which is how life was in the Kraichgau in 1715, the year Greenywalt showed up.

The Kraichgau was filthy with refugees from Switzerland, like our family. New ones came every couple weeks. They were still ordering *Wiedertäufer* "out of Bern or we'll throw you in prison or ship you to the galleys in Italy."

Brother Brechbühl. Now he was one good preacher. Some go so far as to call him "our Moses," because "the children of Israel groaned because of their bondage, and they cried out, and their cry came up to God because of their bondage," as it writes in Exodus. God sent us Benedikt Brechbühl out of Switzerland.

Brother Brechbühl was off visiting Prussia when Greenywalt came into town. It was going to turn out no one wanted to go clear swamps in Lithuania, after they heard about the limestone valleys on the Pequea from Greenywalt.

I was in love with Martin Groff, and that's a sad story. He was a good-looker, and we all, including you, Vetti, thought he'd make something of himself. Like his dad, who owned the one mill in Sinsheim. He was rich—millers always are. We were new in town, and it was hard to make friends at the start because everyone had their circle who came together from Switzerland. We also couldn't go around announcing ourselves, with the Elector's men on the prowl, and when they found a Mennonist, they would extract the Recognition Tax.

I met him at their mill. You were in such sad shape in those days. So broken down from those years in the Insel, lying on the damp stone floor in winter, with chains and a big iron ball. Some mornings it took you an hour to get dressed, with so much groaning and panting. So I did the farm chores, which was fine by me because I liked to keep busy then, just like I do today. You taught me how to harness up our pony and hitch to the cart, and then Rolf loaded it with the wheat and barley we stored in the attic after harvest, and I drove it to Groff's to make chop for the animals and flour for our bread and pies.

Groff fancied me, you'll remember. I was just seventeen, and you hadn't warned me about wolves in sheep's clothes. You just didn't see, I guess. I got taken in by his butter talk: how cute I was and how I was shaped. Did I tell you he actually used the phrase 'delicious'"? I said that was very inappropriate, for which he did at least apologize.

After Groff came along and later Greenywalt, people began to *see* me—as if I'd been a ghost before that. Well, I did start fixing myself up. When we first got to Sinsheim, I wore farm skirts and tucked all my hair under a scarf, but after Groff started coming by, I went into my trunk for some of my dirndls from Langnau. I had to "plain" them. The Mennonist preachers didn't go for ribbons or anything the color red, as you know. And I used a hot iron to make waves in my hair.

Groff was giving me kisses by this point. After a visit in our little parlor, he'd suggest we walk out into the garden and under the pear tree, where the house lamps didn't reach, and he kissed me. Just a stolen one on the cheek, *here*, the first time. But two weeks later, after his "delicious" comment, a hard kiss, and truthfully, when you appeared at the back door and called out to me just then, I was so glad. Groff asked to marry me right after that, as if he'd been planning it all along. I didn't know what to say. The kissing *verhuddelt* me, I guess. I said I'd think about it and ask you. Groff said he could wait.

That's as far as I got with Groff. No hands in the clothes. I'm sorry to talk blunt. What I didn't know was he was all the while going a lot further with Bernadette Faas. She had big tits, which she let him check out, and a whole lot more. I guess she opened up her legs. She wasn't even a Mennonist, so what was he thinking? Why, he could get away with it, that's what he was thinking.

Right about that time, when I'd told Groff I'd get back to him, I met Greenywalt for the first time, at Groff's mill. He was in the mill office, looking at a set of building plans with the miller, when I hauled in with my pony. The miller stopped his conversation and took my cart to the load pulley. I got a good look at Greenywalt in the meanwhile.

Compared to Martin Groff, he wasn't much to look at. His back was turned when he bent over those plans, and I saw he was bandy-legged and about my height, which is short. The chest muscles showed beneath his shirt. I took him to be a customer, and when he turned to look who had come in behind, I was surprised. Such a young face with a tufted beard. He was actually twenty-five.

He looked me up and down and said: "Well!"

I took that to mean he liked what he saw, but I was very pretty, you said so yourself, Vettii, and I had a good figure, and I already knew that and he didn't look like my type. So I didn't make anything of his "Well!" I got a bit uncomfortable from his staring so I turned toward the door. He said: "I'm Klaus Grünewald. From America."

I noted he didn't have a Swisser accent and right off knew this was the man you'd been telling me about for some time, the visitor from America. I kept walking toward the door. Then he said: "Klaus! Klaus Grünewald!" with his arm extended. I didn't shake it.

He laughed his big hee-haw, just like you used to do, so I did respond, "Aebi. Maudlin Aebi." I didn't look him in the eye. I probably looked at his shoes. I was shy around men I didn't know because that was how Mutti taught me.

He withdrew and folded his arms and stared some more. "Glad to meet you."

I went out to check how the milling was coming along, and that's all there was to our first meeting.

The second came the following Sunday because I told you when I got home that I'd met the man from America, and you right off said we must invite him to Sunday dinner. "You can make your gooseberry pie, Maudlin." Of all the things I cooked, my pies were your favorite, and of all the pies? Exactly. The gooseberry! I planted that bush by the garden wall for you.

So Greenywalt came to dinner, and sure enough, he liked my gooseberry pie as much as you did and ate three pieces! We sat around the table: —you'll remember we never had more than five pieces of furniture the entire time we lived there. It was me, you, Rolf, and Greenywalt for dinner. You had a hundred questions about the plantations on the Pequea. That's when I first found out you intended to return to the Emmental and bring your congregation out to a new life. How about the Pequea? What did a farm cost? What crops grew well? What about the Indians?

I wasn't particularly interested in talk of America yet, so I cleared the table and went out to the garden. Of course, we didn't work Sundays, but I thought to pick some pears because storm clouds had built, the wind was picking up, and if they fell—the pears, I mean—they'd bruise and end up only good for pear butter. So there I was, up on a stepstool, in my farm skirts again, a bandana hiding my hair and a bushel half-full of pears in my arms when you and Greenywalt showed at the back doorway.

"Go ahead," you said. Greenywalt came out by himself and started praising the garden.

"What's this?" he asked. "And this?" He pointed at my herb bed.

"Yarrow," I said.

"What's that good for?"

"It stops bleeding."

"And this?"

"Comfrey—that's for upset stomach, ulcers, diarrhea, arthritis. You make a tea."

"And this one?"

"Mullein, —for respiratory. Congestion in the lungs. Tea again. And that's Lamb's ears. For pretty, mostly. Lemon-balm. Spearmint. Peppermint." He pointed here and there, and each time I explained the herb and its use.

"You'd fit in well on the Pequea," he said. "Have you ever thought of going?"

"No. Why would I?"

"You could come with me."

I pretended to miss his pass. I was in love with Martin Groff, after all, even if he'd shown some indiscretion. Of course, we didn't know the whole story yet about Martin, which was about to come out, and if I had, I might have responded different that afternoon. But I was also thinking I needn't tell him about Martin, and if I didn't, I might learn something.

So I said, "What do you have to offer in Peck-Way?"

He liked the question, I guess. He broke out his biggest grin and propped his foot on my herb bed boards and looked up at me on the step stool. My skirts covered my legs, so it wasn't like he was trying to see something.

"My mill," he said. "That's what. A grist mill, like Groff has, because we don't have one and the farmers haul their wheat in bags on horseback to Brandywine—it's just a horse trail, and you can't get a waggon through—to get it ground, and it takes a whole day to get there and another one to come back."

"You have a mill? Like Groff?"

"Not yet," he says. "That's what I'm saying. I need to construct it yet and Brother Groff's giving me the plans for his mill and instructing how to adapt for my location and he's introduced me to his wheelwright in Alsace. I'm getting two burrstones made. I've got the money," he said, "to build the dam and buy the mill timbers and hire a Quaker millwright."

"How much does it take?"

He named a figure that seemed astronomical to me, but I didn't let on that big money impressed me. For five years now we'd lived in Sinsheim with so few creature comforts that a man with money sounded good to me.

"What have you been working up till now?"

He told me of his waggoneering for the Quaker man, James Logan, and his job as a land agent because, he said, "I can speak English like you speak German."

Unawares, I had begun a scenario in my mind of a house like the Fuogs', in the forests of Pennsilvania, by a creek whose mill hummed all day long like Groff's. And in the middle of this picture, I stood in a kitchen, holding a hot gooseberry pie with two potholders, and I carried it out to a proper cherrywood table with carved claw feet, where you sat, Vetti, across from—Greenywalt!

"You got awfully quiet there," Greenywalt said, his foot still propped on the edge of my herb bed.

I'd been building air castles. I felt uncomfortably hot, all at once, which meant I was blushing all over. I stepped right down the ladder and said, "There is definitely a storm brewing!" I pointed over his head at the clouds, which were piled up and black. Right on schedule a blitz of lightning jumped the whole way to the ground, and it thundered. I ran for the back door.

That was July. I thought harder now about Martin Groff's offer. I had options, I came to see. And then in September we got the big surprise, which I'm sure you remember well.

That was the Sunday the ministers called up Martin Groff, and to my shock, he came towing along Bernadette Faas by the hand, who I knew by sight but had never connected her with him because you sometimes didn't know who was eyeing up who until they came out with the banns, and on top of that, she was Reformed, not Mennonist. We never saw such arrangements. Neither side allowed them. But there they stood, in front of the whole congregation, in the living room of the Sinsheim family, where we met now, and I saw clear as a melon the bulge on her beltline, and I guess everyone else did too because you could hear the gasps. Martin Groff 'fessed up. Bernadette was in the family way, and yes, they had been fornicating, and he knew he'd done wrong in the eyes of God and the church. She confessed the same, and the ministers announced the pair had agreed to do the godly thing and get married, and she would get rebaptized first.

I was so rattled I couldn't sing the last two songs. Mostly I was angry I'd been so stupid. I hadn't seen what a Judas that man Martin Groff was, and it would have been me, up there beside him, with my belly sticking out, if I'd let him go where I now realized he intended to go with that "delicious" comment and hard kiss. During the last song right there on that Sunday of the announcement, I made up my mind I would *Never* put my life in the hands of man, which is why Greenywalt knows where he stands with me. Like Midnight, our terrier. I keep him on a short leash.

Things moved fast after that. November 16 at the end of services, Brother Brechbühl called Klaus Grünewald up, and together they introduced the Emigration Plan. The ministers had figured it out the previous evening—or discovered God's will on it, as they put it.

They'd inquired of the Lord regarding the invitation from the Pequea Settlement, by way of Klaus Grünewald, the Settlement representative. The Lord had made a way—which meant they were of one mind on it. We would leave as a group as soon as the Rhine turned passable. With the help of the *Wiedertäufer* merchants in Holland, we would charter a ship bound for Philadelphia. Klaus Grünewald would be our guide, because of his experience with Rhine and Atlantic trips. Because of his familiarity with the road from the harbor through the wilderness to Pequea. Because of his skill with the English tongue, he would broker with the Quaker land agents to buy farms for every one of us in the Pequea Settlement in America.

No one argued with Brechbühl. Nobody said, "Let's not do that." The ministers saw Greenywalt's visit like the Hebrews saw Moses and Aaron in the book of Exodus. God had heard their groans.

People would talk of nothing but the trip for the next four months, but I had other fish to fry. You'd announced over dinner that same Sunday that you would go along and take me. Yet in the next sentence, you talked about your congregation in the Emmentaler hills.

Klaus Grünewald came around the next day, November 17, which is how I remember the announcement was on the sixteenth. He asked me to marry him and said he loved me and did I love him? I said I didn't know. It was all so sudden.

"You could learn to love me," he said. "I'm not such a bad guy."

He knew nothing of me and Martin, so he wasn't comparing himself to anyone. That set him off on a series of chuckles, which he stifled real quick when he seen I wasn't laughing. "Would you ask your father what he thinks? Or—can I come over and ask him? I'll treat you right, Maudlin. I will."

I told you all about it that evening over supper, Vetti.

"He's a good sort. I approve," you said. That comment alone shows how even you, whom I love more than any man in the world, were much too trusting. The fact that you forgave Greenywalt after his dastardly deed a couple years later confirmed it for me.

"And what about America?" I said. "You would come and live with us?"

"No. I'm going back to the Emmental." I'm sure you said, "God told me to go back to the Emmental," but I'm not one to blame God for every commonsense decision that I make, and this was a commonsense decision for you. You couldn't abandon your flock.

"Yes, my dear sheep in the Emmental," you said.

Despite myself—I mean despite how much I hate tears—I couldn't help bursting out when you said that. After fourteen years we'd been reunited as daughter and father, and here you were leaving me again.

I didn't doubt Klaus Grünewald when he said he would treat me right. I didn't realize yet what flesh men are made of. It's weak stuff. It promises more than it can ever deliver. A man resolves, but then those two little glands intoxicate him, and all his promises before God and the witnesses go *poof.* But what options did I have at twenty-one years old, the prime of life, and the two men in my life both asking me to choose? So I did.

Klaus and I got married the first week of the New Year. I didn't love him, but I was starting to admire him. I found sleeping in the same bed with a man somewhat nice because the winters in the Kraichgau get so raw, but I stopped doing *that*—you know—after Benjamin was born. I can't sleep with someone tossing next to me, and as far as *that* is concerned—after what happened with the Girl Janey, how would you feel?

You said good-bye before Saint Nicholas Day. You couldn't even stay for the wedding because you wanted to reach Switzerland before the snows got any deeper.

February brought more big news. A brother from the Emmental arrived to say the Bernese authorities had met you at the border at midnight, tipped off by a spy, and they arrested you and they threw you into Insel Prison again.

Oh my conscience! All I could think was you, Vetti, on your back or side on the stone dungeon floor of that prison, on the island in the swift and ice-cold Aare River in mid-February. Who would look out for you? Make sure you had dry blankets? Food? There was Kirsten and Felix back in Langnau. Sure, my sister and brother, but I'd only met Kirsten once and Felix never until later. They also never became *Wiedertäufer*. Rolf said they talked as if you were a burden, a lunatic of whom the authorities and their friends said, "He's a heretic." In other words, they were ashamed of you.

I told Klaus I couldn't go to Pennsilvania. I had to care for you. I'd come later. Yes, I would, and for me, a promise is a promise. Does a woman have anything more she can give than a promise? He shed tears the last night before I left, February 15. He held my hand between his two, and tears rolled down into his scrawny beard, and he said he loved me. How could he know that after just forty-five days of living with me and eating my cooking? (I will say his tears touched me, but even tears, I learned later, may only say a man is grieving his losses and how lonely he's going to be. Tears are not sure proof of a noble heart.) He brought out a heavy bag, which he said was for my trip, when I came, and he counted them out: a hundred Reichstaler coins.

I thanked him, but I decided not to tell him my other reason for not going on this America trip. Martin and Bernadette Groff, and she as big as a sideways watermelon now, were going along. I couldn't imagine a ship on the Atlantic big enough for me to ride if Martin Groff and his whore were on it. And you know what? He didn't make it in the Pequea either. He skedaddled to Virginia five years later, where I hear he lives on a dog-eared farm with six or seven brats. He has a big beer belly these days. Which kind of proves not all Mennonist chickens do lay eggs.

Greenywalt and I resorted to letters. It's different these days. A letter zips back and forth over the Atlantic in eight weeks, maybe. In 1717 you first needed to find someone to get it down the Rhine to a ship captain in Rotterdam. That was Greenywalt's friend, Horsch. Then there was the ocean, and it was still wartime. The French seized ships for their cargo and for the men. If not the French, then the privateers. There were privateers everywhere, lone ships with pirate crews. If the letter got to Philadelphia, your ship captain needed to find someone who knew about the Pequea Settlement, or cared enough to interrupt his business of selling off his indentures to find that someone.

I sent my first letter the week I arrived in the Emmental.

The Fuogs took me back. Natasha was gone, but Aimee and the brother still lived there with the Reverend. The house wasn't the same without my dear Mutti. It had no soul. I went back and forth in my mind about who I wanted people to think I was. When I visited you, I wore *Wiedertäufer* clothes. On my way home to the Fuogs, I pulled my gay Swiss dirndls out. You begged me to carry messages to your *Wiedertäufer* friends and to Kirsten and Felix. I can't say my sister and brother because I didn't regard them that way. When I went to take your message, I wore my *Wiedertäufer* clothes again, and I wore them proudly.

I got three letters from Greenywalt between the fall of 1717 and the fall of 1718, each by a different ship. He must have spent all his time haggling with ship captains that fall. He had sold a piece of his land to Brother Brechbühl, and with that plus his cash plus the loan guarantee from James Logan, he had laid out the mill site, he said. He hired several men to dam the creek and dig the pond and raceway, and the stone foundation of the mill was already set. He missed me, he said. He was also working on the cabin where we would live, and he couldn't wait to see how I would outfit it. I felt proud I'd married a responsible man.

I sent a third letter at the start of the third sailing season, May 1719. I had lots of exciting news. First of all, your release looked likely, and Felix and I had both been baptized *Wiedertäufer*. I wrote about all that. I didn't know it would be the last letter he would receive from me. They released you on June 2, and two weeks later the hunters broke into the gathering in the hills where you were preaching and snatched you up again, plus Felix. They tortured Felix to learn my whereabouts and came to the Fuogs and wrapped chains around my wrists and ankles in front of the Reverend and Aimee.

The Fuogs had no idea that I'd joined the Mennonists. I hadn't dressed like one around them. I can say truly that I felt no embarrassment when the Hunters chained me in front of them and yelled, "*Wiedertäufer* bitch!" in my ears so I couldn't hear out of one ear for a week. If Mutti had been there, I would have cried, I'm sure. But now that I had you again, my Vetti, did I care what the Reverend, in his very impressive black robes, thought of me? Not one bit. I did feel sorry for Aimee because she was always sweet on me, although not as much as Natasha.

You remember the trip, I'm sure. Us three Aebis were hauled in chains on a waggon to Lake Thun, where the Sheriff gave you, as a repeat offender, your options. If you took an oath of allegiance to the authorities, they would free you. Otherwise it was death or the galleys. We begged you to choose the galleys—there might always be a chance of escape. Felix and I rode along with you on the ship to Venice, so we could be there with you when you died. We knew the trip to Italy and a couple weeks as a galley slave would kill you. A *Wiedertäufer* brother in your congregation, in disguise at the hearing—and I didn't even get his name—took news of the sentence back to the congregation, then downriver to the Kraichgau community, and through them to Horsch, who promised to get the letter to a sea captain going to Philadelphia and from there to Greenywalt.

What we didn't know was that it would take a whole year for the letter to reach Greenywalt, and who should give it to him but the Whore of Pequea, Janey Cameron. In the meanwhile, one more letter from Greenywalt arrived, ignorant of our fate. I received it from the Fuogs when you were released in December of 1719. They'd released Felix and me when we arrived in Venice, since it was only the first time we'd been arrested.

The imprisonment at the Insel and the trip to the galleys and back—although you never rowed a day in your life—broke you, Vetti. We could hardly believe it when we saw you. The Reverend Fuog admitted that he intervened to have us released upon arrival in Venice. Although he hated *Wiedertäufer* and took a regular salary from the Bern Council to distribute their orphans and properties, out of respect for Mutti and her love for me and out of respect for you, her brother, he did it, he told me.

I negotiated with the Reverend, who now regarded me with even more disdain than he did the *Wiedertäufer* child he'd taken in twenty-three years before. If he would let me nurse you in one of the many empty rooms of his house, I would pay for all the doctor expenses. He looked stoat-eyed. I guess he wondered how a refugee girl just out of prison might have any gulden on her but I did, in a bag, my passage money. I'd loosened a brick in Fuog's chimney the day I returned from the Kraichgau, and stowed it back behind there.

It took sixteen months for you to heal. During that time, no letters came from Pequea. The last one I'd received, the letter of 171, the mill was finished and grinding, and Greenywalt begged to know if we'd come the next sailing season. Of course I wrote now again in the spring of 1720, but Horsch seemed to have vanished. I entrusted the letter to a messenger I didn't really know, who did it for money.

In May of 1721, you sat up one morning in the Reverend's house in Langnau and announced you were better. You'd decided you couldn't pastor your little flock any more. We would go back to the Kraichgau. So we did. The remnants of the congregation were still there, including Groff the Miller. The miller and everyone else stared as if you were Peter Klaus the Goatherd, back from his twenty-year sleep.

"They said you were sent to the galleys! You're alive!" Everyone knew the story of the Gerber boys, who were sent to the galleys and never heard of since. They wore men out on the galleys and threw their bodies overboard to the sharks when they died, that's what they did.

The little farm in Sinsheim where we had lived, where my real mother lay buried under the linden, was no longer a possibility. The lord of Sinsheim had rented it to someone else. What was left here for you? You saw the answer was "Nothing" and announced you were ready to go with me to America.

I wrote the letter to Greenywalt in July, announcing our plan, although figured I'd missed the sailing window for the year. I told Greenywalt we were coming, you and I, and we would see him soon.

CHAPTER 19

THE RESURRECTED WIFE,
PEQUEA SETTLEMENT, 1722

I ONCE OWNED a little leather-cover book of Bible stories with pretty pictures at the Fuogs, and I would beg Mutti almost every night for the Joseph story. The covers fell off at last, and she bound the book together with worn-out ribbons from my plaits. In the picture, he's on a camel. Hog-tied, you know, a prisoner of the Ishmaelites. But his head is high, he's looking ahead in this picture. He's looking forward to the pyramids and the stone temples with the pharaohs of stone. The gardens of leeks and onions and melons all around. Mutti said, "He had no choice about coming to Egypt, but fear not, God had a plan for him."

Now I once thought I was different—thought I had a choice about America. But once we got going, we couldn't possibly return. So how was I different from Joseph? We had no money, you and I, Vetti. Your *Wiedertäufer* preacher friends in Holland met us at the wharf and put us on a ship for Philadelphia and paid the passage and food for the trip. They were kind because they remembered you from that riverboat ride with Brechbühl ten years back. Greenywalt is like you in that: people always remember him too. I never said he wasn't a good man.

In Philadelphia, this big man James Logan met us at the Courthouse. He came up just as our ship captain was entering us on the ship log as immigrants and making us take the Oath of Allegiance to their English King.

"It's Missus Greenywalt," the interpreter said to Logan. I understood at least my name in their dreadful tongue, which I have never once desired to learn, but Benjamin—my son and the grandson you never got to see—his father insisted he must read it before he reads our beloved German, since "it's the language of the New World," he says. Benjamin has picked it up and speaks it like a native! That's the bright youngster he is.

This Logan fellow wore a gray wig under his Quaker hat—he was one of them—but when the interpreter introduced me, his face turned a different color.

"Missus Greenywalt?" he says. "I heard you were dead!"

"Well, I'm not. I'm every bit as alive as you, I guess." The interpreter said that back to him for me, and he laughed. That was my first clue that something was amiss.

"Pleased to meet you." Mister Logan recovered, I guess, and shook my hand and yours. (I know you suspected nothing. You were just a shell of your old self and trotted after me everywhere like a puppy dog.) On his own shillings, Logan arranged for one of his waggons to haul us to Pequea, two days out in the wilderness. I found Later it wasn't generosity. He actually charged it off on Greenywalt's account, which shows you how this man got rich enough to build that mansion up in Germantown. He didn't let the small expenses slide— something Greenywalt never learned. Which is why Greenywalt never got wealthy enough to build a mansion like the Mylins built.

It took us two days through forest such as we'd never seen, in a two-horse waggon. The driver—this was the first I seen one of these backwoodsmen who dress and act like the natives. Animal skins and such. Deerskin shirt and his leather hat black from the rain and snow and smelling like something dead. Deerskins tied about his calves to protect from the brambles. A whip and his black-powder musket down through his belt, which caused me to wonder what he might consider to be targets, as he worked for a Quakerman and I understood them to be defenseless folks, like us. But he didn't know our language, so I couldn't ask. Behind him there was me and you on the first bench, our trunk at our feet between us, and behind us on the second the Mennonist family Bowman, who rode down the Rhine with us and were riding beyond Greenywalt's to his brother's on the Pequea. Their little ones, a boy and a girl, slept on pillows on the floorboards between us and them. Behind all that, he carried gunny sacks of salt and pewter plates for Logan's store on the Susquehanna.

We came out of the trees on the second evening. The waggoneer, he turned and pointed his gun and said: "Peck-way," and he checked the horses so we could overlook the pretty picture.

The forest gave way on our right to a field of barley ready to thresh, with glow-worms bobbing up and down across the whole field. It was toward dusk and beyond the barley as one came down the trail out of the woods a log bridge crossed you over to the spot where a lane hooked off to a gristmill, with a pond up behind it, a millrace connecting them, and the big wheel rotating real slow, groaning a high-pitched and regular "MmmMmmMmmMmm," and dripping water and the millstones were making a kind of steady roar. (We'd been listening to locusts for two days, and that's a sound you don't forget. Even at night when they're asleep, I can't rinse their singing out of my head.)

The wheel attached to the mill—well, everyone knows what

mills look like; we have so many nowadays. Except this first one was log set on a foundation of limestones. Beyond the mill, I saw a cabin of new logs, with four window squares cut through and sealed over with grease-paper, and a roof of thatch. Are you remembering that pretty picture? See! I still get goose-bumps remembering that first look we got and how I grabbed your hand, Vetti, and I said, "This is it! It's our house!"

I was twenty-seven, and here I was, here to take possession of my house. But as I said about Joseph, you don't know what's behind the pretty picture until you go through it. Joseph got Potiphar's wife. I got Greenywalt and the English woman.

The driver, he motioned me and the Bowman children to sit down so he could go on driving, which we did. Across Pequea Creek and onto the lane, which angled around the mill front door to the loading dock, where a big-shouldered man who looked Swiss was on top of his waggon, hitching bags to the pulley. The driver stopped right there at the front door.

"Peck-Way Settlement!" he yelled, in case we'd forgotten already.

The mill door opened and a woman came out.

I didn't know at the time I was looking at Hagar, the one who slept in Abraham's bosom. You know the story. She had a pretty face, I'll say that. No pocks on her cheeks or forehead. She dressed Mennonist, like the girls back in the Kraichgau—the blue skirts, the linen blouse with the white apron, but no *Häubchen*, like a married woman. Her hair was in a fat plait. And red, very red.

"Welcome! Welcome!" She came out to my side of the waggon and looked up. "You're here to see the Mister? Greenywalt?" It was good, understandable German. It wasn't her mother tongue. But I'd known that from her face. English foreheads are broader, and their noses run straight or pug, not pinched or ski-slope like our Swissers. Hers was pug.

I stood up. It was my moment to declare it. "I'm Missus Greeny-walt."

Color flushed out of her cheeks and throat, like she'd seen a spook, and I thought it curious, but she recovered straightaway and said, "I'll get him."

I should have smelled a rat, but when you don't expect anything but a hardy welcome to the owner's long-absent wife . . .

She stepped back from the waggon and hallooed the top story of the mill, the window where the grain bags were landing at the top of the pulley run, two floors up on this side, three on the back side.

"Greenywalt!"

His head and shoulders came out through that window, Greeny-walt himself, although a body wouldn't have known it, what with the white mill clothes plus the flour dusting up his beard and all over the hat—he looked like a snowman to me.

"It's Missus Greenywalt."

She said it and ran off for the mill door, as if she'd forgot something, which I discovered shortly was her brat.

This Snowman said something to the farmer on the waggon below, who stopped what he was doing. The pulley also stopped, as I guess he'd unhooked the belt.

"Who?" he hollered down. Imagine! He could see it was me.

"Frau Grünewald." I wanted to add "your wife" but wasn't 100 percent yet it was him. I was so thrilled, standing there in our wag-gon. We'd been a month on the Rhine, twelve weeks vomiting and wishing we could die on the Atlantic, and two days of black-and-blue bum-fiddles on the hard planks of a waggon over stones and ruts through a gloomy forest with wolves howling every night and I was finally here. If I'd been a meadowlark, I would have soared for a nice Hello Kiss, but meanwhile, maybe he was going to fly down first to me.

His arms spread as if to fly, and his mouth fell open. Then he pulled back and disappeared.

You stood up alongside me in the waggon, the most excited I'd seen you for months. The Bowman couple had lowered their children over the side so they could go in the bushes beside the mill.

"It's a very fine mill!" you declared. You pointed this way and that, naming the buildings. I wound my arm around your waist to keep you from tipping over.

Right then Greenywalt came out the front door. It was him, all right, and he stopped and sat down on the front step and stared at me. Aside from his flour makeup, he was the man I had married four years ago. Exactly.

"Yeees? Is this how you greet your wife?" I asked.

"I thought you . . . were dead!"

"You think I'm a ghost?"

"I thought you were *dead*," he repeated.

"Why would I be dead?"

"They told me you were dead. They took you to the galleys. All of you."

"*I'm* alive." That was you talking, Vetti. "You remember me, don't you, Klaus Grünewald?"

"You believe everything you hear?" I said.

He covered his face with his hands, as if he couldn't or maybe didn't want to believe it. I didn't know which, but I was getting a pretty strange feeling.

"It's a very fine mill," you said to him. "They say you built all this? The mill? The pond? The cabin?"

I jumped over the side of the waggon. (When I was twenty-seven I could do stuff like that.) "Aren't you glad to see me?"

He pulled himself together and came to me with his white-floured arms and grabbed my hands.

"Maudlin!"

I could have leapt into his arms, flour dust and all. I'd never felt that way about him back in the Kraichgau. But right as he grabbed my hands, the mill door opened. This little boy showed, not much more than a toddler, with a chubby face. He caught my eye with his. No smile. Very serious. And red hair. Right there was a clue. He caught my eye as I was holding hands with this man and he lunged.

"Who's this?" I asked.

The boy threw his chubby little arms around Greenywalt's leg and said "*Daadi!*"

"Daadi?" I'm sure I whitened like a snowman. "Daadi?"

Greenywalt nodded. He bent down and lifted up the boy. "I made a mistake, Maudlin. I sinned."

We stared into each other's eyes. I'm sure on my side it was more like I goggled.

The young English woman came back out, spied the boy, and ran over for him. Greenywalt said something in English, of which I understood only *No!* She looked terrified. I was going to give her a lot more reason to be terrified. But right now, she took his "No" and went back into the mill.

"Is that the mother?" I said.

"I confessed my sin to God. And to our Meeting, Maudlin." Greenywalt stood right opposite me, holding the boy, who laughed and smacked his beard to make the flour go poof, and I felt sick to my stomach.

"Bod! Stop it. He's a good boy, Maudlin." Greenywalt took the boy's chin between his fingers and towed it around so the boy looked right at me with two very big blue eyes. Of course, Greenywalt has blue eyes. "He's a good boy."

He lowered the boy. "Get Missus Greenywalt a pear, Bod!" He smacked the boy's bottom in the direction of the pear trees up the lane, beside the horse stable, and off he went. We watched him go, with such speed and agility for such a young one. Barefoot, too, on that rough dirt, so he was callused. He pulled off a pear and came galloping back, stopped right at my feet, and held it up to me.

"A pear for you!" The boy said in perfect German.

I took it. "Was that the mother?" I asked again.

"I was lonely," Greenywalt said. "They said you were d-d-dead." He stammered. For the first time I'd ever observed, he couldn't speak straight. "We made a mis- mis- mistake." He also wouldn't hold my look.

"And she's your wife?"

I figure by this time he'd guessed out how things must look to me. We hadn't seen each other for five years, since the honeymoon; he'd somehow heard I was dead; he got lonely so a pretty face reeled him and his fine fortune in, and they fornicated and had a baby; they confessed their sin and now the inconvenient fact—his real wife showed up, in the flesh, alive, three feet away, demanding the truth. What was going on here, Man?

"Is she your wife?"

"No. She lives in the cabin by herself. With him. I promised the ministers and her. I'll raise him like my own. It wasn't love, Maudlin."

I walked past him, sat down on the stone step, buried my face between my knees, and raged. It welled up; I couldn't stop it. I didn't want to stop it. I raged because he'd destroyed my dream. I was going to have a house, a fine house like the Fuogs, except in the wilderness, with my own husband and my own babes, and I'd bake him a gooseberry pie if he liked that, and serve it hot, with milk, and I'd read stories to my babes, like Mutti did.

After twenty-seven years of my life, with all the conditions right, my dream right at the tips of my fingers, we drove out of the forest and into the clearing with the glowworms. It was just as I'd pictured it: the mill, the millpond, the cabin. Oh! And the Other Woman. The Child. And this ugly, ugly weakness of a man I'd entrusted my life to and come five thousand miles to spend my life with. How could he do this?

He put his hand on my shoulder. I scraped it off like poison.

"Don't touch me! I'm going back to Switzerland!"

The boy said something about the pear. It lay on the ground beside my foot, where I'd dropped it.

I sat there on the step, and after a while I stopped foaming at the mouth. My common sense took over. I couldn't go back to Switzerland, or to the Kraichgau. Sailing season was over—it was August. You would not have survived another four-month trip, Vetti. If I had the passage money—I'd make Greenywalt pay it; that was the least he could do—pay for our way back. But even if you were able and we got the money and it was the next spring, what then? What was there in the Kraichgau, other than my mother's grave under the linden in somebody else's field? With Mutti gone, what was there for us in Switzerland except more time in the prisons for you? And surely they wouldn't release you the next time.

Me, wearing the *Häubchen* of a married Palatine woman but returning without the husband, who would be alive back in Penn's Woods with a strange woman? I'd end up a spinster. The longer I chewed this cud, the more I knew I was Joseph in Egypt. No matter what the circumstances here, going back was not possible.

When I looked up, it had gotten pretty much dark. The mill wheel had stopped. The waggon with the Bowman family had gone. You were sitting hunched over on the step, with your back against our trunk, snoring. The red-haired boy was gone, but Greenywalt was there, in the dark doorway of the mill. All I saw was his outline, and the red glow of his pipe coming on and off. He heard me sit up. He came, slow-like, without saying anything.

I stood up so I could look directly into his soul.

"I want her out of my house," I said.

"I want you to stay, Maudlin." He reached for my hand, but I pulled back. I knew now exactly what I needed. I didn't want anyone distracting me from it.

"Bring my trunk in. Vetti! Let's go home." I lifted you up—you'd gotten so frail during the trip that I could lift you. I took your elbow and steered you across the lane to the cabin and pushed open the door and walked into my house.

A betty lamp was smoking, and the English Woman stood there, at the raised hearth, stirring a pot over the wood fire. She stopped stirring and went motionless, her back to me. The boy was in the shadows, playing with a small dog and laughing.

"You'll have to go," I said. "You don't live here anymore."

She went without raising her eyes and led the boy out with her. The dog went too, and his tail was tucked between his legs. Even the dog knew better.

I held up the betty lamp to get a look at my cabin. Who could call it a home? He promised this? Four walls with a fireplace, a table, and two benches. No proper kitchen. No sitting room. One large un-divided room—do you remember how it was? When I heard later that the English woman wanted to convert it to a store, I got it, seeing's how it was then, I got how she came up with the store idea. Although the idea itself, a store on the grounds, was something I shortly came to believe in myself. I never said she was totally worthless.

In a couple minutes Greenywalt appeared with two mill hands. The hands carried in our trunk, and one scooted up the rung ladder to the loft and tossed down rolled feather ticks, which Greenywalt unfurled on the floor, one for me and the other to take to the English woman. Meanwhile the second hand returned from the mill basement, where Greenywalt had been living, with the master's feather tick, which he positioned on the floor by the one intended for me. Greenywalt announced that you would sleep on the rope bed, which the Woman had been using up till then.

Shortly the Woman reappeared. She addressed Greenywalt in her tongue from the doorsill. Then she entered and went to the cupboard and got down wooden bowls, which she filled from the fireplace with stew, and placed them on the table, one apiece for you and me and one across the table for Greenywalt. Then she turned and walked out and didn't come back.

We sat down for our first meal together in five years. The betty lamp threw up shadows on everyone's faces and a lot of smoke, and I felt Greenywalt watching me across the table. He reached across and covered my hand with his.

"You're my wife, Maudlin. I want you to stay." I let him keep his hand there during your immense prayer, which began in the mountains behind the Emmental, traveled to the Kraichgau, down the Rhine to the *Wiedertäufer* Pastors in Rotterdam, over the Atlantic, onto the docks and up the waggon path to the Pequea Settlement, where you circled the property and named each building and ended with thanksgiving for Greenywalt and for the Lord himself.

"In the name of our Lord and Savior, Jesus, Amen."

I removed my hand.

"Tell me about the trip," Greenywalt said.

"Maybe tomorrow," I said.

"It was long," you said. "Nice cabin. Nicer than most of the houses I've ever lived in."

We ate the meal in silence. Her soup was passable, although I make better.

—ⱷⱷⱷⱷⱷ—

I couldn't sleep. Greenywalt lay snoring on the tick, an arm's length from mine. I wasn't accustomed to a man's body in the dark next to mine. More to the point, I'd been cuckolded. Again. First Groff. Now Greenywalt. That promise I'd made myself ten years back in the Kraichgau after Groff, never to trust my life to a mere man? How did I get bamboozled again?

And I was stuck. My mind went round and round on it until I realized: I didn't even know what time it was. He didn't even have a clock. I don't remember any thoughts after that: I must have fallen asleep.

CHAPTER 20

MAKING THE BEST OF IT,
1722

I 'M SURE YOU REMEMBER that first morning on the Pequea. I certainly do. The air felt very, very thick and full of smells. Meadow smells. Woods smells. The cicadas roared and the mill wheel did its part. Do you want to know what I really thought? *I'm in my own house.* That's what I thought!

"Are we really in America?" you said from the rope bed across the cabin.

Greenywalt came in, already in his miller whites, with a white skullcap. "Ohh! We're up!" He had a silly grin, like it was the first cockcrow of his honeymoon again. "Eggs? Pannhaas?"

He fried up a skillet of our favorite Kraichgau breakfast and watched us eat it.

"Show me your plantation," I said.

He obediently took us around. Beneath the house there was a cellar but no inside access. I started a list in my head and put that on it. He took us to the mill, the pond, the millrace, the grinding wheels, the room on ground floor where he'd been living and now, since last night, the home of the English Woman and the Boy. He'd done it all with good craftsmanship. We came to the mill shop last, where he did business with his customers. She sat on a high stool, bent over a set of journals. I remember a lot of cobwebs at the window corners, but he had real glass panes in the mill and only greased paper in the cabin windows. I added that to my list.

"Janey is the bookkeeper," he said. When she looked up, I nodded. I understood the importance of keeping good help. The boy was down on the floor, pulling a waggon with four carved horses, and snorting like a horse.

Back in the cabin, he said he stopped every day at noon for dinner, and he produced a pocket watch to show how he knew when noon was. Sure enough, Janey, as he called her, appeared at the cabin door right on the hour, with a platter of bread and cheese and cold meats, which he carried to the table.

"I've made up my mind," I told him. "I'm going to stay." I said I didn't understand what he had done yet, and I planned to get to the bottom of the story. That would take some time, of course. In the meanwhile, I said, "*The house is not livable.*"

He didn't seem hurt by this. "I gave up working on it when I heard you and your family—" He was about to give me excuses, and I held up my hand. I had no interest in hearing them.

I said I needed walls. The cabin needed to be divided into rooms. I sketched it out on paper: a wall dividing the space side to side, and a second one dividing it lengthwise with a wall to the right of that one to create a kitchen corridor from the front door to the back door. A *Stube* on the other side of the wall from the fireplace, and a five-plate stove to heat the room where we'd do most of our living—he interrupted to say Logan imported German five-platers, and he would get one in Philadelphia—and a bedroom beyond the Stube.

He understood the plan. It was our standard South German house set-up. He would do it, he said.

I wanted an inside stairway to the cellar. It was ridiculous without one. The loft needed to extend over the front rooms to give full ceilings and create attic space, and I wanted a proper stairway to the attic. I wasn't running up and down a rung ladder to store food and bedclothes, like a servant girl.

"Can you afford that?"

"Of course. I'll put my men on it."

"I won't live out of a trunk. I want a clothes press." I remembered the nice hardwood armoires in the Kraichgau homes, although Vetti's house never had one.

He nodded.

I told him we would sleep on proper beds, not ticks on the floor, and I wanted glass, not grease paper, in the windows. I asked for a German clock for the fireplace mantel and finally, a porch swing for you, Vetti. I asked for a garden and pointed out the front door to the spot where it might work well for herbs and vegetables, and reminded him how he'd complimented me on our garden in Sinsheim.

He nodded to everything, and not grimly. I believe he genuinely was ready to kiss the ground under my bare feet if I would just stay. That attitude, more than anything, persuaded me that what he said about the English Woman was the truth. It was over and done.

That was Saturday, my fourth day on the Pequea. Sunday, we drove to the meeting at the Herr House in his waggon. This particular Sunday, it was just he and I and you, although subsequent Sundays the English Woman and her boy came as well, in the waggon back, of course.

We were both astonished to see how the Mennonists gathered in America, without secrecy or lookouts, even in the middle of the day.

Greenywalt introduced you and me all around, and people crowded up to shake our hands and meet "the Resurrection from the Dead," as the minister put it.

I remembered him, Christian Herr, the eagle-eyed hunchback from the Kraichgau. This house where we were meeting was his, he told me. It boggled the mind: three stories of limestone, the glass windows, the cedar shingle roof. It was the only limestone house those days, although a few years out everyone would tear down their log cabins to build houses like his. I saw then that my request to Greenywalt had been modest. A log cabin South German style, with a thatch roof? If I had seen Herr's house first, I might have asked for limestone walls and cedar shingles.

You were in high spirits, happier than I'd seen you since those times when you showed up for Christmas at the Fuogs with your dolly presents. You threw back your head and laughed your old laugh. You introduced me to a man you called "My Friend." There were dozens of "My Friends," families you knew from the Emmental, people who'd come with Preacher Brechbühl in the 1717 Migration. What of Brother Brechbühl? you asked, the one you most wanted to see, the man you'd been chained with on the riverboat ride down the Rhine? Brechbühl, sadly, was dead two years back. Then you entertained Ulrich and Maudlin, Brechbühl's teenage children, with stories of their father from the river ride.

You might say I had the crow's-nest view of how the community regarded my husband. Was he outcast sinner? Not one bit. In fact, most regarded him with some sense of awe, as the land agent who brought the invite from the Pequea Settlement to the Kraichgau and how they could buy farms from the Quaker proprietors. And he'd been as good as his word. I only picked up some footnotes from the leaders, Herr, namely, who said, "Your husband's done well. He's gotten back on his feet." We both knew what had knocked him off his feet.

We got several invites to dinner that day, and I declined them all for now, except for that of Mrs. Herr. Mrs. Hans Herr, that is, the wife of the other land agent. She seemed a specially tenderhearted person, who offered to show me the Settlement soon "with a tour in my pony cart."

"Just call me Frony," she said a week later as we were in her pony cart, riding the length of the Pequea Settlement. She pointed out the farms as we went by. 'Five-hundred-some of us now," she said. "Blacksmith, gun shop, *your mill*, the doctor . . . it's a regular village we have, only spread out. Not all together, like we lived in the Kraichgau."

"How about a store?"

"Not yet. Your husband brings what we order from Philadelphia."

I tucked that cud away for a later chew.

Greenywalt and her man were partners for ten years now in the land agent work. Greenywalt's piece was dealing with the same James Logan I'd met and knew from his letters long ago. Was he a good man? Frony thought so, although she'd never talked with him. He didn't speak our dialect. But that's where Greenywalt came in, as the go-between, she said.

One evening after the mill was shut, I learned how their land business worked when the same Bowman family that arrived with us—him and her, together with his brother—came to buy a farm. Herr and Greenywalt unrolled their parcel maps on our cabin table and did business under the lanthorn with the Bowmans. They reviewed likely spots for a farm, the acreages with each option, who the neighbors would be, where the springs located, with special notes on things like the fertility of the tract, tree sizes, proximity to Indian villages, and so forth.

The Bowmans were eager to part with their money and settle. Janey sat right in the middle of the conversation, recorded the transactions with her quill pen in the land books, and then a couple days later carted her books to Philadelphia, where she and Greenywalt would meet Logan and the land agents to finalize things.

I had to do something about Greenywalt's trips to Philadelphia. Alone in a waggon for two days and a night every couple weeks with a woman whose advances he'd already shown himself helpless to resist? How dumb was that? Why hadn't the ministers said something about that? He was too cheap to stay at an inn on the trip. They slept in the waggon—or she did, anyway. What kept her from snuggling up if it was nasty weather? The more I thought of it, the madder I got.

I asked Frony. She said she'd wondered about the same thing.

I demanded Greenywalt make these Philadelphia trips by himself. He said that was impossible. She knew all the details. All right, she could go by herself. No, the road was unsafe for a woman and he was the middle man; he handled the negotiation. So he could take one of his mill hands along, I said. He complained it wasn't necessary. He'd made a vow before God and the congregation (which only proved how ignorant he was of his own flesh). I think he was more upset about the loss of four days' work for the hand. But by bedtime that same night, we'd come to an agreement that till he came up with something better, this was the plan. He'd take along the mill hand.

As for the girl, she was terrified of me. She knew I could throw her out, that's why. She made a try at cozying up the first week, but I would have none of it. Why should I befriend a slut?

All of Pequea knew Greenywalt was fond of the babe. The boy loved him and came calling, "Daadi! Daadi!" as he'd done the evening I came. Greenywalt would hoist him on his shoulders and gallop around the mill, making horse noises, the boy shrieking like a stuck pig, and all the while Greenywalt laughing his great snort. I would have been thrilled to see it. Except one thing. *It wasn't our son.*

The house progressed rapidly. Greenywalt's mill hands roughed out the room, under his direction, and you and I mudded the inside of the exterior walls into a smooth surface. By early November, the five-plate was connected to the chimney and heating the Stube—and we needed it by then. They'd finished an inside stairway to the cellar, where I stored the hogsheads of cider I'd bartered Christian Herr for, and a stairway to the attic, where I stored bags of dried apple schnitz. Greenywalt had kept his commitment. During those ten weeks, he got no affection from me. No kisses. No intimacy. We did not hold hands again when he prayed the grace. I did not undress with him looking. Of course, Vetti, I didn't want to make you uncomfortable, since there were no walls in the beginning but even after the rooms were done and we moved our ticks into our room and your rope-bed into your own room, I continued my practice.

"I want a proper bed," I said. "I won't sleep on the floor anymore."

"It's your house, Maudlin."

"I want a double bed," I said. I saw his shock. "I want a baby."

Greenywalt could hardly contain his joy. Maybe he thought I'd put the past completely behind. I hadn't. Could any woman, in my situation? Would it just take time and observing him, was that it? I don't know if I could have said so myself. It was excruciating the first time. He watched me undress, from his spot in the new double bed. I blew out the betty lamp.

"Is this the way you did it with her?"

His hands stopped.

"Maudlin. I was wrong. Forgive me. I've asked you over and over now. Forgive me," he said in the dark.

I said I did forgive him, but I couldn't forget. The self-consciousness he'd displayed since the day I arrived disappeared when we came together in the dark that night, and he lost himself in his ecstasy. I couldn't see his face. He couldn't see mine. That was good, because I'm not sure what showed on mine.

In February, Daniel came. He was only twenty weeks, enough to know he was a boy. I insisted on a proper grave and burial and marker in the snow, in the orchard under an apple tree. In June, it was Ezra. The apple tree was in bloom, and the petals blew off in a thunderstorm and covered the fresh dirt. I could hardly breathe, standing there, under the tree, while you said a prayer over the grave. Greenywalt put his arm around me. I let him. It felt comforting.

That night I asked him about the boy. "How did he get the name Bod?"

"Ichabod. That's the whole name."

"Ichabod!"

"His mother gave it to him." He said he wanted me to love Bod, which I knew. He doted on the boy. He said the boy was his son, his only son, and he'd promised the ministers to raise the boy till he was grown. He talked about what it would mean for me to love the boy.

Suppose he was our son? Suppose he lived with us? He'd still have his "mother" around, but he'd live with us.

"He'd need a new name," I said.

"Why? Just because you don't like Ichabod?"

"No," I said. "If I was going to bring him in to live with us, as a son, I'd have to feel comfortable. And I could never feel comfortable with Ichabod."

"What would you call him?"

"How about Luke?"

Greenywalt agreed to it, and Lukey came to live with us and slept in the Stube on a floor tick. Greenywalt didn't say how his mother felt about it, and I didn't care. He just said he'd discussed it with her, that he wanted his son to live with him. For a couple weeks we heard the boy cry himself to sleep at nighttime.

So the dog came back, the black terrier the boy called Midnight, and it slept by the boy so he could put out his hand at night, and Midnight would lick it. That's what Lukey told us. I suspect he let the dog lick away his tears. Oooh, *kusslich*. I could never do that. Who knew what that dog was eating?

CHAPTER 21

THE MIRACLE BABE,
1738

YOU LEFT US IN SEPTEMBER OF '26, Vetti, and I'm grateful you had two wonderful summers in the New Land with us. I only wish you could have met Benjamin, and that's the part of the story I'm coming to.

I had every reason in the world to be content that summer of 1741. After we established our store in '34, the store became the Settlement's gathering spot. Every summer morning, three, sometimes four carts tied up to the hitching rail that Greenywalt posted in the loop of the lane between the mill and the house. I planted several fast-growing willows there to shelter the horses in the summer heat.

Mostly it was the housewives, on summer mornings. They came in towing two or three barefoot little *Bopplin* and paraded by my counter on their way to the fabric bolts in the corner. The men came too, depending on the harvest and crop schedules, but usually their business was with the mill. They dropped off the wife in the store and marched through the partition door to the mill office, where Janey sat on a high stool behind a counter like mine and took milling orders, logged them, and ran up the backstairs to alert Christian and Gerhardt, our mill hands.

I give the English woman credit for the vision of a store. Not in the cabin, though, which was her idea. After I got the cabin all fixed the way I wanted, with real glass windows and curtains and planter boxes with geraniums on the window sills, like we had in Switzerland, I didn't want men with muddy boots in springtime or nosy women tramping through my kitchen every day. I told Greenywalt to divide his mill office in two and give me the front half as a store, which he did.

Success, I found, depended on two things: the right source for goods and the right price. I learned as I went along.

At the start, we got everything through Logan. Logan ran his own store on the Susquehanna, thirty miles off at the end of the Conestoga Trail, where his man took in pelts and mainly supplied tools and liquor in trade to the Shawnee. Greenywalt took me to Logan's warehouse on Fishbourne Street in Philadelphia and pushed me to buy everything there. I said, "Just because Logan loaned you whatever to build the mill and bought your pelts all those years [before that business died for lack of skins] don't mean we have to use him for fabrics and dry goods. Not with dozens of shops in Philadelphia to choose between."

Quaker shops, mostly. Our settlers needed everything: brass buttons, mirrors in frames of various woods and metals, knives for all purposes, boxed scissors, needles and pins in small boxes, forks and knives and spoons of pewter, pepper, English tea, and even cinnamon for very dear prices and eyeglasses from Augsperger in Germany. I even found a shop that carried hairpins like the Swisser women love. Greenywalt made himself useful. I could only point at what I liked but he would get bulk prices for me and pretty soon I was running tabs with a dozen shops. Logan never said boo, just like I thought—although Bod probably told him. He was the one making the weekly trips to Logan now on his own and on the way back hauling goods for the store.

The other thing was profit. If I sourced a set of eyeglasses for X, I marked them up 100 percent and sold them for $2X$. If I sourced a copper kettle at X, I could only sell it for X plus 15 percent because the market for kettles was pretty much glutted. I took Pennsilvania currency or mill credits.

On the way out with her fabric, the housewife could pick up staples as well, which I displayed right up front of the counter in open hogsheads—salt, brown sugar from Jamaica, a barrel of molasses (I did keep a lid on that to keep out the flies), and so on.

The store made me pretty happy. It made Greenywalt happy too, because his ventures weren't doing so well anymore. Other mills had gone up, one on the Conestoga and another on the West Pequea. The land agent business got to be more headache than profit. Once the good land was gone, the price per acre tripled. The newcomers these days often arrived nearly broke, needed help getting started, and tended to fall behind on their payments. So the store was becoming a big plus for us.

But I never knew true happiness until our Miracle Babe.

I'd always suspected Greenywalt's "voices." Where in the Holy Book did it say we can still hear God like Abraham and Noah did? With our ears, I mean? Maybe Preacher Herr knew the answer. He said it was a Voice told him to join the fellowship thirty-some years ago in the Kraichgau—I'm talking about Greenywalt. Then the Voice told him to go back to bring the second wave of settlers. He would say, of course, he didn't hear that with his ears, as such. But some Voice inside told him so.

Anyway, he said one evening, "I've heard from the Lord. We're going to have a babe."

"That's ridiculous," I said. "We've already buried three babies." They're up there under the apple, alongside your grave, Vetti, and I was forty and past the bearing age, and if the Lord had wanted us— well, not everyone who wants gets to have children. Think of Michal, King David's wife. If He had wanted us to, I'd given him opportunity in the past, although not lately. Not in a couple years. In other words. I simply didn't enjoy the mechanics of it with my man. So I said or at least let him know in other ways: I'd had enough of that.

Greenywalt could be so persistent that he turned obnoxious, which means he wouldn't stop talking about something, once he believed it.

It wasn't just him and me doing something, he said. We were first to go to the Minister, Christian Herr, and ask for prayer and laying on of hands, with anointing of oil, as the book of James says. I'd seen them do it, lay hands on the ailing part, as long as it was decent. Much as I respected the man, he wasn't going to lay hands on my womb. Even with my husband standing there. Greenywalt insisted, however, that the Voice said we should do it.

I'm embarrassed to say so now, but I did try spells for a while. After the second miscarriage, Frony suggested I go with her to see a Dr. Mylin, a *Wiedertäufer* doctor with the second migration. He practiced medicine, but if you requested, he would also do charms and spells, and when I told my problem, he rubbed my stomach clockwise three times and pronounced a threefold spell in the name of Jesus. Unfortunately, the third baby miscarried.

Could this Voice be any different? One hardly thinks those verses would have made it into the Holy Bible if God hadn't meant them.

So I submitted, as a wife is supposed to, and we drove to Preacher Herr's house. Herr and his wife and Frony and her husband had all gathered in his Stube—it was still light outside. Preacher Herr read the relevant verses:

Is anyone among you sick?
Let them call the elders of the church to pray over them
and anoint the with oil
in the name of the Lord.
And the prayer offered in faith
will make the sick person well. . . .

He also read the next verse:

If they have sinned,
They will be forgiven.

I shot off an emergency prayer right then. I was feeling regrets I'd let a powwow work me over when I hadn't given the Living God a chance to do the same. Secretly, I added, I was sorry I hadn't given him the first go at it.

Preacher Herr asked Did I want such prayer? I said I guessed my presence showed I did. So he asked the women—which I greatly appreciated—to touch my womb, and he did the cross in oil on my forehead and then his wife did the same on my apron front and I have kept the apron with the oil stain in my cedar chest as a token, because the moment she touched me—and I was believing this could work—a warm ball bubbled up in my womb. We hadn't had relations yet, Greenywalt and I, which we did later that night, but I believe that warm ball was the beginnings of Benjamin. Well of course God can do that! Think of the Virgin Mary.

Your eyes saw my substance,
being yet unformed,
and in your book they were all written,
the days fashioned for me.

As the Book says.

Nine months later, to the very day—a very wet and snowy day in March when I'd just seen the first crocus heads through the snow the day before, another sign, I think—I felt terrible pains, lying there in the dark. I was awake uncomfortable in any position with this enormous belly and Greenywalt had gone back to sleep when the pains started coming bang bang bang and I started screaming my head off and he said he'd get Frony and off he went bareback—no time for a saddle—and brought her on the back of his horse and in the nick of time because Benjamin was done waiting.

Of course, we didn't know until right then if it was Benjamin. I'd also picked Trudi, my Mutti's name, in case. But it was Benjamin. When Frony held him up, he had the little frankfurter. It was light already, almost seven o'clock on a Sunday morning, so we all missed church.

Greenywalt took him from Frony, naked and all, and started sobbing. "He kept his promise! He kept his promise!" He wouldn't let Frony wash him up, and he did the swaddling too. He was very tender to me. He brought me a bunch of fresh daffodils, a week after, which he never did before. Or since. He kept kissing my forehead while I was trying to nurse. As I said, he was very tender.

Greenywalt said to Bod—because he brought him by in the afternoon to see the baby—"What do you think of your little brother?"

I'd never thought of it that way, that they were brothers, as they shared a father. I still refuse to think of it that way.

But Bod, he got excited. "My little brother!" He held him nice-like. Greenywalt showed him how to put your hand under the neck so the head wouldn't flop. I had to give some correction, but Bod did okay until he knelt down with the boy in his arms and said, "See, Midnight! My little brother!"

What does Midnight do but lick the baby's mouth for the milk, and I started screaming, and Greenywalt ripped the baby away. What do you expect from a boy who let the dog lick his own mouth?

(This wasn't the original Midnight, of course. Not the one we met the first day but his grandson, I guess you could call him, because once Bod got attached to a name, he kept using it.)

Before many months it was time for "horsey" and swinging up-side down by the heels and balancing in the hand, all the stuff Bod loved as a toddler. But Benjamin didn't want any of it. He would roll his head my direction, and I saw terror in his eyes, and he began to howl and that's how we discovered Benjamin was different.

Bod was a rumpus-raiser. At three, he rode a horse. At four, Greenywalt showed him how to cradle the rifle and yank the trigger and blow up skunk cabbage balls. At six he shot his first buck. After Greenywalt gave him his own rifle when he was eight, he came home almost every evening with a rabbit, a ruffed grouse, a turkey even, and dropped them on our table, still with the feathers.

Benjamin, now, was a scientist. He would sit very still, with his legs crossed, and examine something, whether it was a spider or a salamander or the parts of a daylily. He pulled it apart and stared at it though his magnifying lens. (Greenywalt put a handle on an extra Augsperger spectacle lens.) He wasn't even a week old when I trundled him to the store and lay him in the cradle Frony gave me because she wasn't having any more and I rocked it with my foot, from my counter stool. After a couple months I moved the cradle under the window, where he played with the sunbeams and studied them, and sometimes he'd clap his hands together on a sunbeam and chortle.

But his favorite thing was words. He said a word over and over, like he was tasting it. "Ci.ca.da." "Hol.y Ghost." "Peq.uea Set.tle. ment." He favored words with two or three syllables, and then he discovered, getting bigger, that a word could also be found apart from someone saying it. I mean written on paper—newspaper, for example, or in a book—and if he pointed at the black-ink characters, one of us would say it. Most folks learn to read in a schoolroom, but he learned it that way, pointing at words. Pretty soon, right around his fourth birthday, I would open up our Bible on the table, the big Froschauer you brought from Switzerland, Vetti. He loved the pictures, but he would also pick out "Jesus" and "Virgin" and "betrothed" and "Immanuel," and he would start in Matthew and say the birth-of-Jesus story. At first I thought he'd memorized it, hearing it so often. But he would read parts we hadn't said. I took the Bible to the store, and he lay on the floor, with the Bible spread out in front of him. He said the story out loud over and over, and customers came in and just shook their heads. They couldn't believe a four-year-old—I just wish you'd been there to see him as a wee one, Vetti.

Anyway, it was too good to last. We were just too happy, I guess.

Bod went through big changes. I said I'd never use that name, but I couldn't, all by myself, make the millwheel go clockwise when everyone else made it run counterclockwise. They wouldn't stop calling him Bod. We called him Lukey while he lived with us, which was up till seven, when he just announced one evening he was sleeping at his Mem's from now on, and Greenywalt said "Okay." I protested

Greenywalt caving like that. Well, he did continue suppers with us pretty regular for a couple years and then even that fizzled out. I gave up with "Lukey" and said "Bod" like everyone else.

Greenywalt doted on him, as you see by that story. There was the problem. The boy got to thinking he was pretty special in his Dat's eyes. He let him drive the team from the time he was eight, and after he hit fourteen, he drove to Philadelphia and back by himself. At fourteen! So who did he meet on the trail? English boys from the Presbyterians on the River, on their way to Philadelphia with waggons too. He spoke English, of course, and that was the difference. Our Settlement boys took their waggons to Philadelphia, but they didn't know English, so they didn't mingle.

Greenywalt, meanwhile, spent more time on the land-grant stuff, dealing with problems, and got elected constable so he could go out to the River with Logan's men and evict the squatters, who he said were everywhere, illegals parked on the Indian lands. He also ran the mill and shopped for store supplies. In my opinion, he got scattered. That was why he didn't make money on any of these projects. But to my point, he lost control of the boy.

Bod came one evening in the full regalia. He'd chucked his Mennonist breeches behind a tree on the trail, I guess, which his mother sewed for him—and he sported the waggoneer look, the wilderness look, all animal skins with the hat to go with it. I was also convinced he'd been helping himself to the stuff he was hauling to town for Preacher Herr, which Herr distilled on his plantation and bottled as applejack. Very strong stuff.

I heard him first and then saw him through the mill window pull up outside the mill about six and right behind a couple teams with drivers I didn't recognize. When I say "pull up," I'm candy-coating it. Coming down the trail across the bridge, he was whipping those horses. Full gallop, pulling a loaded waggon, which was murder on the mares. The other waggon ran neck and neck, but only one could fit on the bridge at a time, so it was all about who got to the bridge first., which he won and he rounded the hook in the lane with the wheels skidding sideways and walloped the hitching post.

I was worried about my goods, so I ran out.

"What's with you, driving like that?"

He jumped off in the full waggoneer outfit he'd been wearing several weeks now. I ran around the back of his waggon and lifted the tarp. As I feared, there were the five very pricey glass pitchers from Wistar in Philadelphia, three of them in pieces. I waved a couple big pieces in his face.

"What is wrong with you, anyway?"

He actually turned red, evidence I'd taught him some manners. He had the presence of mind, right then, to introduce the other drivers. More likely, he just wanted to change the subject.

"Griffith. Aengus. They don't speak Deitsch." He used the back of his hand and said something about me, which caused them each to tip his hat and I knew by that they weren't Quaker boys, because Quakers don't tip their hats to anyone.

"They need to keep moving. They can't stay over," I said.

"Awww! It's practically sunset."

"I'm sorry. Your father won't allow it." In fact, I was mad. Bod walked tangle-footed, like he was bowsy. I was upset about my broken pitchers. His father would pay for it, of course, but it meant a week's delay for the Bowmans, who had ordered the pitchers for threshing season.

I ran back into the mill because Benjamin was by himself in there. It was closing time, but I had something for Janey, and she'd already closed the mill side. I went out the front door, leading Benjamin, and around the mill to her door. She was inside, making our supper.

I opened the door and she looked up.

"About ten minutes," she said. As always, she didn't look fullface but bowed her head as she said it.

"Your boy," I said.

"Bod?" She fixed me in the eye now.

"He's up to no good. I know exactly what these boys are doing."

"He's with some boys?"

"English boys," I said. "From Paxtang. They've been drinking. He broke stuff, driving crazy. You straighten him out, Janey, or I will."

For some reason, she decided to lock horns with me this night. "He's not your son. You don't care about him."

"My husband cares about him, and that's good enough for me."

"*Your* husband. If I had *wanted* your husband—"

"Don't," I said. "You know why he's got *two* sons? You seduced him." I felt hot all over suddenly. We had never talked about this before. "And right now, I wouldn't care if you walked out of here and never came back." I grabbed Benjamin's hand, and we stormed out, the door crashing behind me.

She told Bod. As I expected, she didn't pass on the moral lesson he needed to know. He came by the cabin about seven in a catfit.

"How dare you talk to my mother like that?"

"You straighten out and I won't need to."

He cursed and kicked the door.

When I told Greenywalt late at night, he said, "I don't want you talking with him. Let me handle him."

The snake had thrown its first strike and it was coiled up for the second strike.

A few weeks later and 6:00 p.m. again, three horsemen came onto our plantation. Neither Greenywalt nor Bod was home. I called Janey and asked her to go out and meet them. They didn't look like our people.

Through the mill window I saw for sure they were *not* our people. All three wore breeches with canvas leggings with a row of pewter buttons, instead of stockings, and long coats that looked homespun and rough. The rest of their outfits looked military. I hadn't seen regular soldiers since the French dragoons along the Rhine twenty years back. The French dragoons were snappy. These men made no such dashing appearance. Their military gear looked thrown together from castoffs—old muskets stuck into their saddles, homemade wooden canteens on shoulder straps, farmers' hats with a piece of red ribbon and a pine sprig stuck into each, worn knapsacks, and military belts on which hung *War Hatchets.*

I recognized the younger two—the same Griffith and Aengus who'd come through with Bod a few weeks before, dressed as waggoneers then. The older man looked like an officer. He gave some orders. He sat vertical in his saddle and addressed Janey from there. I couldn't hear but assumed it was English. She turned and pointed at the mill, and at me with my face in the window.

I had just enough time to collect Benjamin before the door flew open, and Janey came through with the older man behind.

"He wants to talk with Greenywalt," she said.

"He's in Philadelphia with Logan."

She translated. The officer—I presumed that's what he was, although we didn't have an army in Quaker Pennsilvania, so who was he really?—sized me up and down. A very severe face and no word of greeting.

"I know where your husband is. He's on the Susquehanna, evicting our people."

Aha. One of the Scotch-Irish.

He slapped the countertop with his open hand and said something, which Janey put in Deitsch for me. "God bless this house, Ma'am, if it's a Christian house."

"It certainly is," I said.

"Reverend John Elder, Presbyterian Church of the Presbytery of Donegal." He stuck his hand across the counter, and I let him shake mine. I would remember that name because of the deeds done in his name years later, but right now I looked in unbelief to see someone with the title "Reverend" carrying a war hatchet with a single banded turkey feather and four red beads dangling from the handle. I'd heard how certain tribes used these clubs on their enemies. I was also familiar with "Reverends," as Mutti's husband was one. Among the Mennonists, we regarded all such "steeple-house people," whether English or German like us, as one notch above the heathens.

"I have a message for your husband."

I listened to Janey's translation and nodded.

"You tell him a war with France could break out any day. When it does, our borders are open to attack by savages. They will come right to your little Settlement. We will not stand by and watch them murder our families and tell your husband if he loves you and that little guy, he won't stand by either. We will purge the land of Canaanites!" Then his neck and face turned red as rooster comb.

"You Germans vote with the Quakers every time, and if Cookson is defeated, . . . if Cookson loses in the fall election, we will hold you responsible for not providing a militia to protect our families."

I didn't respond when Janey finished, and maybe that's what cooled him off. He lowered his voice. "Do you understand me?" He seemed to think he'd made his point, as he wheeled around and marched out. He did march. Straight to the horse his men were holding and up over the saddle in one pretty smooth move.

If he thought he'd scared me, he was very much mistaken. It's a coward intimidates or shouts down a woman or someone whose cooperation he's asking for.

However, I recognized this for what it was: the snake from the next neighborhood who'd been attracted here by the snake living right in our own garden.

CHAPTER 22

BUTCHERING DAY, 1742

I SOMETIMES GO BACK to that hog-butchering day and feel some regrets. Not for Ichabod and Janey, mind you. As you know, the Scripture says:

> Hath not the potter power over the clay,
> Of the same lump to make one vessel unto honour
> And another unto dishonor?
> What if God, willing to shew his wrath,
> And to make his power known,
> Endured with much longsuffering
> The vessels of wrath fitted to destruction?

That vessel of wrath was Ichabod.

It's Greenywalt I'm thinking about, because he took their going so hard and never seemed quite the same after, which I do understand when it came to Bod. He thought of him as his son, even though a bastard and having a legal son, besides.

The boy had a froward spirit; I smelled that early on. He took after the father in a lot of ways: Sharpshooter with that rifle he so proudly toted. A waggoneer. One could say he took the model he was given and improved on it. Friend to all men. And children. And animals. Like Greenywalt in all that.

Yet there was another spirit. He was a brawler, which I'll say more about shortly. Remember Samson and his women? That was Ichabod. When he met up with a lass well put together plus a pretty face, he turned into a hound in heat.

Did I know how far he'd gone? No. But when he brought around the Bowman girl, for instance, and that English girl, he always had his hands rubbing their behinds. I didn't need anybody to tell me how things progress from there.

I'll get private about this. Benjamin was three months or so—holding his head up already!—and I trucked him to the store every morning and put him in the cradle by the window. When he cried, I'd go sit on the stool by the window and nurse. So there we were this particular afternoon, me feeding Benjamin, and Bod busted in, just back from a waggon trip, about fifteen at the time. He was fond of the boy; I didn't fault him for that. Benjie was a pretty child, and he's still got that sensitive look.

Anyway, he yelled out, "Benjie!"

The baby jerked his mouth off my breast—he knew the voice—and for a few seconds my gorged breast pumped my milk out onto the floor. I quick cupped it, but the milk flowed on and squeezed between my fingers. Bod stared and then he licked his lips. As if he was drinking it himself.

Benjamin came right back, greedy as always, but I felt a rush of rage.

"Get out!"

His mother showed in the doorway of her side of the office, and I told her as Bod went by her. "He was staring at me." And I showed her what and she just turned away and I'm sure said nothing after to the boy.

I couldn't root it out of my head. All I thought was this—he wanted what belonged to my son. After that, I began to see more and more signs of that until everything came out at the hog butchering.

—〜〜〜〜〜—

The day we butchered the hogs was a frosty morning late November, and we'd had a week of solid freezes, enough to skim a couple inches of ice off the millpond and pack it in sawdust for the butchering.

But I really need to back up. There were other goings-on that led to this day.

That visit by the Preacher Elder and his militiamen, which is what they were, that visit, as we read in Saur's newspaper, was part of much bigger doings, and the finger points the whole way back to James Logan, the not-so-Quaker Quakerman in Philadelphia. Logan was in a pretty bad way, old and crippled up with rheumatism and a nasty heal of a broken leg, Greenywalt said, anxious to retire, but still pushing to make the Assembly build a militia to take on the Indians and French. It was him that started the rumors that a war was coming.

Why should we believe him? Well, If not," Logan said, "the King of England might revoke our Pennsilvania charter, make us a royal colony like Maryland, and then do whatever His Royal Highness wants."

Our side fired back that this was just the Governor conniving for higher taxes and free labor to build forts. That's how Saur put it in his paper.

Anyway, the Anti-Quakers in Philadelphia—and everyone could see Logan was in with this gang—agitated a group of ship captains and their crews on Election Day. I heard there were eighty-some sailors come ashore to the Courthouse with clubs and canes. At the whistle, they laid in with these to intimidate the Quaker vote, which means our people, the Pennsilvania Dutch. They clubbed down three or four Quaker shopkeepers.

It turns out, however, that us Pennsilvania Dutch outnumbered the sailors that day at the polls 400-some to 80. Our people are mostly nonresistants, but a group including Bod—maybe led by Bod, if you believe him—got access to laths and billies in the Courthouse, and they drove the sailors back to their ships. That's how we won the Election of 1742.

We get Saur's *Bericht* biweekly, of course. But this time we had Bod coming back from his market trip, before the paper was even published, to tell the news in person. I should probably say, to show us in person.

I was serving up breakfast when we heard Jehu arrive—the usual racket and pandemonium from the horse barn! He busted in and landed against the doorframe, with bloodstains all up and down his overshirt, an enormous lip and black and purple eye. He'd flogged his team and come the whole way, sixty miles, since dinnertime noon the day before, driving the whole night by the full moon and very proud of himself as he says, "We showed them what the Dutch can do."

"What's going on, Son?" Greenywalt says.

"They were jawing us with 'Broadbrims and Dutch Dogs Go to Hell!' and we dinged their arses into the River. Then we fished them out and drug them off to jail," he says.

"Whatever happened?" Greenywalt touched his own lip. "Looks like it wasn't just the Dutch that showed what they can do."

"Ha!" he says. "A cobblestone. Those marines were digging up cobbles and lobbing them through the Courthouse windows. Then they went after us, and this chap twitted me."

He showed us where his dogtooth was missing.

"I drubbed him good and put him into the river. I could have trimmed his wick for good, if Pemberton hadn't stopped me."

Bod's aspect and language confounded us both, but Greenywalt said nothing to disapprove or approve, which was part of his pattern with the boy that I just couldn't conscience. I said so, too, about a week later at bedtime, when I had opportunity to say how I saw things.

"This puts you in a bad light with Logan," I said.

"How so?"

"You're Logan's land agent and his constable. He's working to elect legislators to help him pass a militia act. Your son is in Philadelphia on the other side in these riots. You think he don't know about Bod? My advice to you—stay out of this mess entirely."

Greenywalt mulled that a bit. "We've got a friendship," he said, "that goes deeper than how we vote."

"You're sure about that?"

There it was again. His nature was to trust and trust and trust, and then someone took advantage. I could give many examples. If I just say Janey Cameron's name, however, it should suffice. I'm of the belief that we live in a world of charlatans, scoundrels, and pickpockets, and until a man I'm dealing with proves he's otherwise, my purse is snuggled right tight in my armpit.

I also trotted out Bod's line to Greenywalt: "We showed them what us Dutch can do." Was Bod Dutch? I asked Greenywalt. No. He inherited his mother's language and temper and that's why he chummed with the English waggoners. He was a brawler. A brawler like Samson, hiring himself out for the fights. Today it was the Dutch, ooo yes, and tomorrow the Scotch militias? I said. I had no idea then how prophetic that was going to be.

I was only getting started with Greenywalt. I'd been thinking things over, starting with the breast milk, then the militia visit, and now the election brawl.

"I want him out," I said. "It's time for both of them to go. Go to their people. I'm tired of them here."

Greenywalt seemed genuinely shocked, as if he hadn't realized a time like this would come. This was equally amazing to me. I'd known this was coming for years.

"You're asking me to throw out my son?"

"You kept your promise. You raised him. He turned twenty-two in August, right?"

"He's my waggoneer. He's my right hand," he said.

"You'll have no difficulty finding another one."

"No! No, Maudlin!"

"It's them or us," I said. "Me and Benjamin. Bod wants the mill too. He wants to take what belongs to Benjamin—." How did I know this about the mill? I heard him say it himself to his chums, that's what. How Greenywalt promised he'd run the mill someday. Was that a fact? Well, I never heard Greenywalt say it, but if the boy said he did—

Greenywalt rarely got mad. When he did, his neck turned beet-red. It was beet-red now.

"What about his mother? This is her home! The only home she knows in America. I have an obligation."

Obligation? Well, everyone in Pequea neuters their little pigs, and I decided to neuter this obligation animal. "You provided passage, and she worked out her five years. You took her into your bed in a jiffy of passion. She produced a boy that you vowed the ministers you would raise to manhood, and you did. She's not happy. She spends her off-time moping and reading English history books and stories that Logan gives her. Your obligation is done. Let her go to her people."

"You're a hard woman, Maudlin." He threw on his hat and went for the door, as I knew he would.

"And you're a soft man, Klaus."

He could slam the door on me all he wanted.

—◆◆◆◆◆◆—

Hog butchering turned into a family affair on the Pequea, just as it was in the Kraichgau, Vetti. The Herrs and Greenywalts banded together for two days: the original pioneers, their children now married, plus their grandchildren, in the case of both Christian and Hans Herr. Anna—that was Mrs. Christian—and Elizabeth, Hans Herr's John's wife, ran the kitchen during this two-day outing, and the children ran back and forth with food platters to the long tables and benches we set up in our orchard under the Early Girls, which were leafless and finished by now. In fact, depending on the weather, the women and children might eat inside, but we were having a clear and cold day, since it was end of November, so we just bundled up.

Anna raised ducks, the white Muscovies. You could always count on Anna to put together a roast duck and dried-corn pudding meal with pickled everything: cantaloupes, beets, red eggs, sweet gherkins, and sometimes head cheese. Elizabeth baked fruit pies in our outdoor oven, and Old Christian supplied all the cider, including the hard stuff, if you liked it that way, but not all the way to alcohol.

Old Christian was sixty-seven by now. He hardly ever preached anymore, only at Communion, in fact. He also didn't butcher anymore but sat on the porch swing of the stone addition we added to the cabin a couple years back and kept up a steady chatter. He'd always been a talker, as you know. Mostly about the elections and the temperaments of the men running and conversations he'd had with some of them and how Revelations predicted what we were seeing these days.

His daughter Anna was a Mylin, married to the gunsmith, and they were the ones who built the palace, so-called. Three stories of chiseled limestones, at least twelve rooms inside, a veranda and *two* porch swings out front, plus a cellar under the whole house. The ministers conferenced an entire day with Mylin and his dad the pioneer, in his old log cabin, and talked about disciplining them. "The English grumble how rich the Mennonists have become," the ministers said, "yet we won't pay for a militia, and your palace puts a bull's-eye on our backs for the English neighbors and the covetous French." But in the end, they let him go on living in it.

Anna Mylin was working with the grinder, taking the pork pieces Veronica Brechbühl minced. They'd been chilled so they numbed your fingers, and you needed to soak your hands in warm water every fifteen minutes or so. Then she mixed in the spices I'd laid out: salt, sugar, black pepper, nutmeg, parsley (we had to use it dried because the frost killed the bush), vinegar, and fennel seeds.

Veronica Brechbühl. I'll say a little something about her because you knew Preacher Brechbühl so well, her father-in-law. Veronica was Hans and Frony's oldest, now forty-something, I'd guess, and I just felt so for Veronica, wearing a widow's weeds with seven children, although two in Heaven, and her oldest surviving only fourteen. It was so bitter for everyone when Ulrich—one of our best preachers, too—fell off his waggon on the way to market, coming up the bank out of the Brandywine. The wheel and loaded waggon on its way to market ran over his head and rolled it out flat like a pie crust—they did a closed coffin. But the Herrs looked out for her and now that her

John was fourteen and could do a man's work, I was pretty sure she'd make it.

Finally there was us, with Bod and Janey and Benjamin and myself and Greenywalt and one of the mill hands helping. I'd put it at twenty grown-ups, not counting the little ones.

The Herr families rounded up their pigs in the woods, where they'd been fattening on acorns all fall, and carted them over Saturday a week beforehand. The porkers squealed their heads off. You had to wonder if they knew what was coming. Hans and Frony's John had been killing since the day before—a bullet between the eyes and then he beheaded the hog and worked with Bod and Martin Mylin to drag the carcass around to the front of the barn. They winched it up, hind legs first, with a washtub below to collect the blood, and Bod and Mylin took turns pulling off the hide with a skinning knife. Then they went at it with an axe to carve the carcass in two. It's hard work. You know that. Even at these temperatures, the men were down to their undershirts, with the sleeves rolled above the elbows and toweling constantly.

It was a regular factory we'd rigged up on the ground between the horse stables and the cellar of the new stone addition. Every family contributed a table, and Greenywalt put together the work flow. He was good at stuff like that, but I ran the sausage making.

After the slaughter, Greenywalt and Hans Herr did the second step. They dropped the hog halves onto a cutting table, and then went at them with short axes to hack off shoulders, hams, ribs for ground, and sides of bacon. The hams and bacons they dropped into tubs with lots of salt below and above, and our mill hand Gerhardt dollied the loaded tubs to our cellar for the six-week curing. Or he packed them fresh into barrels for the families to take home and do their own curing. The cutters also sliced off the cheeks and ears and trotters for headcheese. Or they diced them, along with the hearts and livers, and us women made a broth of these scraps and mixed in cornmeal to make Pannhaas, which is the last word in winter breakfasts. As the saying goes, "We use everything but the squeal!"

The guts went into a tub for Janey, who made them into sausage casings, an art all of its own that she became an expert in, after I showed her how. She had produced a full tub of casings from yesterday's butchering, which she brined and chilled and now was rewarming for sausage-making.

From the cutting table to the grinding table, which (as I said) Anna Mylin and Veronica ran, using the recipe I'd taught them.

Finally the sausage table, where Frony Herr and I—and we were such good chums for almost twenty years now—were ready to start with the sausage making when dinner was done.

Dinner was a cheerful time. All morning the topic was the news, the election riots, and what nonresistants like us should do. At dinner, we just laughed a bushel.

I was the champion for making sausages, they said of me. Well, all it takes is balance. You need a good mix of fat and meat, and I like 25 to 30 percent fat, and then the spices. That was all set up at Veronica and Anna Mylin's table, and they were processing down the pork shoulders through the grinder I'd picked up at Kaspar Wistar's in Philadelphia.

I slid a casing onto the funnel, and as Frony cranked, the little round casings plumped up and starting looking like sausages, stretching and stretching the length of the table and beyond, some of them ten feet long. Every family would have one to griddle for supper tonight.

The children played hidey-go-seek and red rover under the apples and I kind of had my eye on Benjamin to be sure he was having fun because sometimes he didn't. Old Christian, up on our porch swing, hailed him as he came out of the house: "Benjamin!"

The little ones were terrified by Old Christian's bullfrog voice and the glazed blue eye he fixed on them, but Benjamin always liked talking with grown-ups more than he did his mates.

Christian had a book, the new *Ausbund* Saur had just printed at the request of the Pequea ministers. It was such a blessing that every family could have one now. It carried all the old martyr songs, some by Felix Manz and Michael Sattler, plus the "True Account" of the Swiss *Wiedertäufer* in the generation before yours, Vetti. It made a body's blood run cold to hear how they suffered, and then when you thought about what we got here in Pequea . . . The children needed to know about this. So Old Christian handed the book to Benjamin, who loved books, although he wouldn't be six until the spring, and he said: "Benjamin, I hear you read the Bible. Can you read this?"

Benjamin took the book with both hands and put his finger at the spot Old Christian had indicated. The children immediately stopped hidey-go-seek and bunched around. Everyone had heard how he'd been reading since he was three. How much of that is true? I guess they were thinking.

Benjamin read off the title: "A True Account of the Brothers in Switzerland," and the children looked back and forth and murmured, and then back at Brother Herr to see what he thought.

"In the Zoo—"

"Zurich," Preacher Herr said.

"Zurich district, about the trib—"

"Tribulation."

"Tribulation. Trib.Yu.Lay.Shun." Benjamin sort of tasted this word, as he likes to do even today. "Tribulations." He repeated it to himself. "—tribulation which they underwent for the sake of the Gospel from 1635 to 1645."

Preacher Herr *mutcha'd* Benjamin's hair with his old claw, and Benjamin looked happy with himself. He so liked when others saw his talents.

"Keep going," Brother Herr said.

"They continued and laid their hands also upon four pious sisters, among them Barbara Mylin—"

At the name Mylin, the children erupted. They shook Little Ann and Elizabeth Mylin, Anna and Martin's girls, and got so excited. "That's you! That's you!" It was cute to see. The grown-ups, of course, looked at Anna Mylin because Martin was off behind the horse stables, out of sight.

"That's right!" Old Christian said. "She was your great-great-great—I'd have to write it out on a piece of paper; I think at least five greats—grandmother. Go on, Benjamin."

"Who also had to drink the bitter cup of the Zurich prison; however, the Lord preserved them."

"You see how valuable this is, Children." Preacher Herr took the songbook from Benjamin and cuddled it tenderly. "It tells of our ancestors, who were faithful to the Lord in terrible times. Terrible times are coming again, Children. Has any of you read the book of Revelation? Do you know about the Dragon? The Beast? The Harlot of Babylon? Any of you?"

Benjamin took the book back and went on reading aloud because that's how he is. Once he started, he wouldn't stop until he knew how it was going to turn out. "These thief-catchers, that night, threa—"

"Threatened."

One of the bigger ones over his shoulder was helping him, too.

"Threatened her little children, with bare swords, that they would kill them, if they did not show them where their father was hid."

The other children soon lost interest and drifted back to their game. Preacher Herr complimented our boy and told Benjamin he could keep the book a while. Benjamin never needed a second invitation to do. He ran off to a bench under the apple and went on reading out loud. When he came to a word he didn't know, he just mumbled through, I guess.

The grown-ups went back to their pig work, except Bod, who finally took a break from splitting carcasses. I saw him come out of the horse barn, stripped to his breeches and chemise with the sleeves rolled up past the muscle and the chemise front pretty smeared with blood. I saw he was carrying, of all things, a pig's head, balanced between his palms, which were gripping the ears, looked like. I didn't stop streaming sausage, but I kept an eye out because I suspected something cuckoo. He just couldn't be decent and helpful for an entire day. He lugged the head to a stump in the area of the tables, a couple yards from Benjamin, and propped it on the stump. The children saw, of course, and stopped their game and gathered round and gaped, but it was Benjamin first said something.

"It's grinning." He pointed with his finger.

The children all chimed in. "Yeah! Yeah! It's grinning."

"You know why it's grinning?" Bod said. "It's happy! It's happy it'll be a tasty sausage in your belly tonight."

The children shrieked because Bod can be so funny and charming, especially with children. Then again, so was the Pied Piper of Hamlin, if you remember that story and how that turned out.

"Is it alive?" one of the little ones asked.

"Can it close its eyes?"

"Of course not," Bod said.

Next I saw, Bod leaned down and dipped his fingers in the blood from the bullet hole on the pig's forehead. He painted two red stripes down his forehead across his cheeks to his throat. He hoisted a butcher knife and did the Wah Wah Wah Wah Wah—the war whoop—with one hand clapping his mouth and Benjamin clutched under his elbow against his chest, turning in a circle. He was chanting:

We'll show them we can fight!
They're coming for our mill, Benjie!
Coming for *die Memmies*, Benjie!
Coming Coming Coming!
Shall we stop them?
Yeah!

The second time around, he had all the children chorusing with him.

Everyone at hog butchering had just stopped, and we watched Bod and Benjie dance around the pig's head. Then Bod took the butcher knife and plunged it down through the poor porker's head, up to the hilt.

"There! Don't mess with the Dutch!"

"Don't mess with the Dutch!" the children echoed, and they followed him, lifting their legs, dancing around the head: "Don't mess with the Dutch!"

Greenywalt interrupted, in his usual humdrum way: "That's enough, Bod, you're scaring the children."

From the porch swing, Preacher Herr: "Don't give them the message to fight. We want to give them the message from the book." He pointed at the *Ausbund*, which Benjamin had dropped on the picnic table. As for myself, the whole goings-on disgusted me. I knew I'd be hearing from all of our friends, before the day was out, how outrageous they found it.

"Who said it's going to be your mill, Bod?" I said.

Bod stopped his dance. He eyeballed me like he was a cornered groundhog. "Dat," he said.

"You'll never own a bit of it," I said.

"Why not?" Bod released Benjamin and came tramping right at me. "Here!" He stabbed the butcher knife into the table right at my fingertips, where it vibrated back and forth upright.

"Why would he give it to you?" I said. "It's for his legal son. For Benjamin, that's why."

Bod cursed—I won't repeat the vile things out of his mouth—and took off running down the lane and disappeared around the corner of the mill.

Everyone at the butchering had witnessed it. A half hour before, we were a peaceful village, doing our annual butchering. Then we saw a vision, if you will, of the bloody future. It frightened me. I practically ran to Benjamin, who was crying, and I pulled him onto my lap.

"Bod ran away," he said.

"Yes." I took his hand and walked with him back to the porch to return the *Ausbund* to Preacher Herr. "Sit here by me." I moved a stool next to the sausage table. I was hardly seated when Janey called across the cutting table from the ice buckets, where she'd been working with the casings.

"I heard what you said."

She was addressing me, I figured. "What's your problem?" I said.

"Greenywalt's legal son? What does that mean? The mill belongs to his legal son? Why would you bring that up—for the first time ever?"

I felt righteous indignation rear up and so what if our friends heard? This needed to be cleared up immediately.

"My husband built this mill and this house. This belongs to Greenywalt and our family. You have no right, you and your son, to ask for a piece because of some event twenty years ago. Which I won't mention.

"You worked here"—I stood up and moved around the grinder's bench so I could address her greedy face, twenty feet off—"To pay off your passage money to America. And he still pays you every two weeks, and I know what he pays, and it's twice what anyone else gets for doing that work. You are entitled to nothing more. Nothing.

"Your boy brings the war spirit into our community, and we don't want it. He brought the English boys. And the militiamen. Nobody thinks he belongs here. Nobody. Go join those people at the River. The ones who have the war spirit."

Janey was just an ice sculpture, hearing this, looking me square on for once. And nobody else said anything, and pretty soon she swiped her tears, left and right, and that stabbed me deep in the womb, like a labor pain.

"Don't stand and bawl. We don't want you here."

Old Christian, over on the porch, got up out of the swing. He needed to keep the peace, no doubt. "Now, now. These are very harsh words. Brother Greenywalt, say something."

Greenywalt was on my left about equidistant from Janey, and we made a sort of triangle. He'd been frozen, listening, but now he threw up his hands. "The boy was entertaining us, Maudlin. You make an awful big fuss over nothing."

I, however, saw an opportunity to bring the whole unfortunate affair to a conclusion and shut the door on past mistakes and people once for all. If Preacher Herr spoke, Pequea people knew that's how things would be—the nearest thing in our day to one of the prophets. I'd just tell everyone what I heard him say.

"Brother Herr, you said yourself the other Sunday: 'There's a spirit coming in that we don't want in our community.' He brings it!" I waved down the lane toward the mill. "You said it yourself, am I right?"

Herr lanced me with that glazed blue eye as if I was a mad dog he hoped to stare down. After bit he said, "This is enough. Let's all get back to work."

I knew a dodge when I ran into one, and this was a ruse, a gambit, a ploy.

"You also said she's never really fit in. Am I right? At the meeting with Greenywalt and me my first summer. On a Sunday afternoon in your house. Your wife was serving peach pie with milk, and we were sitting around your table, and you said—"

"Maudlin. I've said things I regret, and I don't remember that statement, but—"

Janey dropped the tub of casings, and I got a look at her face. She had gotten the message, as I had intended she would. She turned white. She gathered her skirts and tumbled down the path her son had taken, toward the mill. I could have told her he was no longer there because I'd seen him saddle up Casper a few minutes before and leave.

That's how I got rid of them, Vetti. All I can say is this: life has been very peaceful since.

Part 5

JANEY'S FLIGHT

CHAPTER 23

FROM THE PEQUEA,
DECEMBER 1742

I RAGED AGAINST THE INJUSTICE in the world, and I damned her and her offspring:

> Happy the one who repays you
> as you have served us!
> Happy the one who takes and dashes
> your little ones against the rock!

Is that too heartless? She cursed me! My "war-mongering son," she said. I will curse her. I assaulted the pillow, and my tears fell unstoppable.

> My tears have been my food
> Day and night,
> While they continually say to me:
> Where is your God?'

Yes, the curses of the psalms belonged to me.

The daylight faded on the greased paper covering the ground-floor windows of the mill, and I was frantic for an answer. What next? Where to from here? Clearly I couldn't stay. I needed to go.

I scrabbled enough strength to go vertical off the cot. I threw another log onto the hearth fire.

"I must pack now. We must go now," I talked to myself. I went down on my knees to grope beneath the cot for the gunny sacks stored there. The old trunk I brought from Lurgan sat by the head of the cot, on my side of the red wool blanket I'd bought to block off Bod's cot, but no, the trunk was out of the question. I couldn't take that.

We would run off on foot, and a gunnysack each would need to suffice for—two days, maybe? To the River. Yes, we would go to the River.

I ripped winter clothes from the trunk and stuffed them down the mouth of the sack—aprons, dresses, blouses. Through the tears, each piece looked like the one before. Blurry. Dark-blue and without ornament. My Mennonist clothes.

We would need food. At least two days' supply to get to the River settlements, and what after that? How long until we found a landing place? A place where someone would open the door and say, "Come in!" I couldn't possibly know exactly, but two pound six in Pennsilvania currency should surely tide us over until we landed wherever we would land. So what?

I pushed the iron arm with the cauldron dangled on its end over the hearth fire and dropped a dozen potatoes with their skins into the already-steaming pot of water.

Bod. Where was he? To the doorframe, and peering out I saw it coming down heavy now, thick flakes that nearly whited out the horse barn only a hundred feet off. The first snowfall of the season on such a night! Would it make our flight more perilous? Or protect us from any who pursued?

I had no qualms about Bod's safety in it. The boy was wise about the forest, summer or winter, and fearless too. He had his gun and his quick wits.

No, it was the decision that troubled me. He hadn't heard me say it. He'd never heard me agree to his dream, which he put like this: "Mama! They're our people on the River, you always said. Scots-Irish, like you. They speak English, like you and me. Their houses are little. Cabins, mostly. No big barns or stone homes like the Settlement. Just log houses because it's the frontier, Mama! They have the pioneer spirit, and the deer roam and the bear abound there like you said it was when you first came here.

"They protect their families with their muskets, and they don't say: '*Rather than take up arms to defend our king and our wives and babes, we will suffer all that is dear to be torn from us,*' as the Settlement preachers say.

"And I'm ready for a wife, Mama. Not a woman that jabbers Deitsch and looks down on you because you're not German blood and your ancestors didn't rot in a Swiss prison. One that loves you, like I do. On the River, Mama! A man can be free on the River!"

"It's wilderness," I said, "a howling wilderness."

"Listen to you. what did folks say in Ireland, before you came? 'The wilderness. You'll die in the wilderness.'"

I couldn't refute him, but I couldn't agree either. He was only twenty. He didn't know yet how it always gaps between the dream and the reality. But I didn't want to argue anymore. It was different after the events today. "You are right, Bod. We have to go."

I closed the door on the falling snow and returned to the pots, over the leaping flames in the mill room losing light. I took our entire cache of sausages out of the barrel where they lay pickling—a month's worth of suppers—and threw them onto two glowing griddles. Immediately they crackled to life.

Bear was on alert before the hearth and pointing the sausages, one black foot lifted in anticipation. Bod would say: Take her, and she'll be our sentinel when we sleep on the forest floor. But no, he was Greenywalt's dog, and I swore it again: not one thing with his name on it, living or dead, goes missing when we go.

What else to do while I waited for Bod to make his way home through the mounting snow?

Would he be surprised by my change of mind? He would be astonished.

For eighteen years, since Greenywalt closed the indenture with his signature—for eighteen years I'd squirreled away that document with the other that held my father's signature, the one he'd signed in the Dublin tavern to get us berth on the transatlantic *Polly Walker.* Every one of those years I could have walked out of this Settlement a free woman, and I hadn't taken it.

Even James Logan couldn't persuade me. I was only thirty, twelve years back, and still in my flower. None of the iron-grey strands I've got now. My figure girlish again. Bod was eight already then.

I was at Stenton, Logan's mansion in Germantown, filing the quitrents for a dozen settlers that Greenywalt handled. His clerk and I were working through the numbers in the office when Logan himself arrived by carriage from the city, hobbled in with the mending leg, and seemed genuinely excited to see me:

"Janey, it's a pleasure! It's a pleasure! You need more books? I've got the new Whiston translation from the Latin of Josephus's *Antiquities of the Jews* and *The Jewish Wars* for you. Absolutely necessary for a serious student of the Bible like yourself. I'll lend one or the other to you but not both. Only one for now. Is the Mister here? No? Excellent! Listen, I have someone for you to meet. Carlyle!"

He gestured for someone beyond the doorway, and the man, who must have been waiting there, stepped out, a beardless and somewhat roly-poly Quaker, dressed as I'd come to expect of the Quakers, in grays with the round hat and waistcoat buttoned the whole way down over the broad expanse of his paunch, and perhaps seven or eight years beyond me.

"Carlyle, this is she I spoke so highly of, Janey Cameron." Then, veering back to me, he said: "Janey, Master Carlyle here owns Carlyle's Fine Glass House on Mulberry, by our Meetinghouse. He imports fine china from Bristol for Quaker madams here, but he's Irish. From Lurgan Towne, like us."

Carlyle extended a pudgy hand, without any bowing or kissing of mine, which is a trait I've always admired in the Quaker.

"And he's a widower. Dear Hannah didn't recover from the voyage. Carlyle, she was too good for this immoral earth. It is such a sadness for Thee. And three beautiful bairns, Janey." It was the first I'd heard Logan use the Quaker plain speech, and it startled me as he was a rather worldly Quaker.

In that trip and my next to Philadelphia, Carlyle made his interests very clear. He wanted a wife. He invited me to dinner at his home on Mulberry Street, a two-story brick edifice with his shop on the first floor and his dwelling above. It was a building that proclaimed him as a man of some means, and he introduced me to the three bairns as Miss Cameron, "Daddy's friend." That afternoon I lamented I didn't have a wardrobe with clothes fit for a woman dining at such a house, only my Mennonist Sunday clothes—dark blue and without trim, as I've said—but he didn't seem to mind and seated me crosswise from him at the dining table. The servant Negress, wearing the plain Quaker cap and dress, brought in a pewter platter with a shank of lamb and the bone sticking out of it. Carlyle placed his hand over mine and thanked me again for joining them for dinner. I saw the oldest child look at his hand on mine, and then his eyes met my eyes, so I wondered what their father had said of me, and I pulled my hand away.

He led me to his parlor after dinner, and we sat down at a tea table, facing each other on fine English upholstered chairs. Carlyle Thee'd and Thou'd me like a regular Quaker. He repeated what he'd heard from Logan about my love for books and the Scriptures, then spoke of his children—eight, five and three—and his plans for them and their education. After an hour, I said I needed to get back to the warehouse as Greenywalt would be finished with his business. "I've only asked the afternoon off, and he'll be impatient to return to the Settlement," I said.

We stood and he stepped around the table and took my hand very tenderly between his two plump ones and asked if he might court me: "Might I dare to dream that one day Thou mightest consider me as Thy helpmeet in this mortal life?"

I regretted that I'd let it go this far, that I'd deluded myself that I could just have a friendship with a man. I didn't need to ask for more time to consider. I said "No" and thanked him. My own son out in the Settlement, I said, had a father he loved dearly, and I could never part him from that father. I thought I heard him weeping behind the door as I descended the stairway.

I could have walked out of the Settlement to live the life of a society woman in Philadelphia, but what about my son, who needed a father?

Greenywalt's love for the boy was the talk of the Settlement and the traders. He taught him the ways of the long rifle and then gifted him one of Mylin's carefully crafted ones on his eighth birthday. They rode, each on a mount, through the mountains north of the Settlement, "Like I did with my own dad," Greenywalt would say. They drove the transport waggon together to Philadelphia, and he introduced him to Logan, the man who would be Governor, as "my son Ichabod."

Daffodil shoots we see every March blossom in the sunshine just like that boy did. He copied Greenywalt. If Greenywalt slapped the backs of his German mill customers and the backs of the English traders in Philadelphia, Bod slapped their backs. He bossed the mill hands like his father did.

"Listen to your father," I would tell Bod. "Learn from him."

I waited all day so I could ask him every night in the dark, "What did you learn today?" I'd pulled open the curtain between us, suspended on its rings from a wire, so we could speak unhindered in the darkness. He would tell me, and it was always "Dat said this" and "Dat did that."

He shook off our troubles with Maudlin like Caspar shook off horseflies. They didn't trouble the bond between the two, even after Benjamin arrived, when he was fifteen.

It was waggoneering that changed everything. He started chumming with the Scots-Irish waggoneers from Donegal. They talked up their primitive frontier life to him, so unlike our quiet life in the Settlement. It sounded to him like freedom compared to the orderly and rigid schedule of the Swissers. Practically overnight he turned critical of the man whose name he carried. "Why'd you say that, Dat? To my Mama?" The first he suggested leaving the Settlement was eighteen months back, and then it became a daily plea to me, but I resisted. Nineteen- and twenty-one year-olds need fathers as much as eight- and ten-year-olds. Didn't I know? I once was one.

The sausages were spitting now, and the aroma of heated nutmeg and fennel perfumed the room something wonderful. It was fully dark, except for the dancing flames in the hearth. I dumped the boiling water off the soft potatoes and wrapped them, one by one, in cast-off pages of Saur's newspaper and snuggled them into the gunny sack. With my back turned to the door and the kettle whistling, I didn't hear him come in. It was the light flash on the wall from his lanthorn that alerted me. Bear traversed the room, snarling, and just as quickly turned to excited yips. But the growls had alerted me it wasn't Bod.

"Where's Bod?" It was Greenywalt himself. "Can I come in?"

He never asked that. For twenty years, as part of his covenant with the elders, I supposed, he only came in if I invited. Tonight he had already stepped in and then asked, stamping the snow off his boots and swatting the stuff from his beard and shoulders with his hat. Bear bounded up and down against his legs.

What to do with my sack? He hadn't seen it yet on the bed, in the deep shadows at the back of the room. I dropped it behind me on the floor and used my foot to push it under the far end of the table.

"Smells good," he said. "Some of that Herr piggy?" He laughed his big laugh, throwing back his chin. "Where's Bod?"

"He not back with Caspar yet. I don't know where he went this afternoon."

Greenywalt, upright and still swiping off snow, situated the lanthorn on the floor between himself and myself, now seated by the fireplace. The lanthorn created goblins whose spectral fingers clawed the wall and ceiling between us.

"He's upset. I'm not here to excuse it," he said. "There is no excuse for what happened today."

Right then the memory of the fateful December snowstorm suddenly overran me . It did what it did every time: it flooded me, and my entire body remembered:

Snow falls heavily. The world beyond the mill goes white, and the familiar landmarks vanish. A man stands in the room and throws off his snow-soaked clothes, peels down to his smock without embarrassment, as if no one else were present. Frenetically thrusts his hands over the flames, and vapor curls out of the warming wool of the wet leggings. His back is to me, and that's me approaching, pity in my heart because I know the sorrow that the letter from Germany has produced. My hands fall on his muscular shoulders and rest there, and his hands come up and seize them. He wheels and pins my body against his, his cold cheeks between my virgin breasts, glowing from the bath, or was it animal heat burning in me?

> Like two fawns, the twin fawns of a gazelle
> That browse among the lilies.

In the moment my whole body relived the climax of my error. He sowed his seed into my womb, the egg that hatches expectant, once a month, and it received and embraced the seed and Ichabod was conceived.

This was a grievous sin against the Lord's commandment, and I have cried out to him these many years: Purge the memory of it out of me! Cauterize the brain tissue! Drain away any pleasure in the picture I have of it! But time and again the memory spontaneously budded, bloomed, and bore its fleshy fruit.

Now Greenywalt stood beyond the lanthorn, and the gamboling shadow of its fire distorted his chin and nose and shadowed his eyes.

"You've been crying. I'm sorry it happened, Janey. That she said, 'We don't want you.' I want you. Both of you. You and Bod."

How could he do this? Come in like this, after his wife's hateful tirade today, butchering day, in his orchard? Did he condemn her tirade today? No, he mumbled about it. I knew exactly why he'd come. He knew I was going to leave. He sensed it. It was all about business. His land business. All those outstanding mortgages and quitrents and patents recorded in my very careful and legible longhand in leather-covered journals, and I was the only one who knew precisely where every settler's debt stood in the abracadabra of due dates and percentages and shortfalls.

I felt no pity for him this time. He looked old to me today. There was white hair at the temples and white patches in his beard. He limped because of the fall off the waterwheel. The Penn brothers hounded him for back rents. The Scots-Irish on the River thumbed their noses as they erected their squatter cabins on land he represented. That was it. Old and useless, that's what he was.

"You can't go, Janey."

There. He'd said it now.

"He's been speaking to me, Janey. Deuteronomy 21, verses 15–17. The right of the firstborn. That right belongs forever to the firstborn, to Ichabod."

"What are you saying?"

"It won't be everything. Probably not even half. But he will get his share. So will you. I promise. The Lord is my witness." He lifted his open hand, like a juror standing before the judge.

"It's too late for such promises," I said, getting up to face him, to cut him off. I would not consider what he was saying. "She's right. We have to go. She won't permit us to stay. She wants everything for Benjamin because he's the offspring of the two of you. I won't fight it. I'm sick of fighting her."

"It's not too late."

"She's turned the whole Settlement against me. Even Preacher Herr. You heard him today. 'My son has a war-mongering spirit.'"

"It's a phase the boy is going through."

"We'll just go."

He froze in the lamplight. Bear had settled at his feet; with out-stretched head and tongue, she licked the melted snow water. Greeny-walt did something strange. He dropped to his knees and clasped his hands over his chest like a child saying bedtime prayers. It caught me off guard.

"Don't go, Janey! He's my son. He'll always be my son. Do you want to kill me, Janey?"

I couldn't believe I had almost relented. I couldn't believe the selfishness of his plea. I was Vesuvius: the rage in me was bitumen, tar, and sulfur that was going to boil over and incinerate him, and I didn't care.

"He's my son too! He wants to go. Will he ever find a wife here in the Settlement? No. The prejudice is everywhere. Does he own any-thing here? Nothing. Even if you say so, can you guarantee he'll still have it tomorrow? She wants everything for Benjamin, you know. The war-mongering spirit? He learned guns and the pioneer spirit from you, Greenywalt. And you'll find someone else to keep your books."

His head shook side to side. I saw a tear travel down into his scrawny beard.

"Janey! This is your home. You have no other home in the New World. They know you in Philadelphia, but it's not your home, is it?" He paused. "Or were you thinking of the people on the River?" But he rescued me from needing to answer or betray my thoughts by saying again, "Janey, Bod will get his share."

"Save his share. Give it to him in your will. When you die."

He got up off his knees. He had given up. His hands lifted, splayed open toward me. I'd convinced him I was leaving. He believed it at last, and there was nothing he could say that would stop me. I was not his indentured servant. I owed him nothing. I owed nothing to the Settlement and its ministers either. He came through the lanthorn shadows, his hand extended.

"I'll do what's right by him and you, Janey Cameron. Where are you going? I'll drive you there with my team." He took my limp hand between his two and shook it.

I didn't respond.

"As soon as it melts. Do you have a place picked out? Someone who will put you up for a couple nights? You're not going to the Irish on the River. Right?"

It was my turn to sink down. My head was underwater. I could sense my thoughts sliding toward chaos, and I slumped into the chair by the hearth.

"I don't know. I don't know where we'll go." Nor would I tell him if I knew. Bear licked the sausage grease on my hand, and her warm tongue brought me back to where I was and who I was talking to. "Someplace they treat me like a sister."

"You'll need cash to get started. It's expensive in the City. Bod can get any number of jobs. Logan will hire him in a jiffy. I'll set up a meeting with Logan."

He stood an arm's length off, and the lanthorn rays lit up both our faces, as long as our faces were toward it. When he turned back toward me, with the lanthorn backlighting him, his eyes and mouth were dark and shadowed.

"You've been good to me, Janey Cameron. You've been like—" He paused. *A wife?* my subconscious spirit volunteered, and I cursed the thought. "How have I been to you, Janey?"

"You've been a father to Bod. The boy loves you, Greenywalt. Even when he needles you. But we can't stay." I crossed my arms. "Not after what she said."

He nodded. He picked up the lanthorn.

"I'll check with you in the morning. We'll work up a plan."

I was thinking, I won't be here. You won't see me again. I don't want to see you again. I don't want to see this house or this Settlement again. If the snow doesn't stop us, we won't be here when you check in tomorrow morning.

But of course, I said nothing. After twenty years, what could be said? I knew the fable of the Three Fates. I'd seen the drawings in my Father's art books, and I thought of these three mysterious women now: Clotho, who spun the thread of life; Lachesis, who drew straws and decided the length of a life, measuring out the yarn; and Atropos, who waited with her golden shears to cut life off when she pleased. I pictured Atropos reaching up even now to cut the thread of our life with the Mennonists.

Was it pagan? Could I worship the Christ who put all things under his feet—dominions, principalities, and powers—and still believe in the Fates?

All I knew for sure was this: I would not see this man's face again.

CHAPTER 24

TO THE SCOTS-IRISH,
DECEMBER 1742

I RECITED THE STORY OF EOCHAIDH as he lay there, sprawled on his back in the haymow. The Death of Eochaidh, the story's called, and so-named for the lake on whose shores my childhood home of Lurgan lies: Loch n-Eochaidh.

We'd scarcely made it inside the barn before the clouds let loose. Rain banged on the shingles overhead. They provided percussion to the throaty gurgles of a dozen pigeons, mostly out of sight in the rafters, by the trapdoor in the alcove.

"He was a brave man, Eochaidh, the son of Maridh, the good king of Munster. But his youngish step-Mama, like Potiphar's wife, lusted after Eochaidh. Day after day she kept up her siren-song: 'Come to me, Eochaidh.' She pressed him hard."

"And the father?" Bod said.

"Maridh. Perhaps he didn't notice. Maybe he was a good man, as the story says, but too busy to pay attention to what was going on right in front of his hearth. At last, Eochaidh did it. He ran away with her—his step-mother—plus his brother Ridh and a vast company of ten hundred men, plus their flocks and herds."

"Ten hundred?"

"Every story has its way of telling. That's how my father told it to me. He eloped with Eibhliu, Maridh's wife, and then they parted— Ridh went west and Eochaidh rode northeast with their train until he reached the Mac Óg. A tall man came and hailed them with 'You need to leave this country now.' Of course, a warlord like Eochaidh paid no mind to fear mongers. But that night, the tall man killed all their horses. On the morrow, he came back. 'Unless ye quit the land on which ye stand, tonight I slay ye all.'"

"Is this a true story, Mama?" He looked up from his bed in the loose hay. My boy, who'd turned a waggoneer and wore the smock-frock of buckskin, gone blackish from the weather. His hat had tipped off, and sticks of hay jutted off the red tangle of his head like light beams from Our Savior's halo in my Father's ancient art books. My son.

"Ach, Bod, it's true in a way, I suppose."

"Like Bible stories, I mean. David and Abraham. They were real, right? Was there actually an Eochaidh?"

"Don't spoil the story. I suppose it had a base. A real man whose story perhaps got embellished."

"Hmm." His eyes closed.

"Eochaidh says: 'Great mischief you've wrought already to us, killing our mounts. Without them we could not, even if we desired it, depart this country.'

"But that very day, Aengus the Mac Óg sent them a great horse."

"Aengus?" The boy's eyes snapped apart. The name of his best chum startled him. "His name was Aengus?"

The eyes drifted shut again, which was no surprise since he hadn't slept a blink last night. Even I, enraged as I was after that woman's insults, fell asleep after Greenywalt left and slept until—it must have been 2:00 a.m. when the boy came home. I told him my decision, and he didn't argue with me. It was over taking along Bear and Caspar that he argued, and I said, "No, we are not taking a dog or a horse or any piece of Greenywalt's possessions so his wife"—may the Lord fill her cup to overflowing for all the gall and wormwood she inflicted on us—"cannot add this to her list of reproaches against me."

Bod knew every step of the way, a fact I marveled since the Conestoga Road was quilted over with new-fallen snow up to our knees, but his boots found the frozen waggon ruts beneath the snow and we shuffled our way along. Without a lanthorn, which he said we couldn't bring, as it would betray our position in the night. The skies cleared by 2:00 a.m., however, so the half-moon refracted on the snow, and the bare-limbed trees reached up their branches and twigs and fondled the ten thousand stars with their fingertips.

I thanked the Lord for every item of clothes upon my body: the muffler wrapping my face and neck, the mittens Frony had crocheted for me last Christmas, the deerskin moccasins that laced to the knees, the raccoon cap he'd thrust on my head before Bod wrapped the bearskin around my shoulders.

Daybreak brought us to the village of Lancaster, which we may now fairly say had become a small city of some thousands. The first stripes of dawn showed the outlines of the stone homes. Like a piece of Frony's scissors art, I saw sharp-edged black silhouettes against the salmon sky, huddled together in the frieze, with smokeless chimneys. Red in the morning spells a warning, the sailors say. The front was coming from the direction of the Susquehanna, large snow clouds.

"They'll wake when it gets light," Bod said. "Hurry up. Somebody's going to see us."

"What can we do?"

"We won't go the River Road." We passed through the Square and the turnoff west to the River. "It's the first place he'll go to find us—the waggon road—and he will come after us. I know him." He hustled us north up Willow, walking through slush and mud now, ankle-deep. "I know a waggoneer," he said.

We arrived at a large log barn, and just in time, because the very icy rain caught us at the door. It was unlocked. He pushed me through, and the sweet-smelling warmth of animal bodies inside enveloped me on the other side. He rolled the door shut and disappeared. In a few minutes he reappeared at the door with the waggoneer, whom I recognized, even in the dark barn interior, as one of his chums. I'd met him at the mill when he came by with Parson Elder.

The boy followed Bod through the door. "Ma'am." He acknowledged me with a nod. He was barefoot, as if he'd jumped straight from bed to answer Bod's knock. He hopped up and down on the cold boards, yawned repeatedly, and seemed only half put together. His "barn door was open," as we say, but I didn't embarrass him by calling attention to that by staring.

"We're taking the forest road," Bod said.

"Then you'll be glad to have this one." The boy led us through the gloom past several magnificent creatures who pawed and thrust their noses through the wooden bars to greet us. "This one."

We stood before the last pen, and the enormous chocolate gelding inside arched his head aristocratically to acknowledge our presence. I don't think I'd ever seen such a colossus. His back rose to the height of his master's shoulders—who was in the pen beside him now—his enormous torso long and tubular, with masses of coarse black hair falling like the Shawnee women wore them.

"He's old," the waggoneer said. "He moves slow, and Pop

doesn't use him with waggons anymore, but he's still dependable and he swims. He'll get you across the Swatty, which is bound to be in flood."

I looked around at Bod, behind my shoulder. "Flood?"

The boy laughed. "Don't worry. You're in good hands with Bod. In the forest, he's the best. His mama, right? Didn't catch that when we came to the mill."

"After we sleep," Bod said, and pointed to the notched log that served as a staircase to the hayloft.

"You do me a favor." The waggoneer clapped Bod's shoulder. "I had to get him back to Paxtang this week."

"Does he have a name?" I asked. I rubbed the forehead of the beast, up to the forelock of the massive head that beetled over mine.

"Eoch."

The nasal Irish sound of it shocked me.

"Eoch?"

"Yes. Means horse. Like the lake. Loch n-Eoch-aidh." He repeated the beautiful Gaelic sound through his nose.

"My home!" I said. "Lurgan Towne in County Armagh."

"We're from the north! County Antrim."

Tears leaped spontaneously from their ducts and drizzled down my cheeks. "God bless you!" Gaelic words I hadn't used in twenty years gushed out of me. "Your name, you said, was—?"

"Aengus. Aengus McClure."

"Aengus! Og! The Tuath god."

"I've heard the story, yes. Our Reverend's from County Antrim. You met him, you know. Reverend Elder. John Elder." He went on, apparently proud to explain: "Did his studies over in Edinburgh, the University of." Bod looked on in astonishment, understanding not even a syllable of it. "The Fighting Parson, we say, since he takes his musket into the pulpit and says, 'Bring yours too.' It's war, Ma'am. The French and the savages, and we never know."

Bod looked me over, his eyebrows raised.

"You're surprised!" I switched to the English for Bod. I had always insisted on English with him, although he used the Deitsch with his father and everyone else in the Settlement. "You didn't know I spoke it, did you? James Logan, too, if you ever gave him opportunity. He's a Fenian."

"Sleep well then!' Aengus waved us up the stairs, such as it was. "I'll be gone when you get up. Delivery in the town."

We crawled across the mow, towing our gunny sacks of clothes, food, and utensils (tin cups, spoons, plate, knives) up the short stairs from the floor and onto the surface of the loose hay. We arrived and spread out.

I could hardly believe our good fortune. Instead of a thirty-some mile slog through the forest on foot with the heavy sacks, we had a horse of tremendous endurance. Instead of strangers at the other end, they were in fact my kinsmen, Scots-Irish from our cherished Lough n-Eochaidh.

"You didn't tell me, Bod! Lough n-Eochaidh! They're just up the east side of the lake a piece."

"What's the story on Aengus? You flared up on his name!"

"There are tales I never told you, Bod. Aengus and the Death of Eochaid. He was a brave man, Eochaid, the son of Maridh, the good king of Munster. But listen! His youngish step-mama, like Potiphar's wife . . ."

The sleet turned to hard rain and then to a drizzle on the shingles overhead, during Bod's sleep. But even with my eyes closed, sleep eluded me. The lad from Lough n-Eochaidh had stirred the long-slumbering coals of my father and his dream of meeting his congregation at the Philadelphia dock. A Pastor from the University of Edinburgh? What great exegesis of the Word must he be capable of? Preacher Herr's sermons were cold clinkers compared to the hot coals my father used to spread every Sunday morning. But then again, a musket in the pulpit?

I made a table of my muffler, laid out two tin plates (my own, not Greenywalt's), and positioned sausages, sliced sourdough, and a cold, boiled potato with a pinch of salt on each. Bod carried a wooden canteen with him, which he'd filled the night before. We'd use that for drinks.

All we needed yet was the guest, and he lay sprawled like a dog on its back in the hay, snuffling noisily with each inhale. His arm cradled his rifle—the way he'd fallen asleep most every night since his eighth birthday. Did he believe he'd need it during the night? During twelve years, perhaps he had on one or two occasions. No, it was just a boy's version of the girl's rag doll.

The bearskin and the man beneath twitched.

"Hey, Mama! What's Aengus have to do with it?"

"You're back!"

He peered down his nose and across the outflung arm to the makeshift table just beyond his fingertips.

"Mmm." He fetched a sausage. "Yesterday's hog?"

"Of course."

"At least that much good from the day, huh?" He sat up.

"This Aengus," I said. I bit into my own sausage. "You heard the part about Eochaid—how his horses were killed. This Aengus appeared, bringing him an enormous horse, a Bucephalus, and Eochaid and Eibhlíu—that's his lover and step-mother—and threw their baggage over its back."

"'*Don't unload the horse on the way.*

"'*Don't make him stop at any time. If you do, you will die there.*'

"That was Aengus, warning them.

"It was a Sunday in mid-harvest month when they set out for Ulidia, the Kingdom of it, the far northeast of Ireland and the birthplace of the Irish heroes Carchelon and Cu Chulinn. They sought the grey bramblebush, and when they finally found it, they all gathered round and threw off their baggage together, and not one of them chose to look back across the way they'd come.

"*Eoch*—for that was their creature's name as well, also stood still, and because it had been quite a long trip, he urinated liberally. It became a bubbling well, over which—"

"A well? You're not going to tell me they drank horse piss?"

"The well produced springwater, the freshest—"

"Only works that way in fairy tales, Mama." He snorted.

"Over which Eochaid built a house, and every night his servant woman put a cap over the well to stop its bubbling up. One night, however, she forgot. The water rose and rose until it covered the grey bramblebush and drowned Eochaid and all his children. And that overflowing created Loch n-Eochaidh."

"Beautiful." He stood up, swiped the bread crumbs off, clapped on his hat, and threw the bearskin over one shoulder. "You ready to go? I think the rain's done."

I shook the crumbs out of the muffler and wound it around my neck again.

Fifteen minutes later we passed the last house and entered the forest with the enormous gelding Eoch. I was somewhat clumsily perched on a blanket athwart his immense back while Bod played the scout a few yards ahead, with a set of reins trailing behind.

The rain turned the snowy path to hasty pudding. There were no waggon ruts here. Only a trail wide enough for two to pass while walking through the leafless hardwood forest, with bare trunks so thick and close that a traveler strained the eyes to see anything beyond a short stone's throw into the trees.

From behind, my son looked the image of the forester, the waggoneer, the pioneer. He passed noiselessly through the trees and snow like a lynx or a catamount. His hips swayed a few inches this way, a few that, in rhythm, even though his feet in their "country boots" sloshed in the melting snow. The rain continued to fall. The bearskins kept the rain off our bodies. I was thankful it was a fur cap and not my muslin bonnet, which I'd stored at the bottom of the food bag for another day. The harder it came down, the more my son reveled in it.

"We waggoneers, Mumi, we love it when there's weather!" Shortly he sang out:

> When first I went a-waggoning, a-waggoning did go,
> I filled my parents' hearts with sorrow, grief, and woe.

He stopped and paused the horse, coming back to rub his nose. By the way he cocked his ear, I saw he was listening for something. I heard water everywhere.

"Hear something?"

"No." He continued the song, singing full-lunged now:

> And many are the hardships that we must undergo,
> Sing woah! me lads, sing woah,
> Drive on, my lads, hi hoah!
> Who wouldn't be for all the world,
> A jolly waggoneer?

He checked the horse again. He cocked his head. Then, abruptly, he fixed me with his eyes. "When we get there, don't say I'm a bastard, will you?"

"Have I ever in all your life said—"

"But they don't know us. Tell them my father died."

By early evening, still light though, I calculated we must have gone twenty miles, if the old standard of four miles per hour was true. As darkness fell, I was figuring how much more track we might have ahead and where we would camp when he slowed, turned in his tracks, and tilted his head once more as if he heard things in the treetops. He cupped a hand behind his ear. He whispered: "You hear him?"

I heard only the steady dripping off the trees. Then, just as I believed I heard *something*, Bod seized the reins and double-timed Eoch off the trail, through the dark wet trunks, and around the back of a massive hemlock, its skirt of green branches as wide as the mill water-wheel, very green and growing branches right to the forest floor, where they flung out horizontally a few inches above the fallen leaves. He pulled me down beside himself, standing by Eoch's head, with his fist wrapped in the bridle and steering the gelding's head away from the road by which we'd just come so he couldn't see whatever was coming, which sounded like it moved on four feet.

"Hold his head like this. Give him chop." Bod thrust the mash bag into my hands. He broke off a hemlock branch and ran back to the trail, dragging it side to side to brush out our footprints as he walked backward to return.

The drumming of horsehooves grew distinct through the trees. I could just make out the trail up which we'd come, a slow ascent to a hilltop another five hundred yards beyond our present point.

"Is it—?" I began.

"Watch."

The animal was galloping, which seemed silly, considering the treacherous path. Now we saw the head and shoulders of the figure above the still invisible mount, a black felt hat such as Mennonist men wore, falling and rising with each stride.

"It's him. . . ."

Bod leaned his face into mine and whispered, "I need to talk with him."

"No! No!" I clung to him. We could not compromise ourselves after coming this far. There was nothing to discuss until we reached the Scots and then—"*No!*"

"I'll say I took you to the River, and I was on my way back—"

"Not today. Someday if you want to go back on your own . . ."

While we argued in whispers, the rider and horse pounded by, and it *was* the Mister, absolutely. Just that fast his horse crested the ridgetop, with the Mister's back square and bulked out with raincoats, and they disappeared beyond.

"Caspar, huh? He took my horse," Bod said. "He'll be back." He pulled the hatchet from his belt. "We'll settle here."

He secured Eoch to a stout hickory and unstrapped our bags. He fed the horse his full rations and then returned to his main task with vigor. Slicing with the hatchet, he downed and trimmed several hickory saplings into poles with Y ends, which he planted ten feet apart, abutting the hemlock and using it as a blind. He strung another pole between the uprights and then a series of poles twelve inches apart that sloped down from the crosspiece to the ground. Another fifteen minutes passed and nearly dark now, he cut and stacked a mesh of hemlock boughs onto the slope of the lean-to, which it was becoming.

The whole thing was built with the slanting roof, so to speak, facing the west and the drive of the rain and also—I marveled and credited my son with the thought—the direction from which Greeny-walt would come again. He led me under it, into the green-smelling but remarkably rain-free room, while he cut more hemlock sprays for bedding.

This time I heard the hoofbeats first. "He's coming back." I felt the boy slide past, going for the horse to keep him from nickering. Could we be seen? It didn't seem possible in the thick brush and closing darkness, but the horse no longer galloped. It was walking. Listening in the woods for us? What would make him look here, of all places?

"Someone up yonder said we ain't passed yet," Bod whispered. I was coming to believe in his prescient grasp of reality on the trail. If he said it, evidence had compelled him to say so, evidence growing out of his knowledge as a waggoneer and hunter.

Our second night out was more like I'd feared. The rain clouds scurried off, and after the rain the woods came alive with night animals. The continuous dripping, like the rhythmic tick-tock-tick-tock of the Mister's mantel clock, lulled me to sleep, and I was almost there when a most bloodcurdling wail curled my spine into a bone ball and cut the hamstrings in my legs. It rose from just beyond the hemlock and filled the treetops. A second wail immediately answered, some hundreds of yards away. Bod's body rocked to upright as he tugged the rifle from between us, and now I heard the horse whimper softly.

"Wolf," he said.

"It's right—" My violently shaking hand pointed. I'd forgotten he couldn't see the hand, here in the gloom of the lean-to.

"Sound closer than they are. Clouds. And humidity. They magnify the sound. Anyway, the rain kills the smell of us." He went out to be with the horse.

I'll never sleep after that, I told myself. Never sleep. All the while I glared at his bold upright silhouette between me and the clearing beyond, for they wouldn't attack through the dense tree cover. Glaring at the rifle Bod cradled, at the raccoon cap proclaiming him a man of the forest, the thought came: I am in good hands, as the waggoneer said. When I thought again, sunbeams streamed through the bare treetops and my body was a hundred years old. I groaned to my feet, one hand on an upright pole and shaking mugfuls of frigid water off the hemlock roof and down the back of my neck.

Bod lay snoring between me and the forest, with the rifle barrel clutched in his fist and pointed outward in the direction of the horse, and his back propped against the bag of food.

I lifted my body over his and found a bush to do my morning business. The horse fixed his wondrous black eyes on me. The forest shimmered, black wet trunks gleamed, and drops of water everywhere broadcast glittering beams as they slid or ran or just fell, sometimes in rivulets, from the leafless canopy. I stood and walked to the trail. Greenywalt's mount had left a violent set of hoofprints in the fresh mud. My eyes followed them to the ridgetop and on beyond to an amazing sight.

Smoke, wasn't it? Beyond the hilltop, a small thin plume smudged the trees and rose visibly white and perfectly vertical above their tops. I sniffed it now, the smell of the burning pine chunks.

Should I wake him? Or check on my own? I lifted my skirts, which hung heavy since yesterday, showing a thick three-inch border of trail mud that slapped my ankles. I started up the trail.

There lay the answer to our questions: a small log-and-wattle cabin huddled in a natural clearing not more than a quarter mile from our lean-to, with a chimney as lively as James Logan's pipe. I stood transfixed on the hilltop, wondering what to do next, when the answer came from behind.

How he got to me undiscovered, I had no idea, but his body hurled downward from an embankment and landed directly by my heels. I felt the brush of his body, heard the impact of his boots in the mud, and twisted to look into an unknown face, European like mine, with china doll blue eyes, twin craters in a face burned the color of pottery, wearing the buckskin shirt the traders and trappers wore when they came into our store. A cluster of foot-long furry things dangled head downward from his belt. The impact of the jump caused him to stagger back a couple steps.

"Runaway?" I hadn't expected English. It was as astonishing as his landing, and the shock smothered the scream on its way to my mouth. "Runaway girl piking it, huh?" He advanced, narrowing the distance between us to an arm's length. "Janey? Answering to Janey?"

Was I more confused by his presence or by hearing my name from his mouth? What about a runaway?

He pounced then and one hand tasting of small animal blood and dirt clamped across my open mouth and spun me around while the other hand pulled his body against mine and dived into my blouse. "Some dollars in you?"

I heard that as I bit down on the finger. I bit to save my life, and he roared and jerked the hand loose while I squealed like the pigs we'd stuck with butcher knives only two days earlier in the Settlement.

This time my hair was caught in his hand and yanked backward until my eyes fixed on the overhead patches of morning mist. I felt my body being dragged backward by an arm around my waist, in the direction of the cabin, with my neck in dire pain. The hand released my hair and the arm came off my waist so unexpectedly that I stumbled backward into him and felt his arms behind me pass my body on their way up, while I recovered my balance with a hand flung out against his chest. Only then did I understand I'd heard a gunshot, and the figure running up the trail toward me, reloading the rifle as he charged, was Bod.

The trapper, when I turned to see if he was dead, crouched on his knees, looking cornered as certainly as one of the muskrats in his traps, his eyes rolling wide and blue as the rifle barrel slid right between my arms and hip on its way into his open mouth. Bod jammed it in, and the black barrel snapped the man's head backward and bulged his cheek outward like a wad of tobacco until Bod lowered the stock, his finger shaking on the trigger, so that the barrel would point directly upward in the man's mouth.

"I'll blow your brains out." Bod's free hand clamped the back of the man's neck and prevented him from pulling his mouth free from the barrel he slavered over.

"Did he hurt you, Mum?" To the man, he repeated, "I'll blow your brains out, you bastard!"

Knowing that any answer but "No" would mean just that, and I had no desire to witness a man's death, I was going to shake my head, but another reason presented now. The door of the cabin ahead flung wide, and three small children, one after the next, pushed out, attached to the legs of a Shawnee woman, and I heard one cry:

"Daddy! Daddy! Daddy!"

"No. No. He didn't," I lied.

"You wicked cull! What ails you, assaulting this woman?"

"He knows my name." I immediately regretted I'd acknowledged that.

"You ever say her name again . . . to anyone," the rifle muzzle lifted the man to his feet and scraped back and forth across the man's teeth as Bod backed him, step by deliberate step, down the hill toward the cabin. "I'll blow your brains out."

The trapper's head bobbled painfully. His eyes popped yes to acknowledge his compliance.

"Get Eoch. And the bags," Bod directed me. I started off. "He had a gun. Somewhere there's a gun. *Where's your gun, bastard?*"

I rushed back with the horse and our bags, flung over the gelding's back. Bod was still back-walking the trapper, and they were at the step up onto the wood-plank porch of the cabin. The woman and children had disappeared inside. Bod gripped the trapper's collar with his left hand, used the rifle as a guiding stick in the man's mouth with his right, and raised his foot. The door latch flew off with his kick, and the man's back went down through the doorway. He sprawled face up, sputtering mouthfuls of blood, his eyes still fixed upward on Bod.

"You come after us," the muzzle drifted upward from the man's face, "you report us to anyone." The rifle cocking cracked the awful silence. My heart froze. Surely not with the man's own children watching . . . I heard the concussion in the room beyond, a large crock, perhaps, because shards flew off, and whatever was inside cascaded to a spreading pool on the floor. The trapper twisted his body into a ball at the concussion and dragged his jacket over his head. The woman was nowhere to be seen, but I saw the children's upside-down legs kicking beneath the bed.

Bod leaped off the porch and came across the clear, grassy area, dragging Eoch now while he himself back-stepped, as if expecting a reprisal. He zinged another shot at the chimney and sent up a puff of pulverized wattle. The cabin door slammed shut.

"Come on, come on. He'll have a gun." Bod ran, pulling me with his arm around my waist into the trees of the trail, and then the cabin was gone as we disappeared over the next ridge.

"Where's the bridle and blanket, the saddle?"

In my haste, I'd left them where he dropped them the night before, on the roof of the lean-to. He jury-rigged a line around the animal's waist and tied our baggage back on top, but I would have to walk now.

My heart wouldn't stop hammering. Gracious Lord, what had I done? What was I to do? Rescued, yes, and grateful for it. But what to do with a boy who wants to blow brains out? Who shoots up a cabin? Without a father to control him. In a howling wilderness. We'd escaped the pursuing hounds only to run straight into the maw of a rabid wolf.

With such dread thoughts and fears, we tramped through the forest for some hours in silence, him in the lead at a forced march pace, Eoch in between, led by his tie-rope, and me following them on foot. We crossed the swollen Swatara on fallen logs, and the horse swam it. On and on.

The trail grew more tortuous, falling and rising more frequently, and finally I had the good sense to suggest dinner. He agreed, this terrifying son of mine. We ate in uncomfortable silence. At that moment, the Lord sent a sign to me, fear-filled Janey, like he sent the angel to runaway Hagar, the concubine. It was the most wondrous sign I'd ever seen.

We sat side by side on a wet, fallen tree, mother and son, eating the last of the sourdough, when I heard it first.

It gurgled and rumbled, as if it were sleigh bells on galloping horses. Perhaps Eoch thought so too. He lifted his head and whinnied. It was not a gentle sound but a wide, deep sound, as if an entire army of horses, each with its neck hung with sleigh bells, advanced unseen across the forest toward us. Or was it thunder? Yet the morning skies were cobalt blue and chilled, after the rain, as they only are in winter in Penn's Woods.

The sleigh bells and rumbling drew nearer. I looked wide-eyed at Bod, and he looked wide-eyed back. He gripped his rifle, the muzzle pointing straight ahead through the trees, as if whatever must come at us down the trail. The trees and rocks seemed to vibrate. In the blink of an eye, we saw them. As far as one could see through the trees in all directions, north and west, ten thousand upon ten thousand gray bodies the size of crows but more graceful, moved en masse like a storm front but not above the treetops. No, they flew *through* the treetops without hitting them, many of them mid-trunk, many more as low as our hands and feet. They were smaller than migratory ducks, more like doves. . . .

"*Amimis!*" Bod leaped onto a fallen trunk, waving his spread hands as if to catch one in each hand.

They propelled through the trees, their wings sweeping so dynamically that the wingtips often clapped together with a sharp rap.

There must have been millions upon millions. Like the quail that fell upon the children of Israel in the wilderness? Only these didn't fall. The angels around the Eternal Throne, more like, ten thousand upon ten thousands, singing the praises of the Ancient and Eternal One. Blotting out the sun and, unlike angels, flinging droplets of dung all around us, like dark melting drops of snow.

The most wondrous thing was their organization: they moved as if connected by invisible filaments to each other, as if they obeyed a master plan. As the head of the phalanx began to lift, the body and bulk of them executed a gigantic pinwheel that covered the entire heaven. The head, miles across, led the army as one unit: now we saw a glistening wall of deep blue as the army turned their backs away from us, and now a rich deep wall of purple as the army breasted us.

"How many? How many?" I called to Bod. He had lowered his arms. "How far? How far?" I ran up the trail. My spirit welled up, like an underground artesian stream seeking a mouth in the soil. I was six-teen once more, running to the top of the mountain in Ulster, and . . . I crested the hill and stopped. Beyond the great broad Susquehanna rolled incessantly, swollen and brown as James Logan's afternoon tea, its waves stretched south, west, and north to the base of the distant cliffs.

"Bod! It's the River!"

Over our heads and even around and past us, the army of *amimi* circled on.

I threw off the fur cap and found a level seat on one of the car-riage-sized boulders. The pale December sun's rays warmed my throat and cheeks. I leaned back to shake my unbound hair loose, long and striped with gray, past my shoulders to the waist.

"It's a sign, Bod! The pillar of cloud by day. He's here. He's with us."

PART 6

THE SCOTS-IRISH

CHAPTER 25

TAKING CARE OF BOD,
JULY 12, 1755

"LOCUSTS MIGHT be shuttin' down a bit?"

It was a question to the Boy Benjamin, seated by him on the high seat of this waggon. Not his second-hand conestoga, parked safely in a shed behind the mill to protect his investment from the elements. No, this was the market waggon, but the same Belgians were pulling it. The second-string Belgians, because my prize team, Neckar and Rhine, and the prize conestoga too, for that matter, were God knows where.

Abandoned it all. They attacked the supply train, and we run for our lives and left everything—our waggons, our pack horses, our flour sacks and kitchen, the panspotskettles, our ammunition and run. With him. Meaning his son. His other son.

The Boy shrugged off the question, without turning his face from the forest path beyond the rhythmically trotting haunches and ears of the Belgians, their tails flinging against the horseflies.

As if to counter his conclusion, a locust sounded in the passing overhead leaves. It began like the toothed and whirling drillbit of Mylin's gun barrel drill, encountering the solid iron—shrill, piercing, disturbing. It grew and grew and the sound merged with the ongoing clamor from the hill to the right and from the grove they were traversing on the left until your head reverberated; and at night, long after they did shut down the whole way to silence, your imagination kept up the ringing.

"*Homoptera*," the Boy said, his face turned now and his eyes riveting behind the two Franklin windowpanes. "*Cicadoidea*. Locusts!"

The fireball in the sky equipoised uneasily on the tiptops of the hardwood forest and dyed the mare's tails over the Blue Mountain.

They'd been driving along the mottled trail since four, when they first entered the forest, the Boy at the reins, himself riding alongside. The maple and oak leaves cut back the light, which offered some protection from the rays, but the air itself clung to them, steamy and motionless and thick with the odors of last evening's downpour and redolent skunk and the tannin of moldering floor leaves. He mopped continuously at the dribbles from beneath his hat with his handkerchief.

The fireball jerked sideways a yard. Tree stump. The left wheel thudded and now the waggon side rose a good foot as it traveled across the stump, and then an equal thud as it hit the roadbed again. The best that could be said about Forest Road was this: one could now drive a waggon direct from Lancaster to Harris' Landing, above the mouth of the Swatara, in an hour less than the time it took on the River Road along the Susquehanna. The worst you could remark was the continuous stumps and rocks because it wasn't used enough to warrant a gang master with a group of slaves to pickaxe and dig-iron a month to remove all the stumps and embedded boulders.

The box behind scraped and slid on the waggon bed as it tilted up on the stump. He reached to steady the leading edge and noticed the black speckles on the broad red cross of the cloth that spanned the box. Crowds of them. *The sure sign of decay.*

"Benjamin."

The Boy's face didn't move. Between his hands, the loop of the longlines lay loosely because the Belgians knew how and at what speed to pull, with very little guidance until they got to a creek or river.

"Hmmm?"

"Shoo them off." Greenywalt gestured at the specks, which walked about and clustered on the flag that covered the box.

The Boy dropped one hand to the whip that propped perpendicular off his right leg. He worried it from its socket and dipped the tip over the horse's rump ahead, the long rawhide dangling almost to the ground. The hand flicked. The rawhide rope snapped along the box. The specks lifted en masse, buzzing in a small blackish cloud.

"Not that way." Greenywalt raised his voice. "I meant a tap. Shoo, I said."

"He don't mind."

"I mind."

The flies circled and shortly they were settling again, most in the same places, where the cloth was discolored. Even on the red cross, the patches of dry blood were as obvious as the shell holes in other places.

"Bluebottles." The boy stuffed the whip back into its socket and didn't look as he gave the rest of his assessment. "*Calliphoridae.*"

Greenywalt had overseen the making of the pine box in Lancaster. Bod was long, a good couple inches beyond the average man. He'd told the militiamen he knew where to get a box tailored for him. This after the humiliating scene at the market stalls, when he'd begged them for the body.

—◦◦◦◦◦—

"Let me take him home. You've made your point. Let me put him to rest in our orchard." He could hardly voice that request; the words were too full of pain. A new grave there beside the wooden tablets with the names of Daniel and Ezra, our babes who never saw the light, and the tablet for Vetti. . . .

"He's ours. Why do you want him?" The militiaman, smelling as sour as he looked, glared.

The Mennonist farmers stood, each one behind his table with his offerings for sale, but no one was buying this morning. The crowd of early buyers in English go-to-market clothes instead pressed around his table to gawk at the incredible sight of a scalped white man, while their women, in poke bonnets behind them, flung their hands to their mouths.

"Because he's my son. I'm Greenywalt. Klaus Greenywalt."

At his announcement, some of the gawkers pulled back. He heard their whispers but stood his ground before the militiaman, Bod's mutilated corpse between them on the table.

"Well, it's out of the question. He's got a family and a church and a whole community in Paxtang that will honor him for what he is—an American hero!"

"An American hero!" the militiaman repeated as he clambered onto the table he'd jumped down from after demanding that the Courthouse bells be rung. He addressed the gathering crowd. "Savages in the hundreds surprised our train. They'd already laid low a thousand British redcoats, and they weren't done. They wanted the supplies, and they come woo-hooing out of the trees and bushes in the still mostly dark when we were sleeping, and he jumped like he'd been watching all night for them and up onto his horse when they come.

"No saddle, just him and that rifle he sleeps with his arms around, giving the camp precious seconds to respond. *Bod Cameron* put his own precious life in the balance to give us time. He rode at them, firing his rifle and whooping back and they killed his horse under him, put a ball through his thigh, and took his scalp."

The militiaman gestured at the head wounds of the man on the table next to the one he balanced upon.

His face glowered darkly. "Tell that to the Broad Brims and their Dutch Dogs. Tell that to the Quaker Assembly sitting mighty and high in Philadelphia that refuses us a militia to rescue our miserable frontier people in the back counties, who now stand exposed around their fireplaces with their babes, peeking out their windows with a solitary musket, because it's coming. *The scourge is coming.*"

"And he survived." The militiaman dropped his voice, looking through the crowd of men at their bonneted wives. "Losing blood." He slapped his own bald scalp. "Nursing a bullet hole." He touched his outer thigh. "'I'm going home,' he said. 'To my family in Paxtang.' We couldn't unpersuade him. We rode after him. It's three days from the Dunbar Camp, and him still losing blood, and then gangrene sets in the wound on his leg, and he's delirious and crying out, 'My family! My family in Paxtang!' And late last night he goes into a coma, and middle of the night . . . middle of the night . . ."

Greenywalt drank down the words of the militiaman because it was his son's story the man was telling, and Bod was alive in his mind, riding into those Indians.

"He went home!" the militiaman said as he flung his outstretched finger over the city steeples and toward the clouds. "Home!" He reeled in and flung the hand at Greenywalt below him. "There's your son. You raised a hero."

The little crowd had more than tripled during this speech, and on that comment, some began to applaud, and it rippled out until they were all clapping, their faces fixed on Greenywalt. The militia-man stopped them with his hand.

"Hold it! Hold it! This story's not done. You!" His hand traveled, trembling, like a curse upon the Mennonist traders beyond and below him. "What about you? This horrible idea of nonresistance we hear about. Will you abandon our backcounty families to the barbarities, or will you get your guns and come with us? Do you believe they won't come after your families next?"

The militiaman's angry rant went on for more than an hour, recycling each time a new crowd gathered, pushing and shoving to see and hear the story of the scalped man. Each time the old crowd faded without buying any of the things they'd come to purchase on market day. He railed on, even when his voice cracked and began to waver.

Greenywalt knew this: he wasn't going to leave his son's body. After fourteen years apart—he put it that way to the other farmers, who had packed their unsold goods back in their waggons and were hitching up the teams again.

"Tell Maudlin what happened here. I'll stay with him to the end."

"What about me?" Benjamin asked. The first couple teams were already trotting out of the Square.

'What about you?"

"I want to go home too."

"And leave your brother's body to them?"

"Why does this man mean something to you? He ran off. Him and his Mem. I don't remember as I was six, but did he contact you once? Did you see him once during the fourteen years in between? That shows how much he cared about you. And Mem says he was violent. 'Live by the sword, die by the sword.' I'm not surprised. Don't be dumb. Let them bury him if—"

"He's my son. That's why."

Did I behave this way at sixteen? Did I ever not give loyalty and respect to my parents, my grandparents, my little brothers and sister?

He felt an impulse to belt the boy, public or not. But no. This was the son he still had. The son who disappointed him now needed more working on. There were other more important things to do right now. He flagged the militiaman when he finished the next tirade and made his offer: he would haul the body to wherever they were going—Paxtang, he'd heard—and furnish a proper coffin for it.

The man leaped from the table. "Aengus McClure." He crushed Greenywalt's hand between the two of his. "We were Jonathan and David, Bod and I. I loved this man!"

Greenywalt reeled him in against his chest. The odor of weeks on the road was much worse up against him, but he wasn't noticing. He was reliving the details of the story he'd heard.

"You loved him and so did I." He saw tears well in Aengus's eyes—a face no older than his own son's, not bearded like his own but heavily stubbled and reeking of campfires—and he reached to brush them off, even as he felt his own eyes burn. "Tell me about his family." He suddenly became aware of his other son, standing behind him, aloof and isolated, and without waiting for the answer, he released Aengus from his embrace and wheeled. "My youngest son, Benjamin."

Benjamin's hand unceremoniously flapped open, and Aengus reached for it.

The Courthouse clock struck one.

"We'll take care of getting a box right now," he said to Aengus and motioned Benjamin to follow.

It took the coffin maker an hour to cut pine boards for an extended box and nail them together. Greenywalt paid, and he and Benjamin each lifted an end of the lidded box and lugged it between them the two blocks back to the marketplace.

There was no privacy in the marketplace, but now that he had the body—if only temporarily in his possession—he let go. He didn't stop the tears.

"Bod! Bod!" He kissed the gray, marble lips and memorized the features again. "He doesn't look like himself. The mouth, Benjamin. It's too sad."

"I don't remember."

"And the eyes." What could he say about the eyes? They were shut, and the blue pools of life had dried up. There was no life to observe.

He opened the breeches to look at the thigh wound. The flesh resembled a log ripped from the fireplace, charred and wooden, blackened, then large discolored patches of the infection with raw reddish blocks on the edges where life had battled the gangrene. Would the leg have been lost either way? Was it better that he didn't face life legless, crippled? He didn't touch it. He only looked and closed up the breeches.

Benjamin observed his hands, wordlessly.

"Let's put him in." They lifted the body like a fire log, one at each end, and down into the box. "Get the waggon now."

Benjamin brought the waggon, and this time it was Aengus and his men who lifted and slid the box, with the lid closed over the man, onto the waggon bed. Aengus leaped up on the waggon bed now and called for the cloth in which they'd trucked Bod from the horse's back to the market table. A militiaman pulled it off the table and went up on the waggon bed to help spread it, the red cross over the blue saltire of Scotland and the red saltire of the Ulster Scots—he'd heard the whole history lesson from James Logan—and now the bloodied, bullet- and brush-torn Jack covered the body of his son Ichabod, and it seemed like a badge of ownership over him.

—⁓⁓⁓—

Light dimmed in the forest, and the evening planet appeared. The little troop—two mounted militiamen several hundred yards in front, the Belgians and the waggon with the coffin, and two mounted militiamen behind—formed a parade as they came out of the deeper woods and into the plantations of Paxtang and Middletown.

Bod is dead. I ride into Enemy Territory, where they hate us and our black hats make us a target. Perhaps this will be the End.

The log cabins south of the Swatara were humble affairs: one room and one floor with a stone chimney, a shingle roof overhanging the front wall by five feet to form a floorless porch and shelter drying buckskins on the walls each side of the doorway, with crude log benches under the buckskins, where one could sit on summer evenings after the chores. Greenywalt compared them to the houses of Pequea, even his own home, Ours started out like this forty years ago, then progressed to two stories with multiple rooms, and on to the limestone houses we're building now. These folks are poor.

Even the fields looked more humble. The third-year drought had hit the whole province, but here the corn was blighted, and mid-July showed barely knee-high stalks, with shriveled leaves and nubby ears. No one sat on the porch benches of the cabin they were passing. The farmer was in his oats on the south side of the road, swinging a great scythe in the early dusk, while his tow-haired children ran behind and gathered the cut grain into small piles for their mother to tie with a single handful of stalks and leave in a row of standing shocks.

Does he own this land, or is he living here under squatter's rights, so-called?

Glowworms blinked here there over the new shocks of oats. Alongside gathering the grain, the children ran after them, guessing where the bug would reappear while it was flying darkly.

The farmer ceased cutting. He came toward the waggon, his arm overhead in greeting, and the wife followed.

"We heard."

He'd seen farmers like this one in Philadelphia. The man wore a waistcoat, open in front to reveal his tanned chest, with breeches and leggings of deer hide and leather moccasins like a Shawnee's. Over his shoulder, even while harvesting, a powder horn dangled on a rawhide strip with a shot bag flapping clumsily alongside against the man's waist. A third child, no more than five, darted from a tree with a musket, which he thrust into his father's outstretched hand as he came across the field.

"We heard." The farmer gestured at the trail with the musket. "Your comrade came by thirty minutes back. Is *he* in there?"

The forward militiamen had paused the waggon, and Aengus himself rode back alongside. "You want to see?"

The farmer nodded and clambered onto the waggon because the contents of the box were only partly visible to a man standing along-side. Aengus stretched out from horseback, ripped the stained flag and its contingent of flies off the box, and pushed the lid aside.

"It's Bod all right." The farmer addressed his wife. "You should see."

"And the children?" she asked.

"Yes, the children, too."

They climbed up and encircled the coffin. He saw the children pinch their noses, and the mother swiped their hands down.

"Children, it's Captain Cameron," she said. "He fought for us."

The father extended his hands both ways, one to his wife, one to his oldest son, and the family stood like that, around the box on the waggon, as if they prayed or meditated, he couldn't tell which. No one said anything, but Greenywalt felt a surge of warmth toward this man who was honoring his son.

"Here, you put the Colours back." Aengus tossed them to the farmer, who closed the lid and spread the flag. His children pulled the edges taut and re-set the flat rocks that anchored it on each corner.

"Where you bound to?"

"Harris' Landing."

The family came down and stood in front of their cabin, in a row that slanted oldest to youngest, their faces now sullen and fearful, as the waggon rolled away.

But the next cabin was different. The farmer and his wife came out of the cabin, and he shook his fist at the waggon.

"Sons of bitches!"

"Did he mean us?" Benjamin asked.

"Who else?"

An oncoming waggon nearly ran them off the road and into the trees. He stared in astonishment at the woman who cracked the reins on a single horse's back to keep it galloping and stood feet widespread at the front of the waggon in a balance as good as any sailor's, her gray hair flying from beneath a blue bandanna to her waist, bouncing against her back. The waggon swerved past them and its righthand wheels tilted in the six inch drop from the trail to the oat field.

Aengus, sitting stalled on his horse, turned completely around to see if the waggon would make the maneuver.

"Where you going, Goody McKnight, with the bairns?" Five children of various ages rode flour sacks in the waggon, together with two more women who straddled bags of wheat and held duck fowlers pointed outward.

"Lancaster."

"Where's your man?"

"Harris' Landing. Her man too. And hers. They're coming, you know. The savages! Who'll fight for us?" The waggon rattled by. "For our daughters? And our sons? And our houses?"

They were gone.

The alpenglow on the hilltops they'd passed faded to charcoal, but the horses, with the instincts of night creatures like deer or possums, drove on.

"Is that Bod Cameron?"

Out of the dark maw of a cabin, a settler emerged, his pine-knot torch lighting his path to the waggon, which Aengus had paused in recognition, it seemed, of people's need to honor his comrade.

"I'll take a look."

The settler threw himself up onto the waggon bed. The torch cast huge shadows that climbed the tree trunks around them. He lofted the torch, popping and burning with a smoky orange flame, high overhead, illuminating everything—the waggoneers, the rumps of the Belgians, the coffin before him. Aengus pulled the Colours and the lid again, and the man thrust the torch downward, lighting up the very white, chalklike features of the slain militiaman.

"It's the Captain, all right."

"Murphy, is that you?"

"Yeah, it's me. Same sonofabitch as the last time. Same piece of land the Devil himself won't farm."

"Here. Cover him up again."

Murphy did so, ending at the fore end of the coffin, where he turned and brought his torch down within a foot of Greenywalt's backward turned face.

"Yeah, I thought so. I know you."

The man looked little different from the last farmer, but the hostile voice stirred a memory.

"You remember me, huh? I see it in your butter-boy face. Conestoga Manor, right?"

It came back to him. Conestoga Manor, William Penn's own private reserve along the Susquehanna, the last place of refuge for the Delaware peoples as the settlers and squatters gobbled land—and this man had pitched his cabin right there, illegally, by the stream. Within a mile of fifteen other illegal Scotch-Irish cabins.

"You torched my cabin, do you remember that? You stood there and watched it burn."

"It was there illegally. Probably like this one, I'd guess." Greenywalt gestured at the cabin, whose outline showed in the dark trees. "You built on Indian land."

"Were they using it? No. It was wasteland that God Almighty give us. You torched my cabin, while me and the wife—"

"James Logan ordered them down. Your own countryman."

Murphy poked the torch at him. "And a scaly Quaker. We've got a problem with you, Dutch Dog. You and the Quakers, who say if a pack of Scots-Irish get killed, no loss."

"I didn't say that and I wouldn't."

"Move along, Murphy." Aengus pushed his musket barrel between them, swatting Murphy's torch with it and, with a cascade of sparks, sending it flying over the waggon side and into the dirt. Murphy leaped after, retrieved the torch, and stood erect, shaking the torch furiously at the men in the waggon.

"We ought to tar and feather you, Dutchie. Captain, you listening?"

"I heard you."

"Where you going?"

"To the Parson. Let him decide," the captain said.

"Yeah, let him decide. I think I'll come along and see to that." Murphy disappeared into the cabin, which sat at the trail's edge.

Beside him on the bench, Benjamin sat stone-still, the lead lines fumbling back and forth in his hands. He whispered, "Are we prisoners?" He cracked the lead lines, and the waggon lurched forward.

Murphy came back. They saw him following, between the waggon and the mounted militiamen behind them. His flintlock stabbed upward with every step, and his hound ran ahead, along the right side of the Belgian.

In that way, a farmer here and a farmer and his wife there, the parade grew. By the time they arrived at the banks of the Swatara, twenty-five or thirty armed farmers and a few wives clustered behind the waggon, ahead of the rear militiamen. They walked silent and grim. Their hounds, however, were not silent. They circled in a pack at the riverbank and bayed as if they recognized the stench of death.

Greenywalt got off the waggon to ford the Swatara.

The bank was almost waist-high above the river here, but grooved from many previous horses and waggons. His hand felt the coffin scrape slowly forward and guided the coffin until it bumped against the waggoneer's seat. Water rose around his legs to mid-calf.

The night had the feeling of a party. Twenty-five men and women, some on horseback, some wading, with pine-knot torches aloft here and there. The light from the torches flickered on the heavy vegetation on the other side, looking impenetrable because the rhododendron bushes, sycamores, and river birches came right to the water's edge, and their outlines merged in the darkness. The dogs romped in the water. The two militia horses led the way, and suddenly the waggon path opened up before them, and their waggon came up the opposite bank.

CHAPTER 26

"YOU DON'T HEAR it on your side," the Boy said. From the Swatara, they had entered the forest again, and they progressed, in the dark, in the middle of the procession of settlers.

"That farmer, the one whose cabin you tore down—?"

It was an advantage he'd used for years in business, the Deitsch dialect. After forty-five years, it was not exactly the southern German of the Kraichgau anymore. Among the Mennonists of the Pequea, the dialect was spotted with words and phrases from the Swiss valleys and corrupted with Quaker English phrases. But still, it was completely incomprehensible to the Quaker traders in Philadelphia and to these Scots-Irish farmers.

The Boy clutched the reins against his chest, bolt upright on his seat. "There! There!" Listen to him!"

Under his own torchlight, the Settler Murphy gestured with huge sweeps of his flintlock, his shoulders rubbing those of the two settlers striding alongside. He stabbed his musket forward at them on the waggon. The Boy interpreted the words lost in the rumble of waggon wheels.

"The pillory, he's saying. The pillory, Dat."

He'd heard there was one at Harris' Landing now, just as they'd erected them in Lancaster Square (and every other colonial town), and you could see a different runaway servant there every weekend, his hands and head pinned between the hinged wooden boards after his upper body was stripped, and yes, the girls as well, and given the Welcome Lashing by the sheriff's men. Then they padlocked the offender down, and it was a free-for-all as the townsfolk competed with each other to pour rotting tomatoes, potatoes, rounds of horse and dog excrement, or just the contents of the night chamber pot over the offender's head and body.

"Says they're gonna send a message to Lancaster, Dat."

"We'll see."

In the sky ahead, above the treetops, a rosy pyramid of light appeared, and a few minutes later the orange haze of a large fire somewhere below.

"Harris' cabin!"

"They're under attack!"

Their militia escorts spurred their mounts ahead, their muskets leveled. The procession of settlers on foot and on horse ceased movement around them. The settlers stared away through the trees and gawked at the burning sky ahead.

"Drive on!" He urged the Boy. They emerged alone from the forest into a treeless meadow. Five hundred yards beyond ahead a succession of timbers with pointed tips ran the entire width of the meadow, rising to the height of his own eyes from their perch on the waggon seat. From here the length of Harris' cabin roof rose above the stockade, visibly dark and separated from the flames by a hundred feet.

"It's not the cabin!"

Great orange tongues leaped and gyrated side to side above the timbers. Their gleam backlit the two riders who came at them in the darkness from the direction of the stockade. Their militia escort rode by, hallooing the settlers still hunkered down in the woods.

His waggon arrived at the gate of the stockade, a wide gap without a door or way of closing it, and a militia materialized directly in front of the Belgians as they reached the opening. The militiaman's musket pointed the way while his free hand came up to seize the bridle of the left side horse. The whole action didn't slow their movement. The team accelerated their trot through the gap in the stockade. The Belgians sensed food and water.

The long meadow ahead sloped away and downward toward the void another five hundred yards out, where a ghost image of the bonfire bobbed and moved in shreds and slivers on what he knew was the River. Between here and there, his eyes took in the Harris plantation, the accomplishment of two generations of Harrises over fifty years.

Harris himself—no, not him but the son—stood at the edge of his welcome fire, a heap of locust or pine logs teepeed and incinerating with a roar that cracked and detonated and threw upward a burning golden orange-rust pillar and flicked glowing embers like billiard shots at the darkness. A host of moths and mayflies and night insects circled the pillar continuously.

Forty years ago he'd ridden packhorses here to trade for bundles of fox and marten and beaver pelts from Harris, Senior, in exchange for English store goods from James Logan. That was all before the Mill. There were only a few buildings then. In addition to his cabin, Harris had a pelt house then. And now? Thirteen buildings? Fourteen? The cabin had more than doubled in size as well.

"You see that mulberry tree?"

The Boy had dropped the reins to let the militiaman steer the team past the bonfire toward the watering trough.

"Yes. Is it a mulberry?"

"They tied Old Harris up to that and threatened they'd burn him to death. The Oneidas. Just shows not to believe it every time someone bullies you."

"He got away?"

"The Shawnees across the River rescued him."

He didn't see a pillory anywhere in the compound.

The man Harris met them with his upraised hand, just at the edge of the bonfire. He resembled his Old Man, now deceased and his body buried at the foot of that same mulberry tree, but seemed less of a rustic. Harris Junior looked cleaned up, too clean to be a fur trader and frontier militiaman, with a white ruffled ascot about the neck, a spotless waistcoat, and a wig under the tricorn. A wig!

Harris walked around the back of the waggon and stepped up onto the waggon bed with another militiaman, who lit the way with his torch. Four or five more of them came jogging from the cellar now, all with their muskets.

Harris gestured the box. The militiaman tore off the flag with one long swipe of the arm and tilted the torch downward. Harris knelt over the box, examining but not touching. He straightened again.

"It's him all right. Gaaaaawd!" Harris stared around, shaking his head. "Gaaaawd! What did they say when they saw this in Lancaster? Where's Aengus?"

"Sir." That militiaman trotted his horse around to the front of the waggon.

"Well?"

"They gawked."

"That's all? They gawked?"

"When I said Captain Cameron. Said what happened. How he saved us all. Some applauded."

"Some applauded?" Harris pointed his riding stick. "Take him off."

Another militiaman clambered up and together, one embracing each end of the box, they hoisted it clumsily, the loaded box looking like more than two hundred pounds, up onto the side of the waggon and then steadying it there as the four on the ground lifted the box. Then under instructions from Aengus, "Hup! Hup!" they moved the box from the waggon at a rhythmic pace, past the horses' heads to a set of sawhorses set a few feet apart, between the bonfire and the cabin, with the dead man's head pointed toward the River.

Harris stalled on the waggon bed. He took the torch from the militiaman's hand and lofted it over the faces of the waggoneers.

"At least you come to see for yourself what we're in for!"

Greenywalt had been mulling it over. He would announce himself as the slain man's father. But now, abruptly, the scene erupted with shouting and a hurly-burly of activity at the gate.

The procession of settlers behind them had just arrived at the gate, and the first settlers passed through, firing off their fowlers overhead while their hounds bayed, and they drew toward the enormous bonfire as certainly as the moths.

"Mennonist?" Harris asked, staring sharply down at Greenywalt and his son. He didn't wait for an answer. He lifted an elegant leather boot onto the waggon rail and leaped over the side.

The militiaman by the horses' bridles wanted to escape the oncoming crowd. He led the team away smartly beyond the bonfire to the well and wrapped the reins around the windlass supports.

Greenywalt stood, nodded to his son, and they scrambled down.

The horses had already found the empty iron trough and thrust their noses about in the bottom in anticipation. The pail splashed in the well bottom far below their feet, and the militiaman winched it up, splashing water liberally as he tipped it over and into the trough. The horses slurped the entire pailful in seconds.

"They'll need grain," Greenywalt said.

"We have plenty."

The Boy unharnessed the team. After a third and fourth bucketful, he led them off in the direction of a corral, while the militiaman disappeared into one of the sheds for grain.

Greenywalt climbed back onto his waggon seat. The settlers had formed a huge semicircle that began beyond the upraised coffin on its trestles and swung around the bonfire and down the other side. The left end of the line had their backs between him and the bonfire, effectively blocking its heat from him, which was just fine. The summer night air needed no additional heat.

Harris was about to address them. He'd positioned himself on a small horseless cart on the other side of the well, a few feet from the coffin, his feet about the same distance from the ground as the bottom of the box.

"Give 'em each a cup of kill-devil."

A short, squared-off militiaman balanced a small keg backward against his chest and thighs while a second opened the bong each time to release a stream of the dark liquid into the mugs that he'd toted out on a wheelbarrow, each one nestled in straw to prevent breakage.

"Straight from Jamaica! Now . . . you've heard the story. Forty Indians with their French commander are boating down the River to loot and scalp and burn . . ."

The shadowy figures standing shoulder to shoulder around the bonfire gave witness to the fact that they had heard it. They were here.

Their eyeballs shone wide, and every one of them, at least the men, carried a musket, which most wouldn't permit to touch the ground but held them cradled, as if in the next ten minutes the unseen bank of the River, whose waters rolled unseen from this vantage point, would suddenly crawl with human cockroaches, each one capable of springing up with a tomahawk or pointed gun to unleash pillage, rapine, murder, and kidnapping on all that the settler held dear.

"You heard the report, and is it true? Montour?"

The man who stepped out at his call was a man Greenywalt had never seen before. A white man, apparently by his features: the thin straight nose, oval eyes, pale coloring, Six-foot height. His clothes looked European as well: the white shirt with ruffles across the breast around the neck, crimson damask waistcoat, and breeches, shoes, and stockings of a proper British officer. But something was off. The round ring of red paint that circled the perimeter of his face; the twin shafts of lead, each an inch long and cinched together by the ring that dangled from his nose; his scalp, shaved back to the midpoint in a line with his ears and the shave covered with the same red grease and black stringy locks that hung down from there beyond his shoulders.

"They're assembling on the west fork of the River," the man Montour said. "So, no. The story's not true. You'll see no one for at least a week."

When his mouth opened, no flawed grammar, no foreign sounds fell out, but smooth clipped English such as a Philadelphia Quaker from Bristol or Belfast might speak.

Greenywalt felt no animosity toward this man standing by his son's coffin. He's on our side. He wasn't one of the killers.

"We Six Nations must let you know that it was the pride and ignorance of that great General from England. He's dead now, but he was bad when he was alive," Montour said.

The settlers hissed.

"He looked upon us as dogs. He would never hear anything what was said to him. We endeavored to advise of the danger he was entering with his soldiers, and he never appeared pleased with us—"

The settlers moved about uneasily, murmuring.

"Who is this cull?"

"Hey, why do you wear that paint?" The settler slapped a mosquito on his neck as he said it and pinched whatever had survived the slap.

"It keeps the bugs away. See my face? Look at yours."

It was true. The settlers laughed. The tension in the crowd melted away.

"Montour here is a friend of Colonel Washington. That means he is a friend of ours. He was at the Battle of Monongahela with Braddock. Were you?" It was Harris again, addressing the settlers from atop his cart. "Listen up if you want to survive. We'll take friends wherever we can get them, and Montour here is a friendly."

Harris turned back to the coffin off his right side. "Go ahead. Go ahead." His waving hand gave his blessing to the settlers on this end of the line, who had queued up to pay respects to the slain man in the box. A militiaman stationed himself at the head with a pine-knot torch that cast a flickering light downward into the box for each oncoming settler to see the man's features, the hands folded across the blood-streaked shirt, the begrimed face, the black gap at the top of the head where the red hair frizzed away from the sad gouge.

Most of the settlers gazed silently. They shuffled past and touched fingertips against the man's breast or even the forehead.

But the middle-aged settler's wife, old enough to be his mother, wailed, "Look what they done! They scalped him."

Harris continued his address. "You heard André. They're only now assembling on the West Branch, his people say. That means we have some days yet. I dug loopholes today in my cabin walls, the ones facing the River. I need a few men to finish the stockade. You see it, halfway done, although we've got the ditch the whole ring around. This is no time to flee! I intend to stay until the last extremity. Bring your families in until we know how things stand. André will bring his. Right?"

The white man/Indian nodded.

"And I've got a shed full of rum. Give 'em another cup if they want it."

Beyond the semicircle, Greenywalt sat on the high waggon seat beside his son, who had joined him, watching from the outside. Overhead, the million million stars spilled like milk the whole way back past Philadelphia.

"This was a mistake," the Boy said. "Can we leave? No? We're stuck?"

"We're staying till the end," he said. "I won't let him out of my sight."

Back in the semicircle, Harris called instruction to someone in the cabin that none of them could see. "Bring the family, Elizabeth," Harris said. Two women emerged from the cabin front door, facing the River, and turned toward Harris. They appeared to be daughter and mother, their arms intertwined, and the younger lady came first, leading the older.

Their clothes seemed out-of-place for an endangered frontier settlement. They wore Sunday clothes, as if to celebrate an important occasion. The younger one wore the hooped skirts and bodice with exposed cleavage fashionable these days in the French and English courts and a jaunty flowered hat. The older one also wore broad skirts but a modest mantilla around the shoulders and a white organdy cap with white ribbons looped beneath the chin, her unbound hair falling from it loose across her shoulders. The older woman towed a boy, eight or so, who in turn held his sister's hand, and she held the hand of her own friend, a girl about the same age.

The crowd parted to let them pass, and the older woman took the lead now, striding to the coffin. Using her arm like a mother hen's wing, she encouraged the children along with her.

From his raised post on the waggon's high seat, Greenywalt could see her past Harris' shoulder. He saw her face come up over the side of the box, her eyes searching its contents. He saw the shock of recognition cross her face, saw the hand fly to her mouth and cover her nose, and he heard the outcry: "Ichabod!"

He knew the voice.

The children's hands appeared on the edge of the box. The sawhorses stood three feet high and the box another eighteen inches, so someone was lifting them up to peer in. No, the boy was on a stool, standing solitary, and one of the militiamen lifted the girl.

The girl glanced once and commenced screaming: "No! No! Let me go! Let me go! It's *not* Daddy."

The boy, in contrast, stared across the coffin edge. He stretched one hand and touched the face of the slain militiaman. He straightened and addressed Harris in a flat, emotionless voice: "I'm gonna kill 'em. I'm gonna kill 'em back."

He saw an image from the past. The red-haired child was Ichabod at eight, in every detail. The voice of action. The erect figure. The determination.

"She said *Daddy*," he said to the Boy on the high seat beside him. Somehow, in all of his daydreams and brooding on his son since that day in December thirteen years ago, the idea that *Ichabod has children* had never entered his mind. "I'm going to meet them."

"Don't be stupid. They don't want to see you. You heard the man Murphy."

"I'm going to meet his mother." He began his step down. "You want to come along or stew here by yourself?"

He walked around the end of the semicircle, past Harris' cart now and directly toward the coffin. The eyes of the spectators around the circle were palpable. *They see my beard. They see the Mennonist hat. And they know. I'm not one of them. If the Indian is different, I'm double different.*

"Hey! Who invited him?"

"Go home, Dutch Dog!"

She was beyond the coffin, kneeling by the hysterical small girl, her arms sheltering her. The child, like a small terrified puppy, had ceased trembling and sobbed quietly and nodded her head to inaudible comfort words. The woman lifted her face at the hoots and jeers, and he saw her face across the coffin. She stood as he came to the lip of the box opposite and passed the child's hand to the younger woman.

He didn't watch her anymore but looked directly below his hands, where the slain man's face lay shadowed. The militiaman thrust up the torch, as he had done for all the mourners in the queue. He touched the nose and cheeks. He traced the mouth with his fingertips.

"Son! Son!"

The older woman watched his moves. It was a comfort to her to see grief over her son, and although he didn't see it, tears coagulated and trickled down her unflinching face, fixed toward Greenywalt.

"It's his son!" She lifted her face toward Harris and then out in a sweep toward the settlers, she raised her voice: "He's the father. Klaus Greenywalt."

Greenywalt didn't shift from his position or look up in response. His head and shoulders bent leaden and stiff over the coffin, his own tears landing on the slain man's face. His heart felt fatigued and weighed down, and there was no strength available to acknowledge anything other than the loss that now surged back on him, like the incoming tide that began at his feet and deepened to flood around him until it reached his throat, and he choked for air.

He was in this bubble of time and air together with the face of the Beloved below. They were locked together. That bubble was going to burst very shortly, and that face would sink down forever into the ground in its flesh form while the spirit—where was he, even now? His son—where was he? He felt no affinity for people who thought the spirits of the departed hover just overhead in the clouds or just behind the shoulders, watching. No, the spirit had separated from the flesh, and this was not his son. This was a wood-carved, decaying, mocking representation of his son. And yet, it was all that he had left of him.

O God. O God in Heaven.

Does God know?

When the Son said, "My God, why hast thou forsaken me?" did God hear? The father couldn't watch it anymore. Turned his eyes away. Couldn't bear to watch the spirit peel off the earthy body of his son and the son's head drop lifeless and the body hang broken, already cooling, starting to putrefy, stiffen. Yes, he knows. He knows what it's like to see a son, the most beloved Son, murdered.

"The father, Goody Cameron?" Harris said, loud enough for the woman but too low for most of the crowd to hear. "Bod always said . . . we were friends, me like his older brother. He said his father died."

"It was my pact with Bod." She stood defiant, her chin up. "We would say it that way when we got here." Her voice rose. "But he's the father." She gained certainty of the rightness of telling this story now to the whole assembled crowd of settlers.

"This man raised him on the Pequea. He taught him how to shoot, and that beautiful rifle, which you saw how he hit the playing card at how many yards—where's the rifle?" She interrupted her own story with the logical question and looked around at the militiaman for an answer.

"Lost at the Monongahela," the militiaman said. "A savage got it."

"His birthday present to him at eight. He made him his waggoneer, back and forth to Philadelphia from the time he was fourteen. And these are his grandchildren."

Greenywalt lifted his head at this unbelievable piece of information. Grandchildren? He looked at the face across the coffin. The same face of Janey Cameron, his indentured servant for five years, his hired hand and keeper of the books for fifteen more, the mother of his slain son. He saw an indomitable face, whose resolute eyes met his. He saw the obstinate set of the mouth. She stood like an ancient Pequea oak on the other side of the coffin.

He nodded.

"It's all true."

His hand still rested on Bod's forehead. She stretched one hand now and laid her fingers on top of his. He didn't want to look up to see what was written on her face, but he couldn't stop himself from it. His hand lay unmoving beneath her fingers. but his eyes shifted upward and took in the determined face opposite.

What did it mean? What did it mean?

He couldn't say. He could only say that his heart lifted, and some terrible burden rolled off his chest.

"The father, she says," Harris announced in his clarion voice. "Fritz Greenywalt."

"Klaus," Janey corrected.

"Klaus Greenywalt."

A hand clapped somewhere in the semicircle, and now a couple more, and then the applause took on a life of its own and built to a crescendo.

"Captain Cameron," Harris said.

"Hip, Hip, Huzzah!"

"Captain Cameron!"

"Hip, Hip, Huzzah!"

"Ichabod Cameron!"

"Hip, Hip! Huzzah!"

He dropped his stare to his son's face again, the man's forehead beneath his hand. He watched her fingers pull away.

"There's work to do," Harris said. "It's past midnight. Take the man inside. They'll be washing the body, and the Parson will come in the morning to bury him, and he'll tell us all what to do."

Greenywalt intended to go after her, around the head of the coffin, to meet those children whom Mrs. Harris was already hustling back into the cabin, but the smell of bear grease and the man's hand on his shoulder checked him.

"I didn't see him fall," the man said. "I heard though. We all heard the news when we got to Dunbar."

He wheeled. Montour's bejeweled, stippled, and painted European face hung inches away. The odor of bear grease seemed overpowering but no stronger than the odor of putrefaction in his nostrils for the last twenty minutes. It seemed sweet to him, now that he grew aware of it.

"Your son was a warrior!"

What could he say? A warrior? What baptized Mennonist wanted a warrior for a son? The man had meant it as his highest compliment to the fallen captain. Greenywalt took it that way. "I thank you," he said, and then immediately he remembered who was with him.

"My other son," he said. He'd been conscious of Benjamin, spitting distance behind him during the entire dialogue with Janey Cameron. He pulled the Boy's arm forward.

"Be like your brother!" Montour said. "Be a warrior!"

It only seemed right to make the next move. He reached with both arms and seized the hands of the half blood.

"Room in the cabin for all the women," Harris said, still balanced on the cart. "The rest of you can stretch out, wherever you find six feet of clearing. I have blankets, if you need one, although . . . ?" He eyeballed the overheated starry sky. "Yes, it will chill off."

They trudged to the waggon, he and the Boy. They climbed and found spots on the waggon bed, full flour sacks for pillows, and covered themselves with the same blankets they'd used last night in Lancaster Square.

"We got lucky," Benjamin said. "Lucky that Harris shut 'em down."

"It wasn't luck. It was Him. Protecting us."

He knew that the Boy knew who he was speaking about. He knew the Boy was not going to say anything about Janey Cameron and her speech because he hated her, just as his own mother hated her. Not because he had personal reason to do so but because he'd drunk that hatred into his body. He'd drunk it down with his mother's milk. But maybe the evening had given him something good to think about.

CHAPTER 27

A FUNERAL, INTERRUPTED,
JULY 13, 1755

T HE THUD OF SHOVELS WOKE HIM. He pushed off the wooden slats of the conestoga. Each vertebra, each hipbone, and each shoulder blade presented a twinge or soreness. He pulled himself up with the aid of an overhead waggon hoop and rolled back the pale canvas, its upper side wet with the night's dew.

He faced the River and the broad, very flat, slow-crawling water that stretched a mile, empty of all life, to the Cumberland County shore. A bold golden brushstroke already shellacked the water for several hundred yards out, and the quiet water hardly ruffled the shape of the reflected image of the July sun. It couldn't be more than twenty minutes into the new day, and the locusts had already begun their vibrato in the trees behind him.

Beyond the half-dozen waggons by the well, last night's bonfire had collapsed into a foot-high mound of lumpy ashes and some charred log ends that still sent up wisps of smoke. The other waggons sat scattered, in some the drivers visible as silent knolls of clothes and blankets, in others the drivers and their families out of sight under canvas-covered hoops.

He saw the shovelers now in the long shadows cast by the horizontal sun over and through the sharpened tips of the palisade logs. Only their heads and shoulders were visible. They bent over their hole and now reappeared, first one, then the other, with a flying shovelful of dirt over the shoulder and onto the heap of dirt on the east side.

They're digging a grave for my boy. They're going to plant him in the ground and praise him as a warrior, and then they'll throw that dirt back on top of him, in their fortress.

Greenywalt was thirsty. He'd taught his son: when you thirst, so do your horses. He lowered himself over the waggon side. It was the Boy's task, but the Boy lay curled in the waggon bed, his body wrapped around a sack of flour like a lover, his Mennonist hat concealing his eyes.

Benjamin. This isn't Benjamin's day. This is the day to remember Bod.

He led the horses to the trough and cranked the windlass. The stream caught the passing sunbeams and glittered as it tumbled musically from the wooden staved bucket to the trough. He stripped his shirt, and when he brought the third bucketful, doused his head and bared back and assaulted his face with the chilly stuff.

"I'm hungry." The Boy was sitting up in the conestoga. "Why are we here, anyway?"

"Because your brother is here. Throw me the shirt that's under the seat."

"I smell bacon." The Boy looked off in the direction of the cabin.

"Let's go together. Wash yourself."

He shouldered open the door to the log cabin and motioned the Boy to go in ahead. Yes, bacon crackled noisily at the open hearth, where two Negress girls stirred enormous kettles and a third turned a hundred pieces of bacon in an open skillet.

"Here!" Mrs. Harris ladled out two bowls of oatmeal. She swiped her forehead with a backhand sleeve and looked overheated and perspiry, as if they'd been going at it a while now. "There's milk in the barrels. Find a seat where you can. You're looking for Janey and the children, I'd guess? In the cellar."

"Captain Harris?"

"He's breaking out the benches and tables. We're feeding a powerful lot of people. Did you get your bacon? Emmy, give 'em each a couple sticks of bacon."

They took their bowls of oatmeal, still too hot, with the bacon sticks riding sideways across the bowl tops, and descended the stairs toward the cellar. He pushed the door at the bottom, and the air lofted up damp and chilled and redolent of earth.

"Feels good, huh?"

The cellar resembled their German cellars, large limestones mortared into a five-foot-high wall around the sides, with a ceiling that arched upward another foot and a half in the center and a packed dirt floor. The small windows were paneless but too narrow for even a child intruder. The windows let in stingy light, but the whole room seemed funereal, with the coffin resting on a set of wooden trestles at the far end, crosswise with the room. Two half-consumed candles, each in a pool of melted wax, burned at the head of the coffin, one on either side, and Janey sat beside the left candle, on a wooden chair. She turned from the coffin as they reached the cellar floor.

"I couldn't sleep after we finished. I couldn't sleep for remembering," she said.

Her eyes looked fatigued and ancient. She sat bent, with one hand down into the box, perhaps resting on the man's shoulder. She didn't look disheveled. She wore clothes similar to last evening: the broad gray skirts, the mantilla around the shoulders, but with the white organdy cap covering her now-coiled hair and tied beneath her chin with the ribbons. She must have changed because they'd washed Bod, and the man-sized wooden tub still sat behind the box, an inch-deep residue of reddish-ochre water in it.

"Can we see him?" He'd set his untouched bowl of oatmeal on a hogshead of cider and motioned Benjamin to do the same.

He stepped to the edge of the coffin. The man had been cleaned of nearly all evidence of battle and wounds. She'd dressed him in a fresh captain's outfit, a black frock coat with parallel pewter buttons on the cuffs above his folded hands and the buttons on the frock in twin vertical rows the whole way to the immaculate white ascot that tied at his throat. His hair had been brushed back, and his head sank into the embroidered pillowcase so that the head wound was only barely visible.

Even in death, he looked clean-cut and noble, yet more like a marble statue than a man.

"He loved his family." She didn't speak as he had expected, mournful or monotone, but with her usual lilt. "He loved me and he loved his children. When he saw the threat, it was like a wolf or a bear coming for us. He had to go."

"He loved us too," Greenywalt said. "When Franklin came to Lancaster to conscript a waggon and a driver, he took Benjamin's place."

"He was a Paxtang Boy. They'll all show here today. Them and Parson Elder—he's their captain."

He believed in you. Be merciful, Lord. Preacher Herr baptized him, and then he strayed. He ran away. He left the faith, the Mennonists say. But the Calvinists say he can never be plucked out of your hand. Who is right? *Be merciful, Lord.*

He backed away and bumped into Benjamin by the hogshead,

finishing his oatmeal. He couldn't think of his own stomach right now.

"Children!" Janey called out.

The children descended the cellar steps, dressed for the day. The boy held his sister's hand and led, a step in front of her. They crossed the cellar toward Janey, at the far end, and the girl twisted his hand, trying to shake loose.

The boy didn't go to Janey but released his sister's hand and turned in Greenywalt's direction. He stopped and stared at them.

"You're my grampa, Granny says."

The boy had fine blue eyes in his steady gaze, a face open and freckled, and his throat encircled by a white ascot over a white shirt, like the ones his father wore right now.

"Come here," Greenywalt motioned from his seat on the horizontal hogshead. "You're a fine lad." He extended his hand, and the boy nibbled, moving tentatively his direction, like a colt whose curiosity overcame its fear of the larger creature. He took the boy's hand. "What's your name?"

"Wallace." The boy glared. "I'm eight and I shot three deers. A buck through the heart. A doe through the lungs, and Father and I chased until it fell. And another buck. Here." He tapped his forehead.

"You have a gun?"

"Not here. At home."

"Come, sit on my lap."

The boy sidled against him but wouldn't climb up. He stared into Greenywalt's face.

"I'm your grampa, that's right, and I didn't know about you. You know what?"

"What?"

"When I look at you, I see your daddy. I loved your daddy."

The boy slanted away and pointed out the girl, who had buried herself in Janey's skirt and peered out and away and again out and away. Each time she caught their eyes, she averted hers toward her grandmother's skirts and giggled.

"Annie Laurie's scared," Wallace said. "She believes in the banshee, that it will come and get our papa." His laugh was high-pitched and tinkling. "There's no such thing as banshees."

"Where's your mum?"

"You mean Granny?" Wallace flung out his arm and pointed.

"No. That's your grandmother. Your mummy."

"She's with the angels. She got consumption and died, and now it's just the three of us. Granny says she'll take care of us. But I'm going to take care of her because I'm a deadeye."

"I'd like to see that. Come visit us on the Pequea."

"And him?" Wallace asked. "Who's he? Will he be there?"

"Benjamin. Your daddy's brother. Your uncle."

Benjamin put down his empty oatmeal bowl and nodded to the lad.

"Yes, come and visit us on the Pequea," Greenywalt said, over Wallace's head, to Janey. "We'd like that."

At that moment, light flooded the far end of the cellar. They heard the complaining hinges and doors thumping open at ground level. Two militiamen clattered down the wooden steps.

"The Parson is here. We're going to start!"

Janey led the way out of the cellar, towing the two children. The stockade yard was a riot of commotion. Breakfast had finished. The women washed down the hastily arranged plank tables. The men lifted the benches away from the tables and set them up in a new configuration at right angles to the rising sun and facing a set of saw-horses, where Greenywalt supposed they would place the coffin.

Like Mennonist gatherings, men dressed alike and women dressed alike, but instead of the dark blue or black breeches and frock coats of the Mennonist men, men here wore white linen, deerskin breeches, and the familiar tricorns of Philadelphia. Was there any meaning to the fact that some decorated their hats with one or two turkey feathers, and others with the plumed white and brown tuft of a whitetail? Circles of muskets stood butt-downward by the coffin, something he'd never seen at a Mennonist gathering, where even one musket in the hands of a sentinel would be a rarity.

He had no trouble identifying the Parson. His waggon had been arrested just inside the east palisade gate by a militiaman who held the bridle and protesting head of the Parson's single horse, while a second militiaman assisted the Parson's wife—he had to assume—in finding her footing as she swung down, the hooped skirts blocking her view of her own feet. Beyond the horse, the Parson would be the man tugging a long black gown over his head and shoulders while one of the stockade sentinels, his musket in hand, reviewed the Parson's appearance and straightened the upturned collar.

Is that what he preaches in? He remembered the Reverend at the Heilige Geist Kirche in Heidelberg. He dressed in robes like these. But he had a splendid cathedral with a thundering pipe organ and five hundred parishioners. This Parson looked the same, but his church was a hurriedly constructed stockade in the forest, with locusts instead of an organ and no more than fifty parishioners. The robes triggered his negative comparison.

Mrs. Elder passed the horse and her husband on her way to Janey.

"I just can't believe it, Janey. It's such a big loss." She threw her arms around Janey's shoulders and pressed her cheek, with the hat twined with black ribbons above it, against Janey's. "And the children here with you. Ohhh, Chickies." Mrs. Elder crouched and pulled the children against her breast. "Motherless. And now fatherless."

The Parson came right behind, past the milling settlers without stopping to address any of them but intent on reaching the family in their grief.

"Janey!" He squeezed her hand between both of his. "Janey! He was a man of the Old Cameronian blood. Like his name, Cameron. It's what I'll always remember Bod Cameron by. He went to meet the threat head-on."

Greenywalt stood apart but near enough that he could be taken as part of Janey's family. Or was he?

This close, Parson Elder cut an impressive figure The wig lay snug over his forehead; the brown wig hair was pulled straight back to the black ribbon on his neck, with two tightly curled rolls at each temple, over his ears. The man's ruddy chin jutted, resolute, above the black robe with felt lapels that traveled the whole way to six inches above his black boots, which were only dusted by the stockade dirt. His ability to maneuver his generous girth and stocky body under the robe gave the impression of unusual vigor and ebullience for a man he guessed past fifty.

"I'm Klaus Grünewald." He extended his hand, stepping out.

The man turned and fixed fierce blue eyes on him.

"The father. Yes, my boys told me." The Parson gazed directly into Greenywalt's face. His eyes cut downward because of the eight-inch difference in their height. Like Bod, the Parson exceeded six feet. The Parson extended his hands. "Yours is a terrible loss, too, Greeny-walt. But not for naught. The first great law of Nature is self-defense, and Captain Cameron has inoculated us forever from the infection of Quaker nonresistance. You're not a Quaker."

"We're Mennonist."

"Ahh, yes. Your farms are the toast of Colonial America. Lush. Fruitful. Fertile. The lines have fallen for you in pleasant places, as the psalmist puts it." The Parson bunched his fingers as he elevated his voice in a rhetorical flourish.

"My son, Benjamin."

"You grieve too," the Parson said. He crushed Benjamin's hand between his. "The loss of a beloved brother. My own father lost his older brother in Scotland's wars, and he never recovered from the loss."

"John, they're ready for you." Mrs. Elder projected a good-natured laugh and distributed it around to all in the circle. "He gets so lost in the current—" Still turning, she caught the arm of the militiaman behind them by the empty trestles. "The family should sit in the front row here. Seat them in the front, will you?"

Greenywalt eyed the rows of benches that had filled with settlers, and Mrs. Elder led the way to the seats she had chosen for them, a few yards from the still-empty trestles.

He watched the backside of the Parson's sepulchral figure head away and wondered, Is he an ally? Mennonist history said *No*. It was the Calvinist clergy, his wife told him, who enforced heresy laws in Switzerland, clapped Mennonists in prison, auctioned off their lands, and distributed their children to foster families and orphanages. Calvinist clergy collaborated with the Council of Bern, chained her father to the riverboat floor with Benedict Brechbühl, and sent them down the Rhine. Calvinist preachers in the Kraichgau arm-twisted the Elector Palatine to sign laws that contained the Mennonists, kept them from growing, fined them with the Recognition Fee, broke up their secret assemblies. My own grandfather, the Calvinist elder . . .

But here on the frontier, who cared about ancient history and tribes? Aren't we all in the bateaux, and if we paddle together we survive, and if not, do we overturn and drown? Us and the Quakers, we want to disarm the threat, use peaceful means. The Scotch-Irish come with their guns. Even Montour, the Iroquois. Aren't we all in the batteau together?

Then there's my son, who brought his gun, and they're making him a hero.

Everything seemed muddled. Only one thing seemed clear to him. We are here to bury Bod, all of us.

The militiamen, six of them, arrived at the top of the cellar steps, Bod's coffin riding on their shoulders in the steady left-right, left-right movement of men who have drilled together. They reached level ground now, and their faces turned toward the Parson, who waited with his back to the seated settlers. The Union Jack unfurled with an audible snap over their heads, catching the faintest breeze off the River as it lifted, lashed to the pulley rope that John Harris hauled up the barkless tree, above the cabin roofline now.

The Parson's voice boomed out the high note:

God save our glorious King
Long live our noble King . . .

The settlers joined with the words and tune of the newly famous anthem.

Parson Elder turned back to the settlers and continued:

I am the Resurrection and the Life,
saith the Lord.
He that believeth in me, though he were dead,
yet shall he live.
And whosoever liveth and believeth in me
shall never die.

He recited the memorized words and then led at a procession pace to the sawhorses. The militiamen followed and swung the coffin down onto the trestles. Aengus, the head militiaman at Lancaster yesterday, retrieved a new and folded Union Jack from inside the coffin and spread it over the lidless top of the coffin.

The Parson returned to face the seated settlers. He opened his black-robed arms with his hands spread downward and outstretched, to bless them.

> Infinitely great, glorious and incomprehensible God, the Eternal Spirit, complete in all perfection and happiness of boundless power, wisdom, and grandeur, today we commit the soul of our beloved brother, our captain, Ichabod Cameron, into your eternal arms.

Greenywalt was seated, but he felt a charge of dark blood course through him. "Mmmm." He dropped his hand onto Benjamin's leg. The Boy looked up.

"Dat?"

The Parson lowered his arms, took out a small pocket notebook, opened it at arm's length, and began his eulogy:

> A mighty warrior has fallen today. We gather today to commemorate, nay, to celebrate our Caleb, a man who possessed a different spirit. Your son, Janey Cameron. Your father, Wallace and Annie Laurie. Like his clan name, Cameron, he represents the Cameron blood that coursed the veins of brave Scottish Covenanters in the Killing Time.
>
> Today I want to exalt the life of our brother. [The Parson punctuated with one hand overhead.] At the very mo-

ment when our frontier inhabitants here and everywhere are quite sunk in despair and dispirited—and since the defeat of the mighty British Army under General Braddock, in terror of the attack of the enemy—many seem inclined to seek safety rather in flight than oppose the savage foe.

I am no Adept at politics and have seldom troubled my heart about that science, beyond reading the common newspaper. It has long been my unhappy lot to be a spectator of the distresses and suffering of our fellow subjects in our neighboring provinces of Virginia and Maryland. But suddenly, one July afternoon, year of our Lord 1755, suddenly the storm gathering in the back counties of Pennsilvania for some fifteen years now unleashes with unspeakable fury in our beloved province and threatens all who have settled along the Susquehanna—my heart bleeds for us.

My heart also bleeds over the City Quakers, safe in their taverns and their beds a hundred miles from the frontier, and that spurs me on to speak my sentiments on the turn of events and the life of Bod Cameron.

Greenywalt moved uncomfortably on the front seat, without looking right or left. How unlike the spirit of our Preacher Herr, who told us to hate the war spirit! We don't permit it, and for that reason I sent my Ichabod away.

The crack of the musket overhead interrupted.

"Canoes on the River! French on the River!" Someone shouted.

When they drove in last night and he'd pointed out the mulberry in the darkness to the Boy, Greenywalt hadn't noticed the sentinel, hadn't even seen the platform circling the trunk top of the huge mulberry that loomed over the cabin. But now he stood, and so did the other settlers, all staring at the sentinel, sixty feet up, bent over the parapet of his platform and gesturing with telescope in hand toward the River.

The sentry bellowed, "At least four canoes. I see them clearly."

Greenywalt saw the man John Harris sprint for the tree. He saw him rip off his wig and smart military coat and toss them at the base and leap off the ground for the low limbs, his boots clawing the trunk. The settlers stood petrified for only a moment before Parson Elder shucked his own robe and threw on the military coat that the militia-man extended as he ran up. Harris reached the treetop and steadied the telescope against his trained eye.

"The lily flag. And savages. Four canoes full of them."

"Fire a round!" Elder shouted. His tricorn hat clapped over his wig now, he looked every bit the role of commander of the men, who responded like disciplined soldiers. Every man ran for his musket, which Aengus distributed, tossing each man his as the owner identi-fied it. Four of them ran without muskets to the twin cannons lo-cated beneath the flagpole. They rammed the wadding and the heavy cannonballs—already piled there in waiting—down the throat of the cannon and prepped the powder.

"Fire at will!" the Parson commanded.

The militiamen touched the fuse holes with burning tapers and clapped their ears. In the open stockade yard, the blast didn't seem frightening, but the roar of it would certainly carry across the width of the river, wouldn't it? The balls splashed harmlessly somewhere be-tween the bank and midstream.

"They've noticed!" Harris shouted. "They're shooting off their own."

CHAPTER 28

VISION OF LOCUSTS AND THE SAVIOR

THE LEAVES ON THAT MULBERRY TREE, each shaped like a man's hand, lay listless, green sides out, unmoving, not even a tremble because the day hung airless. The sun pitched at its zenith and blasted their heads. The pale white haze of the morning hours had burned up, but he still seemed to sit in a porridge of palpable but invisible air, filled with smells of moldering earth and bacon and running streams. The soup worked like a magnifying glass, concentrating the incoming rays onto his black breeches and dark blue shirt, which clung to his chest and back, soaked.

Greenywalt stood by the bench as long as he could, his eyes fixed on the sentinel in the treetop.

The militiamen strutted about the stockade yard, but mostly in twos and threes they patrolled along the trench on the embankment that overlooked the ten-foot-descent path to the River. From this trench Harris' still unbuilt west-side palisade was promised to rise, but now the only thing between them and the French and Indian party, if they chose to cross, was that ten-foot bank. Of course, the party couldn't cross the mile of water in secret, as they all knew. The Parson stood in the trench himself, his musket butt resting in it, in

355

heated discussion with Captain Harris, while several settler men hung around them, their own muskets level and pointed at the River.

He'd sent Benjamin to water the horses again, and now he thought he should sit, that his head was wobbling, and yes, he should sit.

But when he sat, the Image of Death also sat with him. He saw his son's face, Bod's face, on the forest floor, perhaps pinned there by his fallen horse and face upward, gazing at the knife poised over him and the pitiless eyes of—who? A Delaware? A Shawnee? A French-speaking white who'd adopted this barbaric practice? Did his son feel fear? Did he even feel the horrendous, pouring shot wound in his thigh? Never! He was sure he could stave off the knife, and then the knife came down. He saw it come down on his son. It lifted away, and the shout of exaltation over the blood-drenched trophy came simultaneously. But the scene wasn't done. It began again before his eyes. The knife uplifted. The descent. The roar of exaltation and his son's answering scream of pain.

I can't chase it away. I plead: O Christ, take away the Image, but when I least suspect, it gallops across my vision like a nightmare, vivid and relentless.

"They're gone. They're out of sight,." the sentinel shouted from the crow's nest.

"We'll continue the service," the Parson said. He crossed the yard to the front of the coffin, still wearing the rose-madder dyed jacket of His Majesty's officers, distinguishing him in this crowd of homemade linen hunting frocks. He pointed west. A cloud the size of a mulberry leaf had puffed up over the horizontal purple smudge line of the Blue Mountains. "We'll see a storm here yet." He used a handkerchief to mop his neck and forehead and cheeks, which glowed ruddy and wet.

The settler men brought their muskets back to Aengus, who stacked them, while the women corralled their children. They towed the children in, then sat and fanned their faces and the faces of the smaller children with whatever they could find: their hands, an extra cap.

Greenywalt felt the pulsing under his breast pocket. He noted he wasn't sweating anymore, that his arms below the rolled-up sleeves were dry to the touch and flushed.

"You're red," Benjamin said.

"Get some water."

"Our brother Bod Cameron." The Parson was continuing to the reassembled settlers. He stood with his back to the coffin as he spoke.

What can we learn here today? I've spoken of his courage. But there's another lesson for us, and we just saw the sign: enemy canoes a mile off.

The Indian looks with contempt on us. We're a pusillanimous pack of old women, divided amongst ourselves, without a spirit of resolution to call him into account, letting him commit what outrages he pleases upon us.

Cato, the Roman, expressed it well: "Whoever will pretend to govern a people without regarding them, will soon repent of it."

The supineness of the provincial authorities of Pennsylvania—our man Aengus said it—"They are more solicitous of the welfare of the bloodthirsty Indian than the lives of the frontier families." In their blind partiality, bigotry, and religious prejudice, they will not hear the demands of a different religious faith, the faith of us frontier

Presbyterians. At their feet we lay the reign of horror and devastation that has occurred in the neighbor provinces and now threatens—you saw them just now on the River—threatens our own settlements.

What about the Christian Indians, you may say, the supposed converts of the Moravians and Penn's Quakers, a band of them not forty-five miles down this river in Conestoga Manor? Do their wigwams harbor deadly foes? Do they conceal the night assassin of the forest? The villain who with savage ferocity tears the innocent babe from the bosom of its mother, where it was quietly resting, and hurls it into the fire of the cabin he has torched?

With that, the Parson paused, turned, and dramatically pointed his outstretched forefinger downward to indicate the man in the box behind. "The mangled body of our friend cries out for vengeance."

Vengeance?

My father lay on his chest in the entry of our home, where they'd drug him in, the back of his head crushed by a mighty stone, and the brain and blood draining onto our floor while the perpetrator stood in the doorway with his friends and gave his story, and did Mutti and I believe it? Not a word of it. But could we prove it was him? Not at all. Until I confronted him in the Tavern, "I heard you say just now—." And he, "You heard nothing, and no one would believe anything you said." There's an admission of guilt, I thought, but I'd prayed to the Lord and Hans Herr heard me say, "I will release the man. I will forgive as Christ forgave his crucifiers," and I did. I forgave him.

The ball and chain fell off that day. I got released to come to the New World and start life again.

And now? And now?

I sit before another mangled body, and the man says, "We will seek vengeance."

Greenywalt's body recoiled. Spasms hit both temples, and his entire head, under the straw hat, throbbed. His son's face before him presented double and blurred around the edges.

"Are you all right?" Benjamin asked. "You're very red."

"The image of death, Benjamin. I keep begging the Lord. Blot it out! Save me from it!"

"The image of death?"

"The knife. And the scalping."

The locusts had also elevated their chorus. The sound seemed to come from all directions. From where, exactly? The forest beyond? The woods to the right? The mulberry? Was this their seventeenth year? How did they know when it was seventeen and time to crawl out of the earth, as the big brown bugs did, and dig their hooked feet into a topside branch and split their shells and out they tumbled, leaving the papery husk propped like a kelpie self on the branch? Did the heavenly bodies tell them when? The alignment of the stars with the sun?

"There's a storm brewing," Benjamin said.

The small puff towered now in the west, a superstructure with a white head and an amorphous dark-gray butt that dragged itself steadily, slowly, toward the east. As it came, it morphed into ever larger versions of itself.

"I give you Bod Cameron," the Parson said. "He took it as his personal call to raise the drooping head of Pennsilvania and restore it to health and vigor.

"I call on my boys, the Paxton Boys!" He scanned the settlers, and Greenywalt felt the man's eyes traveling, felt them cross his face and move on. "Rise up like Bod Cameron! Let's honor our friend one final time."

He set the black tricorn on his wigged head.

Simply moving on his suggestion, the settler men organized themselves again in little more than a minute. Aengus ran to the teepeed rifles and distributed them. The five designated men paused on both sides of the coffin, their hands resting on its lip, until Aengus finished and joined them as the sixth, and with one grunt from him, they swung the coffin up onto their shoulders.

Parson Elder led the procession, the coffin at his heels, the company of settler men with muskets behind the coffin, all in march-step with the Parson, and the women in a loose undulating band behind them. Mrs. Elder led the women. His granddaughter walked between her and Janey, her hands in theirs, and the Boy Wallace march-stepped beyond, by himself among the women.

Greenywalt had uncorked himself to stand when the Parson gave the call for the procession, but his legs wouldn't cooperate. It was a couple hundred yards across the back of the stockade yard to the hole the men had dug this morning. The entire crowd had passed now, and their backs were to him. The women were singing.

The Lord's my shepherd,
I'll not want.

"I need to go with them, Benjamin."

He pushed himself upward again, his hand and shoulder against Benjamin's body, but his knees buckled. "I'm dizzy. I can't walk."

"Then wait. Drink some water." Benjamin pressed his canteen against his father's lips.

"The locusts."

"What is it?" The boy cocked his head sideways.

"They're coming from the well. Up out of it. It's the bottomless pit. The Angel has unlocked it."

The Boy stared back across the yard toward the well, three hundred feet in the other direction, the direction of the River. "You see locusts? I don't see anything."

Yes, he saw them. At first he didn't see them individually. He faced away from the well, watching the massed skirts of the women as they surged at a slow, measured pace up the path, to the rhythm of their song.

It didn't matter whether he looked back at the well or not. The well belched a cloud, and he knew it, a dark plume like the cloud of furnace smoke that rose over the Pequea limekilns. The cloud was vast. It stretched back and back, across the River, a mile wide, to the Blue Mountains ten miles off, the breadth of it several miles and the depth of it, over his head, several hundred feet.

He heard them, here in the darkness that they created because they blocked out the sun, which appeared now and again through shifting holes in the cloud. The sun hung black and bedraggled, like the Quaker Logan's wig on its stand. He heard them gnawing, chewing as they flew. He heard the clanking of steel breastplates, and he realized they were commanded by a general like Marlborough, the commander at Blenheim, the battle every Palatine boy knew like his ABC's. The great English general had saved them from Louis XIV's army, and he'd done it at Blenheim. He threw his massed Hussars on horseback, their terrible curved swords aloft as they flung themselves against the French lines, and their swords devoured the French.

But these weren't Marlboro's Hussars. They were locusts.

And out of the smoke came locusts upon the earth,
and unto them was given power,
as the scorpions of the earth have power. . . .

And the shapes of the locusts
were like unto horses prepared unto battle.

Yes, yes.

And on their heads were as it were crowns of gold,
and their faces were as the faces of men.
And they had hair as the hair of women,
and their teeth were as the teeth of lions.

"Teeth of lions," he muttered. He hobbled, one hand on Benjamin's shoulder, toward the mass of skirts ahead on the path. "The sound of their wings was as the sound of chariots of many horses running to battle," he said.

Benjamin squinted sideways at him.

He had the sensation that he was not walking, but a locust had hooked its talons into the shirt on his shoulders and both lifted his feet several inches off the ground and propelled him forward, his toes still kicking against the stones. These were monster locusts, the size of eagles, and the locust twisted its head in flight to glare directly at him. Her visage was human, yet demon-like, the eyeballs globular like a cicada's, her teeth greatly out of proportion and fanged in the gapped mouth that hissed and flicked greenish-black spittle over his face. The crown was golden that capped the unbound waist-long hair—but why say "waist"? Her body was rippled and scaled, like an insect's thorax. . . .

The women pulled back, and the path opened ahead to let the two of them pass. The grave lay directly before them, with rangers standing on three sides of it, but none in the front. The coffin sat on the ground between him and the hole.

He knew he should warn them.

"The day of his wrath has come," he said, "and who is able to stand?"

"What did he say?"

Benjamin hurried his arm. "Dat! Dat!"

Parson Elder stood on the far side of the hole as well, between his militiamen. He'd passed his musket to a militiaman, and now he removed his hat as well and crossed his chest with it. The rangers all straightened, their muskets upright by their legs.

The man Aengus came forward, lifted a corner of the Union Jack, and snatched it away.

From the far side of the hole, Parson Elder extended one arm out over the hole toward the coffin and over the crowd of women and over the several settler men who were not part of his militia. The men pulled off their hats.

"We commend into thy hands, most merciful Father, the soul of this our brother departed. . . ." The Parson read from his little notebook. The leaves on the mulberry rattled, and the treetop swayed several feet under the sudden gust. The sentinel crawled over the edge of his crow's nest, and began a hurried descent. The settler women craned upward at the oncoming storm.

Greenywalt arrived and propped himself against the side of the coffin and looked down. The immaculate uniform was black, which made the contrast with the dead captain's chalky face all the stronger.

". . . in sure hope of the general Resurrection in the last day and the life of the world to come, through our Lord Jesus Christ."

The Parson placed his hat back on his head, which cued all the other men to do the same.

"Prepare for the salute."

The ranger beside the Parson handed him his musket, and the

assembled rangers, the Parson included, lifted their muskets, the muzzles pointed uniformly toward a spot in the sky several feet above the roofline of Harris' log cabin, in the direction of the River.

He heard the roar and saw the muzzles belch a line of sparks and flames. A white, acrid cloud materialized above the flash holes of the flintlocks, and a shapeless white haze moved slowly toward the crowd in the now abruptly motionless air again.

In the smoke, a most marvelous thing happened that he would remember the rest of his life. He would tell about it, at first with great hesitation and fear of ridicule and laughter, and then with joy as he grasped the full meaning of it.

He saw the Savior. He knew it wasn't reality because the rangers moved all around him, reloading their flintlocks, yet it seemed real. He *knew* it was the Savior by the crown of thorns on his head, pressed down into his scalp, and large droplets of blood that coursed continuously across his forehead and fell into his beard, which had no white hairs in it, and the Savior's eyes were locked on his. Only then he saw more: his wrists were still nailed to the Cross, yes, it was through his wrists, not the palms of his hands. The Savior appeared confused. He'd toughed out the night of temptation in the Garden. He'd endured the mock trial and the scourging, the mockery, and the nails. Now his eyes gazed piteous and empty, and the eyeballs rolled up suddenly as he cried: "My God, my God, why hast thou forsaken me?"

But he saw more.

Behind the Savior on the Cross, another cross loomed in the gun smoke, and Bod was there, hanging, his arms—in the black captain's uniform—spread like the Savior's, and blood coursed, . . . *no*, deluged from the terrible hole on his scalp. It streamed across his cheeks and nose and fell onto the white ascot, the black uniform front, and the white shirt beneath it, and he saw his son's eyes, cornflower blue and wide with confusion. He'd made irreversible decisions. He'd enlisted and led his company into Braddock's battle, and on the last morning, leaped on his horse and charged, solo. Had he done wrong?

The Savior's face moved behind Bod now—and how that happened, how he escaped the nails and came behind, and how Bod himself escaped the cross, he didn't see—the Savior's arms with the bleeding wrists rose through his son's armpits and supported the man, and he saw the Savior's face over his son's shoulder. The furrows of sorrow were more hideous than the trails of lifeblood. Tears trickled along those furrows, mixed with the blood, and ran pink.

"Today shalt thou be with me in Paradise."

Bod hung limp in the Savior's grasp. His eyes rested shut, and a trace of smile seemed to break. Was the man alive? Yes, the chest was heaving slowly.

His legs wobbled. The Image of Death had been scrubbed away by a new image, his son with his eyes resting shut, a very small smile breaking, and he saw it now, not in the vision but on the face in the coffin below him, a very faint smile.

The dark blood erupted upward from his chest to his own brain. It was going to blot out the terrible vision he'd just seen, which he hoped would not continue because he didn't think he could bear any more.

"My Son! My Son!"

Parson Elder called the rangers around him at the coffin.

"What happened? Get him out of the box. Is he breathing? Get him over in some shade. The mulberry. Under the mulberry."

The bolt of electricity shot out of the incoming fortress of dark clouds, and the instantaneous thunderclap sounded in the woods beyond the stockade. The locusts hushed.

"No, not beneath the tree," the Parson said. "Take him inside."

The settlers sprinted toward the cabin, and the militiamen, under Aengus's direction, tapped the lid onto the coffin and roped it down into the hole.

PART 7

THE SECOND SON

CHAPTER 29

JANEY AGAIN, THE PEQUEA, SUNDAY, JANUARY 4, 1756

SOME SAY I HAVE UNUSUAL POWERS. Unlike many people, I remember everything I see or hear. I see a word and remember how to spell it ever after. I meet a man, and years later I remember the clothes he wore, the warts or freckles or pockmarks on his face, the accent on his English, and the exact words he spoke in response to my: "Benjamin here. Benjamin Grünewald." Is that really so unusual?

I also keep journals, which I bind up with needle and thread, one journal for the plants in our Pequea forest, one for the quadrupeds of all sorts and reptiles, and one for the poems and proverbs I have written. I think my memory is not magical so much as the cultivated results of keen observation, reflection, and the keeping of records that I review from time to time.

Three things do give me unmingled delight:

1. A book of narration, such as the book of martyrs, whereby I taught myself to read, with good explanatory pictures. I have also read the historical parts of the Bible, but I steer clear of the prophecies and psalms. Information and facts are what I want, not sentiments.

2. A thunderstorm in frown masses lifted up and discharging electrical fluids. I have read much of Franklin's theories and discoveries and journeyed to the Pennsilvania State House to see the upright rods of iron on the roof, made sharp as a needle and gilded to prevent rust, and from the foot of those rods, a fat wire leads to the ground, to draw the electrical fire silently out of the rod and secure the building from terrible mischief. It is my firm intent not to become a miller, like Dat, or a waggoneer, like Ichabod, but a man of science, like Franklin.

3. The presence of Charlotte, who is exquisite as a dewdrop, modest, and quiet. Were I to brush her garments, as we stand in the meetinghouse on those rare Sundays when her family comes from their home in Manor Township, I don't know if I would be joyful or miserable. I was tempted several times to come near and touch her hand, but her gentleness forbade the least approach of rudeness. Her sister Clarissa is slim and sweet, yet cross-eyed, which mars the charm of her expression, but Charlotte is voluptuous and full-developed. I have yet to speak my first word to her.

How I learned to read I know not, but it occurred without a teacher, piecing out the ab ab's in my mother's *Ausbund*. I was four, Mem says. I learned to read German first, although my father discouraged it and kept the books out of my way because he intended I learn English, the language of the thirteen colonies, he said.

But I found a book of martyrs, in German, and without help of an alphabet or spelling book, I applied myself. In a short time I was able to comprehend and read the volume with facility. It held the narrative of martyrdom and persecution from the stoning of Stephen until toleration was established for Anabaptists in Holland in 1660, with many gruesome pictures.

I had already reached my ninth year, I believe. Mem insisted that I read books of "pious reflection" and introduced me to John Bunyan's book, but I was able to obtain Aesop's *Fables* and the writings of Josephus, and from there I progressed to Homer's *Iliad* and Plutarch's *Lives*, which I dearly love to this day.

But nothing held me like *The Bloody Theater, or, Martyrs Mirror of the Defenseless Christians*. "Do not expect that we shall bring you into Grecian theaters, to gaze on merry comedies or gay performances," wrote Mr. Thieleman van Braght, compiler of the martyr letters and composer of the reports.

> We shall lead you into dark valleys, even into the valleys of death (Psalm 23:4), where nothing will be seen but dry bones, skulls, and frightful skeletons of those who have been slain; those beheaded, those devoured, others strangled at the stake, some burnt, others broken on the wheel, many torn by wild beasts, half devoured, and put to death in manifold and cruel ways; besides, a great multitude who having escaped death bear the marks of Jesus, their Savior, on their bodies, wandering about over mountains and valleys, through forests and wilderness, forsaken of friends and kindred, robbed and stripped of all their temporal possessions, and living in extreme poverty. . . .

"And who knows," our Preacher Herr and lately Preacher Hirshi would say, "after a hundred years of rest from the worst of these torments, how soon we shall again come to a time of martyrs?"

Such words seemed remote to me, pure speculation or, at worst, the old trick of frightening the flock into a state of spiritual panic, into which the Preachers might introduce a solution: the necessity of repentance, the misery of the wicked, the unspeakable perdition of the lost.

I hardened my heart against such appeals as I came into my mid-teens.

But then came the events of 1754–55. Ardent hostilities broke out between the English and French, and both nations determined to send reinforcements to their colonies in America. The Delaware and the Shawnee, aggrieved by the English settlers and their cruelty, were stirred up by the French, who promised "to restore their lands." England countered the French intentions by sending General Braddock and his 2,100 men westward over the Allegheny Mountains. And Braddock's death on July 13 of this past year, along with 26 of his 86 officers, over a third of the privates he led into battle, and my own brother, Ichabod. That defeat inspired the enemy and dispirited our provincial people.

What bloodthirsty cruelties, like those recounted in our book of martyrs, might we now see with our own eyes?

My subscription to Franklin's *Pennsylvania Gazette* showed its value, for Mr. Franklin published letters from our provincial authorities that provided more substance than the rumors that quickly dominated every public meeting of two or more persons.

Here in my library I hold the Petition of October 22nd to Governor Morris, signed by seventeen of the settlers of Penn's Creek who escaped the bloody events of the Sixteenth:

> That on or about the Sixteenth of this instant October, the Enemy came down to the said creek and killed, scalped, and carried away all the men, women, and children, amounting to twenty-five persons in number, and wounded one man who, fortunately, made his escape and

brought us the news, whereupon we, the Subscribers, went out and buried the dead, whom we found most barbarously murdered and scalped. We found but thirteen, which were men and elderly women, and one child of two weeks, the rest being young women and children we supposed to be carried away prisoner.

The House we found burnt up, and the man of it, namely Jacob King, a Swisser, lying just by it; he lay on his back barbarously burnt and two Tomahawks sticking in his forehead, one of the tomahawks marked recently with the letters W.D., we have sent to your Honor.

The terror of which has driven away almost all these back inhabitants except us, the Subscribers, with a few more who are willing to stay and endeavor to defend this land, that as we are not able of ourselves to defend it for want of Guns and Ammunition, and but few in number, without assistance we must fly and leave this Country at the mercy of the Enemy.

As it happens, this Jacob King came to Pequea last fall under the name of Jean Jacques Le Roy, as he hailed from the French territories of Switzerland but a Dutchman, like us., and together with a party of Mennonists purchased a tract on Penn's Creek off the West Susquehanna, from Abraham Herr, the brother of our former Preacher Christian, now passed to his reward, and brother of my father's business partner, Hans Herr. King left his oldest daughter with the Herrs, her good fortune as she would else have ended the bride of a painted Delaware like her younger sister Marie, had she been on Penn's Creek that morning. Or perhaps a slave—the fate of that girl and the others seized has not been found out.

Panic ensued and has continued down to this very hour.

I also hold this letter from the *Gazette*, a letter from Weiser, the Indian translator for our Governor Morris. On October 30 of this past year, the letter states, Weiser alarmed the settlers of Berks County. The farmers—more than two hundred, armed with guns, swords, axes, pitchforks, *et cetera*—formed a posse that gathered at a farmer's house near Weiser's place. Weiser sent for his Lutheran clergyman neighbor, who gave an exhortation and a prayer, after which Weiser divided the men into companies of thirty, and they marched toward the Susquehanna to secure the Tolihaio Gap on the Swatara, where it was supposed the enemy would come through the pass in the Blue Mountains. On arriving there, they received news of further attacks on the John Harris burial party by some savages painted in black and that the enemy had already passed the Gap, so the posse men concluded it were better they go back and protect their families at home.

Rumors! Rumors!

Those days last fall, every day we heard fresh news of a settler murdered here, a family scalped there. The Courthouse bell in Lancaster rang continuously, it was reported, sounding the alarm.

In November we learned that the Governor had issued a bounty of 150 Pennsilvania dollars for every hostile Delaware captured and brought to the authorities and 100 for his scalp alone. The Governor also invited the Friendlies to lay down the hatchet and meet for treaty talks.

Meanwhile, the Governor announced a chain of forts to be constructed from the Delaware to the Susquehanna, one every twenty miles or so, each manned by twenty to thirty provincial militiamen. In Lancaster, a blockhouse was to be put up at the north end of Queen Street, with a deep ditch around it and a drawbridge for those wishing access—like the castles in the Song of Roland—"and we will place our girls and children within," promised the Governor.

"These are fearful times. God only knows when they will end," he said.

Which all brings to mind the *Martyrs Mirror* and our Preachers' prediction of bloody times again.

I commiserated on this with Sholley, our tenant's son, as we drove the waggon shortly thereafter, early November, I believe, to Lancaster with barrels of cider, some of Herr's applejack, and the usual bags of flour with our mill's imprint, for the market.

Sholley became my friend when his father and mother and their thirteen brats moved into our old cabin. He cut a wild and solitary figure, with his perfectly gray locks, although only a year less than I, uncombed and tangled in fierce knots about his neck; and with his way of stalking off by himself into the words "for a good hike," as he would say. I was reminded of Ossian, the wandering hero the gray Scottish Highlands, whose life I have read about and admired.

"Benjamin," Sholley said, "I think I'll enlist."

We were in Lancaster Square that day, as I said. The militia passed before us, two companies of marching men under Colonel Weiser and a company of light horsemen, all marching in time to the deep tones of a baton swung against an oversized bass drum slung about a foot soldier's neck, and to the notes of a second foot soldier who piped on his flute and pierced me sweetly. But the Colonel himself paled, I thought, in comparison with the memory of my own brother, Ichabod, on his stallion. Weiser was old, maybe sixty, with a potbelly and none of the swagger and strut of my brother.

They marched across the Square and up Queen toward the site of the proposed blockhouse, and Sholley stood on our market stand in a state of rapture.

"What a brave and noble band! To shoulder a musket like that and march to the defense of our women and children."

I got a sudden impulse to tweak him because his idea of enlistment seemed puerile to me. "Maybe Charlotte too," I said.

Sholley's throat and cheeks crimsoned. He was as smitten with her as I, and he turned round and punched me solidly in the breast.

"What do you know?" he said. He wrestled me down, and we rolled once or twice before I managed to seat myself on his chest and threw my weight forward to press his arms flat on the cobblestones. Although I was thin, all of me was muscle from toting bags of flour at my father's mill.

He rutsched his wild locks back and forth beneath me, and he seemed like an unbroken colt, beautiful in his natural wildness. But I had him pinned.

"Uncle?" I cried.

He rotated his head to and fro again on the cobblestones to indicate negative, and I couldn't bear to see him lose his unrestrained freedom, so I rolled off.

"Do you really mean it?" I asked. We were both seated, brushing off the dirt and irregardless of any customers at the stall because there weren't any. Everyone had gone to gawk at the militia. "Enlist?"

"Why not?"

"Have you ever seen a dead body? People die in war. Could you shoot a man dead?"

It was perhaps the wrong question to ask because Sholley was not of the nonresistant persuasion of the Mennonists. His people belonged to the Scottish Presbyterians on the Octorara. Those were things we'd talked about, hypothetically. But now the real issues of defense or defenselessness marched, as it were, right up the streets of our town.

"No, but I wouldn't let them come and scalp my mum and little brothers. I'd fight first. Wouldn't you?"

Face to face with this question, I found that I couldn't view it from my usual objective stance of marshaling all the facts, retreating into the mill with my clay pipe to measure my reading time—how many pipefuls did a book take?—and letting the verdict of history arise out of the facts and present itself to me. There wasn't even the possibility of a pipe today, and I stared at him. The silence between us seemed to stretch until he pulled a *Sholley* on me.

"If it were Charlotte?" he asked. He smiled, and when he did, it flashed like the flash of light in an opening doorway. His smile revealed all his teeth as his mouth opened to its maximum stretch.

"I don't know," I said.

But his father forbid him to enlist, at least for now, and so he was available when my next mission came.

It arrived the first week in January 1756. Christmas had passed, and the recent snow lay mounded everywhere around our mill and house. The roads were mostly cleared because of the passage of waggons into and out of our store. The mill itself was shut because of the deep freeze, although the store stayed open every weekday, but it was a Sunday afternoon, the first one of the New Year.

We sat in the *Stube* around the five-plate stove, and I was working on Virgil's *Aeneid*, in Dryden's translation, and without my customary pipe, because Mem hated the stink and only allowed it in the office of the mill or in the fresh air. She was in the kitchen, shuttling popcorn seeds in a hot skillet because Dat liked the fluffy white kernels with salt.

My father lay half-reclining on a wheeled bed, the self-same bed he'd been occupying since we carried him in from the waggon five months ago. He spoke these days, although with some slur of his words, and walked at least twice a day around the house with the aid of a cane and my arm. Perhaps he was reading the big Bible, which lay open on the plaid blanket that covered his lower body, or perhaps he napped. I don't remember.

"Someone's here," Mem called me from the kitchen, "Go see, Benjie."

Once I extracted myself from Virgil, I heard the noise myself. On opening the door, I found a single horseman right outside, with a saddlebag flapped open on his lap as he rummaged through it.

"Grünewald?" he asked.

When I said I was, he handed me the letter. He declined to come in to warm himself, although I figured that he hailed from Lancaster, a thirty-minute ride when the roads were clear.

I noted the address to my father and brought it to him. His eyes opened at the sight of the letter, and as I expected, he said, "Open it. Read."

I did so with a penknife while my mother came with the popcorn, in a woven Indian basket. I read the signature aloud: "Jane Cameron."

"What does she want?" My mother made a sour face.

"*Greetings in the name of our precious Savior,*" I read.

"Get on with it," Mem said.

"*Things have changed for us, since the sad passing of your son. The calamities on the Susquehanna have forced us, as well as most we know, to leave everything behind and take refuge in a secure place.*"

"*We are all in Steitztown at Light's Fort.*"

"I know the place," Dat said.

"*Sixty families.*"

"Just a house," Dat said.

"*Wallace and Annie Laurie are safe with me.*"

"His children?" my mother asked.

"*Just writing to keep you abreast, in the event you would like to meet again, as you stated before your accident. We pray the Lord is restoring your health completely. Jane Cameron.*"

"You promised that?" Mem asked.

"Yeees." Dat appeared incapable of any other response to this news. His eyes drifted, crossed my face, and paused.

I knew all of the family dynamics, all of the untouchable topics, all of the items that might instigate an explosion of words or accusations between my mother and father, but I felt a compulsion to respond.

"We could help them, Dat!" I said.

"Oh my conscience," Mem said. It was her favorite phrase of mortification, the words she reached for when she reached the absolute end of toleration. "There are families without homes everywhere. The preacher said this morning again: They want food and clothes for those poor folks in Tulpehocken."

Dat came alive. He waved his good hand and twisted to look at Mem's face, behind him.

"But we know Jane."

"We need to do this, Dat," I said. "Doesn't it say: 'Naked and you clothed me, sick and imprisoned and you visited me'?" I wasn't a Bible scholar, but those verses about the sheep and the goats brought up one of my favorite images.

When you are eighteen, you sometimes change your mind because the facts have piled so high that the scale suddenly drops on the other side. What you once believed is exposed as a half-truth. This was not something I came to one afternoon over a pipe in the mill.

Perhaps it began that morning in Penn Square in front of the man I admired more than any preacher or businessman, Mennonist or otherwise. That man was Benjamin Franklin. I had heard my father, in English, because none of his fellow Mennonists could or wanted to articulate his thoughts in "that cursed tongue," as Mem calls it, argue for our people and their nonresistant principles to Benjamin Franklin.

Then the man whose name I'd heard reviled in our home for fourteen years rode out in the flesh that day, on the back of his stallion, a hero to his own men, the object of awe by my peers, and he took my place *against my will* at the side of our waggon and team on their way to battle. Then the events of July, when they brought home his mangled body.

I witnessed this man, my father, in the camp of the warmongers. He would not leave the body of his son. Despite threat of the pillory, despite the armed militia on every side, despite his appearing as out of place as a redcoat officer speaking Pennsilvania Deitsch. He did so, and along the way he went toe to toe with Captain Harris and with the Fighting Parson himself, Parson Elder. Fearless. Beaten down by his tragedy and loss but not broken. Overcome by the sun and the clot in the channels of his brain and dark visions, but he held on till the end.

This man, I now realized, was a good man, maybe a great man. My mother would always be my mother, but I was done with fighting on her side in the fratricidal conflicts of our home. Why should I take sides ever again? Could I love them both, equally?

I didn't know the answer to that yet, but right now I knew what my father would want for Jane Cameron and her two children. He'd called them *"my grandchildren."* Was there a man alive who didn't love his grandchildren as if they were chunks of his own soul?

Only one thing remained outstanding in my calculations, and that was his opinion of me. I was the second son. Not the beloved son, who had died. But in the Providence of God, at that moment, when I'd said what I did about helping Jane, he leaned out of his recliner toward me, where I sat on my chair, and I went to catch him, to prevent him from falling to the floor, which I presumed was happening. But his hand avoided mine and instead grasped my arm above the elbow, very hard. His eyes were riveted on mine, and I saw tears there. He was without speech, but I saw he was expressing his thanks.

He remained half-sitting on his bed, punctuating the air with punches of his hand.

"The waggon," he said. "Load it. Cider. Blankets. Sausages. Bread. Butter and eggs from Frau Herr. I'll pay you." He fell back, exhausted, whispering, "Sixty families!"

My mother pushed herself between the stove and his outstretched feet, her back to the stove. Her mouth fell open, and I waited for a storm of recrimination.

"Take Sholley," he said.

My mother shook her head, a sort of shake of disbelief. "My conscience!" she repeated. That was all she said. For the first time in my memory, she appeared to have nothing else that she was ready to say.

PART 8

GREENYWALT'S JUSTICE

CHAPTER 30

BENJAMIN AND THE WILL,
SUNDAY, JANUARY 11, 1756

SHE PEELED THE QUILT BACK from his shoulders to lay bare his arms. He watched the quilted flowers and birds retreat: two-inch high tulips whose purple petals embraced red-and-yellow cores, the flowers themselves rooted in red-rimmed hearts and hung on branches that looped gracefully over vermilion birds with yellow eyes, their bodies large and their tail feathers long like those of the native turkey, but their necks and heads smooth and unpatterned, like those of turtledoves.

Throughout dinner he'd watched wordlessly from his cot because, as seated, the adults' backs were turned toward him. The children, on the other hand, occupied the corner bench against the wall facing him, but they only came visible from time to time through the shoulders of the adults, as they shifted over their dinners. Maudlin announced each dish as she carried it in triumphantly from the kitchen and the hearth stove there.

"The duck!"

"Squash from our garden!"

"Frony's cantaloupe pickles!"

His mouth watered at each announcement. The small plate of minced duck breast and boiled squash she'd spooned onto his tongue were unsalted and seemed without taste to him.

The five-plate stove threw off prodigious bursts of heat, enough for the whole room, and he felt warm enough, for now, but he couldn't stop the tears that continued to trickle.

"What now?" she asked, bending over him. She took the white handkerchief and wiped down his cheeks. "You should be happy. You got your way. They've come."

It wasn't that at all. It was the humiliation. It was the diaper cloth between his legs that she checked every time she came. It was his head, shaved bald, although the doctor had made one kind allowance. "We won't need to shave the beard." After forty years of rubbing the hair on his chin and cheeks and viewing them in the mirror, it would have felt like public nudity.

Everything hurt. His grandchildren—and he hadn't even known he had any six months ago—were visiting! These beautiful chips of the son he loved sat thirty feet away, and here he lay, hairless, diapered, eating unsalted squash mash.

She wiped his bald scalp with a damp towel.

"The barber is here."

How had that happened? He hadn't heard the man enter. Perhaps he'd fallen asleep. The heat from the stove was so pleasant. The case clock behind the stove chimed through the full set of up-down notes and bonged twice. Past the end of the table, through the windowpane, large snowflakes swam up and down, as they always did at the beginning.

"How are we?"

The barber was a clever, bony-faced man with a cocked hat set on his wig. The precisely fit, knee-length waistcoat over his short frame and the perfectly knotted blue ascot made him look like a fussy man. That was probably a desirable trait in a man who wielded a six-inch razor and an assortment of bloodletting tools in the leather apron that buttoned to his lower vest and covered him from the waist to his knees like an apron. He set the small satchel on the bedside chair and unsnapped it.

"Any change since last week, Ma'am? The usual confusion still?"

Maudlin nodded. "Some speech. We only understand about half of it."

"The blood?" he said. "That's why I'm here, of course, but have you noticed anything?"

"He's got a plethora again," Benjamin said. He joined his mother at the far side of the bed, addressing the barber, who stood on his right side, pulled out his tools as he spoke, and placed them on the blanket covering Greenywalt's legs. "He overheats. He perspires, and we have to change the sheets several times a day."

The barber began his usual routine. He swabbed both of the patient's arms with soapy water and then once more with a clean rinse cloth. He wound tourniquets around the muscles of both the right and left arms. Then he produced an elegant six-inch high ceramic jar from the satchel, labeled LEECHES, the turret-like top perforated with numerous air holes in the shapes of diamonds and hearts. The barber set the top aside and thrust one hand inside to retrieve a dripping metal tube.

He rested the tube against the patient's arm, flapped a small hinged door down, and the nearest leeches within, smelling blood, inched forward. He blocked the passage of all but the first one, which moved past his posted finger in a series of humping moves to a spot on the crook of the elbow where the vein showed blue beneath the skin. The leech settled and burrowed its head downward. The barber moved the tube a few inches to a new spot and released the second, and then to a patch of skin over the wrist for the third leech.

The grandchildren, driven by curiosity, bunched in front of Benjamin, who was on the far side of the daybed from the barber.

"What is it?" the boy asked. "What's he doing to Grampa?"

"Oooh!" The girl whimpered, pushed around Benjamin's legs, and thrust her face into Maudlin's skirts.

"My! My!" Maudlin rubbed the girl's capped head and looked across the room toward Janey, who had paused in the table cleanup to watch.

"She hates creepers," Janey said.

"Just leeches," Benjamin said. "*Hirudo medicinalis.* They'll help Grandpa get better. See?" He went down on one knee beside Wallace.

"Put one on me!" Wallace extended his arm toward the metal tube and rested it on the quilt over his grandfather's chest.

He gazed down on the boy's hair, the color of sumac in October, and observed the bold thrust of his arm. It was true to form. Like his father. The boy's eyes burned the steady blue flame just off the wick of a candle. The leeches pinched as they set their mouths in his arms and began their long drink, but he didn't notice because of the children. Wallace. It had a foreign sound. He knew lots of Quaker Englishmen, but no Wallaces. The girl, what was her name? He sorted through his memories and recalled the exact moment he'd first met her in the cellar of Harris' cabin, and he pictured her grandmother Janey speaking to her that day, but no name came forward, and right now he didn't know how to ask the question.

The boy's arm lay flung out across his belly, with the lone leech the barber had put there, black and segmented and stationary, in the crook of his arm.

"It tickles," the boy said.

"Tickles!" Greenywalt echoed the boy, and it caused him to smile hugely.

Maudlin applied the damp towel against his forehead and swiped upward.

She's gotten old. Her cheeks droop. Her *Häubchen*, it hides her forehead completely, and I want to see her hair, whether it still has any of the old color. She wore a bandana, white polka-dots on blue, that day in the Kraichgau. She stood on a step stool, with the lower branches of the pear tree surrounding her, ripe pears hanging against her body, in the garden behind her father's house.

She'd gazed down at him below her, his shoe up on the board edging the herb bed, and she called out the names of the herbs in the beds as he pointed to them. He saw the strands of hair, the color of unstained cherry wood that escaped from the bandana. She wanted a stone house like Preacher Herr's, she said, although that was much later. He'd built it for her. *I kept my promise to you.*

"I'll treat you right," I said. That I did say in the Kraichgau, at her father's table, after the news of the Atlantic trip. How about that? How did I do? I held a grudge because you rejected Bod, the child of my mistake with Janey but here, look, Janey is back, with our grandchildren. Ours, yours and mine. You didn't forbid their coming today. I said they must come, and Benjamin took the sleigh to get them, and you didn't forbid it. Does that mean things are different? Does that mean you can open a room in your heart . . . ?

He lifted his hand, trembling, toward her face, which still bent over him.

"Maud—"

She took his hand and guided it down. "Keep your arms still so they can do the job. The leeches, I mean. I want you to get better."

Her hand still pinned on his, she said, "Do you smell the pie?" A small smile played on her mouth, and she lifted her eyebrows. "It's gooseberry. You can have a mouthful."

"Sor.Ry," He said.

"You're sorry?" she echoed. "You're sorry, I'm sorry. Let's get you back on your feet before spring so you can start up the mill when the pond melts."

"It's getting red," Wallace said, just left of his stomach. "Look! It drank my blood."

"Let's take it off before you get dizzy." The barber reached across and took the boy's outstretched hand in his. With his free hand, he used a mallet to tap both ends of the leech, which immediately curled up. He flicked the leech, let it roll across the quilt, then pincered it and dropped it back in the ceramic jar.

"Look! It bleeds by itself," Wallace said. The wound continued to weep.

"That's the leech's secret," Benjamin said. He took the towel offered by the barber and wiped the boy's arm. "Hirudin in its saliva, which keeps your blood from making a clot so the leech can keep drinking."

The barber bandaged the boy's arm.

"Are you dizzy, Grampa?"

The sound of the boy's voice was musical. He smiled hugely again and looked away toward the table, at Janey. She stood beside Frony, over the wooden tub, her sleeves rolled up and her hands plunged into the water. Frony toweled off the clean plates.

How would they get home? The snow was falling thick now. How could he tell her how happy it made him that she'd accepted the invitation and she'd come? How could he say it before she went away? The whole room lay between them, and words failed him today. Benjamin had reported the distressing conditions at Light's Fort, with sixty families back-to-back over the three floors and cellar of the house, all cooking and eating together and sleeping like Palatine refugees on straw ticks, with blankets pincered by clothespins to wires between each and the next family. Benjamin insisted that they do something, invite the family over, and they'd come. But he wanted to say a private word to her. When he lay immobile, how could he say a private word? In addition, there was Maudlin.

It was snowing hard. Maybe it would make a snow squall. Squall, squall. It was a snow squall that night I returned from Philadelphia, soaked to the skin by the wet snow, and there she stood at my fireplace, cooking my dinner, a young woman . . . I refuse to dwell on the happenings of that night and that weekend. It's my pact with Him. Everything changed because of that night, her life, my life, Maudlin's dreams, and the Boy himself and his destiny. I promised the ministers then I'd raise the Boy, and I did. I kept my promise, but there must be more. That verse in Deuteronomy—where is it? The number is gone, washed right out of my brain. But there is a verse on the right of the firstborn, isn't there?

I will take care of you, I told her, the day before they ran off.

Hans Herr alone knows the spot in my mill, second floor, where the stone pulls out and the box with fifty gold guineas (with the King's bust and the royal seal) fits in. But what is fifty guineas compared to all that I own and will pass to Benjamin?

The clock sang its familiar tune again and struck three.

Hans Herr. What would I do without him? Like everyone I know around here, he's turned old. He hobbles and pokes up our pathway with his cane, and right now he sits at my feet, watching the bloodletting, with the reading pipe stuck into his face and little smoke puffs rising out of his white beard. He rode the raft with me and our nags across the Neckar that day and bought me a pint at the tavern on the south shore and said one little word: America. Here we are forty-five years out. One afternoon out of all the afternoons of my life. One man of all the men I've done business with. Only this man said *America*, and only this man said *Forgive*. Go to the man who killed your father and forgive. I said I would. *And I kept my promise.*

He also keeps the will I've drawn up. The will for that day, whenever that day comes, and now I think—the will, it doesn't say enough. I could have done much more for Bod. I was stingy. When I left the Kraichgau, Mutti gave me everything. My grandchildren, what do they need? Can Janey clothe and put my grandchildren in the school on a box of golden guineas? Is it too late to change what's written?

Benjamin interrupted by announcing, "Puppies!" He came through the doorway from the kitchen, toting a wooden box with low, slatted sides. Pieces of straw dropped from it as the animals inside rolled about, blindly, their noses thrust up, their mouths flapped open in huge pink yawns or grimaced as they mewled. The mother, a descendent of Bear and Midnight before her, kept up a nervous trot round Benjamin, scampering past the box and thrusting her head sideways to see inside until Benjamin lowered the box on the floor beside the cot. Then she leaned in to lick the foreheads and small furry bodies.

The children were on the move from the instant they heard "Puppies," and they raced around the foot of the cot to reach the box. Greenywalt rolled his eyes down to see them, past the barber, who sat attentive in the bedside chair.

"Let me see!"

"Let me pet them."

"Their eyes are still shut," Benjamin said. "So don't touch their faces."

"Or their eyes will fall out," Frony said. Maudlin had turned the table chairs around, and the three women sat in a row, with Frony between, holding the hands of both Maudlin and Janey.

"No!" the boy said. He looked up in disbelief. "That's not true."

"We used to say that," Frony said.

"Here. Sit like this, with your legs crossed," Benjamin instructed. "I'll put a puppy in your lap. Here—one for you. One for you. Just don't touch their faces."

The girl squealed. "It's licking me!"

The clock chimed the half hour.

From his elevated pillow, Greenywalt gazed down at the children and marveled that Bod's children, the only mementos he had of him, played on the floor of his Stube, while the snow continued to fall heavily. It wasn't the same floor Bod had played on with his dog. That was over in the log cabin, where the English tenant family of Sholley lived. But it was the same picture.

"It's looking like a squall," Frony said, addressing Hans Herr. His head nodded—was he asleep? She stood with her palms on her hips before the window that faced the mill below on the left and the old cabin to the right.

Maudlin got up, went away, and returned shortly with a box covered with a wallpaper of hundreds of tiny pink roses. "I've got something to show you, children," she said, and then to Benjamin, "That's enough of the puppies for now."

"Okay, say good-bye to the puppies."

The children chorused "Good-bye." He carried the dogs away.

Benjamin returned through the bedroom, which brought him out at the left side of the bed. He stopped on the wall side of the bed and looked across the room at the women. Frony and Janey were still seated side by side, clasping each other's hands in Frony's lap, like women do, talking. Maudlin had pulled her chair around to face the children on the floor, with her back to the cot and Greenywalt. She lifted the box lid.

"It's my ribbon box." She addressed Annie Laurie.

"I'm freezing," Greenywalt said.

"It's a good sign," the barber said. He hovered over his patient, regularly taking his pulse. "Close to syncope."

"Syncope?" Hans Herr asked. If he had dozed off, he was awake now.

"Fainting, in ordinary English. It means the humors have reached a balance."

Benjamin leaned down, his eyes fixed on Greenywalt's eyes. He spoke just above a whisper. "We need to take care of them, Dat. It's the right thing."

Greenywalt glared at the boy. What was this? What madness? He looked toward Maudlin. Her back was to him as she fished long strands of red, pink, and cobalt blue ribbon from the box.

"Which do you like best?" The girl responded by pointing, but the boy seemed disinterested.

"They shouldn't go back to the fort," Benjamin murmured. He searched his father's face for a response.

"'Ess!" The malformed word exploded out of the old man.

"I don't need all this land," Benjamin said. He glanced at Hans, whose eyes followed him, emotionless, like an old turtle's. "I get the stone house, the cabin, and the mill. I get the team and the waggon. We have five hundred acres. What am I going to do with more than a hundred acres? Give her a piece of it to build a house on. Or sell, if she wishes."

Greenywalt stared, immobile because his body seemed as lifeless as a chunk of firewood now that the leeches had been draining it for ninety minutes, and they lay rotund and scarlet against his pale arms. Everything within him said Yes to this.

"'Ess," he said, his eyes fixed on Benjamin.

"South of the road along the creek," Benjamin said. "We can build her a cabin when spring comes. Look at all the English on the Pequea now. The tavern. And the Huguenots too. The children can go to an English school."

"'Ess!" Tears filled his eyes. His head wobbled. He fought to keep his focus on the boy's face before his eyes. He wanted to say more. He made a hoarse sound.

Hans Herr lifted his hand. "I heard. It's a wonderful idea, Benjamin. Your father likes it." Hans paused and pointed toward the west window. The snow against the window was piled three inches deep on the window ledge. "What about tonight? There's some wind out there. If it picks up, it will drift, and either you and your sleigh won't find your way to Light's Fort, or you won't find your way back afterward. Didn't she used to live in the mill? Is that—"

"'Ess! The mill!" Greenywalt's head sank back into his pillows, heavy. A deep sense of peace flooded him, warm. It was the right thing, after all, and he hadn't come up with it. The Boy had come up with it. The Boy that he loved because the Boy had become a man since last spring. Strange how this happens. Once a boy, and then a set of events, and a boy modifies into a man. Like the caterpillar into the moth. As I myself modified many years ago in the Kraichgau, when that man at the end of the bed there said, "Forgive the tavern keeper, Ziegler," and I did. The sense of peace resembled a soak in their cedar tub after a day of driving the team and conestoga through driving snow and shifting drifts of it. He found himself in a land between activity and unconsciousness, a place where the faces of people flickered on and off around him like glowworms over the meadows of the Pequea.

The case clock chimed the hour.

The barber leaped up. He snapped the bloated bodies of the leeches off his patient's arms, one after the other. "Syncope!" he said. He seized Greenywalt's arm and fumbled for the pulse.

Halfway across the room, Maudlin had braided the pink ribbon into the little girl's ringlets, and now she leaned back to look at her.

"Show the madam how you dance," Janey said. "Come." She led the girl into the center of the room and knelt beside her. She began the song and nodded to the beat, her eyes on the girl.

> . . . where early falls the dew,
> and it's there that Annie Laurie
> gave me her promise true.

"Come, Annie Laurie! Will you do it for Grandma?" Annie Laurie started hesitantly, a tentative step, then another, reading the faces that were turned toward her. Her grandmother clapped the rhythm. "See, you can do it!"

> . . . Gave me her promise true,
> which God will ne'er forget,
> and for bonnie Annie Laurie,
> I'd lay me down and dee.

That was it! In the gloaming, the shadowy twilight where the faces flickered on and off like glowworms, he heard the name he'd forgotten: Annie Laurie!

The dancer stopped and shot coquettish glances at the women around her.

"Aren't you pretty!" Maudlin said. The girl stared at her.

"Water!" the barber shouted. "Here. Hold this cloth." The pungent odor of ammonia rose out of his bottle, and Benjamin fell into a coughing spell, even as he held the ammonia below his father's nose.

"Greenywalt!" Maudlin scrambled to her feet.

Their faces encircled him and bent in toward him. They no longer flickered off and on like glowworms. They glowed steadily, in a ring, and their mouths opened and closed and opened again, but he couldn't decipher the sounds, if they made any. He saw that, even as his eyes rested shut.

Then the circle parted, and the boy with hair the color of sumac in October came toward him. The boy's eyes burned steady and blue, and he felt his heart melt, as if it had been a frozen block and now dissolved like the snow that was evaporating all around them. White crocus petals poked up here, there, everywhere from the mounds that were still intact. He extended his hand, with the Mylin rifle. It was a treasure, the gift of a lifetime, with scrolled feathers on the stock and the initials M.M. engraved on the gun metal.

"It's for you, Bod. Take good care of it."

The boy reached with both hands and took the gun and cradled it. A large smile broke below his eyes, like the first blaze of dawning sun over Mine Ridge east of the Settlement.

—⁓⁓⁓—

GLOSSARY

amimi—The passenger pigeon, in Delaware Indian dialect. In the 18th century America travelers regularly reported mass migrations of millions of birds. Overhunted, their breeding grounds destroyed, the last known passenger pigeon died September 1, 1914, at the Cincinnati Zoo.

banshee—A female spirit in Gaelic folklore who makes an appearance or wails to warn a family that one of them will soon die. *bean sith (anglicized as "banshee")*—is a Scottish fairy, seen as an omen of death and a messenger from the Otherworld. For a superb film version of the banshee, see *Darby O'Gill and the Little People*.

batteau—A shallow-draft, flat-bottomed boat used to ferry freight, especially furs, on rivers like the Susquehanna River in the colonial period. Plural: batteaux.

Betty lamp—A simple iron or brass lamp that burned fish oil or fat trimmings and had a wick of twisted cloth.

Boy Ruprecht—One of the companions of St. Nicholas. Knecht Ruprecht in German.

Calvinist/Reformed/Presbyterian—Calvinists are proponents of Reformed theology, a Christian belief system associated with the 16th-century John Calvin. This theology is summarized in historic church confessions such as the Westminster Confession of Faith. In the British Isles, this tradition is associated with the Presbyterian Church.

carroty-pate—18th-century slang for "Redhead."

Colours—The flag. In colonial America, the flag of the Thirteen Colonies was the Union Jack of Great Britain, colloquially called the Colours.

Conestoga—This heavy covered waggon is reputed to have been developed by Mennonite German settlers to transport heavy loads from their farms to the city. First mention of this waggon is Dec. 31, 1717, in the accounting log of James Logan. The conestoga was used extensively during the 18th and 19th centuries in America.

Deitsch—A variety of West Central German spoken by the 17th-and 18th-century immigrants to Pennsylvania from southern Germany. Also known as Pennsilfaanisch Deitsch, the traditional language of the Pennsylvania Dutch people. How is Pennsylvania Dutch/German different from *Standard German*? In summary, it consists of a simplified grammatical structure and several vowel and consonant shifts. The influence of American English upon grammar, vocabulary, and pronunciation is also significant. The dialect is still alive and well among modern Amish, Old Order Mennonites and in rural ares of Pennsylvania counties, Lebanon and Berks. See also Pennsylvania Dutch.

Elector—The Elector ruled the Electoral Palatinate of the Rhine in the Holy Roman Empire from 915 to 1803 AD. The Electors had enormous power. The religious affiliation of the Electors moved from Calvinist (Karl I and Karl II, 1648–85) to Roman Catholic (Philipp Wilhelm and Johann Wilhelm, 1685–1716).

Emmental—A valley in west central Switzerland, part of the canton of Bern. The hills around the Emme River sheltered Anabaptist (*Wiedertäufer*) believers in the 17th and 18th centuries.

General Edward Braddock—British commander-in-chief for the Thirteen Colonies at the start of the French and Indian War. Best remembered for his command of a disastrous expedition against the French-occupied Ohio River Valley in 1755, in which he lost his life and the majority of his army.

Goody—Title used in addressing a married woman in the Colonies in the 17th and early 18th centuries, such as Goody Cameron.

Grünewald/Greenywalt—The name comes from *grüne Wald*, green forest, which certainly fits Greenywalt's new home on the Pequea. When anglicized by Quaker land officials, Grünewald became Greenywalt, a nickname that stuck.

Harris' Landing—Trading outpost established by John Harris, Sr. in 1705. In 1733, rights to operate a ferry across the Susquehanna were granted to Harris by the Pennsylvania Assembly. Now called Harrisburg.

Häubchen—The most important female head covering of the 18th century was the cap. It was worn by women of all classes and stations almost all the time. The best and most widespread material was fine, bleached linen. Mennonist women also wore the *Häubchen*, usually a kerchief of homemade linen with corners tied under the chin. In the Palatinate, only married women wore it.

Hof—Country house, yard, and group of buildings.

Indentured servant—Indentured servitude was a labor system in which people paid for their passage to the New World by working for an employer for a fixed term of years. After the term expired, they became free to work for themselves. About 50% of the white immigrants to the American colonies in the17th and 18th centuries were indentured.

Jäger rifle—Very accurate rifled muzzle-loading gun developed in Germany and thought to be the inspiration for the Pennsylvania (Kentucky) long rifle. It required longer loading time for its patched ball but was far more accurate than nonrifled contemporary muskets.

James Logan—William Penn's Secretary in charge of the province of Pennsylvania, later mayor of Philadelphia and chief justice of the province. Logan was a gentleman-merchant, a Quaker, fur trader, slave owner, and book collector.

kelpie—A water sprite of Scottish folklore that enjoys or effects the drowning of travelers.

kill-devil—Jamaican rum, in 18th-century slang.

Kraichgau—The Kraichgau, formerly a part of the Palatinate, later a part of northern Baden, Germany. The fertile Kraichgau region, devastated in the Thirty Years' War, was repopulated at the invitation of Elector Karl Philip to many Swiss Mennonite exiles, who settled from 1652 onward on the estates of the imperial knights.

land patent—Land patents were exclusive land grants made by the British king to William Penn and in turn by Penn's agents to settlers. The official land patent granted right or title to a piece of real estate.

lanthorn—1580–90, an early term for the lantern. (Lanterns formerly had reflectors made of translucent sheets of horn.)

Louis XIV—*aka* The Sun King, King of France from 1643 until his death in 1715. Louis's reign was characterized by an overbearing foreign policy with the goal of adding territory to Catholic France at the expense of its Protestant neighbors. French court dress, arts, and the splendor of his palace of Versailles inspired a generation of European rulers to bankrupt their own treasuries to imitate Louis's style.

Mac Óg—"Young son," a designation for Aengus, the Old Irish god of love, youth, and poetic inspiration.

Martyrs Mirror—Thieleman J. van Braght's collection of stories and testimonies of Christian martyrs, especially Anabaptists (*Wiedertäufer*). Van Braght's book of more than 1,100 pages was translated from Dutch to German and published by the Ephrata Cloister for the immigrant Mennonite community in 1749. Next to the Bible, the *Martyrs Mirror* has historically been the most significant book in Amish and Mennonite homes. In English: http://homecomers.org/mirror/

Mennonist—Alternate form of "Mennonite."

Mutti—A term of endearment, "Little Mother, Mommy."

navel-tied—18th-century slang for "inseparable."

Palatinate—In German history, the lands of the Count Palatine or Elector, a title held by a leading secular prince of the Holy Roman Empire. Nearly the entire 17th century in central Europe was a period of turmoil as Louis XIV of France sought to increase his empire. After the harsh winter of 1708–9, the stage was set for mass migration. Between 1708 and 1750, tens of thousands of Palatine families fled bad conditions and settled in New York, Pennsylvania, and the Carolinas.

Pannhaas—My friend Dan Ness describes it this way: "After the hog-butchering is complete, all the scraps of meat including the head, if not made into headcheese, are placed in the iron kettle with water and cooked till soft. The meat is strained out and becomes puddins or puddings which are packed in small crocks or sealed in glass canning jars. Cornmeal is stirred into the remaining broth and it becomes pannhaas (PA Deitsch for 'pan rabbit'). This is poured into pans to harden. At breakfast the pannhaas is sliced, browned in a pan and eaten with puddings spread over the top. Sometimes the pannhaas is eaten with apple butter or syrup. In some areas, cornmeal is stirred into the meat and broth without straining out the meat, then poured into pans and this is called scrapple which I think is more Lancaster County." Mmm mmm good.

Paxtang/Paxton Boys—Frontiersmen of Scotch-Irish origin from along the Susquehanna River in central Pennsylvania who formed a vigilante group to defend their communities. The group was founded by Parson John Elder and is perhaps best remembered for the Conestoga Massacre of 1763.

Peace of Westphalia—A series of peace treaties that ended the Thirty Years' War (1618–48) between warring European states. The Peace established the principle of *cuius regio, eius religio*—the religion of the reigning prince determines the religion of that state. As such, the Catholic Church, Lutheran Church, and Calvinist (Reformed) churches were legitimate options. All other peoples, such as Jews, Mennonists, and gypsies, were not "legitimate" and were open to regular harassment and discrimination.

Pennsylvania Dutch—17th- and 18th-century Pennsylvania German immigrants from South Germany to the USA. In this usage the word "Dutch" refers not to Dutch people but represents Deitsch (Deutsch, German), the Pennsylvania Germans and their dialect, Pennsylvania German, related to Palatine dialects.

Peter Klaus the Goatherd—Hero of the German folktale that inspired Washington Irving's short story "Rip Van Winkle." Peter Klaus followed his goat into an underground cavern, where he met dwarfs who supplied him with wine. He awoke twenty years later.

Plantation—The term 'plantation' in the 17th and 18th century American colonies referred to the large farms that were the economic base of the colonies.

plethora—An excess of any of the body fluids. The four-humor theory of body health was first propounded by Hippocrates in 5th-century-BC Greece. Hippocrates's theory dominated medical theory until modern research replaced it in the 19th century.

quitrent—An annual land tax imposed on freehold land by the provincial government of Pennsylvania and other colonies

Redcoats/British lobsters—Soldiers identified as British by their standard-issue uniforms in the 17th and 18th centuries, also nicknamed British lobsters. The color red was chosen because red dye was one of the cheapest to produce.

rumkicks—18th-century slang for knee breeches laced with gold or silver brocade.

shambles—Originally a word for a slaughterhouse. In Colonial America, a marketplace.

soul-case—18th-century slang for the body.

Steitstown—Now called Lebanon, Pennsylvania.

stone—The stone as a unit of measurement is now equal to 14 pounds. The stone continues to be used in Britain and Ireland to measure body weight, but the metric system has replaced it in all other instances.

Stube—A room, often a sitting/living room.

syncope—Fainting. The goal of bloodletting by the use of leeches. Bloodletting was a central part of early modern medicine.

Täufer—"One who baptizes." Another name for the *Wiedertäufer*.

Teufel—The Devil.

Union Jack—The British flag, a composite design made up of three national symbols: the flags of England, Scotland, and Ireland.

Vetti/Vettir—"Father" in the Swiss dialect of German.

waggon—18th-century spelling for wagon.

Wiedertäufer—"Anabaptists" or "those who baptize again." These ancestors of the modern Amish, Hutterites, and Mennonites were given this nickname because they rejected the baptism of infants and insisted on only baptizing confessing adults. During several centuries after their 1525 origins, Anabaptists/*Wiedertäufer* were heavily persecuted by state-church Protestants and Roman Catholics. Anabaptist churches are typically composed of baptized believers only, in contrast with the state-church model of Lutheranism, Calvinism, and Catholicism.

ACKNOWLEDGMENTS

If Academy Award winners are permitted to gush about all the contributors to their careers, surely you will forgive this writer for doing the same! My deepest thanks to the following:

ACFW Scribes—This wonderful national group of practicing Christian writers review each others' fiction works-in-progress and make comments. I benefited greatly from the Scribes in early stages of my novel.

Carolyn Wenger—Carolyn is a priceless treasure of the Mennonite Church. As archivist and former librarian of Lancaster Mennonite Historical Society, her work in preserving historical documents and artifacts and introducing them to the curious public enrich us all. Through the pages of *Pennsylvania Mennonite Heritage*, I found the marvelous diaries of Benjamin Herr.

Schowalter Foundation—This Newton, Kansas, based foundation provided a scholarship to launch research on the novel in 2009.

John Ruth—Ruth's *The Earth Is the Lord's* was a magnificent inspiration to me. I was astonished to find it. I underlined paragraph after paragraph of this great history. Then I joined Ruth and TourMagination for one of his many two-week tours in a big purple bus up the Rhine to visit the Mennonite Roots, including the Unterbiegelhof, historic home of the Herr family, members of the 1710 migration, and Christian Herr, the builder of the Hans Herr House.

TourMagination—Audrey Voth Petkau and her team provided me with a scholarship that enabled Patti and me to take the Ruth Mennonite Roots Tour across the Netherlands, Belgium, Germany, Switzerland, and Austria in 2011.

Linda Arbaugh and the Milpitas Public Library—The Library's Interlibrary Loan service brought great and rare books right to my backyard, where I could take them out on loan for three weeks. (For interested researchers and writers, I can make available a bibliography of books used in the three years of research stage on *Both My Sons*.)

Herb Reed—My brother Herb's enthusiasm for the project often equaled mine! As my partner on the Port to Paradise tour several hot days in July 2014, we rode for several days in Herb's car from Philadelphia to the Pequea Settlement. We explored the Scots-Irish connection and sites together. He also raved over the final book, but that's what brothers do for each other.

Chuck Faust and the Rangers—Colonel Chuck is a leader in the reenactor community for the French and Indian War and the Revolutionary War. He introduced me to Donegal Township Riflemen and their histories and to the John Harris reenactor, Pastor Dave Biser. Chuck also led me to the Pennsylvania Archives and contemporary maps and the priceless "Diary of Colonel Burd," builder of Fort Shamokin in 1755.

Rosalind Beiler and Caspar Wistar—Rose's scholarly work *Caspar Wistar, Immigrant and Entrepreneur: The Atlantic World of Caspar Wistar* inspired the Old Country portion of *Both My Sons*.

Ted Hazen—A modern spokesman for milling who called himself a "master miller, millwright, millstone dresser." Ted taught me most of what I know about gristmills, flour mills, and waterwheels and where to find operating mills today. Sadly, Ted left us in 2013.

Readers/critics—Dr. John Roth, Everett Thomas, Carroll Yoder, Julia Yoder, Nancee Cline, Dr. Rose Rolon Dow, John and Alice Lapp, Carolyn Wenger, and Herb Reed all lent their critical eyes and gave valuable feedback to the project.

Publishing Team—The capable Masthof Team—Dan Mast, Lois Ann Mast and Liz Petersheim, have been fantastic to work with. They believed in this book and made it happen!

Marketing Team—Merle and Phyllis Good contributed their years of publishing and marketing savvy. I throw my hat up in the air for them.

Patricia—As Proverbs 31 puts it: "A good wife, who can find one?" I am so lucky. Patricia has been my best critic. She heard every word of the novel at least twice, and her keen comments, born out of her counseling profession, deepened the characters.

Other books by Ken Yoder Reed . . .

MENNONITE SOLDIER

Mastie and Ira Stoltzfus, Mennonite brothers in Lancaster, Pa., face the draft in World War I. Ira chooses the traditional Mennonite position of conscientious objection to war. Mastie, on the other hand, joins the Army and is excommunicated from the church. As the story shifts back and forth between Ira and Mastie, you will be caught up in a powerful examination of love and war, duty and conscience, and the starkly different experiences of two boys from the same Mennonite home. This classic retelling of the prodigal son story set in World War I America includes a thoughtful foreword essay on Mennonites and the military by Professor Joel Hartman of the University of Missouri. Reprinted so a whole new generation can enjoy!

HE FLEW TOO HIGH

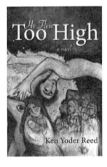

Saul McNamara believes God is telling him his work as a Korean War nuclear bombing strategist is evil. For this reason and with moral support from the Mennonites and their leader, Bishop Krehbiel, Saul leaves his career, marries the Bishop's daughter, and falls in love with her pacifist Mennonite community. However, Saul grows disillusioned because he believes 1950s prosperity has lulled the Mennonites into a dangerous sleep. This suspense story with a strong spiritual undercurrent tells of one man's quest to bring an awakening to a reluctant people. But will Saul lose his community, wife and family, and even the voice of God in his life?

Books available from . . .

MASTHOF BOOKSTORE
www.masthof.com | 610-286-0258
219 Mill Road, Morgantown, PA 19543

The New World

The Pequea Settlement
in Greenywalt's Boys

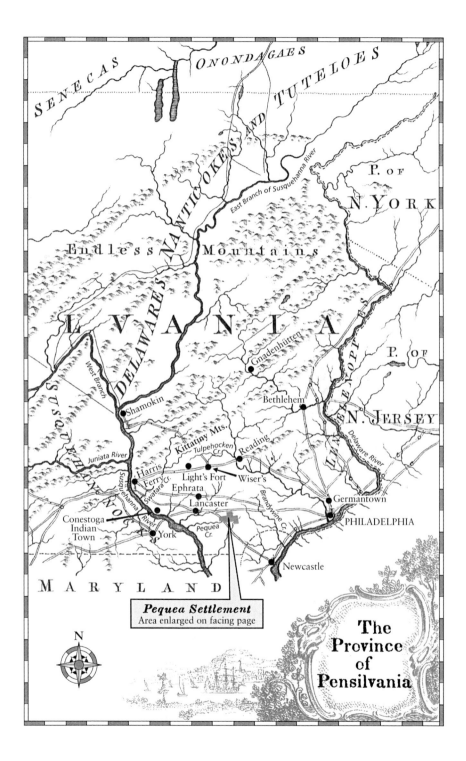

Pequea Settlement
Area enlarged on facing page

N

The
Province
of
Pensilvania

THE AUTHOR

KEN YODER REED likes Pannhaas (scrapple) with his eggs. However, it's not available in Silicon Valley meat markets around his home in San Jose, California. Reed calls himself a refugee Mennonite. He spent his boyhood in Lebanon County, Pennsylvania, near Swatara Gap. After eight years of education in Mennonite schools, a stint with MCC Japan and a period of free-lancing for Mennonite publications, he moved to San Francisco and became a recruiter for high-tech firms. He and his wife Patricia affiliated with the Presbyterians (ECO) in Milpitas, CA some years ago and he serves as an elder there. Reed's previous historical novels, *Mennonite Soldier* and *He Flew Too High* are available through Masthof Press.